VOLATILE CONJUNCTION

ROGUE JUSTICE | BOOK TWO

MARY ASHE

Ebook ISBN: 979-8-9882484-2-2

Paperback ISBN: 979-8-9882484-3-9

Cover design by Miblart.com

First published in 2023 by Merry Spinster Studios, LLC

www.maryashe.com

*For my parents
(Just don't read the spicy bits, okay?
Or at least, don't tell me.)*

1

AMARYLLIS

So many rich dicks, so little time. She was here to do a very specific job. If she weren't, Amaryllis Vertè would have already stripped the jewels dripping from the necks and wrists of the smug individuals attending tonight's black market auction and disappeared.

Unfortunately, she wasn't here for the low-hanging fruit. She was here to steal some engine prototype thingy that would supposedly change space travel as they knew it. Blah, blah. Boring. If it didn't sparkle or weigh down her pockets with credits, it was of little use to her. Besides, there was always some kind of revolutionary engine or rocket or system that would change space travel forever. She'd believe it when she experienced that revolution for herself. For now, it was enough that Lore wanted it, and that there'd be multiple hells to pay if Amaryllis didn't get it for her.

Why Lore wanted the damn thing rather than letting Amaryllis clean out the pockets of the rich and corrupt wandering around this massive cavern underneath the Vanid estate, she didn't know. But as head of a coalition of mercenaries called The Cabal — members that included pirates, assassins, thieves, and smugglers — Lore was the most cutthroat of them all. She played the long game. Everything she did was either to expand The

Cabal's reach, make money, or secure her power base. Somehow, this prototype fit into at least one of those categories.

But, honestly, beyond grabbing it and delivering it to Lore, it didn't really concern her. She didn't care beyond getting the job done and wasn't about to delve into the motivations behind the theft. Lore had her reasons for doing what she did, and you questioned her at your peril. At least the prototype thingy was compact enough someone could spirit away it with relative ease once it left the cavern.

Taking a slow lap around the underground space, she spared a moment to admire the balls it took to run a black market auction literally underneath the feet of some of the most powerful political figures in the galaxy as they danced and drank the night away at the Full Moon Ball, hosted annually by the Vanid matriarch on her island estate. Of course, many of those rich and powerful individuals snuck away from said party to attend the secret auction currently taking place. Everyone in attendance was masked, making identification challenging, though not impossible. And everyone here was also loaded, credits dripping from every orifice. Starting bids alone on the items up for auction were enough to make her eyes water. Hells, she could buy a whole-assed ship with the reserve price on the pair of yellowgrass earrings she'd strolled past. These people had far too much money, and her fingers itched to relieve them of it.

She'd never been inside the palatial island home of the Vanid matriarch, would never be invited to something as exclusive as the Full Moon Ball but, considering the expense that must have gone into making the cave underneath it functional, she might have to steal a ticket next year just to experience the opulence for herself.

Dripping with stalactites, the main cavern soared at least thirty feet overhead. They'd leveled the stone floor, most of the stalagmites removed except for a few artfully scattered around the outer edges, forming little alcoves for privacy. Evenly spaced lanterns cast flickering shadows on the dark stone walls. It was giving prison-lite vibes, as if designed by someone who'd only seen prisons on a vid screen. The actual prisons she'd been in were darker, damper, and didn't have roaming servers offering tasty treats and bubbly to inmates. They also didn't smell like leather and old money. More like harsh industrial cleaner and misery.

She ran a hand over the silk of her simple floor-length gown, enjoying the smooth feel of the fabric against her fingertips. Real life prisons also didn't have pretty dresses that emphasized her curves and made her feel like she temporarily fit in with this glittering crowd, even though she quite obviously didn't.

Snagging a purple berry cut into the shape of a flower from a passing server's tray, she circled a tall black plinth. A spotlight illuminated a small but detailed painting of a pale, delicate-looking woman with long honey blonde hair, a contented look on her face as she soaked in a deep stone tub filled with a milky pink liquid, red flower petals strewn over the surface. At first, it looked like nothing other than a nice painting of a woman bathing, but when she leaned closer for a better look, she spotted the sharp knife, a smear of blood across its surface, dangling from the woman's fingers. Barely visible behind the tub lay a limp, pale male hand. Attached to the bottom of the ornate gold frame, a small tag proclaimed the painting's title to be *Peace at Last*.

A smile brushed across Amaryllis's lips. *Good for her.* Sometimes, the only way to get the peace you needed was to shed a little blood.

The guard stationed next to the painting's plinth cleared his throat as she leaned too close. Giving him a haughty look, she straightened and ambled towards the stage area where an auctioneer called out bids for a three-tiered necklace of lapis lazuli and astatine. Pretty, but she wasn't here to get involved in the brewing bidding war over the piece. No doubt it was stolen from some conquered civilization or archeological dig. Seemed to her that rich people just loved owning things pillaged from other cultures, especially when those societies had been crushed under someone else's boot heel. Her lip curled at the thought.

Under the guise of tucking a braid back into place, she

brushed a finger along the edge of her ear, activating the team comm. "Status report," she murmured, weaving her way between the masked attendees in their fancy outfits, her fingers twitching as she walked by a particularly tantalizing necklace of gleaming azure begging to be lifted off the soft neck it embraced.

Next year, she promised herself. Next year, she'd return not to the auction in the dark cavern below, but to the fancy party above where she'd wear a gorgeous gown, dance with handsome celebrities and power brokers alike, eat and drink delicious offerings, and walk away so loaded down with jewels, she'd sink straight to the ocean floor if she fell in the water. This year she had a job to do, one she couldn't deviate from or there would be serious repercussions.

However, if all went according to plan, by this time next year, she and her crew would have enough saved to buy a stake in The Cabal, becoming full-fledged members with voting privileges, the ability to bid on the jobs they wanted, and to turn down Lore's "extra assistance", also known as her spying on them. Or maybe, if they did really well, they could afford to leave altogether, strike out on their own, and forge their own path without the anchor of The Cabal weighing them down.

But the latter was a pie-in-the-sky kind of dream. Lore did not let people go easily or cheaply, especially not people she considered hers, like Amaryllis and the *Dog's Day* crew. Right now, all four of them were still obligated to follow orders, no matter how they felt about them.

"Ground team in place," Von responded. His voice held more of a growl than usual. She didn't blame him. He'd drawn the short straw and had to deal directly with two of the three meatheads Lore forced upon them for this job.

Skip, Kenny, and Andrea — gods forbid if you didn't pronounce her name An-dray-ah and, no, Amaryllis did not like any of them but especially the snotty woman who took every opportunity to look down on Amaryllis and her crew — were aggressive, trigger-happy mercenaries who put her entire crew on edge. Amaryllis had tried to explain to Lore that the job would go so much smoother with just her small team running it. As usual, Lore paid her objections no mind, saddling them with the violent trio, claiming they'd need the extra muscle.

"Babysitters with blasters," Von said upon hearing of the team's unwelcome additions. He said they were only part of the mission to make sure Amaryllis and her team did what they were sent there to do and nothing else. Amaryllis didn't disagree, though she wanted to believe Lore was merely being overprotective, rather than distrustful and controlling.

After all, Lore had saved her, had taken her in after her parents died in a plague that killed nearly everyone on board their colony ship. She'd raised Amaryllis, cared for her in her own way, and taught her how to survive in the cutthroat world of The Cabal and its collection of ne'er-do-wells.

"Your getaway driver is ready and awaiting our speedy departure," Trick said, much more chipper than Von. Of course, he'd be happier than Von. He was alone in the submersible, watching the galactic rugby semi-finals, waiting for them to complete their task, rather than dealing with Lore's goons.

"All clear. No abnormal chatter or alarms anywhere in the area," Dagby said from her position on the *Dog's Day* as it carefully skimmed along the exosphere to avoid detection from Badin's planetary defenses. It was a rare pilot who could keep a ship hidden within the thin layer of atmosphere without flashing a wing into space or dipping down into the thermosphere and tripping the sensors, but Dagby was just that good.

"Auction's starting," Amaryllis said, taking a sip of the bubbly. She made a face at the sour flavor and scanned the crowd. *Wait. Was that...?* She choked, her eyes tearing up as her drink went down the wrong way.

"You okay?" Trick asked.

"What happened?" Von said.

She coughed again to clear her throat, lifting the edge of her black filigree mask to dab the tears from the corners of her eyes. "Nothing. Thought I saw someone I knew."

If it truly was who she thought it was, he'd blow the entire job. Ivan Halonen. The most annoying man in the galaxy. A man who went out of his way to interfere in her life, jack up her jobs, and aggravate the shit out of her until she wanted to scream and punch him in the throat. Or throw him down on a bed and fuck his brains out. At this point in their acquaintance, either option would do, as long as it got him out of her hair and her system.

But it couldn't actually be him. Surely her eyes were playing tricks on her. After all, what would he be doing here in this ridiculous cave surrounded by all these treasures, anyway? The *Laughing Dragon* crew tended to work more at the living, breathing beings end of the mercenary business, and nothing here fit in that category. Nothing she knew of, anyway. She wouldn't put it past the organizers of this highly illegal auction to dabble in the sales of sentient creatures. Anyone who ran a gathering like this had a rather loose grasp of morality and minimal ethics. Most likely, they wouldn't blink at crossing another line if it filled their accounts with credits.

After her last run-in with Ivan, which, as per usual, had ended in an explosion, he and his team retreated to Gastez Station to avoid a nosy Starguard cruiser while her crew burned a jump to shake the 'Guard off their tail. So, for him to be on Badin, on Vanid Island, at the same gathering as her was improbable, right?

Not impossible, though. After all, Ivan's captain and friend, Quin Sidron, and that fugitive woman, Bea Farsirus, were likely still on Badin. Just the other day, she'd spotted the pair of them at the spaceport, lost them, then picked them up again at a shabby hotel in one of the sketchier areas of Badin's capital city. The *Laughing Dragon*'s captain had claimed that Bea wasn't there, and there was no sign of the woman in Quin's room when they searched it. And there had been no indication of Ivan lurking around at the time, either.

While collecting the bounty on Bea's head would have been a

nice bonus to her trip, Amaryllis didn't have the time or the patience to sit on Quin until the woman turned up. So, yeah. It was entirely possible that Ivan made his way to Badin after Amaryllis's chat with Quin, especially if his captain needed him. Dammit.

Narrowing her eyes, she surveyed the crowd, but didn't spot him again. She let out a soft sigh. Maybe she'd caught a glimpse of a tall, broad-shouldered someone with red hair out of the corner of her eye, and her brain had immediately categorized them as Ivan. After all, natural redheads were relatively uncommon in this sector of the galaxy. A man as large as him didn't just disappear into thin air. His height and build alone made him stand out. Top that with his shock of ginger waves and thick beard, and there was no way he could just blend in, even in this crush. Was there?

2

IVAN

I f he never had to make his way through another pitch black, tight-assed tunnel again in his life, it would be too soon. Even here in this little pocket of space that led to the main cavern, it was too tight for him to take a full breath, much less stand up straight.

But Ivan had been in far worse situations, including some pretty harrowing spots during his time with the Starguard. A long, dark crawl through tunnels filled with nothing more than sharp rocks, slimy bits, and a broad collection of insects didn't even make the top ten. Still sucked, though.

"Ivan, scout ahead. See where this tunnel emerges and what's in store for us," Quin Sidron, his captain and best friend, said, barely sparing his Number One a glance.

Ivan rolled his eyes. The man was completely entranced by the woman standing next to him. Bea Farsirus. Amazing how quickly Quin had turned from a cocky rake who thought nothing of slinging Bea over his shoulder when she wouldn't cooperate during her rescue to a man so deeply in love with that same woman he could hardly take his eyes off of her.

Ivan was happy for his friend, especially considering how destroyed Quin had been after that debacle with Jannette, his last girlfriend. Ivan had been worried her betrayal had shattered the man's heart so completely he'd never recover, so he was pleased to see Quin enraptured with this lady. And Bea was an absolute delight. Not only was she brilliant and lovely, she was fearless about calling Quin on his shit, which Ivan highly enjoyed.

Giving Quin a nod — one he barely noticed — Ivan stripped off his protective coverall and worked his broad shoulders through the narrow opening, emerging into a small alcove edged by stalagmites. With efficient motions, he brushed off his plain black suit, ran a hand through his hair, and slid a narrow black mask over his eyes before casually joining the milling crowd. He plucked a glass of a pink bubbly liquid from a passing server's tray and took a sip. His lip curled at the sour-sweet flavor. Gross. Give him a beer any day. This chi-chi stuff was repulsive, no matter how expensive it might be. Useful as cover, though. No one paid him any attention as he strolled around the space like he belonged.

He was surprised by how sanitized the cavern was. Someone had smoothed the flooring so no one would trip on a stray stone and removed most of the cave's mineral formations, leaving just a few for what he guessed were esthetic purposes. Even the walls were manicured, their sharp edges carved away, leaving just enough roughness for atmosphere. Add in the flickering torches and fancy lighting and you had a cave-like feeling without what this crowd would probably consider the "icky bits". He fought to keep the disdain off his face, thankful for the beard and mask to help camouflage his true feelings about the types of people who would attend the black market auction held beneath the mansion of one of the most powerful families in the shipping and ship-building business.

Ivan and the team were there for two reasons. One, verify that Bea's propulsion system prototype was indeed being auctioned off here tonight and retrieve or track it, depending on access and ability; and two, deal with Arden deVan, someone they'd thought deceased until quite recently.

After hearing Bea's story about how Arden's death was verified with a solitary tooth found in the ashes of her workshop, Ivan'd had his suspicions. After all, this was the man who romanced Bea for a year only to turn around and steal her prototypes, burn down her workshop, fake his own death, and set her up to take the fall for those crimes. And now, here he was, selling her groundbreaking work to the highest bidder. He was scum and deserved to rot on a prison moon.

Faking a sip of his drink, he frowned at the squishy noises and breathless moans he was hearing through his comm. It took him half a second to figure out what was going on. Quin and Bea, at it again.

"You two better not be doing what I think you're doing," he grumbled. "I'm coming back in like five minutes and don't want to see you swapping spit." Seriously. Those two just couldn't keep their hands off each other. He'd think it was delightful how in love they were if only they'd keep the pawing to a minimum.

Bea giggled, then their comms went silent. Ivan knew they wouldn't stop what they were doing in the dank of the tunnels, but at least he didn't have to hear the noises that came along with it.

A throat cleared over the team comms. "Are they...?" Cormac asked.

He let out a sigh. Lucky man. Cormac was thousands of miles above the planet's surface on the *Laughing Dragon* and didn't have to bear witness to the happy couple's constant displays of affection.

"They haven't been able to keep their hands to themselves since I've been with them. I've learned it's best to just pretend it's not happening." Surely this honeymoon phase of their courtship wouldn't last forever. Could it?

Cormac made a sound of commiseration and didn't probe any further. Smart. No one needed to know the details of their captain's love life.

Ivan surveyed the crowd at the auction with practiced efficiency. While he appreciated the anonymity that came with wearing a mask, everyone was wearing similar masks, which made it extremely challenging to identify anyone visually or with tech. That, of course, was the point, but it was still annoying. How was he supposed to find Arden deVan if he couldn't identify him beneath his mask? Beyond that particular stumbling block, nothing jumped out as immediately dangerous.

Pulling off his mask, he slid back between the rocks to the small space where Quin and Bea waited for him. His captain had a very pleased air about him.

"Really?" He raised an eyebrow at their rumpled state. They didn't even have the good manners to look shamefaced about it. He sighed to himself. Truly, it was a burden to be right, especially at times like this. "Well, at least you were quiet about it."

Bea blushed. Quin gave her a wink, wrapping an arm around her waist, drawing her close. "Report," he said.

It was all Ivan could do not to roll his eyes at the pair of them. Instead, he focused on the job at hand. "We're safe to proceed. It'll be tight, though. Auction hasn't started yet, and there are plenty of people there already, so we should blend right in," he said. "I'll slip in with security. Easier than carrying a tray. People are always bothering you when you've got free food and drinks." His report given, he squeezed his way back into the main cavern. Bea followed at his heels, Quin bringing up the rear.

When she emerged into the light, he spotted something that had caught a ride on her shoulder. He reached over and plucked the fat gray spider from the strap of her dress before she noticed. He didn't know if she was a screamer when it came to arachnids, but best not to find out in a space where they were trying to blend in.

"What? Do I have something on me?" she asked, twisting around to check herself.

With a shrug, he casually deposited the spider on the stalagmite behind him. "Just a bit of cave junk, nothing to worry about."

"Thanks." She gave a quick spin, the skirt of her dress flaring. "Anything else?"

"All good." He tugged at his cuffs. "Wait here for Quin. It's a tight squeeze for us big guys."

This time, he didn't grab any of the food or drinks being offered. Nor did he put the mask back on. He shifted his cover from guest to security, squaring his shoulders as he took position next to the unguarded plinth he'd scouted earlier holding a landscape painting. Clasping his hands in front of him, he adjust his face to read "professional badass: you break it, I'll break you" as he scanned the crowd. Once in place, he said, "I'm to your left when you finally enter the cavern."

Out of the corner of his eye, he saw Quin emerge from the tunnel to stand beside Bea and slide a black mask over his eyes. When Bea ran a hand over Quin's shoulders, straightening his suit, Ivan couldn't resist adding, "Don't worry if you're a little rumpled. It'll look like you disappeared for some nookie in a nook before the auction starts." He snickered quietly at his clever play on words.

"Ivan," Bea protested, taking Quin's arm as they began their stroll around the space.

"Are you two finally ready?" Cormac asked, his voice tinged with a hint of irritation. The man got pissy when he couldn't see everything that was going on and when he discovered there weren't any easily accessible cameras in the cavern to ride, his grump emerged.

"Affirmative," Quin said. "Do you see him?"

"Not yet. But he's here. I can feel it," Bea said.

A feeling was good. Ivan appreciated and depended on feelings and instincts, but it wasn't enough. They needed to get their hands on Arden so they could bring him to the authorities and clear Bea's name, eliminating the warrant out for her arrest and the ridiculously high bounty on her head.

"Nothing over here." Ivan scrutinized the attendees as he scanned for a pale blond man with a smug demeanor. Irritatingly, about half the men had that annoyingly smug way of carrying themselves that those with power and money had, and too many of those had some shade of blond hair. Since he'd never met the man and couldn't speculate which one Arden might be among the gaggle of lookalike blonds, he switched from search mode to defensive mode, mentally playing out possible escape and evasion scenarios. If Arden was present, Bea would find him, of that he had no doubt.

"Copy," Quin said. "Let's do a circuit."

Ivan watched them as they skirted around a blonde woman in a bright red dress who was loudly flirting with anyone who entered her sphere and made their way through the forest of plinths, pausing to examine the offerings as if they were interested. No one appeared to be focused on them except for a couple close to the auctioneer's podium. But their interest was to be expected. After all, it was Dai Farsirus, Bea's sister, and Rhain Sidron, Quin's cousin, both of whom had a vested interest in the outcome of tonight not only for Bea's sake, but for some secret mission that Quin's team had been warned away from interfering with on pain of death.

Fine. They had more than enough on their plates already. They absolutely did not need to get involved in whatever shenanigans had lured Rhain from his base tonight, no matter how intriguing they might be.

Cormac cleared his throat. "We don't have eyes inside the cavern, Quin, so make sure you're checking in."

Ivan snickered at Cormac's pissy tone. The man was out of luck if he thought that was happening. Quin was not about to narrate his moves and nor was Ivan.

"Stop being such a mother hen. They've got Ivan down there with them. They're going to be fine," Navi said.

Godsdammit, Navi, he thought. Did his brother ever consider his words before he spoke? One absolutely did not say things that could bring the wrath of the goddess of luck down upon them. Ivan sketched a protective rune to counteract the jinx.

"Godsdammit, Navi. How many times have I told you never to say those words before or during a mission?" Cormac growled, saying what everyone else on the comm with them wanted to say.

"Mother hen?" Navi sounded confused.

Ivan shook his head. Navi. He loved his brother, but Navi could be such a dingbat sometimes.

Across the room, Bea paused, her eyes widening. Ivan followed her gaze to where a cone-shaped device on a plinth near the back of the cavern. Bea's prototype. Though she told him it was a scaled-down version of what would eventually help power a ship, it was a lot smaller than Ivan expected. The brassy-colored device with its flat, circular panels ringing the surface could fit in a large rucksack. Despite its smallish size, it looked heavy and too awkward to sneak out of the cavern without anyone taking notice. Maybe they could grab it when it was transported out of the cave.

"Can you snatch it? You don't want to leave it there, do you?" Navi asked.

"No to both questions," Bea said in a firm voice. "But it'll be taken care of."

If she gave any more details, Ivan didn't hear. He'd spotted an unwelcome someone, and his entire focus was on her. Amaryllis Vertè.

She was stunning, as always. Even though she'd covered up her verdigris markings with either makeup or a holo-glamour, her deep copper skin still glowed. Her black silk dress pushed her ample breasts up so they nearly spilled out of the neckline, then nipped in at her waist before flaring out over the curve of her hips and falling to the floor. She'd twisted her braids into a crown of purples, blues, and pinks upon her head. She probably thought she was blending in with that mask and simple black dress of hers, but she elevated it, drawing admiring stares as she glided through the space like she owned the place.

Of course, Amaryllis was here. Ivan cursed. "Navi, you asshole. You did jinx us. Look at who's standing by the bronze statue. What the fuck is she doing here?"

"Is that Amaryllis?" Quin asked.

Ivan abandoned the plinth with the painting and slid along the wall towards her. "Yep," Ivan said. "Stay on mission. I've got her."

"Let me know if you need assistance," Quin said, turning Bea so her back was to Amaryllis and his to a wall.

Ivan appreciated his captain left it at that and didn't try to talk him out of it because, as per usual when it came to Amaryllis, he was about to do something stupid.

3

AMARYLLIS

As she tried to convince herself she was seeing things, she spotted Andrea in her red pantsuit, her icy blonde bob skimming the edge of its high collar. The woman so desperately wanted to be Lore, she'd taken to dressing like her.

Amaryllis rolled her eyes as the woman tipped her tall glass of bubbly in her direction. Could she be any more conspicuous? The goal right now was to blend in with the crowd, not stand out. That lurid red in a sea of primarily black and white was not blending in. Nor was getting drunk and loudly flirting with anyone wearing a tuxedo. Not a lick of sense in that brain of hers, but plenty of ambition and the misplaced belief that she was both in the right and in charge.

If it came down to it, Amaryllis would ditch Lore's merc in a heartbeat. She wasn't about to get caught by security because one of the very unwelcome additions to her team had no clue what undercover meant. Maybe Andrea just didn't give a shit. The idea that Lore had sent her here to fuck up the operation flashed across Amaryllis's brain. But why would Lore do that? She wouldn't. Lore said she needed this prototype thingy, and there was no profit in purposefully sabotaging the job that Amaryllis could see. She shook the thought from her head.

"How are the appetizers?" Dagby asked, her husky voice refocusing Amaryllis on the mission at hand.

Turning away from Andrea and her annoying display and firmly telling herself that her mind was playing tricks on her regarding Ivan, Amaryllis snagged a round puff and popped it in her mouth. "The seafood snacks are pretty good, but the bubbly is shit," she said, giving Dagby the code they'd agreed upon to switch to their private comms so she could do a quick check-in with her small crew without Lore's hangers-on noting every word and reporting back to her. She double tapped her wrist and slid a finger up towards her elbow, opening their private channel.

"So, spill. What's the situation really like down there?" Dagby asked.

"Andrea is making a spectacle of herself, and I get the feeling that Von is going to knock out either Skip or Kenny or both before too much longer." She decided not to mention Ivan, knowing they'd only tease her about seeing that man in every shadow. Bad enough they'd agreed with Quin earlier when he offered to get them a hotel room so she and Ivan could bang it out. Although, she wouldn't say no to a free room on Badin, even if she had to share it with Ivan. Hotel rooms on the pleasure planet weren't cheap, and she was trying to save every credit.

"Hopefully, he'll wait until we're done to do that," Trick said. "Give us time to come up with a plausible story and dispose of any bodies."

"Yikes. So, just as we thought, then." Dagby wasn't jazzed about Lore's mercenaries either, but there wasn't much they could do about it and stay in Lore's good graces.

No one wanted to be on Lore's bad side. Getting on her bad side meant they'd be in the shit with The Cabal, and those bastards would take any excuse to get in a jab and a slice whenever possible.

"You know, this would have been so much easier without Lore's little spies hanging around, sticking their noses where they weren't wanted," Trick said, the indistinct murmur of a sports announcer and crowd noise in the background.

Von grunted in agreement. Since he said nothing, Amaryllis assumed Von hadn't lost his temper yet and tossed Skip off a cliff or snapped Kenny's neck and ditched his body under one of the giant yews that formed the hedge maze.

Though, if something happened to them in the course of doing the job, Lore really couldn't be too upset, could she? After all, accidents and death happened on these types of dangerous jobs all the time. Not much you could do about it. For the moment, however, at least one of the two mercenaries was still alive and close enough to Von that he couldn't safely communicate on the crew's private channel.

"So, did you find it?" Dagby asked.

"It's here," she said, her voice tight with excitement. After all her time searching, she'd finally found it. While Lore might have sent the team to get their hands on an engine prototype, Amaryllis had a secondary goal for this particular job. She was here for the Ibiana Diadem, a filigreed tiara encrusted with flame stones and black opals worn by the Verdet matriarchs as a symbol of their power and status.

Stolen from the Verdet clan home on Pavan during a mostly unsuccessful incursion by Melorian forces a century ago, the diadem disappeared only to resurface at tonight's exclusive black market. Amaryllis wanted it because it belonged with the Verdet people — her people, not that there were many left in the galaxy, and none she knew of personally — not hidden away for another century in yet another rich dick's private collection. With no living relatives, she desperately wanted that connection to her ancestors.

But Lore didn't care about restoring priceless relics to their rightful owners, not even when they belonged with the family Amaryllis lost over twenty years ago. So Amaryllis hadn't even mentioned the diadem, though she was certain Lore knew it was up for auction. Come to think of it, it's probably why Lore decided her team needed babysitters for this job, so they wouldn't go after it as well and risk the job. Dammit.

Lore's insistence on sending her own people to tag along on this job was really jacking up Amaryllis's plans, especially with Andrea stalking around the cavern as her supposed backup and drawing unwanted attention. If Andrea had just stayed outside with Von or even on *Dog's Day* with Dagby, it would have been simple to switch the real diadem for the fake one she had stowed away under her skirt. She could've snagged it before it left the island with its new owner and still had plenty of time to grab Lore's prototype.

"It's really there?" Dagby's voice pulled her focus back from her musings.

Feeling Andrea's eyes on her, she strolled past the plinth holding the diadem and ground her teeth. So close and yet so far. "It is."

"Oh, no. I recognize that tone of yours," Dagby said. "What's the problem?"

"Andrea." Amaryllis grimaced. "Too nosy, too close, too loud. I don't see how I can make the switch without her noticing."

"I can swim ashore and help you hide the body," Trick offered. "Give me like ten minutes, and I'll be there."

She huffed out a quiet laugh. "Now, now. We can't solve every problem with violence, as much as I'd like to take you up on it in this instance."

"Offer stands. These babysitters are getting on my last nerve."

Von let out another grunt of agreement.

"Do anything other than the assigned job, and she'll report it back to Lore," Dagby said.

"Exactly. And because this is in addition to Lore's job and not in any way approved by the boss..." Amaryllis trailed off.

"She'd be pissed beyond belief." Dagby understood why Amaryllis felt beholden to Lore, why she still, after all these years, worked to impress Lore and earn her praise. Both of them wanted to prove their worth to Lore, to show that they were deserving of the sanctuary she'd granted them when they were younger, and the time and training she'd put into both of them.

Looking for protection from some decisions that had led her down the wrong path and were coming back to bite her, Dagby joined The Cabal about twelve years ago. The Cabal, already filled with less-than-law-abiding citizens who were used to evading the repercussions of their own poor choices, was an ideal place to hide, especially once Lore found out how good a pilot Dagby was. With only a few years separating them, Dagby and Amaryllis had immediately bonded, becoming soul sisters, together through thick and thin.

Both Von and Trick also understood Amaryllis's motivations since they, too, had been "rescued" by Lore, given sanctuary when they most needed it, and welcomed into the rough arms of The Cabal. Lore was good at finding lost souls who needed a home and who, because of that, felt as if they owed her their loyalty and even their lives. Luckily for Amaryllis, she'd found a genuine family with Dagby, Von, and Trick.

"Dagby, once this thing is over, you think you can find out who bought the diadem for me?" They'd have to go after it later, after they ditched Lore's spies and handed the prototype over her. Lore didn't need to know what Amaryllis did in her spare time without her approval.

"Absolutely." She paused, then added, "I mean, maybe? Though I have to warn you that I wasn't able to crack the list of attendees. If there's that kind of security on the buyer list, and I have to imagine there is, then most likely not. Sorry."

Scanning the crowd for any sign of Ivan, Amaryllis let out a disappointed sigh. Not ideal. If Dagby couldn't track the buyer, they'd be back to square one, with the diadem once again vanishing into the hands of a private collector.

But she had faith. She'd found it once; she'd find it again. If Dagby couldn't dig up the information she needed, she'd just have to find someone who could. At least this time, they had a starting place.

"But I didn't really put my all into it, you know?" Dagby hurried to reassure her. "I'm like fifty-six percent sure I can get the info we need if I focus and have more time."

"We'll worry about that later. Right now, we'd probably better drop the private chat and return to team comms." They'd already been off team comms for too long, and Andrea was giving Amaryllis suspicious looks.

"Right. Don't want them to have anything to tattle to Lore about." There was a quick squelching noise as Dagby switched all their comms back to the full team.

"Teams, check in," Amaryllis said, carrying on as if they hadn't had a whole entire private conversation without Lore's mercs.

"No change for the solo aquatic team; Vanid patrols still following established routes and schedule," Trick chimed in.

"Ground team in position," Von said. "Maze is clear of watchers; we've got eyes on security bots patrolling the gardens. Ready with the diversion on your go-ahead, Cap."

"Primary team has eyes on the prize." Amaryllis took up position near a bronze statue close to the tunnel exit. "Our item is up for auction soon and, if it follows the pattern of the other items, will leave the cavern shortly after, so be ready."

While the map Lore provided showed a second tunnel leading from the cavern, only the main tunnel was accessible to guests. It led into the center of a large hedge maze a fair distance from the house. Von and his team were posted right outside the maze, monitoring the area.

Auction winners who wanted to transport their new prizes themselves were escorted through the maze to a private landing strip on the edge of the island with armed security. The plan was that the ground team would make their move at the landing pad, snatching the prototype before it was loaded onto a purchaser's shuttle.

Andrea slid up beside Amaryllis, a half-finished drink dangling from her fingertips. "All the pretty jewels here tonight, and you're not allowed to touch a single one. So sad." She made a little moue of disappointment. Amaryllis's love of sparkly things and her deft touch when it came to attaining them was well known among The Cabal.

Clenching her jaw as she fought against the urge to punch the annoying woman in the nose, Amaryllis crossed her arms and ignored her.

Andrea continued. "I saw you eyeing that ugly tiara. Lore would not be pleased if you ruined the mission to grab some useless trinket."

Did she just call a thousand-year-old diadem a "useless trinket"? Amaryllis narrowed her eyes at Andrea. "We're done here. Go meet up with Von and the rest of the team. I'm right behind you."

"Don't think I won't tell Lore everything that happened here tonight," she said, an ugly glint in her limpid blue eyes.

With a casual shrug, Amaryllis said, "Go ahead. You'll just make a fool of yourself if you try to spin it like I've done something wrong or disobeyed Lore's orders. We're following those orders. We're here for the prototype and nothing else." She took a step forward, her folded arms bumping against the shorter woman's chest, driving her backwards a step. "Don't forget, Lore's not here, and we're a long way from base. I'm running this job. I'm in charge here. You're merely a lackey, a kiss-ass trying to ingratiate yourself with Lore. It's not a good look, Andrea."

The woman opened her mouth to protest, but Amaryllis cut her off, leaning close to whisper in her ear, "If you don't follow my orders, I'll make certain you meet with a fatal depressurizing accident on the trip back home. No one will contradict my story. Do you understand me?"

Andrea paled. A muscle jumped in her jaw as she worked to compose herself. Finally, with a haughty toss of her hair, she said, "We won't have a problem as long as you do what you're supposed to." She almost pulled it off, but Amaryllis caught the tremor in her voice.

"I know my job. Now, go do yours." She flicked her fingers at the woman in a shoo motion, biting back a triumphant grin as the woman shot her a dirty look and scurried off. She'd wanted to tell that chick off since she stepped foot on board *Dog's Day*. That felt so good.

"You tell her, boss," Dagby whispered in her right ear.

"Why are you always so mean, Rilly?" a man whispered in her left ear as he covered her mouth with one hand and with the other, grabbed her around the waist, trapping her arms, before hauling her off down the tunnel behind them.

Oh, fuck, she thought, struggling against the forearm of banded steel wrapped around her middle. *Ivan*.

4

IVAN

Why he thought grabbing Amaryllis and dragging her away from the auction was a good idea, he'd never know, especially considering the headache doing something similar not too long ago had caused his captain. *You'd think I'd learn from his experience*, Ivan reflected as he booked it as fast and as far as he could down the exit tunnel before Amaryllis could recover from her surprise.

He was already regretting his impulsive move. Because, while Bea, the woman Quin manhandled during her rescue, had literally bitten his ass and kneed him in the balls as retribution, Amaryllis was from the "grab it, twist it, pull it off" school of thought. *Idiot. What was I thinking?* he asked himself.

"What just happened?" Cormac squawked over the team comm. "Talk to me, people." Maybe if the rest of the *Laughing Dragon* crew hadn't arrived at the planet too late to outfit Ivan and Quin with cams, he wouldn't be so pissy, always demanding more information from the ground team. But Ivan didn't answer. He had more dangerous things to worry about than a cranky crew member.

He released Amaryllis as soon as she turned into a writhing mass of pissed off hellcat and took a step back, his hands up.

"Now, Rilly. Let me explain," he said, as if his overtures would diffuse the situation he created.

And what exactly was he going to say to her? That he dragged her away from whatever crime she was doing at this highly illegal auction so she wouldn't spot Bea and mess up their mission? As if that would get her to cooperate or forget what he just did.

Maybe he should have tried to pay her off first or gotten her to leave a different way. If he'd stopped to think for even a second, he could have come up with a better plan. But no. When he spotted her by the statue, her multicolored braids twisted into a crown, her gleaming copper skin on display above the low cut of her black dress, and her eyes glaring daggers at someone other than him for once, his common sense disappeared into the aether, and he wound up making a stupid move that might very well lead to Amaryllis twisting off his balls. They shriveled, tucking up close to his body just thinking about it.

"Ivan just removed Amaryllis from the area," Quin said over the comm, the irritation in his captain's voice coming through loud and clear. Understandable, considering he'd put a crimp in tonight's plans. By grabbing Amaryllis, he'd effectively alerted her to his team's presence while also removing any assistance he might provide to said team. A royal fuck up indeed.

The very hellcat of which they spoke whirled on him, practically spitting fire, the skirt of her dress swishing against his legs. Then she hauled off and punched him in the nose.

His head snapped back, and he let out a pained grunt, his eyes watering.

"What the actual fuck, Ivan?" She ground the words out, flags of furious color shading her cheeks a dark rose gold. She shot a glare back towards the main cavern, that single look scaring away the servers who'd stuck their heads out of their makeshift cave kitchen, curious about what was going on. "I am here on a job." She threw out an arm back towards the auction, as if he wasn't aware of what she was talking about.

"Ivan, you good? Need backup?" Quin asked over the team comm.

He made a sound in the negative. "Good," he answered, spotting a server speaking with a pair of guards and gesturing in their direction. *Shit*.

His attention diverted, he missed seeing Amaryllis ball up another fist until she nailed him in the stomach with it, driving the air from his lungs with an oof. "But you know," he wheezed, eyeing her as she danced away, then darted back in to take another shot. He leaned to the side to avoid the next blow, her knuckles grazing his jaw. "Rilly was never one to go easy."

He kept his hands raised, unwilling to do more than dodge her blows and let her vent some of that righteous anger of hers. He supposed he should be happy she hadn't pulled a knife on him. Yet. The night was still young.

She narrowed her eyes at him, slowing her footwork and dropping her fists to her hips. "Is that Quin? Tell that rat bastard he can visit all three of the hottest hells along with your entire crew, who I assume are also listening in. His interference in my job is really pissing me off."

Stifling a grin, he passed her message along to Quin, "She wants you to know that she doesn't appreciate us fucking up her heist."

"Noted," Quin said in a dry tone.

"No, I absolutely do not." She paused for a moment, listening to her own comm. "And my crew agrees with me."

Of course they did.

The two members of the security team dressed in plain black suits similar to his approached them. "Ma'am, are you alright? Are you in distress?" the young guard squeaked, his heavy brows drawn together over his brown eyes in concern.

Ivan held his breath. This could go so wrong in so many ways, all of them depending on what Amaryllis did next.

Turned out, she didn't appreciate their interference. "First, not a ma'am. Second, this is absolutely none of your business.

This is a disagreement between me and this annoying man here. Be on your way." She flicked her fingers at them.

He winced. Not the best idea to piss off security.

At her abrupt dismissal, the older guard puffed up like a bantam rooster, his chest straining the buttons of his white shirt. He double-tapped his wrist and pulled up a holo. "What are your names?" he asked, attempting to look down his nose at them. Unfortunately for him, he had neither the height nor the air of authority required to pull it off.

"I have no reason to give you my name." She slowly edged her way down the tunnel towards the exit.

Ivan stayed quiet, quickly reviewing and discarding plans on how to diffuse the situation. Clearly, an outright confrontation with security this close to the auction was in neither of their best interests.

The older guard gave her a condescending look. "If you won't give us your names, I'm afraid we're going to have to escort you off the property." He gestured to his partner. "Jason, call for backup. These two are leaving. Authorities will be waiting at the Katash dock to take you into custody for trespassing and criminal mischief."

In one swift, smooth motion, Amaryllis palmed a short-barreled blaster, aimed it at them, and pulled the trigger. She didn't even give Ivan a chance to move.

He heard a crackle in his ear.

The older guard's holo flickered and died. Both guards let out a squawk, frantically tapping their wrists to no avail.

He slapped at his own comm, trying to wake it back up. "What in the hells? What did you do?" he asked her. The comm was fried. "You could've killed me."

With a casual shrug, she tucked the blaster back into her pocket, grabbed his arm, and tugged him along after her as she made for the exit at the other end of the tunnel. "Concentrated EMP. It'll knock out their communication devices and any other nearby tech until they can get them reset."

"Well, you got me, too," he grumbled, though he allowed her to drag him along behind her. In fact, he wasn't certain he could pry her fingers loose from his arm. That was quite a death grip she had there.

Since they were moving away from the guards, Bea, and the prototype, he decided to play along until he had some answers about what she was doing at the auction. Besides fucking up his life, as per usual that was. Quin and the team would be worried when they didn't hear from him, but what was he supposed to do? There was no way he could return to the cavern now, not with security already on alert. His presence would only stir up the watchdogs more and draw unwanted attention to Quin and Bea.

And he could kiss his ass goodbye if his return fucked things up for Rhain and Dai and whatever nefarious shenanigans they were up to on the island. Known to most only as the Knight, leader of the Shields, Rhain was someone he didn't want to be on the bad side of. Dai, Bea's sister and an ex-spy, was at least as dangerous, if not more so.

Also, Quin would absolutely murder him if his actions led to him having to deal with a pissed off Rhain. The *Laughing Dragon* crew just erased the last favor they'd owed the man. There was no way any of them aspired to be on the Knight's naughty list.

Quin knew he could handle himself. It would be fine.

"Don't you know to move out of the line of fire when someone aims a blaster near you?" she asked, picking up their pace to a run. "It's a wonder you've survived as long as you have."

With security hot on their heels, they booked it down the tunnel and up the stairs before bursting through a door that spit them out in the center of the estate's hedge maze.

Ivan ducked as a blast hit the edge of the stone folly, showering them with chips of granite. He and Amaryllis exchanged a glance and separated, him going left and her right. Behind them, Jason and his partner followed suit.

With practiced ease, Ivan spun on the ball of his foot, slamming the other foot into Jason's head. He felt a twinge of remorse as the young man crumpled into a heap, knocked out cold. He turned to watch Amaryllis grappling with the older guy, wincing in sympathy as she nailed him on the chin. The man shook it off and swung at her.

"Did you punch me in the tit, you piece of shit?" she shouted, scaring the man into taking a step back.

"Would you like some help?" Ivan offered, feeling magnanimous. After all, he wasn't doing anything else at the moment except acting as backup in case more security arrived.

She spared him a glance. "Done with yours already?"

"Yep." He toed the downed man. Still breathing. "I must have gotten the lightweight." He shrugged off how easily Jason had gone down. "Offer stands."

"Nah," she said, gathering her skirt in her hands, giving him a flash of her deliciously thick thighs. She caught him looking and gave him a wink, lifting her skirts higher to reveal more of her silky copper skin.

His cheeks heated, his face turning red. The curse of being a ginger bit him in the ass yet again.

"I've got this." She ducked a wild swing. "Wait right there, Cherry."

He blushed harder at the nickname. Fuck.

She kicked out, her foot connecting with the stocky guard's solar plexus. Wheezing, the man folded at the waist, his arms moving to cradle his torso protectively. She darted in and, with a graceful leap, slammed an elbow against the back of his head. In slow motion, he sank to his knees on the gravel pathway and toppled over, unconscious.

Nice, he thought. A pang of loss swept through him as she dropped her skirts and shook out the wrinkles, covering up a sight he hoped to see again soon. *No. Fuck*. He absolutely did not want to see her naked. In fact, he'd be thrilled if she disappeared from his range of notice entirely. She was too much of a pain in his ass already. Just imagine what she would be like if they slept together. Gritting his teeth, he did his level best to ignore the pulse of lust that shot down his spine and straight to his cock at the idea of her naked and writhing under him while he made her come.

But that would never happen, especially not with their contentious history. Or maybe Quin was right, and they needed to bang it out in that hotel room he'd offered up not so long ago.

Again, no. Fuck. He needed to halt that train of thought in its tracks. He did not want to get any more entangled with Amaryllis than he already was.

"We need to move, to get out of this maze and away from here," the bane of his existence said. "These two might be down, but those servers were nosy as the three hells. They'll report to security about what went down and then we'll be swarmed."

She wasn't wrong. "I'll just move these two out of the way," he said.

Grabbing Jason under the arms, he hauled him behind a well-groomed bush. Then he did the same for Amaryllis's guy. Not an ideal hiding spot for the unconscious men, but at least they'd be out of direct line of sight of anyone entering or exiting the area.

Straightening his suit jacket, he eyed her. Better to get what he needed to do out of the way now, rather than later. After all, isn't that what he told Quin? He wasn't about to be a hypocrite because he couldn't follow his own advice.

He cleared his throat. "I need to apologize for my actions at the auction. They were impulsive and out of line."

She cocked her head, eyeing him. "What?"

Well, this sucked. Was she genuinely asking what he was apologizing for or just fucking with him? He inhaled deeply and said, "For grabbing you. I shouldn't have done that. I'm sorry."

Her eyebrows rose, and she stared at him for a beat longer before doubling over with laughter.

She laughed at him. Laughed. What the fuck? He apologized and here she was, practically rolling on the ground.

See, this right there was one of the many ways in which this particular woman drove him absolutely out the airlock. "The fuck, Rilly? I'm trying to be sincere here and you're laughing?"

"You," she said, taking a deep breath to clear away the giggles, "apologize to me? Why? For grabbing me and fucking up my job?"

A muscle jumped in his jaw as he gave her a tight nod.

"Ivan, you idiot." She pointed a finger at him, then at herself. "This is what we do. If I'd spotted you first, I would have done the exact same thing."

He'd like to see her try to pick him up and haul him down a tunnel, but sure. Let her believe she could. He crossed his arms over his chest and raised an eyebrow, not seeing the humor in any of it.

She sighed. "Fine. If it gets you off my back, I accept your apology, as unnecessary as it is. Now, if we're done here, can we get a move on? I doubt you want to get busted any more than I do." Not waiting for an answer, she picked up her skirts and took off through the narrow arch of hedges and into the maze.

Taking a second to gnash his teeth, he followed her. Remembering when his grandfather taught him how to get out of a maze without hitting any dead ends, he trailed his left hand over the sharply manicured branches, the needle-like yew leaves tickling his fingers.

"What do you mean, 'this is what we do'?" he asked. Why wasn't she pissed at him? Did she really think this was all a game between them?

She tossed a glance at him over her shoulder. "You fuck up my jobs, I fuck up yours... it's our thing."

Huh. He hadn't really realized that they had a 'thing'. He thought that they so strongly disliked one another, they went out of their way to piss each other off. That could be considered a thing, he guessed. Or was he that bad at reading intentions? He didn't think so. Maybe it was just with her. "So you're not mad that I stopped you from completing the job you were pulling here?"

Slowing, she moved to his right side and looped her arm through his. It wasn't a friendly gesture, though. Just one of convenience and disguise, as she gave the well-dressed couple strolling past them through the maze a close-lipped smile and a bob of her chin. As soon as they'd rounded the corner, she dropped his arm and sped up again. "You stopped nothing."

He kept pace, sparing her a questioning glance. "What do you mean?"

"I mean, I was about to leave when you grabbed me so you hauling me from the cavern only accelerated my plans." The corner of her mouth quirked up as she tilted her head up at him. "Sorry if that disappoints you."

He grunted in response. He'd gone at it intending to pull her from the playing field, not necessarily to fuck up her job, though that would've been a delightful bonus.

At the sound of raised voices behind them, Amaryllis grabbed his arm in her death grip again and hustled him along. "Faster, you slow-moving mountain of a man. Do you really want them to catch us here?" She tugged at his arm. "No doubt they'd happily ship us off to a prison moon in a heartbeat."

"That certainly wouldn't be ideal, so no," he grumbled, jogging alongside her. "How big is this damn thing, anyway?"

Without skipping a beat, she said, "Made up of over ten thousand yews imported from the now-closed planet of Dathria, the Vanid maze covers just over one square kilometer." When he gave her a look, she shrugged and said, "What? I do my research. If you were as thorough as me and my team, maybe you'd have known that bit of important information."

"Okay, princess. No need to be snarky."

"Princess?" She scoffed. "Do you really believe that title suits me?"

He shrugged. "Well, you're wearing a crown."

"That's my hair." She reached up and touched her crown of braids, as if to confirm it was still there and intact.

"And you've got the superior attitude down pat."

"Thank you." She took it as a compliment. Of course she would.

"So, yes, princess fits."

"I'd rather be queen." She took a sharp right turn and almost knocking a pale woman in a mustard yellow dress made of some kind of floaty material into a hedge. Amaryllis ignored the woman's squawks of protest and kept moving. "The queen, she's the one who holds all the power. A princess, while she gets to wear pretty dresses and flit around doing princess-y things, a queen rules. I much prefer to be in charge, in control of my own life and my own choices." She shot a look behind them, then gave him a smile. "Like now." She took another right and, with the exit in view, she released her grip on his arm, hiked up her skirts higher, and took off.

He looked back at three very pissed off members of the security team hot on their heels. "Fuck. Wait up," he growled, lengthening his stride.

But the woman ran like a gazelle, dashing down the greenway and out the exit. Of course, she'd try to ditch him now that they were out here in the open, away from his team and without any nearby assistance. Well, she wouldn't get away from him that easily. They still had things to discuss, like why she was here in the first place. It certainly wasn't because she wanted to drink crappy alcohol and eat crab puffs. He needed to know if she was there for Bea or for the prototype because, if she was, they were going to have a serious problem that he had to figure out how to handle.

Running was not his favorite activity, but a surge of irritation and determination carried him down the path after her. He burst out of the exit and paused for half a beat to scan the area. Between the full moon and the artfully placed accent lights, the gardens were lit up enough that he could see without night vision goggles, yet dark enough to cloak those who wanted a sense of privacy in the shadows.

No security bots nearby, which meant either someone had disabled them or they were responding to another issue somewhere else on the property. To the right, a winding, flower-lined path lead through the extensive gardens and up to the main house. Straight ahead, a black sand beach, a small fishing vessel anchored off shore. To the left, he spotted Amaryllis, her flowing black skirts flaring out behind her as she ran. If he recalled Navi's map correctly, that direction would take her to the estate's secondary landing pad. According to Rhain's people, that was where the auction items would be loaded for those who didn't want to depend on the auction runners for a swift and safe delivery. Amaryllis and her team must be planning to snatch their prize at the landing pad. Smart.

Behind him, the guards yelled at them to stop. Ahead of him, a woman in a bright red dress materialized out of the shadows, blaster in hand. Ivan felt a sharp pain in his thigh and stumbled.

At the first blast, Amaryllis spun around. "No!" she shouted, spinning on her heels and running back towards them. "Andrea, don't shoot him!"

But the woman didn't listen. Ivan saw the muzzle flare again, then he couldn't breathe, and finally, darkness.

5

AMARYLLIS

Horrified, she watched him fall in slow motion, a giant tree crashing to the ground. The three guards behind Ivan also dropped, crumpling where they stood. Her vision coated in a haze of red, Amaryllis slammed into Andrea's back, tackling her to the ground and knocking the blaster from her hand.

"You stupid cow." She smashed her fist into Andrea's nose, a satisfying crunch under her knuckles. "I told you not to shoot. You need to follow orders when I give them." She grabbed a hunk of the woman's hair, hauling her face close to hers and giving her a shake before letting go. "Do you understand me?" She was so mad it took physical effort to hold herself back from repeatedly smashing her fist into Andrea's annoying face. Though the first time was satisfying, once was not enough. Still, she resisted.

Now flat on her back, the smugly superior expression wiped clean off her face, Andrea nodded weakly, blood from her nose spilling down her cheek and staining her blonde hair.

Strong arms hauled Amaryllis the rest of the way off Andrea and set her on her feet. "Okay, Captain. I think she gets it," Von said, staring down at the prone woman. He didn't offer her a hand up.

Amaryllis shifted her glare to him, her hands fisting her skirt. "I'm not sure she does. She seems pretty hard-headed to me, considering we recently had a very serious discussion about the repercussions of her not following my orders."

But deep down, she knew her reaction wasn't only about this snake not following orders. It was that Andrea shot Ivan. Ivan, who blushed when he caught a glimpse of her thighs. Ivan, who growled when she tormented and teased him. Ivan, who she wouldn't mind taking to bed to see if his entire body turned red when he blushed. She didn't want their — whatever it was; not a relationship, surely not that, but connection? Situationship? — thing to end, especially not like this.

The woman paled, her skin turning ghostly white in the moonlight.

Her heart pounding, Amaryllis looked over to where Ivan lay still on the ground, not moving. "I swear to all the gods, if you killed him, I will follow through on my earlier threat," she snarled at Andrea, her tone low and venomous.

Hurrying over to Ivan, she dropped to her knees beside him and, bottling up her anger and concern and locking those emotions down, she did a quick field assessment. Upper chest wound and another to his left thigh. Leaking blood but not gushing, which most likely meant the shots hadn't hit any arteries. She hoped. Based on the locations of the wounds, there would be internal damage though. They needed to get him into a medi-bay and quickly.

Von checked on the three guards sprawled on the grass and shook his head. "Gone."

Motherfucking son of a backstabbing cretin. The bottle broke on her anger, filling her up, her heart pounding hard in her chest. She clenched her fists so hard her knuckles turned white as she fought against the urge to shake the ever-loving shit out of Andrea. She'd managed to jack up the entire job, which had actually been salvageable up to this point.

Because now there were five guards out of commission. They

wouldn't have much time before someone came looking for them. Meaning they didn't have the time they needed to wait at the landing pad until the auction ended. Meaning they couldn't boost the prototype as it was loaded onto a ship, bound for its new home. They needed to leave before security locked this place down and security swarmed everywhere. Their countermeasures wouldn't be enough to halt an emergency response.

And then there was Ivan. She was not about to leave him behind, bleeding out on the estate's perfectly manicured lawn.

Skip and Kenny ran up to them. "Another guy was tailing you. Not security. One of the guests, I think. Wearing a real fancy suit," Skip said. "We took care of him. Didn't even see us coming, he was so focused on following you."

"You didn't kill him, did you?" Von asked, his brows drawing together like black thunderclouds.

Kenny swallowed hard and shook his head. "You were pretty clear on the no murdering part of the job. Only knocked him around some."

Having heard everything over the team comms, both Skip and Kenny shot dark looks at Andrea, sitting on the ground pinching the bridge of her nose in an effort to stop it bleeding. She was in the shit with everyone on the team, not just Amaryllis. She'd be lucky if she made it back to base in one piece.

"He mighta been unconscious when we left him, but I'm practically positive he was still breathing," Skip added.

Amaryllis raised her eyes to the starry skies above, hoping for an extra dose of patience to make it through the night. None of this would've happened if it had been just her crew on the job. Well, Ivan would have, since he would still have been there, but not the murdering. Damn Lore to the netherworlds and back. Why couldn't she trust that Amaryllis knew what she was doing? Now they were going to have to leave here without finishing the job and, of course, Lore would blame Amaryllis for it all going sideways.

In truth, it was her fault. It was her job. She was running it.

She sighed. *Good to be the queen, my ass*, she thought. *Maybe I'd be better off as a princess. At least that way, I could blame someone else for the fuck ups.*

She pointed at Skip and Kenny, then at Ivan. "You two. Grab him. He's coming with us." When Kenny opened his mouth to protest, she cut him off with a swipe of her hand. "He needs medical attention, and we can't leave him behind to be arrested. He'd give us up in a heartbeat." He wouldn't, but it was a good enough reason to convince Lore's people that Ivan had to come with them. She was responsible for him getting shot and, as annoying and frustrating as the man was, she didn't want him dead.

"What about the job?" Trick asked, his voice making her jump. She'd been so focused on the people in front of her, she'd almost forgotten about Trick and Dagby. Dangerous in her line of work. Another reason to dislike working with the untrustworthy people Lore kept sticking her with. Too much attention had to be paid to them, pulling focus from the job at hand and her core team.

"Fubar-ed to the three hells," Von said, his hands on his hips as he eyed Andrea, still sitting on the ground, still pale and quiet. It wouldn't be too long before she bounced back to her old, bitchy self. Obviously, Von thought the same.

"We need to get out of here before the security bots show up," Amaryllis said.

Von grunted. "Our diversion won't keep them from their regular patrols for too much longer and, once they spot the bodies, this entire island will go on lockdown."

This was why she loved her crew; they were on the same page.

"Acknowledged," Trick said. "On my way. Pickup in three."

Skip and Kenny struggled under Ivan's weight. "Do we really have to bring him? He weighs a literal ton," Skip whined, his breath coming out in short pants.

Amaryllis raised an eyebrow at Von, who shrugged.

He frowned, considering the situation. "I could do a shoulder-carry, but that would put too much pressure on the wounds, and he might bleed out before we can get him back to the ship."

"Grab his feet, and I'll cover our retreat?" Because she sure as hells didn't trust Andrea to do it.

He nodded. Once they had Ivan repositioned and his weight better distributed, they took off to meet up with Trick and get the hells off Badin before anything else went wrong.

THE LEADER of The Cabal sat behind her desk of polished steel, her hands folded together as she watched Amaryllis, who stood at parade rest exactly six feet in front of her. There were no chairs in Lore's office beside the one she sat in, no hint of comfort or softness. Weapons of all shapes and sizes were artfully displayed on the gray wall behind her. The scent of brimstone or possibly clove hung in the air.

Lore wore one of her ubiquitous pantsuits, this one in a saturated blue that emphasized her creamy white skin and drew the eye as the only splash of color in the room. Her honey blonde hair was slicked back into a severe bun at the base of her long neck, not a hair out of place. She was considered a handsome woman by many, her sharp features bold and unflinching. She was also scary as the three hells and no one, not even the biggest, baddest Cabal member, wanted to be called to Lore's stark office. Not even Amaryllis, who most believed Lore was grooming as her successor.

As if Lore would ever willingly hand over the reins to the empire she spent the last thirty years building. Sure, Lore had rescued her from the wreckage of a colony ship all those years ago. She adopted her and took her under her wing, making sure the traumatized thirteen-year-old was fed, clothed, and educated in the ways of The Cabal and the wider galaxy. And, having survived the plague that swept through their ship like wildfire, her entire family dead because of it, running out of food, and alone on a dying ship, young Amaryllis saw Lore as not just her rescuer and mother figure, but her hero for many years.

It wasn't until she was in her twenties that Amaryllis realized that, while Lore felt affection for her — maybe even loved her, in her own way — she loved her Cabal more. And she certainly wasn't grooming Amaryllis to take over. Whoever started that rumor obviously didn't know Lore as well as they thought they did.

When it came down to it, Amaryllis was merely another piece on Lore's massive chessboard, just like the others Lore rescued and brought into the violent arms of The Cabal. Lore offered refuge and protection to the desperate and hopeless to fill her ranks. Because of her beneficence, she gained a group of individuals who were deeply loyal to her, many of whom would do almost anything for her approval.

Amaryllis certainly had. For many years, she'd done whatever Lore asked with minimal questioning. She still had that core of loyalty, though she was less than willing to do anything for Lore's approval these days.

On the heels of her realization, it became more and more challenging to remain under Lore's yoke and not buck against her restrictions. It was one of the reasons Amaryllis was working so hard. She wanted to buy her crew full membership in The Cabal. With that elevation in status, she and her crew would have the freedom to choose their own jobs and to refuse Lore's additions to their team.

And, to be perfectly honest with herself, she also wanted to show Lore she was more than capable of running her crew successfully. Even as she yearned for independence and freedom, she still felt beholden to the woman who rescued her and raised her after her parents died. She still wanted her approval and her favor, her love, and her affection.

But it looked like she wouldn't get any of that today. Her stomach filled with knife-tipped butterfly wings as Lore gazed at her with glacial eyes.

"Tell me again why I don't have my prototype?" Lore asked, her quiet words bouncing off the smooth gray walls and black marble flooring.

Her nails digging into her palms, Amaryllis told herself not to respond, not even to defend herself. There was no point. The question was rhetorical; the answer already provided by Andrea, the snitch, who stood to her right, that smug smile firmly back on her stupid face. It didn't matter that Andrea had been the one to put the final nail in the coffin of their job. As leader of the mission, Amaryllis was responsible for the actions of all her team members, even those she didn't pick, didn't know, and didn't trust.

"You'd think that, after all this time, you would know how to run a team, dear," Lore said. "I trained you better than this."

Amaryllis gritted her teeth. She wouldn't react, no matter what buttons Lore pushed. The woman she stood in front of didn't appreciate displays of emotion, but she did enjoy prodding at the painful spots to see how much someone could take before they finally reacted. Hells, she'd kept the entire *Dog's Day* crew on lockdown, unable to fly or leave her base for an entire week before finally meeting with her. Amaryllis was already stewing, but she was practiced at not letting it show.

Lore gave her a small nod of approval for her stoicism, and the butterflies in her stomach lost some of their sharp points. She was in trouble for not completing the mission, but it wasn't the end of the galaxy. Still, she didn't let herself relax. One didn't relax when one was called onto the proverbial carpet.

"Andrea reported the mission a complete failure," Lore said.

Andrea straightened her shoulders, unable to resist shooting Amaryllis a look of triumph.

"Is this true?"

Ignoring Andrea, Amaryllis kept her tone calm and even. "Not entirely. While we failed to procure the prototype, before we left the area, Dagby tagged the ship transporting it. It jumped outside of Melorn airspace and is currently docked at Cora

Station. I was about to send Trick in a hopper to the station to track where the prototype went from there."

An expert-level tracker, Trick had an uncanny ability to follow a lead to the very end. If anyone could track that prototype from Cora Station, it was him. And if he wound up at a dead end, Dagby was hard at work flexing her tech skills and digging up everything she could find on the auction and those who attended. If they were very lucky, she might even uncover a purchase list. But Amaryllis didn't mention that part of their plan because Dagby wasn't hopeful about her chance of success there, and none of them wanted to go to Lore with another failure. Still, it would be useful to get their hands on that list if for no other reason than it would make a suitable gift for Lore.

Andrea whipped her head around to glare at Amaryllis. "You didn't tell me that," she said, her voice sharp.

"Why would I? It wasn't any concern of yours." Amaryllis didn't bother looking at the woman, keeping her eyes focused on the curved edge of the kajita sword mounted on the wall above Lore's head. She saw her well enough out of the corner of her eye.

Andrea made a choked sound of protest, her face going red.

Lore shifted her gaze. "Andrea, remind me again what I said when I assigned you to this job?"

She snapped to attention. "Lore..." she cut off whatever whiny excuse she was about to unfold at Lore's look. Clearing her throat, she said, "You said that I was being assigned to this job to learn how a strong team functioned."

Amaryllis's heart jumped at Lore's words. *Had she really said that my team was strong? Wow.*

"And?" she prompted.

"And that I was to follow Amaryllis's orders because she was running this job. That I needed to learn how to listen to those who were in charge, even if I didn't think they deserved to be there."

Ouch. Shot to the heart, Amaryllis thought. Of course, Andrea was one of the people who thought she'd gotten where she was because of Lore's nepotism. What she didn't seem to realize was that no one got any help from Lore, especially Amaryllis.

"Correct. And did you follow Amaryllis's orders, Andrea? Did you listen to what your captain told you to do? Or, in this case, what not to do?"

Oh, this was not going well for Andrea, Amaryllis thought. She'd heard that tone before. It was the "patient but not really because this person was about to learn why Lore was so fucking scary" tone.

"I... I..." Andrea stammered.

Lore slashed a hand through the air. "The answer is no. You did not. This was your final chance to prove yourself, Andrea, something I also informed you of. I was very clear about what would happen if you failed."

"Wait," Andrea said, her voice desperate, her eyes searching the room for any sort of assistance and finding none. "I can do better. I'll follow orders next time."

But Lore was done listening to Andrea. "By not following my orders or your captain's, you blew the mission and nearly compromised the team." She pulled a sleek black weapon from under her desk and shot Andrea between the eyes. "Like I said, no more chances."

Amaryllis jumped at the sharp crack of the blaster, her eyes wide as she watched the woman's body fall to the floor.

"Unfortunate," Lore made a moue of disappointment as she tucked the weapon away. She sighed at the expression on Amaryllis's face. "Don't look at me that way. I'd given her so many chances. Too many, in fact. I can't have people thinking I'm going soft, now, can I?"

Goddess forbid, Amaryllis thought.

She clicked her tongue. "Such a waste. I tried to guide her to the right path, but she refused to listen."

"So I guess coloring her hair and dressing like you wasn't enough?" The words just tumbled out of her mouth before she could stop them.

"Not nearly enough," Lore said. "A strong leader knows when to cut away the dead weight, Amaryllis. Andrea was a drain on our resources."

Amaryllis made a noncommittal sound. If that's what was required to be a strong leader, she didn't want it.

"Now, inform Trick he has no reason to go to Cora Station. Christophe and Deno will take it from here."

"What?" Surely she'd misheard her.

Lore tapped a sharpened nail against the smooth metal of her desk, her only sign of impatience. "You're no longer on this job, dear. Did I not make that clear? And here I thought you were sharper than that." Lore tsked. "You failed. Therefore, I can no longer depend on you to get the job done." Lore swept a finger along the edge of her desk, pulling up her holo-computer, and began clicking through something. "Oh, and I want to see my uninvited guest as soon as he's mobile."

Frozen, Amaryllis stared at her. Of course Lore knew about Ivan. She tried not to look at Andrea's body laying on the marble floor. But Lore wouldn't hurt him, would she? No. The Cabal and the Shields recently signed a cease fire, laying down their proverbial swords in an effort to reduce the violence between their factions. Attacking each other's ships was costing too much, especially with the Starguard sticking their noses in things that didn't concern them. Bad enough Andrea had shot Ivan but if Lore did anything else and the Knight took that as a breach of the treaty, the space between planets would become a lot more dangerous and costly for everyone. Lore liked her money far too much to allow that to happen.

Lore looked up, one perfectly sculpted eyebrow rising. "Dismissed."

Fuck. Gritting her teeth, she spun on her heels and walked out.

6

IVAN

Ivan felt like he'd been run over by a speeder. Last he remembered, some mean-looking blonde woman shot him with a blaster. Surprisingly, it hadn't been Amaryllis doing the deed. A glance at his surroundings told him he was in a medibay. Given its small capacity, it was most likely on a cruiser of some sort rather than a space station or planetside. He could tell immediately it wasn't the *Laughing Dragon*. Unfortunately.

Double-tapping on his wrist, he tried to bring up his comm to no avail. Not good. Maybe because of Amaryllis's pulse shot, he needed to get it reset. Or he was somewhere that blocked his comm altogether. He hoped it was the former.

He removed the monitor cuff from his arm, ignoring its sad beep of protest. On the plus side, with no guards present and no restraints on him, it didn't seem to be a prison ship.

Sitting up, he swung his legs over the edge of the narrow bed, his bare feet landing on the cold floor. He scrubbed a hand over his bare chest and frowned when his fingers encountered fresh scar tissue between his shoulder and clavicle. Another freshly healed wound cut across his upper thigh, far too close to his important bits for his liking. He frowned at it, tracing a fingertip over the star-shaped scar.

"A few inches higher and you'd be of no use to me whatsoever," an amused voice said from the doorway.

He looked up to see Amaryllis grinning at him. *Shit.* He hadn't even heard the door open. There must be pain medication or something coursing through his system and dulling his senses for him to miss it. Not good in enemy territory. He couldn't have Amaryllis or any of her ilk sneaking up on him when he wasn't functioning at optimal levels.

Walking into the room, she tossed his clothes next to him on the narrow hospital bed. "Laundered and repaired." She poured a glass of water from a tall pitcher on the counter. "Sorry one of my team members shot you. She's been dealt with." A strange look — if he didn't know better, he'd call it regret — crossed her face. She handed him the glass.

He could feel his face scrunching up into a frown. Her being, well, maybe not nice, but at least apologetic, was throwing him off-kilter. Needing a moment, he stared down into the clear liquid.

"It's not poisoned. Promise." She winked at him.

Did that mean it was or wasn't poisoned? He shook his head, trying to clear it of the muzziness. He must be more doped up than he initially thought.

"Oh, for the gods' sake." She snatched the glass from his hand and drained it dry. Then she filled it back up from the same pitcher and handed it to him. "Drink it. It'll hydrate you and help clear your head. You're no fun when you're loopy from pain meds."

He did as ordered, the cool liquid easing the fire in his throat.

"Good." She nodded her approval. "Now get dressed. Lore wants to see you."

He coughed, the last sip of water squirting out his nose.

"Yeah, that's what I said, too," she said with a small huff of laughter.

"I'm on Lore's base? The *Ephemeris*?" He looked around the small room, confused. Then why was he in this tiny medi-bay?

Lore's base was a decommissioned battleship, which meant that, unless she stripped it to its bones and sold everything off, it should have big, state-of-the art facilities. At the very least, he'd expect a medi-ward that could handle more than three people at any given time.

"You are." Amaryllis toyed with the end of a purple braid. "But at the moment, you're also on *Dog's Day,* in our medi-bay. We brought you here after Andrea shot you. We decided it best to keep you here rather than move you more firmly into Lore's clutches."

"You what? Why?" he asked, cocking his head as he examined her. She'd restyled her hair, the braids at her temples twisted together and the rest loose around her shoulders. It softened her somehow, made her feel more approachable. Of course, that was probably the drugs talking. But even without meds on board, he didn't mind admitting she was a stunning woman.

"You know, I asked myself that very same question." She looked down at the braid she'd wrapped around her fingers and unwound it before returning her gaze to him. "Honestly, I couldn't leave you back there, bleeding out on the grass."

Interesting. "Why?" he asked again.

If she'd left him, one of three things would have happened: he'd have been found by Vanid security and arrested, Quin would have found him and scooped him up, or he'd have bled out from his wounds before anyone found him.

But instead of rolling the dice, she'd hauled his unconscious body onto her ship and brought him here. To Lore. What possible reason would she have to do that? Unless he was a hostage. Which would really suck, because the last place he wanted to be was in Lore's hands.

She crossed her arms over her chest and gave him a look. "I didn't bring you here for Lore, if that's what you're thinking. I didn't even stop to consider how Lore would react to my decision to bring you aboard my ship and, in turn, hers." She let out a puff of air, a soft exhalation that spoke volumes. "I saw you laying there, not moving, two holes in you, put there by one of my team, and I just reacted."

Huh. He wasn't sure what to make of that, either. Had she been worried about him or merely worried about what would happen if he died because of her team member's actions? He wanted to say the latter, but he had the strangest feeling that it was actually the former. "Thanks for saving my life," he said.

She looked away as if embarrassed and shook her head, dismissing his thanks.

"What about Quin? What happened? Why aren't my comms working yet? Does my crew know what happened to me?" Quin was probably so pissed that Ivan had disappeared on him. Did Bea get her prototype back? What about Arden? He had so many questions but held off asking them, unwilling to show his hand. He'd find out when he got a hold of Quin.

"Your comms are functional but blocked because we're on the *Ephemeris*. And don't you worry your pretty little head about Quin or your crew." She winked. "I sent word that you're fine, that you're in my safekeeping for now."

"Oh, I'm certain that brought them comfort, considering we've been trying to kill each other for the past, what, three years," he grumbled.

She snickered. "Hey, I wasn't trying that hard to kill you. Anyway, Quin said to tell you everyone was alive and safe, if that's what you're worried about. That they had things well in hand."

Ivan breathed a sigh of relief. "I need to contact him."

Her face lost all emotion, her eyes serious. "Not here. Not now. It's not safe."

He studied her for a moment, then gave a sharp nod. He still didn't trust her, but she'd kept him alive while he was vulnerable in the medi-tube. He'd follow her lead for a while longer. "Fine. But as soon as it is..."

"Yeah. As soon as it is." She tugged at the hem of her black shirt and smoothed a hand over her hips. "Look, I put Lore off as long as humanly possible but, considering we're currently docked in her hangar deck and not allowed to leave until her business with us is concluded, I need you fully functional, okay?"

"Fully functional, got it," he said, setting the empty glass on a shelf next to the bed. *Fuck.* He was absolutely not clear-headed enough for a visit with the head of The Cabal. He needed to be on his best behavior, despite the fact that he'd happily ring Lore's neck for what she did to his brother.

Navi had been sucked into The Cabal in his early twenties with a friend, beguiled by the promise of easy money and plenty of adventure. Unfortunately for him, Lore found out that not only was he an expert marksman, but he had an affinity for getting into secure places that stymied others. She'd plucked him out of the crowd, promising the riches and excitement he was seeking.

When he'd finally called his big brother for help, Navi was in so far over his head, he was drowning and almost out of air. The friend he'd joined The Cabal with was dead, Navi hopelessly entangled in Lore's web. While Navi was an adult and absolutely responsible for his own actions, Ivan knew without a shadow of a doubt he wouldn't have been in so much trouble if it weren't for Lore and her scheming.

He loathed the woman. She was manipulative, she used people up until they were either dead or mere husks, and, if she had any morals or ethical values at all, he'd never seen evidence of them. But, despite his very real objections to the woman, if Ivan said or did anything to piss Lore off and fuck up this shaky cease fire Rhain had spent far too long negotiating, he may as well find another galaxy to live in.

He scrubbed both hands over his face, dragging them down over his beard with a groan before picking up his pants. Raising an eyebrow, he shot Amaryllis a look. She knew he was naked under the sheet.

"Don't let me stop you," she said, gesturing at him to continue as she leaned against the counter and crossed her ankles.

She wanted a show? Fine. He had nothing to hide. The bedsheet slid to the side as he stood, freeballing and letting it all hang loose in front of Amaryllis. He made sure to move slowly so she could take him all in. He wouldn't want her to miss anything before he covered it all back up again. After all, she'd asked for it, right? He slid a glance in her direction, pleased to see her watching him, flags of rose gold staining her high cheekbones.

The show wasn't quite as impressive as he'd hoped when a wave of dizziness hit him as he bent to put on his pants. A gauzy frame of black clouded his vision. He lost his balance and crashed to the floor, his bare ass hitting the cold tile flooring with a splat.

In a flash, she crouched at his side. "You okay?" she asked, in a concerned tone.

But it was the glimmer of laughter sparkling in her eyes that irked him and made him feel ever so slightly petty.

"I could use some help," he said, making a show of pulling himself up to a standing position with a hand on the bed for balance. She grabbed his arm to steady him, helping him rise. He gestured to the pants on the floor. "Seems I'm not quite up to the task yet. What kind of drugs did your doc-in-a-box give me, anyway?"

With a small frown, she picked up his pants from where he'd dropped them. "Just the regular kind, I think. Maybe it gave you a higher dose because you're so big."

Sadly, she didn't look at his cock when she said that. Disappointing. Only semi-feigning weakness, he swayed a little and dropped onto the mattress as if his legs couldn't hold him. It irritated him it wasn't all fake. Merely hauling himself up onto the bed left him breathless. But annoying Amaryllis helped fire him up.

She watched him for a beat before letting out a frustrated sigh. "Fine," she said, readjusting the pants in her hands and crouching to hold them open for him. "Let's go then."

Her hair brushed against his legs, tickling his knees as he slid one leg in his pants and then the other. Despite the meds, he felt his cock stir and firmly told it that this was absolutely not the right time to leap into action. He just wanted to torment her a bit, nothing more. Nothing to get excited about.

She slid his pants on, her fingers skimming over his calves and up his thighs as she rose slowly, trailing her gaze along his body as she did so. When the fabric reached the edge of the bed, she paused. "Stand," she said, her voice husky. "Place your hands on my shoulders so you don't lose your balance again."

He did as ordered, his hands resting on her shoulders as he gazed down at the top of her bent head. Unable to help himself, he brushed his thumbs over her clavicle, her skin soft against his. This close, her spicy-hot scent teased his senses, and he again had to send word to his lower bits to settle the hells down. Yes, she smelled good. Yes, she was close enough that if he dipped his head a little, he could kiss that irresistible curve of her neck. No, they were not doing that now so no point in getting all excited about it only to have to deflate on their own because there was no way in any of the three hells he was going to pump one out in the middle of enemy territory.

She straightened, the movement putting her forehead just inches his mouth. He gritted his teeth, resisting the impulse to press his lips against the lightning-shaped verdigris marking streaking its way along the edge of her temple and disappearing into her hairline. From the information he'd gathered on her people, depending on which of the Verdet family branches she was from, the markings on her skin could be poisonous. He had the unreasonable inclination to see if her verdigris marking was as beautifully deadly as she was.

Her fingers blazed a path over his sensitive skin, sliding around his waist to pull the pants up over his ass. Involuntarily, his glutes flexed under her touch.

She inhaled, a deep breath that brought her breasts in contact with his chest, the material of her shirt silky against his skin. She blinked up at him, her spicy-hot scent flooding his brain, clouding his thoughts. This close, he could see the speckles of forest green in her dark gold eyes. If he wasn't careful, he could get lost in them.

With a smirk, she gave his pants a solid yank, surprising a little eep out of him. Her grin widened. "You good? I'm assuming you can fasten your own pants without fainting?"

His cheeks heated under her gaze. Reluctantly, he released his steadying grip on her shoulders and did up his pants. "Thank you for your assistance," he said, returning her smirk.

She licked her lips, her gaze skimming over his bare torso before meeting his eyes. "Anytime, Cherry." She stepped away from him, moving over to the pitcher and pouring herself a glass of water.

He didn't know what had just passed between them, but he knew that, despite the snark, she felt its effects as much as he was. *Something to explore at a later date*, he thought. For now, there were more pressing matters to handle.

"So," he said, pulling on his shirt and reaching for his boots. "Lore." He absolutely wasn't ready for this, especially not with the lingering effects of the drugs the doc-in-a-box fed him, but if meeting with the woman was the only way he would be allowed to leave, he had little choice.

Amaryllis rolled her shoulders and drained her glass, setting it back on the counter with a loud clink. "Yes. Lore." She took a deep breath in before slowly releasing it. "Follow me."

7

AMARYLLIS

She almost kissed the man. She knew better than that, especially considering where they were. Yes, technically they were on *Dog's Day*, but it was docked on the *Ephemeris* and while they were in Lore's domain, nothing was secret, nothing private. Lore employed plenty of sneaky folks who made it their business to burrow into every nanobite of information that passed within her walls and pass it along to her.

Which is why it was dangerous that Amaryllis almost showed her hand. If Lore thought Amaryllis didn't hate Ivan, didn't see him as an enemy combatant in their ongoing skirmish — albeit under cease fire at the moment — against the Knight and his Shields, she wouldn't hesitate to use Ivan. Use him and throw him away. Bad enough, Amaryllis had helped him when he was injured and brought him here. At least that could be explained away. Kissing him, however, showing tenderness or caring? That would be a lot more challenging to explain.

Nevertheless, she was hyper-aware of the man walking next to her, his head on a swivel as he took everything in. Of course, he'd report back to his captain about everything that he'd seen and that information would make its way back to the Knight. However, since Lore didn't seem to be bothered by that, Amaryllis wouldn't concern herself with it either.

Anyway, it wasn't as if she was going to take him on a guided tour of the entire battleship that Lore had transformed into her base and give him access to their armaments or combat center. Their path from the hangar bay at the aft of the ship where *Dog's Day* was docked to Lore's command room at the fore, just off the bridge, was a hike but a relatively straight shot, avoiding all the classified areas.

Out of the corner of her eye, she watched him stalk along, people instinctively moving out of his way. For such a big man, he moved quietly, as if his heavy boots didn't make full contact with the floor. When she helped him put on his pants earlier, she'd felt almost delicate standing so close to him. Her forehead barely crested his chin, for the gods' sake. Standing at six feet in her bare feet, she was used to being the tallest women — if not one of the tallest humans — in the room. Not only that, but with her broad shoulders and the muscles she'd worked hard for, she could go toe-to-toe with practically anyone in The Cabal.

But if she went up against Ivan, she had the feeling that, though she would put on a good show, he'd win their bout. The man had to be at least 6'6", with much broader shoulders than hers. He had the kind of meaty, muscle-y build that smaller individuals bounced right off of when they came at him. When he was mad, he radiated serious "fuck off" vibes. She'd seen him clear a room with an annoyed grunt and the curling of his fist.

What they didn't know was that when embarrassed, the man blushed a red that rivaled the cherries the grandmother she barely remembered used to grow in her garden, or that he was mostly bluster until someone pushed that final button, and he detonated on them.

"I need to contact Quin as soon as possible. My crew will be searching for me," Ivan said.

She'd told him this before. Seemed she might actually need to recalibrate their doc-in-the-box. A slight frown creased her forehead. "Your captain knows where you are and what landed you here. I told you this."

Quin had been none too pleased to find out that his Number One was on board Lore's base, but when Amaryllis guaranteed Ivan's safety, he'd relented. He had no other choice, since he couldn't storm the *Ephemeris* without serious repercussions.

"Okay, yes. I remember you saying that. Damn drugs still fuzzing my brain." Ivan grimaced and shook his head. "How did he react when he found out I was in your clutches?" he asked, his voice curious.

"Not particularly well." She slid him a glance, noting the tick of a muscle in his jaw. "Did you know he came after you, concerned that you were getting your ass handed to you by a girl after hearing all the pitiful grunting and groaning you were doing?"

He snorted. "He should have known better."

"I believe it was the woman, the fugitive, he was with who pushed him to come rushing to your aid after you lost comms."

"Bea." He smiled when he said her name and shook his head. "Sounds like something she'd do."

She felt an unexpected and unwelcome jolt of jealousy at the warmth with which he said Bea's name and the gentle smile that spread across his lips at the thought of her. She should have tracked that fugitive down and claimed the bounty when she had the chance. Irritated, she shoulder-checked a guy who didn't move out of her way quick enough.

"But the disabled comms are your fault," he said.

She growled at him. "Don't blame me. You're the one who didn't move out of the way when I pointed a blaster in your direction."

He made a noncommittal noise.

"Amaryllis. Hey, wait!" A white woman of average height and toned build waved at them from down the corridor that lead to the living quarters. Her long brown hair was swept forward over her left shoulder in an intricate braid. The right side of her head was shaved to show an equally intricate tattoo of swirling vines that trailed down her neck and disappeared into her bright blue shirt. A tattoo of stylized bolt of lightning danced over her wrist.

Amaryllis slowed, moving out of the flow of traffic so her crewmate could catch up to them. Ivan followed suit.

"Hi," Dagby said, giving Ivan a once-over. "Good to see you up and about, Ivan."

"Thank you," he said. "And you are?"

"Oh!" She bounced on her toes. "Dagby Jaklic, pilot on *Dog's Day* and Amaryllis's best friend." She stuck out her arm. "Nice to officially meet you."

"Nice to meet you, Dagby, Amaryllis's best friend." He clasped her forearm in greeting and gave Amaryllis a side eye. "Best friend, huh? Didn't think you'd have one of those, what with you being so prickly."

"I'm not prickly." She folded her arms over her chest.

"Ha. She had no choice. I made it through her prickles with the force of my vivacious personality alone." Dagby elbowed her in the side. "So, what's the sitch?"

She tipped her head in his direction. "Lore wants to meet him."

"Ah." Dagby chewed the inside of her cheek, clearly holding something back. She knew better than to say too much in Lore's halls, too. Not only did the walls have metaphorical ears, but every individual in the vicinity was gathering intel, waiting for the opportunity when it might be either worth something or be put to good use. There were multiple reasons Amaryllis avoided returning to base unless absolutely necessary. It was hard to always be on guard, never to trust anything or anyone here.

She nodded. "Exactly. So, is the *Dog* ready?"

"Restocked, refueled, and ready to go when you are, captain," Dagby said with a jaunty little salute. "I was just coming to tell you that."

"Excellent." Out of her small team, she was the only one who still had quarters here, the same ones Lore had assigned her when she'd first rescued Amaryllis all those years ago. For the longest time, it was the only place she felt safe. Now, she mostly used it as a spare closet. "Round up the guys and let them know to be ready. Hopefully, we'll be out of here today."

"I was hoping you'd say that." Dagby bounced on her toes again, something she did to relieve tension. She'd had some unpleasant experiences on base and preferred to spend as little time here as possible. "Good luck with Lore." She gave Ivan another sweeping look, then gave Amaryllis a grin and a parting wave as she bounced off towards the hangar.

"Good luck with Lore indeed," Amaryllis muttered. "Come on. We're almost there."

For the second time in a standard week, Amaryllis was standing in front of Lore in her cold room at parade rest. That was two times too many in her book. If she had it her way, she'd never have to see this blasted room again. It reminded her all too clearly of the trouble she'd gotten into when she was younger and all the KP duty she'd earned because of her shenanigans. Now that she was firmly in her thirties, she had better control over her temper and her impulses, though not always as much as she'd like. But every time she was called to the carpet — or bare floor in this case — she was immediately returned to her wildly rebellious teenaged years. And even though it wasn't her being called to task this time, the sharp-winged iron butterflies still made their presence known in her stomach.

Taking his cue from her, Ivan stood at parade rest beside her, a blank look on his face even as he absorbed every detail. He kept his mouth shut, waiting. Smart. Lore'd called this meeting. Best to let her take the lead.

Silence sat like a weighted blanked over the room, its heaviness oppressive and claustrophobic. Despite the cold chill of Lore's preferred temperature, Amaryllis felt prickles of sweat forming along her temples and at the small of her back.

Lore narrowed her eyes at Ivan, tapping a pen on the bare surface of her metal desk in a slow, steady beat.

The sound of each tap stabbed into Amaryllis's eyeballs until she wanted nothing more than snatch that fucking pen out of Lore's hand and snap it in half. Ivan didn't seem to have the same kind of reaction as her, his breathing deep and measured as he waited. In fact, he looked like he was about to fall asleep. Maybe, when she grabbed that pen, she'd stab him in the shoulder with it, just to see if that would elicit a reaction. She let out a miniscule sigh. No, of course she wouldn't snatch the pen or stab Ivan with it. But she did enjoy envisioning the chaos of it in the comfort of her own brain.

"How's Navi?" Lore finally asked.

Ivan's entire body clenched, and Amaryllis didn't think it was because Lore finally broke the silence. It was more the question she chosen to shatter it with. Amaryllis was aware of Navi as one of Quin's crew. He'd joined the *Laughing Dragon* about four years ago, if she recalled correctly. But how did Lore know Navi, and why did Ivan have such a reaction? She wracked her brain, trying to remember where else she knew Navi from.

"He's fine," Ivan said through clenched teeth.

Having broken the proverbial ice, Lore relaxed in her chair, twirling the pen between her fingers. "We certainly do miss him and his skills around here. Don't we, Amaryllis?"

Amaryllis blinked, shooting a wide-eyed glance at Ivan. "Um, yes?" She internally winced at the question in her voice. Lore didn't like that. *Be definitive in your answers, Amaryllis. No one respects an indecisive leader.* How many times had Lore drilled that into her brain? She cleared her throat and tried again. "Yes, we miss Navi."

Fuck. The name sounded so familiar, but she couldn't remember who in the second hell Navi was in relation to Lore or The Cabal at the moment. No matter. She'd be damned if she contradicted Lore, even if it pissed Ivan off. She was protecting him as much as herself by doing so. There'd be time to explain and get the details later. Right now, not agreeing with Lore would be bad for the both of them.

"My brother is beyond your reach." Ivan's voice was low and harsh. "You're never getting your hands on him again, so back off, Lore."

Oh, shit. Navi was Ivan's little brother. The pieces clicked in her brain. She remembered him now. She hadn't realized he was Ivan's brother. Except for a playful if somewhat cheesy reversal of their names, the two looked nothing alike. Ivan was quiet, more introspective, and a giant ginger mountain of a man. The dark-haired Navi was cheerfully outgoing, with more of a fencer's build. No wonder she hadn't realized they were related.

And she remembered him from before, too. If memory served, he'd come to The Cabal with Pete, both of them young and looking for adventure. As with many who were woefully unprepared and swimming out of their depths, they'd gotten way more than they bargained for, unfortunately.

She and her crew had hung out with them a couple of times at the bar on base. She didn't really remember much about Pete, but both were sweet kids. Far too naïve to be hanging out with Lore's rabble. As she'd done with several other misguided kids who found themselves somewhere they didn't belong, she'd tried to gently steer them away from the path they were on. As most of the others, they'd brushed aside her concerns, cocky and certain that The Cabal was where they'd find what they were looking for. Last she'd heard, Pete was killed during a job gone wrong. She hadn't heard what happened to Navi. Seemed he'd found a way out before it destroyed him, too. Good.

Lore smiled, the points of her sharp teeth glinting in the room's bright light. "Of course, Ivan. Send him my regards."

"Absolutely not," he ground out. His entire body practically quivered, his muscles were clenched so tight. "And if you reach those claws of yours in his direction, I will snap them off and stab you with them."

Fucking fuckety-fuck, Amaryllis thought, holding herself still, even though she wanted to slap a hand over Ivan's mouth and drag him from the room like he'd done to her not too long ago. She didn't want him to face the blowback from Lore's wrath.

But instead of exploding, Lore merely tsked, the sound echoing through the cold space. "Now, now. Let's not forget our manners, Ivan. Here I am being polite, asking about the family, and you respond with threats? I'm certain your Shields' protective Knight would not be please to hear of you threatening the woman he recently treated with. It would be heartbreaking if that agreement were broken. So many lives would be lost." She didn't sound worried, which concerned Amaryllis. What was Lore playing at here? Was she trying to provoke Ivan into violence so she could claim the cease fire broken, their negotiations towards a formal treaty dissolved? Why?

Amaryllis could almost hear Ivan's teeth grinding as he bit back everything he wanted to say. Luckily, he was intelligent enough not to let those words flow. She understood his anger though, had felt it herself, especially as the shine of her rescue tarnished, and Lore allowed her to see more of her calculating nature.

"What do you really want, Lore? Why am I here?" he asked, his tone flat.

She blinked, her eyes wide, as if shocked by his questions. "I merely wanted to inquire about your brother, our former Cabal member, and to make certain that Amaryllis was treating you well, overseeing your recovery and such. After all, it was a member of her very own team who attempted to kill you at the Vanid estate."

Seriously, Lore. What are you up to? Amaryllis thought, keeping her eyes focused on the sword secured to the wall above Lore's head. Why was she going out of her way to make it seem like Amaryllis was the bad guy? Not that she was exactly the good guy in any of sense of the word, but it wasn't like she was truly out to get Ivan.

Lore cocked her head. "What were you doing there, anyway, Ivan?"

He took a deep breath, his chest rising and falling as he exhaled. "My business is none of your concern, Lore."

"It is when it interferes with my own business or puts my people at risk."

Ivan stayed silent.

Lore narrowed her eyes. "Don't worry. I'll find out what you were doing there." Picking up the pen again, she made it dance through the tangle of her fingers. "Dismissed. I need a word with Amaryllis alone."

Great, Amaryllis thought. *Why can't I go, too? There is no need for her to "have a word" with me right now. We just spoke.*

Ivan sent her a hooded glance before glaring at Lore. Spinning on his heels, he left, the door shushing closed behind him.

Lore turned her attention to Amaryllis. "Don't get too attached to that man."

"I'm not attached," she said. *Shit*. She must have shown too much concern for him that Lore twigged to it. "I merely enjoy tormenting him, as you well know." She kept her tone light, waving a careless hand through the air as if to brush away Lore's concerns.

She hummed a neutral sound that made the hairs on the back of Amaryllis's neck stand up. "Drop him at the nearest space station. You contacted Quin to let him know his crew member survived and is in no present danger?"

"Yes."

She tapped the pen on her desk. "The clothes you had repaired for him, you added a tracker?"

One of Lore's more annoying traits was to ask questions she already knew the answer to but still required verbal confirmation from the person she was asking. Amaryllis forced her jaw to unclench. "Yes," she said.

"Good. I want to know why he was at the estate for the auction. Find out. If it has anything to do with my prototype, they will have to be dealt with." She swiped at her desk, pulling up her holo-computer.

Dealt with? That meant eliminated in Lore-speak. Quin and his crew might not be members of the Shields officially, but everyone knew they were connected and under the Knight's umbrella of protection. Amaryllis's heart beat hard in her ears. This was so not good. Would Lore really dissolve the cease fire with the Shields because of this damned prototype? What made it so important to Lore? What was her game here?

Just like last time, Lore looked up and lifted a perfectly sculpted brow as if it surprised her to see Amaryllis still standing in front of her. She flicked her fingers. "Dismissed."

Amaryllis spun and walked out of the room on shaky legs, collapsing against the wall as soon as the door locked behind her.

"What? What happened?" Ivan appeared in front of her, his brows knitted. "What did that woman say to you?" He glared at the closed door, bracing himself as if he was about to storm back into the office and confront her.

Before he made any foolish moves, Amaryllis pushed off the wall and grabbed his arm. "Say nothing here," she said in a low tone, dragging him down the corridor.

"Why?" he asked. "Rilly, tell me. What happened in there that made all the color drain from your face?"

Oh, gods, she thought. That better not have happened in front of Lore. A reaction like that would give Lore too much information. *Fuck.* She dug her fingers into his arm and hissed at him. "Shut the hells up. Not. Here." She was moving faster now, her feet leading her to the closest safe space in this entire fucking ship.

Ivan finally caught onto her urgency because not only did he stop asking questions, he matched her pace.

After what felt like an eternity, they made it to her old quarters. She all but shoved him inside, setting the lock so no one, not even her own crew, could get inside without her permission.

When he opened his mouth, she held up a finger to stop him. "No," she said. "Not yet. Keep your mouth shut."

He crossed his arms over his chest and stood in the middle of the room, watching her as she set about securing the place. It was a deceptively complex task, each piece disguised to look like something innocuous in her space, but once everything was connected, the tech cloaked the room in a veil of protection that not even Lore's best hackers could crack.

She was so mad at Lore for her manipulations and ridiculous games. She hated feeling trapped in her life, unable to move forward because of her obligations and the underlying drive to please Lore, to impress her. Anger at the whole situation flooded her system. She needed an outlet. Screaming didn't let off enough steam. A long session with a punching bag helped, but only partially. There was another option.

Protections up, she turned to him. *You know what?* she thought, giving him a head-to-toe look. *Fuck it. I need this.*

He dropped his arms as she moved with purpose across the room, his eyes going wide as she backed him up until the bed hit his calves.

She gave him a hard shove, pushing him onto the bed, and crawled on top of him.

"What are you doing, Rilly?" he asked as she ripped open his shirt and ran her fingers over his chest.

"What do you think I'm doing, you idiot?" she asked, lowering her mouth to his.

8

IVAN

"Rilly, are you sure you want to do this?" Ivan asked. He groaned as she trailed her tongue down his chest, paying attention to one nipple than the other. "I can see that you're angry right now, and you might regret this choice later." Why was he saying this? He had a gorgeous woman on top of him, doing lovely things with her mouth, and he was encouraging her to stop. He must be out of his damn mind.

She nipped the skin at the hollow of his neck, then sat up, the heat of her core rocking against him as she shifted. "You're right. I am mad and frustrated and irritated, and I need to burn off some of this anger before I do something stupid that might get us both killed." She leaned down, her hands splaying over his chest, the tips of her nails pressing against his skin, and whispered in his ear, "Fucking you won't kill me, but I'm guessing you've got it in you to give me at least one little death. Is that alright with you?"

With a groan, he wrapped a handful of braids around his fist and pulled her mouth to his. She opened to him, her tongue darting out to meet his in a kiss that inflamed his senses. He tugged her shirt from her pants, sliding a hand under the fabric and over the silky skin beneath as she moved from his mouth to trail nips along his jawline, her sharp teeth grazing over his skin.

A better man might say no to an angry fuck with this woman, but he was not that man. The very least he could do was give her what she wanted, help her work through all that anger and frustration. "What do you want, Rilly? What do you need?"

She paused, her fingers skimming the waistband of his pants. "I need to feel you in my mouth, to taste you," she said, licking her purple-stained lips. "Then I need you to take control, fill me up, and make me come." With a snap of her fingers, she undid the fastenings and slid a hand down his pants.

He groaned when she wrapped a hand around his cock, stroking its length. *Goddess-fuck.* He wouldn't survive this, he thought as she bent to trace her tongue over its head, licking along his shaft like she was catching the drips of a melting popsicle. She sucked him down, her cheeks hollowing as she did so, and he threw back his head with a deep groan, his hips bowing up to meet her. If she kept this up, he wouldn't last long enough to fill anything other than her mouth. He desperately wanted to confirm that her pussy was as hot as her mouth. "Fuck, Rilly. You've got to stop, or this is going to end far too quickly."

Her hand slid up his shaft, and she raised her eyes just enough that she could watch him as she stroked him with both her hands and her mouth, teasing him, ignoring his words.

She wanted him to take control? Fine. He could do that. Reaching down, he grabbed her under the arms and pulled her up his body, her mouth releasing his cock with a little pop. She watched him with wide eyes as he tossed her on the bed next to him and rolled on top of her, caging her beneath him. She struggled, straining her body, trying to buck him off.

He lay down, draping his body weight over her. "Do you want me to let you go?" he asked.

She shook her head, still squirming under him. "No," she whispered.

Typical Amaryllis, never one to give in easily, even when it was what she wanted, what she asked for.

He buried his face in the crook of her neck, breathing in her spicy-sweet scent, and gave her a little nip on her earlobe as she squirmed beneath him. "What do you need?" he growled. He shifted, pushing his hard cock against her pussy.

"I want, no, need all of it." She bucked against him again and gave a little wiggle. "All of you." Her voice was low and breathless as she shimmied her body, rubbing herself against him. "Inside me."

He could do that. He wasn't fueled by anger like she currently was — not that he wasn't pissed at Lore and frustrated with Amaryllis for dragging him into this mess — but years of her tormenting him had him pretty pent up. And that hot mouth of hers had him ready to explode.

Still, he wasn't about to just go at her like some rabid teenager. No, he needed to live up to her expectations of at least one orgasm. If he was very, very good, he was pretty sure he could exceed those expectations. Plus, a little payback for all her teasing.

He grinned down at her, a hint of wicked promise peeked through the widening of her eyes and the stilling of her movements beneath him were any indication. "You sure?" he asked as he shucked off his shirt, giving her one last chance to end things, to take back the control she'd handed him.

Biting her lower lip, she nodded.

She was still fully clothed, which wouldn't do. He tugged the soft black shirt over her head and tossed it to the floor along with her bra. His fingers skated over the triangle embedded in her shoulder, a visible signal she was both on birth control and vaccinated against known STDs. He cupped her breasts, kissing the rounded mounds, her brown nipples hardening into peaks at his touch.

He unfastened her black pants and yanked them and her underwear down her legs in one swift motion that made her gasp, dropping them next to her shirt. Then he sat back on his heels, raking his eyes down the length of her as he took a moment to appreciate the dangerous feast laid out in front of him.

Golden eyes darkening with desire, she licked her lips, her long legs moving restlessly against the sheets.

"Take off your pants," she said, her voice husky with desire as she reached for him.

He grabbed her wrists, pinning them above her head with a hand, and tsked. "I'm in charge, remember?"

She stuck her bottom lip out but nodded, shifting under him.

"Grab the headboard." He guided her hands up to it. "And don't let go until I tell you. Do you understand?"

Following his orders, she nodded again, her eyes wide.

She was right, though. The pants needed to go. Backing off the bed, he slid his pants down his legs, kicking them off and adding them to the clothes scattered on the floor, before reclaiming his position above her. He stroked a finger down her cheek, tracing the edge of her verdigris lightning strike as it snaked its way down her neck, branching out into smaller tendrils along her torso. "I read that, as you grow in age and wisdom, so do your verdigris markings." He licked a streak of green lightning that curved along the bottom of her breast.

She gasped, releasing the headboard to push at his shoulder. "Careful. Those are poisonous. I don't want to kill you, just fuck you. So, best to keep your lips away from my lightning."

"Didn't you know? I drink poison for breakfast." He placed small kisses on the forks of lightning trailing along her neck. Thanks to his time in the special forces branch of Starguard, he had some enhancements added that made him a lot less killable. Most toxins had minimal effect on him. Hers made his tongue tingle. Must be a pretty powerful poison to get even that level of reaction. He shouldn't be surprised that she was both beautiful and deadly, even when disarmed and naked.

"Ivan..." she said, clear warning in her tone.

With a laugh, he said, "Never fear, princess. It would take more than your poisonous markings to kill me, I promise." He skated his hand down her side, making her shiver. "You let go of the headboard."

"Oh, yeah?" She grinned up at him, a challenge in her eyes. "And what are you going to do about it?"

He tightened his legs, holding her in place as he grabbed his shirt from the edge of the bed. In a smooth motion, he wrapped the material around her wrists and loosely bound her hands over her head. "Just a reminder to stay where I put you. Next time you disobey, I'll make sure those bindings are more secure."

"Promises, promises." Her smile widened. "You'll be lucky if you get a next time."

He tweaked a nipple, making her squeal. "Then I'd better make this one count."

She moaned as he captured her mouth again, her tongue meeting his.

Nipping her bottom lip, he kissed his way down the column of her neck and across the curved mound of her stomach, sliding down her body. He parted her legs and settled between them, giving her a grin.

"Ivan..." she began, only for her breath to catch in her throat when he stroked a thumb over her clit.

"So beautiful." He replaced his thumb with his mouth, sucking hard on the sensitive bud of nerves. Reveling in the taste of her, he worked her with his tongue, delving into her warm heat.

She bowed up under his ministrations, gasping out his name as he slid a finger into her core, her slickness coating the digit.

"More?" he asked, adding another, curling his fingers as he stroked her, eliciting the most delightful noises from her as he teased her senses.

"More. Keep going," she gasped, writhing under his touch. She clenched her thighs around his head, holding him in place.

If she killed him while he was face down in her, it would be a glorious way to die, he thought, licking and sucking her clit as his fingers pumped into her.

Her thigh muscles tightened as an orgasm flooded through

her, her inner walls pulsing around his fingers. "Oh, fuck me," she said as her grip on his head loosened, and she went boneless.

One orgasm down, he thought with satisfaction. Not giving her time to recover, he flipped her onto her stomach, sliding an arm around her waist, her head pillowed on her twisted arms, as he lined up the head of his cock with her slick entrance. "Still with me?" he asked, sucking her earlobe.

She wiggled her ass against him, pushing back against his cock. "Abso-fucking-lutely," she moaned.

Ever so slowly, he sank into her heat with a groan.

"Holy fucking goddess of sweet divinity." She slid her knees farther apart, drawing him deeper into her. "Don't go slow now, you idiot."

"So bossy, even when you're tied up and spit-roasted on my cock." He adjusted his grip on her hips for better control. Just to torment her, he slowly withdrew before leisurely sliding back in. It took all his focus not to speed up, not to give into the temptation to fuck her hard and fast.

She twisted around the best she could, glaring at him over her shoulder. "You sonofabitch. Is this payback?"

Bending forward, he nipped her shoulder, the muscle tense beneath his teeth. "Of course it is, princess. Now, hold on because I'm going to make you come so hard, you'll see stars."

With a snort, she said, "I'll believe it when I feel it. Bet I can make you come first."

He shifted in her, making her gasp. "Challenge accepted," he said, sliding back out of her before torquing his hips forward and picking up speed, making certain that his cock rubbed over the spot deep inside her that he knew damned well was practically guaranteed to make her explode.

She squeezed him tight with her inner muscles, nearly making him lose control on the spot. But he wouldn't fail at this challenge, no matter how badly he wanted to come. She might be using him to burn off some of her anger, but he was the one in control at the moment. He shifted a hand so he could stroke her clit as he pumped his cock deep into her delicious heat.

She gasped out his name, her knuckles turning white where she gripped the headboard.

He felt his balls draw tight against his body as he drew closer to completion, but he wasn't about to go without her exploding first. Adding a little twist to his hips, he added some pressure as he thumbed the bundle of nerves at the apex of her pussy. Her body tensed, quivering as she went to pieces around him. With a shout, he joined her, losing himself in her.

Once they caught their breath, he reached up and tugged his shirt from her wrists before rolling onto his back. She collapsed next to him, a well-satisfied look on her face.

"I win." He grinned.

She reached over and pinched his nipple, making him squeak. "Pretty sure I emerged the winner in that round. Twice, in fact."

"Can we call it a draw?" He rolled his eyes. "Why does every-thing have to be a competition with you?" Granted, he had been all in on the race, but good goddess. He'd just given the woman some mind-blowing orgasms, and she wouldn't even let him claim the win? See, this is why she bugged the fuck out of him, little things like that. Except...

"Blame Lore," she said, interrupting the stray thought. "Grew up vying for her attention and approval." She scooted off the bed and started dressing.

Godsdamned Lore, he thought. Lore was the beginning and end of so many problems. He knew a little of Amaryllis's history gathered from bar room gossip. Amaryllis felt like she owed the woman for saving her and giving her a safe place to grow up during her teen years. Understandable. Even Lore's base, the *Ephemeris*, was better than suffocating on a dying ship or being "rescued" by someone who would then turn around and sell you to the highest bidder. Slavery was highly illegal within United Body of Planets space, but unfortunately, it was still something he saw far too often while in the Starguard.

But Lore was a greedy, grasping individual, a mob boss who used people up and threw them away when they were of no more use to her. He'd seen it happen with Navi's friend Pete. It almost happened to his brother. And he didn't want to see it happen to Amaryllis, despite the fact she was a part of The Cabal, despite her still following Lore's orders, despite them being on opposing sides. Yes, she was his bane, his nemesis but, in his heart of hearts, he also knew she was not Lore or The Cabal.

Idly rubbing a hand over his bare chest, he looked up at the ceiling. *Was that?* He squinted at the poster above the bed. "Why do you have a poster of Vanilla Pants on your ceiling?"

The boy band had been hot about twenty-ish years ago, their perky popcore songs, colorful hair choices, and puppy dog eyes making them popular with young folks across the galaxy. Apparently, Amaryllis was one of their fans. Huh. Unexpected. Learn something new every day.

"Hey now, they had some excellent songs and were quite talented, musically," she said with a sniff. Although he didn't completely disagree that their music was fun, he noticed she wouldn't look at him when she said that. Was the unflappable Amaryllis embarrassed by her younger self's musical choices? But she didn't give him a chance to delve any deeper. She pulled on her shirt and threw his pants at him. "Get dressed. We need to get moving."

"Where are we going?" he asked, pulling on his clothes. She was certainly in a hurry all of a sudden. Guess she scratched her itch, and that was it. He felt an inexplicable tug of sadness and frowned, puzzling over his reaction.

"Lore ordered me to return you to your people, so that's what I'm going to do." She pulled out two knapsacks and started filling them with clothing and seemingly random items in the room, pawing through a dresser, sometimes removing something and stuffing it in her pack before slamming the drawer shut. "We should have gone straight to my ship, rather than wasting time here," she muttered to herself.

He didn't think he was supposed to hear that. Acting like he hadn't and that he wasn't oddly hurt by that comment, he bent to fasten his boots, keeping an eye on the whirlwind Amaryllis had suddenly become.

It was when she pulled a stuffed troll off her shelf and placed it on the bed next to a nearly full knapsack that he realized she was stripping the room of everything she held close to her heart. Did she not plan to return? Why would she be doing that now, after all these years? Or was she just completing a move from base to her ship? Rumor had it that she was Lore's heir apparent. Had something changed?

He desperately wanted to ask, but instead, he picked up the ratty-looking troll doll and asked, "Who is this?"

Her eyes soft, she plucked the stuffie from his hands and ran a gentle finger over the gray troll's thinning mane of orange hair. "This is Wocks."

"Wocks?" Unusual name for a troll toy, but kids were weird and named their friends the oddest things.

She nodded. "I couldn't say my r's when I was little so, yeah. Wocks." After zipping Wocks into her pack, she gave it a pat. "He's the only thing I have left from my parents," she said quietly before giving herself a shake.

"Why does it feel like you're saying goodbye to this place, Rilly?" he asked in a low voice.

Pressing her lips together, she turned her back on him and continued pawing through the dresser.

So, she didn't want to discuss personal matters? Fine. "Okay. Then why were you at that auction? What was it that Lore sent you after?" He moved to stand between her and the dresser, pausing her frenzied sorting.

With a glower, she shifted away from him and started packing the items she'd piled on the bed.

"I need to know, Rilly. You weren't there for the jewels." He picked up a shimmering pink rock from a pile on her bookshelf. "All those sparkly, expensive pieces and not a single one made it into your pocket. On her orders?" When she didn't answer, he continued. "Okay, so, no to the jewels. Based on the lack of decor in her very scary office, Lore most likely wouldn't be interested in the art or statues that were up for auction." He bounced the stone in his hand. "I'm sure there were some things for sale that were not out on display but, if that was it, you wouldn't have been casing the room. You would have headed directly to wherever they were storing the thing you were after and snatched it there."

She paused long enough in her packing to shoot him a dark look.

So he was on the right track. He felt a thrill of triumph. "Other than jewels, art, and statues, there wasn't much else there."

In fact, there were only three items that didn't fit into any of those categories: a clutch of dragon eggs, though he doubted they were actually dragon eggs, considering the creatures had been declared extinct on every known planet; a case of wine salvaged from a ghost ship that appeared near the moons of Melorn every hundred years; and Bea's propulsion system prototype. While the other two were both unusual enough to pique Lore's interest, he didn't particularly care if she was after them.

What he needed to know was if Lore was after the prototype and, if so, why she wanted it. "So, I'm guessing, Lore sent you there to collect the propulsion system prototype."

When she froze, he knew he'd nailed it. *Fuck. Not good.* For one, it would put Rhain and Lore head-to-head once again, threatening the fragile peace that they'd worked so hard to attain. For two, Quin would have a shit-fit, wanting to immediately squash anything that upset his Bea. For three, Lore having that kind of tech in her hands nonfunctional though it currently was could be exceedingly dangerous, even disastrous.

"What does she want with it?"

Amaryllis threw one of the knapsacks at him. "Not here," she said, taking another glance around the room.

"I thought you had protection from..." He twirled a finger

instead of saying "listening devices". She was making him paranoid. Of course, he should be on edge. He was trapped on Lore's base with no way off except with a woman who just anger-fucked him not ten minutes ago. A precarious situation deserving of all the paranoia, for sure.

"I do." She huffed, the frustrated sound loud in the room's quiet. "But this is absolutely not something that needs to be discussed anywhere on *Ephemeris*. I haven't been here for a while. It's entirely possible that my protections are no longer up to snuff or that someone managed to access my space and fuck them up or whatever." She slashed a hand through the air. "It doesn't matter. This is not something we're talking about right now. Right now, we need to get on my ship and get away from here."

"As long as I get my answers," he said, glowering at her back as she strode out of the room, a pack slung over her shoulder. Seriously, the woman had no call to be as grumpy as she was after a pair of orgasms. Usually, that made women smiley and sweet. Agreeable, even.

But then, Amaryllis was not really the sweet, smiley type, so acting out of character like that would actually be quite scary and mean something was really wrong. She was merely back to her usual self, and he was foolish to have expected anything else. He shook his head. *Foolish, Ivan.*

Besides, as much as he hated to admit it, Amaryllis was right. It wasn't safe here, especially not for him. However, he wasn't certain how much safer he'd be on *Dog's Day*. Still, he had little choice in the matter. Until he got off this base and contacted his crew, he was dependent upon Amaryllis. He didn't like that. Nope. Didn't like that at all.

Grumbling to himself, he hefted her second bag over his shoulder and followed the bane of his existence back to her ship, a small smile curling his lips as he watched her delightfully perky ass encased in black leather sway along in front of him.

9

AMARYLLIS

I t wasn't until the clamps released, and *Dog's Day* flew out of the landing bay unaccosted that Amaryllis finally breathed a sigh of relief. She flopped back in her captain's chair and flipped her legs over the arm with a groan. "Thank the gods," she said, watching the *Ephemeris* recede from view on the trio of large displays covering the forward wall of the command deck. Her nerves couldn't take another session with Lore. The battleship she'd once called home now felt fraught with traps, ears listening to every word that left her mouth, every interaction observed in the hopes that she tripped up and fell out of favor.

What she wanted to tell them was that she had no desire to head The Cabal, that Lore wasn't actually grooming her to take over, merely playing more of her frustrating games. Instead, she stayed away from Lore's base the best she could and avoided The Cabal's other factions and members whenever possible.

"For now." Trick leaned back in his chair and scrubbed his hands through his short-cropped brown hair. "But what's our plan? Are we really going to just let those dicks snag our job out from under us? You know how much I want to punch Christophe in that stupid face of his."

She didn't blame Trick in the least. Christophe and his partner, Deno, were slimy sycophants, always trying to ooze their way into Lore's favor so she wouldn't come down too hard on them when they broke the rules or stole other people's jobs. This wasn't the first time they'd stolen a job from the *Dog* crew, but it was the first time Lore had officially taken one from Amaryllis and given it to them. She didn't like it. Didn't like it at all.

"Absolutely not. No way are we giving up this job, especially to those boot-lickers." Dagby idly rubbed at the lightning tattoo on her wrist.

Dagby had designed the tattoo of a jagged bolt of lightning in a show of support and solidarity when Amaryllis's own verdigris began to grow. Dagby wasn't Verdet, but she knew how much the appearance of the verdigris markings meant to Amaryllis and to the Verdet people. It was a symbol of adulthood, usually ushered in with a big family celebration. But no blood relatives meant no canonical ceremony. So, with Amaryllis's permission, she designed a lightning bolt logo for their crew that mirrored the lightning-shaped verdigris spreading across Amaryllis's skin and had it tattooed on her wrist. Trick and Von had followed suit; Trick adding his to his arm, and Von getting it emblazoned over his heart.

"We're family," Von said when she'd asked them why they'd gotten them. "These are a visible symbol of our connection, letting everyone know that, if they fuck with one of us, they fuck with us all."

"You might not have your bio family around anymore to support you, but we're your family now and you're ours. We wanted to show you and everyone," Dagby had added.

The assholes made her cry. She appreciated the gesture more than they'd ever know. Every time she caught a glimpse of one of their tattoos, it reminded her that she wasn't alone. Now, instead of just representing the family she'd lost and the heritage she knew so little about, her markings also exemplified the chosen family they'd created and the depth of their bonds.

"Fuck those guys if they think they're taking that job from us, no matter what Lore says," Von said. He narrowed his eyes, his thick black brows coming together like dark clouds. "Bad enough we got stuck with the Trio of Uselessness on that job." His disgruntled tone said he still wasn't over being saddled with Lore's goons. "Now that shit-for-brains Christophe is supposed to grab the prototype for Lore? I don't think so."

"You're right. I definitely think we need to finish the job. As long as everyone agrees." Amaryllis dropped her head back, giving her neck a stretch before turning so she could see her whole crew. "Because by doing this, we're taking the very real chance that it'll piss off Lore and, by extension The Cabal, and you know how that goes."

"I'm in," Dagby said with a clap of her hands. "We can handle anything that comes our way. And we won't fail. Lore will have her prototype; Christophe and Deno will lose. We win."

Trick raised a hand. "I vote to finish it. I'm all about completion."

Von inclined his head, a black wave of hair falling over his forehead. "And with me, that makes it unanimous."

"Alright. Good." Amaryllis nibbled on her bottom lip as she took in her crew watching her with bright eyes. "Which brings me to this: I'm concerned about why Lore wants that prototype. It's supposed to be some new fancy propulsion system, right?"

Dagby brightened, her love of all things ship-based shining through. "I've been digging. There's not much out there, since the engineer who invented it wasn't working with anyone else and is extremely private..."

"She's that bounty we went after, the one on the Intrepid, right?" Trick asked.

Amaryllis nodded. "Bea Farsirus. And she was on Badin." A spark lit up in a dark corner of her brain. Had Ivan been at the auction because of Bea and that prototype? Gods, she wasn't usually this slow on the uptake, but it had to be. With those questions he asked while she was packing, the curiosity about if the prototype was what they were retrieving for Lore. And then, once he puzzled it out, he wanted to know why she wanted it. That's when she'd snapped at him. She felt a little bad about that, especially after what he'd just done for her but, seriously. He was too curious about things that could get him killed.

Well, if Ivan was there for the prototype, that meant that Quin wanted it and if Quin wanted it, then most likely the Shields were involved somehow. Oh, this could go wrong in so many ways.

Dagby didn't notice Amaryllis's brain exploding as she sorted through the possibilities and made connections. "So anyway, word is that this prototype will make space travel more accessible to the galaxy's population because it doesn't use those stupid-expensive pellets the Vanid system requires." She shrugged. "But that's all I know. Like I said, there isn't much info out there about it."

Amaryllis rubbed the tips of her boots together, pondering. "I think Ivan was at the auction for the prototype, too," she said.

Everyone started lobbing questions at her.

She held up her hands to get them to settle down. Once they settled back into their seats, she summarized her guesswork. Then, with a sigh, she said, "I don't know for sure; it's just a theory, but it fits."

Von frowned. "And if he was, if the *Laughing Dragon* crew is involved in this..."

"Then does that mean the Shields are involved? This could go very badly if they are," Trick said, putting voice to her own concerns.

Dagby whistled. "If so, that means the message boards were right: this prototype could be the real thing. That would be so cool." Her eyes shining, she bounced in her seat. "Cheaper space travel for the win!"

"More affordable space travel would be amazing, I agree." It would allow ships to explore more of the galaxy. It would open up more trade routes and give more individuals the ability to travel between planets and move out to the colonies on the outskirts of explored space. Hells, they could explore more of the galaxy than they'd ever been able to before, maybe even beyond. Cutting the cost of travel and boosting a ship's efficiency and capabilities would send explorers deep into the unknown. Quite honestly, if the prototype became a real, functional propulsion system, it absolutely would revolutionize space trade and travel as they knew it.

Amaryllis sat up and leaned forward, her elbows on her knees. "But why does Lore want the prototype? The Cabal isn't involved in any industry, unless it's to steal cargo or liberate a shipment of fuel pellets." The group wasn't a business in any sense of the word. It never had been. It didn't own things or run things. It was a group of like-minded individuals who appreciated the added protection, power, and income it provided.

She looked at her crew who shook their heads. "This has got to be one of her ridiculous chess games, where she's planning her moves ten steps in advance. Somehow, the propulsion system is a piece in that game." They wouldn't figure this out without more information, information they had no chance of prying from Lore. If they wanted to know, they'd have to uncover it another way.

But did they even want to? She wasn't sure. What was the benefit for them? Why not retrieve the prototype and let Lore play her games? That was a choice as well. She sighed quietly, deciding she'd play it by ear. If they learned the reasoning behind Lore's machinations, great. But she would not put her crew or their future at risk for those answers. It just wasn't worth it.

"Lore and her constant fucking games," Von said.

She'd used him as a chess piece far too many times. They all had been used too often. But enough was enough. They had to do something to take control of their own fates, rather than continue to be used as pawns in schemes they wanted no part of.

Amaryllis shot a finger in Von's direction. "Right? So I was thinking we get our hands on this thing before anyone else does, then we'll have some leverage."

"Leverage?" Dagby asked, cocking her head.

"If it's something that can change an entire industry, then that prototype's got to be worth at least as much as what we need to buy our stake in The Cabal, right?"

Slow nods from everyone on deck.

She took a deep breath. "Or, in addition to the credits we've saved, it might even be enough to buy our way free entirely. If we want, that is."

They'd talked about it, tossing the idea out during one of their many post-dinner drink conversations. More in a "dare to dream" kind of way than anything but, what if it could be a real possibility? It would be dangerous, going out on their own without The Cabal to back their moves, but the freedom to run their own lives without having to answer to Lore or The Cabal could be worth it.

Still, there were massive risks involved. While it was relatively easy to join The Cabal — you just had to be desperate enough to sign up as a foot soldier or come with enough treasure and experience to buy your way in as a full member — Lore didn't like it when people tried to leave. Less so when she considered those people "hers", like Amaryllis. But if this prototype was important enough to her, well, it might be enough to let Amaryllis and her crew walk.

But she wouldn't do it on her own. Her family had to willingly go with her.

Silence reigned as everyone chewed on her words.

Dagby spoke first. "I could get behind that." Her voice was soft. "I mean, Lore and The Cabal were there when I needed help, but..." She bit her bottom lip.

"But a lot of things have changed in the last few years and not necessarily for the better," Von said, the rasp of his fingers over the stubble covering his jawline loud in the quiet room. He wasn't wrong. "I wouldn't be opposed to exploring the option of breaking with The Cabal. Or, at the very least, speeding up our schedule to buy a full stake in it so we won't get stuck with assholes like Andrea and Skip again or have even bigger assholes like Christophe and Deno steal our jobs."

Thirty years ago, Lore hammered together a group of space pirates, smugglers, and privateers into The Cabal, forming what was in essence the most dangerous guild in the galaxy. Full membership meant voting rights, first dibs on a variety of legal and not-so-legal jobs, and lawyers on retainer when pesky legal issues arose from said jobs. Lore's initial reasoning behind forming The Cabal was survival. Between the Starguard's crackdown on illegal activities, the rising cost of fuel pellets, and bloody conflicts between crews that usually resulted in the destruction of one or both ships, it'd been tougher and rougher to survive. By joining together, they pooled their resources and created a more united front.

Of course, it wasn't a perfect solution by any means. A guild of pirates was still a group of bloody-minded individuals who preferred anarchy to rules, but they did like money and the power that came from their united-ish front. Through her cold-blooded determination and ruthless handling of the issues that arose, Lore and her Council made it work.

But something was changing within The Cabal that made Amaryllis uncomfortable. She wasn't sure if Lore was behind it or someone else, but it wasn't running as smoothly. There had been more dust-ups between crews and individuals lately. Jobs that should have gone to one crew went to another. Things like that. Nothing major she could put her finger on, but enough minor things to make her and her crew twitchy.

Trick nodded. "I agree. I think that, if this thing really could be our meal ticket to change our lives, we should grab both the prototype and the opportunity. Whether it's buying our full stake or cutting ties completely, I'm with whatever we decide in the end."

"Okay." Amaryllis looked at each of her people in turn. Her stomach fluttered at the tantalizing idea that a life-changing opportunity was within their reach. "Okay. As long as we're all in this together."

"Always," Dagby said. Trick and Von nodded in agreement.

Von sprawled back in his chair and scrubbed a hand through his hair. "Now, we just need to figure out where the prototype went, sneak into a place that most likely has top notch security system to keep people like us out, and steal that shit before Christophe's team can get it."

With a shrug and a flick of his wrist, Trick said, "Pfft. We've got this. No problem."

And just like that, the seriousness dissipated, evaporating from the deck as if it never existed.

"Sounds like a plan to me." Dagby clapped her hands together in glee.

"Good, because you're the one who needs to figure out where we're going after we drop Ivan off." Amaryllis sat up and rubbed her palms over her eyes. "Dagby, you've got until we reach Gastez Station to get us the intel we need."

"And where is that ginger mountain of yours anyway, Amaryllis? You didn't drug him so you could get away from him, did you?" Trick teased.

Dagby cocked her head, looking closely at her friend. "No... No. Tell me you didn't." She flopped back in her chair, a hand over her mouth. "Did you?"

The way she said it, Amaryllis knew she wasn't talking about drugging Ivan. She felt her cheeks heat. "No, I did not drug the man. He agreed to spend a cycle in the medi-bed to finish healing." She avoided looking at Dagby, whose blue eyes saw too much, especially when it came to her best friend. "He'd barely finished getting patched up when Lore ordered him in front of her, and I'm pretty sure he overextended himself."

"Girl," Dagby said, her tone filled to the brim with suspicion. "Exactly how did that man overextend himself? You didn't have anything to do with it, did you?"

She studiously ignored Dagby, pulling up her holo-computer

and flicking through her messages. Von and Trick looked from one woman to the other, identical looks of confusion on their faces.

Bouncing in her seat like an over-sugared toddler, Dagby gasped and pointed at her. "You did!" she squealed, slapping her hands on her thighs. "Ooh, you naughty girl. That man was shot twice, had just left the medi-ward, had a probably less than pleasant face-to-face with Lore, then you go and do that?"

"Do what?" Trick asked, his brows drawn together.

"Look," Amaryllis said, giving Dagby a glare. "We'd just left Lore and I was pissed and he was there and more than willing... it just happened, okay?"

"So? Don't leave me in anticipation. How was he?"

With that question, Von's eyes widened as comprehension dawned.

Amaryllis pointed at him. "Don't." She moved that finger to Dagby. "And it's absolutely none of your business. I'm not going to tell you that." She couldn't help the wicked grin that lit her face. She still had beard burn on her thighs as a reminder of what turned out to be an excellent way to work out her anger issues. "But it should give you some indication when I tell you that he went into the medi-bed willingly, with minimal protest, and was asleep before I even turned it on."

"Damn, Amaryllis," Dagby said. "Now that's the way to work out those anger issues of yours. You might should try that kind of cure more often. Maybe you'd be less grumpy."

"Hush, you." She shook her head, waving Dagby off.

"Wait. I'm so lost," Trick said. "What happened?"

"Oh, you poor innocent soul." Dagby reached over and patted his knee. "Amaryllis finally banged Ivan. Sent the man back to his hospital bed, it was so good." She gave Amaryllis a proud grin. "That's my girl."

"Oooh," Trick said with a slow nod. "About damn time. Anytime those two are together, it's like fireworks in a munitions bunker."

Von snorted. "Indeed."

"Okay, okay." Amaryllis waved them off. "You've had your fun."

"You certainly had yours." Von bumped fists with Dagby.

Trick snickered. "Good one."

She rolled her eyes. "I'm going to go check our supplies are properly secured before crashing for a bit. Dagby?"

"Considering I didn't participate in any exhausting extracurricular activities like you obviously did and already had myself a good old rest, I'll start digging, see what I can't turn up on our mysterious buyer."

"Course locked; Gastez Station is our destination." Trick swiped across his holoscreen and gave her a grin.

"Great. We'll meet in the mess in a few hours, then."

"Don't forget to check that your man is on the mend," Dagby called after her. "You might have need of him later."

Amaryllis raised a middle finger high for all to see as the door shushed closed, laughter chasing her steps.

10

IVAN

With a low hiss, the domed top of the medi-bed retracted, and Ivan blinked up at the ceiling, assessing the results. The angry scars from the blaster now felt as if they were several months old, and he no longer ached from head-to-toe. He'd take that as a win.

Going back into the medi-bed had been a good idea. Yes, it had been Amaryllis's idea. She'd pretty much forced him into it as soon as they came on board. Yes, he realized she most likely cared more about getting him out of her hair than his full recovery so she could plot nefarious schemes with her crew, but he didn't care. Whatever her reasons, a cycle later, he felt like a new man. Or at least a man who hadn't been shot and nearly died, faced down a woman who was almost scarier than Rhain, and helped assuage the anger and frustrations of a dangerous woman by giving her multiple orgasms. Busy, busy.

The question was, should he have gone to bed with Amaryllis? The answer was, he had no idea. It might have eased some of the tension between them. But did it change anything? She was still following Lore's orders to drop him off at Gastez Station. Which, fine. He wanted to get back to his crew anyway. He still didn't trust her any farther than he could throw her. There'd been no pillow talk. She hadn't revealed Lore's reasons for wanting the prototype. He hadn't confessed his love of romcom vids.

No matter the result, it had happened. He was a big boy who'd made his choice just as she had. They'd handle with any fallout as it came.

Sliding out of the narrow bed, he stood up, pleased his legs no longer threatened to collapse beneath his weight, and pulled on the clean clothes someone had left on the counter next to a pitcher of water. Last time he'd been in this room in this position, Amaryllis had been waiting for him. This time, there was no one else in the medi-bay.

Once dressed, he strode over to the exit. If this was locked... But it wasn't. It slid open with a soft shush when he approached. So, not a prisoner. He poked his head into the corridor. Empty. Not even a watcher posted.

He stepped back into the medi-bay and double-tapped his wrist, bringing up his comm. The holo 'puter popped up, ready to go. He eyed it suspiciously. That seemed too easy. Or was he overthinking it and being paranoid? Shaking his head, he decided it was the former with a strong dash of the latter.

"Contact Quin," he said, flicking the holo onto the flat white surface of an upper cabinet. He poured himself a glass of water while he waited and hoped the call connected. It was entirely possible that the signal was blocked, and his call would go nowhere. Or, depending on where both of them were in the galaxy, there might not be a strong enough connection to do a face-to-face, and he'd have to bounce a message out.

He really hoped Quin was close enough, though. When he'd removed Amaryllis from the cavern, by extension, he'd removed himself as well, leaving Quin and Bea without immediate backup. It had been a boneheaded move on his part and far too impulsive. If he'd been using his brain rather than reacting to Amaryllis's unexpected presence, he wouldn't have done it in the first place. You don't leave your wingman.

But he had and, until he saw Quin to assess for himself that

Quin and Bea were fine, he couldn't relax. Sure, Amaryllis claimed to have messaged his captain and that everyone was okay. Still, he needed to see it for himself.

Running a hand over his beard, he paced, eyeing the holo as he counted his steps. The flashing text in the center of the blank screen claimed to be connecting, which meant Quin was somewhere in the same sector as Ivan. He cracked his knuckles, prowling across the white flooring, spinning, then striding in the other direction. Why was it taking so long?

He'd practically worn a groove in the floor before the call finally connected.

"Ivan." His captain's voice crackled over the comm.

Ivan's head shot up, and he let out a sigh of relief as Quin's face flickered into view. It wasn't the best connection in the galaxy, but he didn't care. "Cap. Good to see you," he said, stopping in front of the holo, slipping automatically into parade rest.

Quin's voice held the same note of relief as Ivan's. "Damn, man. It's good to see you, too. We were worried about you."

Worried about him? Aw, he was touched. "Same."

Bea stuck her head into the frame and waved. "Hey, Ivan! Boy, are we happy to see you. We were afraid Amaryllis had killed you and dropped you somewhere in the black of space and we'd never recover your body. But you're not dead, so yay." She raised the remains of a sparkly pink drink at him.

"Not dead yet," he said. "And neither are you, thank the goddess." Amaryllis said they got off the planet fine, but he didn't realize just how much he needed to see the both of them with his own eyes until the wave of relief swept through him.

He cocked his head, looking them over and trying to see what was behind them, something that would give him a clue as to where they were. It certainly wasn't the *Laughing Dragon* or Gyan Station. Both Bea and Quin were wearing lightweight, flowing clothing in bright, colorful patterns. For the life of him, Ivan couldn't imagine Quin would feel comfortable enough to wear something like that around Rhain's space station, rather than the dark colors he normally preferred. He looked more relaxed than usual, too, though there were some more grays sprinkled in amongst that brown hair of his. Quin was a handful of years older than Ivan, and Ivan did his best to give his friend shit about aging any chance he got. No matter how he got those additional grays, Quin looked happy. Hard to tease a man who looked that content.

They were sitting outside in bright sunshine, a deep blue sky above them, birds were singing, and... were those waves he heard in the background? "Where are you?" The words popped out before he could stop them.

"Safina's murder cabin. Got here this morning. It's vacation time!" Bea giggled and drained the rest of her drink. "I'll let you boys chat a bit while I get us another slushie."

Before she could slip away, Quin looped a hand around the back of her neck and pulled her down for a kiss. "Thanks, Daisy." He smacked her on the ass, eliciting a squeal and a look that promised retribution before she left Ivan's view.

It was surprisingly good to see their displays of affection still going strong. "Murder cabin?" he asked, raising an eyebrow.

"Inside joke," Quin said with a shrug. "Though Safina lent us a beach house, so we could have a little recovery time before getting back to it."

Ivan held up a hand. "Don't say too much and no specifics. I'm on *Dog's Day*."

"Oh, I'm well aware," Quin said, his brows drawing together. "Amaryllis sent word about what happened." He gave Ivan a long look. "You okay, man?"

"Fine. Shockingly, she didn't take the opportunity to finish me off," he joked. She could have left him to bleed out or ditched him on the *Ephemeris*, but she didn't. He didn't quite know what to think about that.

"Yeah, I was pretty amazed, too. I was preparing to storm that ridiculous base of Lore's when we got her message. The only reason we didn't come for you was because she guaranteed your safety."

"And you chose to trust her." Surprising, considering.

"Yep. Look, man. You're the one who clashes with her and winds up dragging the rest of us into your battles."

Ivan opened his mouth to protest, then closed it again. Quin wasn't wrong. It stung, but it was the truth.

"I get it and I support you, but Amaryllis and her crew, they're actually pretty decent. For pirates, that is. So, yeah. I chose to trust her. And Navi vouches for them. But she knows, if anything happens to you, I'll hunt her to the ends of the universe and personally eliminate her from it." He gave Ivan a long look. "Okay?"

He nodded, strangely choked up at Quin's words. "Okay."

Quin got up off the lounger and headed inside, moving into a sun-drenched room decorated in bright pastels. Bea was singing a peppy song he didn't recognize somewhere in the background.

Ivan rubbed the back of his neck. "So... you're not going to give me shit about what I did?"

"Oh, I will. But it'll be way more fun in person, so I'm holding onto my best material."

"Great. Can't wait." And he'd deserve every moment of it. He got mad at himself all over again.

Quin laughed. "Ivan, seriously? You can't possibly think I'm upset at you for what you did. You did what you were trained to do. You spotted a problem, then removed the obstacle that might have blown everything Bea needed to accomplish that night. Granted, you almost got yourself killed for it and worried the fuck out of your entire crew, but you're alive... even if you are still in Amaryllis's talon-shaped clutches."

"I left you with no backup." He couldn't let it go.

Quin saw that and narrowed his eyes at his Number One. "Ivan. We had a plan. Cormac and Navi were watching everything from *Laughing Dragon*. Safina and her team were off shore and came when we needed them. You didn't leave us stranded. We had backup."

Ivan grunted. "I fucked up. Big time."

"Okay, if that's how you see it," he said, rolling his eyes. "I mean, you were impulsive, sure, but that always happens when your nemesis is on the scene. It's like all your common sense slides out of your big brain directly into your little brain when you see her. That's why I think you should bang it out, rid yourself of that temptation once and for all." He smiled up at Bea as she handed him a drink with a kiss on the cheek and did a little finger-waggle thing at Ivan.

"Oh, I'm pretty sure that's already happened," Bea said, taking a seat on the wide arm of Quin's chair.

"What?" Both Quin and Ivan exclaimed, looking at her.

She nodded, gesturing at Ivan. "I mean, look at him. For a man who supposedly was mostly dead just a few days ago, he's looking exceptionally healthy."

"Hey, I just got out of a medi-bed," he said.

"Oh, friend." She snickered. "Okay, but that particular look did not come courtesy of a medi-bed." She gave him a sly smile, one that was far too knowing. "One might even say he's glowing."

He opened his mouth to protest, but nothing came out. He couldn't lie. He closed it again with a click of his teeth.

A broad grin transformed Quin's face. "Ivan, you dog! And when you were injured, too. Please tell me she played sexy doctor for you."

Bea smacked him on the back of his head. "Gross, Quin. No."

Quin had the good sense to look shamefaced.

Ivan could feel the blood rushing to his cheeks and cursed. "The others don't need to know."

"Oh, but I think they absolutely need to know," Quin said, a grin lighting his face.

"Especially because we need to check who won the pool," Bea added. "What?" she said when Quin nudged her and shook his head.

"What pool?" Ivan dared to ask, though he could guess. Those bastards.

"Um..." Bea took a sip of her drink to avoid answering.

Quin tickled the back of her knee when she wouldn't answer and said, "We bet on you, Ivan. When you and Amaryllis would finally bang one out." He shrugged at Ivan's death glare. "What? We all knew it was going to happen sooner or later. Nemesis or not, every time you two so much as caught a glimpse of each other, you could cut that tension with a knife. You can't possibly be surprised that we started a pool."

He wasn't, of course. But still. Closing his eyes, he drew in a deep breath, counted to ten, then slowly released it. Nothing he could do about his useless, backstabbing, gambling shipmates right now. No, right now, he needed to focus on the job at hand rather than bets about his love life or the way Amaryllis felt when she came around his cock. He took another deep breath, this time willing away the pulse of lust that was encouraging other parts of himself that did not need encouragement at this time, thankyou-verymuch.

"Anyway," Ivan said, his voice booming across the comms, startling Bea. Her drink sloshed.

Quin hid a smile behind the mouth of his glass, his eyes sparkling with humor over his lurid orange-colored slushie drink.

"Did we accomplish what we needed to, remembering that there are most likely several very interested ears listening to our conversation?" And that they'd heard everything, including what had happened between him and Amaryllis. Fuck.

Bea nodded. "We did. String tied, sandcastle kicked, cock-womble in custody. I even got to dose a guard with one of Safina's toys." For someone who had never been a soldier or a spy, who spent the majority of her time fiddling around with engine parts and tech that was way above his pay grade, Bea was surprisingly decent at giving coded details about their job.

Quin wrapped an arm around her hips, giving her a squeeze. "Proud of you, Daisy."

Ivan decoded her statement to mean that Bea successfully planted a tracker on her prototype so they could follow it to whomever bought it, that she'd managed to make sure whomever purchased her work wouldn't benefit from it, and that Arden deVan, the man who'd set her up and ruined her life, was on his way to a cold prison moon. "Excellent work, even without me to back you up," he said, feeling a pang of regret and guilt that he hadn't been there for all that.

She beamed. "We're just waiting for word that the warrant for my arrest is nullified and the bounty is gone, and I'll be able to get back to my life and my work."

Quin squeezed her again.

She kissed him on the top of his head. "With a few changes, of course."

Bea and Quin exchanged soft smiles. "We wouldn't have been able to do it without your help," she said. "So thank you, Ivan."

"It's not over yet. Seems Amaryllis was there to steal the prototype for Lore." He took a risk saying that aloud, but Amaryllis's small crew was as tight knit as the *Dragon*'s and most likely knew everything she did. He needed Quin to know the immediate issue.

Quin's eyebrows disappeared into his hairline. "Lore? What in the three hells could The Cabal possibly want with a nonfunctional propulsion system?"

Ivan gave him the stink-eye. "Well, for one, they might not have known it was nonfunctional until you just told them."

Quin shrugged. "Oops."

"As for your question, I'd very much like to know that as well," Ivan said. "And you..." he gestured, not wanting to say it out loud. Amaryllis was smart enough to connect the dots, but he didn't want to make it easy for her.

Bea hummed her agreement. "Same. I don't want my work to be misused or co-opted. It's supposed to help people, not help line the pockets of some rich cockwombles."

"Cormac's monitoring things, but we can't make a move

safely until Bea's name is cleared and that bounty is gone, thus the vacation," Quin said, looking fondly up at his lady love. "We're going to need some help answering our questions."

He nodded. Though he wanted to get back to his crew and the *Dragon*, they needed intel, including what Amaryllis knew, Lore's plans, and what part Bea's prototype played in them. They also needed to retrieve Bea's system, thus eliminating any threat of reverse engineering her work. She might have done a good job of sabotaging that prototype, but it was better to be thorough.

Amaryllis might think that she was going to dump him at Gastez Station and be on her merry way, but she had another think coming.

A plan was forming in Ivan's brain, a way to make up to his captain for abandoning him during a job — not acceptable, no matter what Quin said — and to make sure that Lore didn't get her hands on Bea's work. "Send me what you've got. Fully encoded, my eyes only," he said, a broad grin spreading across his face. "I'm about to fuck up Amaryllis's little plans."

11

AMARYLLIS

The fabulous smells wafting through the ship drew Amaryllis from her cabin and down a level to the mess. She loved it when Von decided to cook. The man had the magic touch in the kitchen, presenting his crewmates with unusual concoctions that rarely failed to delight.

Dagby and Trick were already there and greeted her with raised drinks. They perched on stools at the pass-through counter between the galley and the mess, watching Von put the finishing touches on the meal.

"You've got to try these things." Trick handed her a drink. "Von, where did you learn how to make these again?"

Von placed a plate filled with small, round pastries in front of them, smacking Trick's hand away when he reached for one. "Not yet." He twirled a pastry bag tight before squeezing a dollop of white cream on top. "And the drink is called a 'Smitten Kitten' — made with Valintian gold liquor, fermented peach juice, a dash of sparkling water, and a twist of lime. A mixologist over in Waroc's Midtown taught it to me years ago." He carefully added a small sprig of green on top of the cream before giving them the go ahead to dig in.

Dagby stuffed one in her mouth and let out a groan of appreciation. "And you're only just now sharing it with us? Why are you holding out, Von? I thought we shared everything."

"A man's allowed to have some privacy, Dagby," Von said. "And I thought we had this discussion about talking with your mouth full."

She blinked at him, then opened her mouth wide, sharing the contents. He rolled his eyes and turned his back to her, moving on to his next dish.

"Gross girl," Trick said, shoving a pastry into his mouth.

She gave him a bright smile, flicking her long brown hair over her shoulder. "At least I don't carpet-bomb the command deck with my farts every morning. I mean, seriously, Trick. You eat the same foods I do. How is it you can produce such noxious gas? Maybe you need to spend some time in the medi-bed to fix whatever's wrong with your insides."

Trick threw a pastry at her, which she caught. She bared her teeth at him before popping it into her mouth.

"Okay, children. That's enough." Amaryllis snagged a pastry before they all disappeared. Some days, she felt like she ran a daycare instead of a crew of fearsome pirates. Not that they were actually all that fearsome, but they had a reputation to maintain. What if Ivan walked in and heard them bickering? What would he think?

Where was the man anyway? She checked her comm for the time. Huh. Medi-bed should've finished with him nearly an hour ago, and there was no way he could miss the delicious scents coming from the galley. It wasn't like he was a prisoner. "Anyone seen Ivan?" she asked, keeping her voice lightly curious.

"Why? You looking for your boyfriend?" Trick teased.

She huffed. "Not my boyfriend. Mortal enemy." It sounded impressive, calling someone a mortal enemy. Every true pirate ought to have a mortal enemy, especially one who landed on the "do-gooder" side of the sliding scale. She wasn't sure he fully fit the definition though. Mortal enemies despised one another, went out of their way to try and kill each other. Sure, they may have tried to kill each other a couple of times, but not for a while now. It felt like they'd evolved beyond mortal enemies. So what would that make him then? Nemesis, maybe. Giant pain in the ass, for certain. Ruiner of jobs, destroyer of a good time?

She huffed out a quiet laugh to herself. Ivan did have a stick up his ass when it came to her, that was certain. She wasn't sure why it had been insta-hate between them, but she made sure she gave as good as she got. Mortal enemies, indeed.

"Oh, so now we bang our mortal enemies, do we?" Dagby reached for the last puff but Trick was faster, pouncing on it with a triumphant cry. She stuck her tongue out at him.

"This was the only time," Amaryllis said, nodding her thanks to Von as he refilled her drink. She didn't even remember finishing the first glass. Truly, she needed to get her mind off Ivan and back in the game. They reached Gastez tomorrow. There, they'd drop him off, and then she wouldn't have to worry about him until their paths crossed again, hopefully in the far distant future. She'd even take never again, thankyouverymuch.

Von raised an eyebrow. The man might not be overly verbose, but he could communicate entire paragraphs worth of information with a single arched brow. This one said he didn't believe anything she had to say when she denied her attraction to Ivan or when she claimed she wouldn't ever sleep with him again.

Because of course she'd bang him again if the chance arose. The things that man had done to her, how he'd made her moan with his talented fingers and his flexible tongue and, oh gods, that deliciously thick cock of his... she shifted in her seat. "This drink of yours is warming me to my toes, Von." She fanned her face to cool down. It didn't work.

His other eyebrow rose as if to say, "You sure about that? Doubt it's the drink, Captain."

She glared at him and his eloquent brows. Clearing her throat, she said, "So, no one has eyes on Ivan, then?"

Granted, he wasn't a prisoner, but it was always a good idea to keep an eye on your mortal enemy when he was loose on your ship. You never knew what he might be up to. If she were better at being someone's enemy, she'd have made sure one of her crew was watching him at all times.

"Just who do you think I am? You might not have locked him down, but I'm not about to let him wander around the place all willy-nilly." Dagby scoffed. She checked her holo. "Anyway, he's still in the medi-bay. Just finished up a call with his captain."

"Trick, help him find his way down here, would you? I don't want him telling that captain of his that I starved him," Amaryllis said.

Grumbling, he got to his feet, pausing at the door. "Don't start without me."

"Then get a move on," Von said, gesturing at him with a large kitchen knife. "Everything will be ready in five minutes."

Amaryllis turned back to Dagby. "And? Don't leave me hanging. What did they say?"

"Unfortunately, Ivan guessed that, even though he wasn't blocked from making contact with his crew, someone would be listening to those calls."

Smart man. "So, you didn't hear anything?" Disappointing, to say the least. She wanted to know if they talked about the prototype or anything she could use.

"Of course I did. Got us a full transcript right here." She double tapped her wrist and pulled up a transcript of the conversation, enlarging it and pointing at a few lines. "Look where that fugitive chick says, 'String tied, sand castle kicked, cockwomble in custody'. They're speaking in code, thinking we can't figure out what they're talking about."

Amaryllis snorted. "'Cockwomble.' That's a good one. I'll have to remember it." She skimmed the text, rereading the part where Bea said they got what they needed to accomplished. "What does 'string tied, sandcastle kicked mean', do you suppose?"

"Kicking a sandcastle could be them stirring shit up." Dagby shrugged. "Though I'm pretty sure we did a better job of that, considering what happened with the guards."

"You tie a string to hold something together or to connect," Von added. Silverware clinked against the dishes.

She plucked at her bottom lip, thinking. Bea's coded words could mean a lot of things, but Amaryllis had the sneaking suspicion the prototype was at the heart of it. Ivan was interested in it. He'd come to attention like a pointer dog when he figured out that Lore wanted it. First chance he got, he told his captain. So, hells yes, the prototype was involved. Also interesting that Quin said the prototype was nonfunctional. She wondered if Lore knew. Probably not. It actually made her feel a little better about retrieving it and handing it over. If it didn't work, Lore couldn't misuse it, right?

And she hadn't missed the part where Ivan said he was going to mess up her plans. Even more reason to dump him at the space station and bounce before he could raise a fuss. So far, he hadn't made any trouble, but that was only because he didn't know she planned to find and steal the prototype herself. It was only a matter of time before he made a play. The peace and quiet couldn't last forever. Nor did she want it to. Things would be much calmer and simpler without him all up in her interests, but as much as she fussed about it, she actually enjoyed their little games of destruction and deception.

"Do we know anything about who this cockwomble might be?" she asked.

Dagby shook her head. "No chatter from that night beyond a run-down of the who's who in attendance at the ball and what they were wearing."

With a swipe, she enlarged a photo of a brown-haired woman in a strapless teal gown, her tanned skin glowing in the candle-light. She smiled and waved with an arm stacked with glittering bracelets of precious gemstones that crawled up her arm. A single gold band encircled the other arm's bicep. A stocky man in a perfectly tailored tuxedo stood a step behind her, a possessive look of avarice on his face as he gazed at her.

Dagby pointed at the woman. "That's Decima Vanid, CEO of Vanid Enterprises and eldest child of Acacia Vanid, matriarch of the Vanid family. Just look at all those lovely sparklies, just waiting for someone to grab." She sighed, her eyes going soft. She enjoyed relieving the wealthy of their sparklies almost as much as Amaryllis did. "And the dress is pretty, too."

"Who's the guy?" Von asked, tilting his chin towards the holo of Decima posing on his counter.

"Decima's husband. Bob, I think his name is? Or Pete? Something like that." Dagby waved the image away. "Not important. Definitely not interesting enough for the gossip rags to talk about, so I don't know much about him. Can look into him, if you want."

Amaryllis shook her head.

Dagby shrugged. "He doesn't have anything worth stealing anyway. He was just there with his wife as moral support, I guess."

Von lost interest, turning back to finish plating the food. "Where are Trick and your guest, Amaryllis?" he asked, irritation in his voice. "Dinner's ready."

The common room door swished open at his words.

"We're here." Trick jerked a thumb over his shoulder. "Found your lost puppy, Amaryllis."

"I didn't need a guide," Ivan growled. He shouldered his way into the room, taking everyone in with a quick glance. "I knew exactly where I was going."

"Man would have wound up in engineering if I haven't steered him the right way." Trick waved Ivan towards the open seat to Amaryllis's left before grabbing the full plates Von set on the pass-through. He served everyone, then took his place next to Dagby with a wink.

"*Dog's Day* has a similar layout to the *Dragon*," Ivan said, still grumbling over Trick escorting him to dinner. He picked up a fork and poked at the offering. "I was on my way here when your man here bumped into me."

"I believe we're an H-class cruiser, while your ship is an older F-model." Amaryllis nodded at Von as he took the seat across from her. "And we've made some improvements, as well."

She wasn't sure why she felt the need to tell him that except she was proud of *Dog's Day*, and how they'd fixed her up into the sleek cruiser she was today. Plus, with the adjustments Dagby'd made, she was one of the most maneuverable ships in The Cabal. But Ivan already knew that, having experienced her capabilities from the other side.

"Von, man. This is delicious," Dagby said, her cheeks stuffed full like she was tucking it away for later. "Your best yet."

The corner of Von's lips curled up as he accepted her praise with a small nod. He cut a slice of meat and ate it, his eyes distant as he absorbed the flavors.

For a brief moment, silence reigned as they tucked into the meal Von prepared for them. Tank-grown meat that was tender enough to cut with a fork. Fresh greens seasoned with butter and garlic. Tiny potatoes roasted until crisp, their insides soft and fluffy. There was even a loaf of freshly baked bread. So much better than what the *Dog's Day*'s auto-oven could produce, even though it used the items they supplied and the recipes they programmed. Von claimed it was because he cooked with love.

"This is delicious." Ivan stuffed a forkful of greens into his mouth. "Best greens I've had in forever."

"Thank Von," Trick said, shoving a thumb in his direction. "He's the chef. Sadly, he only cooks when he feels like it."

"But we sure are thrilled when he does." Dagby leaned back in her chair with a contented sigh. Her plate was so clean, it practically sparkled.

Amaryllis didn't say anything, just watched as Ivan interacted with her crew, her family. He got them telling stories about past jobs, laughed in all the right places, and didn't treat them like the scum of the galaxy the way most people did when they realized they were part of The Cabal. It was the most pleasant, non-combative interaction they'd had with a member of *Laughing Dragon* and, tangentially, the Shields. Maybe they had more in common than she thought. Or maybe Ivan was on his best behavior because he was trapped on a ship with a bunch of pirates. Whatever the case, she appreciated his good manners.

When she got to her feet and started to clear the dishes, Ivan jumped up to help. "You're a guest," she said, waving him away. She tried to grab the plate from him, but he held tight. She glared at him. "Let go. We've got this."

"Guest or no, I always do my fair share." Ivan picked up Von's empty plate and followed Amaryllis into the galley.

With Ivan's broad shoulders and big presence, the already narrow galley shrank. She couldn't move without rubbing up against him. An arm touch here as they stacked the dirty dishes in the washer. The brush of his hand there as they placed the silverware in the sonic cleaner. Even the smell of the man, a subtle combination of cold mountain air and aspens, surrounded her as they worked in companionable silence to clean up the galley.

By the time they'd finished up, her entire body was tingling. If her crew wasn't mere feet away in the common area, she might very well have pulled him to her for a kiss. Her toes curled in her boots imagining him standing between her legs as she sat on the counter, his big body caging hers as his tongue invaded her mouth.

Fuck. She had to get out of here before she did something stupid. Wringing out the cloth and tossing it in the recycler, she tried to push past him, but wound up wedged between the counter and his round ass.

"Godsdammit, you giant mountain," she said, smacking at his wide back with no real force. "How are you taking up so much space? Move." She poked his side.

He squeaked, his torso bending away from her finger.

"What was that noise?" she asked. How did a man as big as

him even make that squeaky toy sound? "Are you ticklish?" An evil grin spread across her face as she eyed his waist.

"That was a very manly reaction to someone unexpectedly jabbing me in the side with her pointy finger." He cleared his throat, throwing a glance at her over his shoulder. "And no. I'm absolutely not ticklish. You just surprised me, that's all," he said, pressing forward to give her enough bare inches to scoot past. "There. Now you can get by."

She poked at his side as she slid past.

This time, what could only be described as a high-pitched giggle burst out of the man's mouth. He whipped his head around, glaring down at her. "Stop that."

With a snicker, she raised her fingers and waggled them at him. "Does this mean if I need to torture you, all I need to do is use these?"

"You wouldn't dare," he said, wrapping his arms protectively around his waist.

"Annoy me and I just might," she teased, taking half a step closer, close enough to feel the heat of his body. "After all, these fingers have plenty of ways to torture you. Learning that you're ticklish just adds to my arsenal."

A muscle jumped in his jaw. He looked behind her, his eyebrows coming together like thunderclouds.

Shit. "They're all right there, watching, aren't they?" she asked in a whisper. Damnable bunch of Nosy Nellies.

He nodded. "If you torture me, I have witnesses," he whispered back.

"Fine." She dropped her hands and stepped back. "I guess that means it's time for dessert."

12

IVAN

He let Amaryllis shoo him out of the galley so she could make tea. After a surprisingly nice dinner, complete with pleasant conversation and delicious food, Ivan found himself seated on a loveseat in the common area and, once again, the center of attention.

Oh, they tried to act casual, settling into the u-shaped seating arrangement in the space just beyond the community table in the mess. Dagby pulled up her wrist comm and with a flick of her fingers, put the galactic rugby finals on the large screen that filled most of the far wall. Trick relaxed onto the couch with a groan, his long legs splayed over the entire space. Von and Dagby each claimed a cushioned recliner, Dagby flipping hers out and snuggling into it while Von sprawled in his. They gave the impression that they were totally relaxed after a good meal, not a care in the galaxy. But while Amaryllis puttered in the galley, they were watching him.

He slung an arm over the back of the small sofa and spread his legs wide, taking up the space, aiming to look as at ease and comfortable as possible. Always a smart idea to show the enemy you weren't afraid, especially in their home territory. Not that he actually thought they'd try to murder him. They'd had plenty of chances to do that. He was waiting for Amaryllis to join them so he could get some answers as to what was actually going on. He wasn't relaxed; he was plotting his next move. But he didn't want them to suspect.

Trick waved a lazy hand towards the game on the screen. "The Space Dusters are about to get their asses handed to them."

"Ha. In your dreams. Dusters are will smash the Flux Capacitors into the dirt," Ivan said, his eyes on the game, but his attention on the room's occupants. The Space Dusters were Quin's favorite team, and he turned the entire crew into fans. One of their favorite things to do when they weren't on a job was to get a bunch of snacks, some cold beers, and watch the team play their weekly games during the season.

"Care to put some credits where your mouth is?" Trick asked with a slow grin.

Ivan shook his head. "I don't gamble."

"Why? Afraid your team's going to lose so badly, you won't be able to hold your head up?"

"Yeah, that's it." Trick didn't yet realize he wouldn't be able to goad Ivan into doing what he wanted. Only his younger brother could get a rise out of him like that. *And Amaryllis*, he reminded himself, watching her sashay her way into the room, her tight black pants hugging her hips.

Her hands full of steaming mugs, she paused, clocking everyone's position and the one open seat next to Ivan. She set the mugs on the low table at the center of the seating arrangement.

"I guessed you took your tea bitter and black, Ivan," she said, giving him a wink as she leaned forward with the tea. Her loose white shirt, top three buttons undone, gaped open as she bent, revealing her breasts cupped in the delicate white lace beneath.

She certainly enjoyed trying to get a rise out of him, flashing those deliciously plump assets of hers every chance she got. He didn't mind. If she wanted to give him a show, who was he to deny her the pleasure?

Accepting the mug with a grin, he said, "I like my tea strong, but a little sugar once in a while is a nice change of pace."

A little snort escaped Dagby.

Drinks dispersed, she paused, trying to decide where to sit. Trick stretched out his arms over his head and crossed his booted feet as if to say, "No room here."

Ivan patted the space beside him. "Looks like this is the only spot open."

"You do realize my hips won't fit in that tiny space you left," she said with a toss of her hair. "I'd wind up sitting on you."

He wouldn't mind that either.

Instead of taking Ivan up on his offer, she smacked at Trick's feet. "No boots on the furniture. And sit up. We've got a guest." With a groan, he shifted, and she plopped onto the long sofa next to him.

"Yeah, Trick. You lounge around like that, you'll forget where you are and shove your hand down your pants," Dagby said.

"What? It's comfortable." Trick gave her a wounded look. "And my hand's not really down my pants; it's just tucked into my waistband. Gives it a place to rest and keeps my fingers warm."

"You're so embarrassing." Dagby took a cookie from the plate Von had placed on the low center table.

Ivan sipped his tea as he watched the interplay between the crew. He'd never spent any downtime with them as a group before. Brawling in a bar didn't count. They were completely comfortable with one another, much like the *Laughing Dragon* crew.

Of course, it was hard not to be when you spent so much time together in a confined space. Crews who couldn't get along broke apart or made deadly mistakes during jobs because they didn't like or trust one another. Crews like Amaryllis's and his, though, they became family. And family looked out for one another, supported each other. If they wanted to keep something secret, they would.

Which meant to get what he wanted from them, his best bet would be to catch them off guard, put them on the back foot, so to speak. "So," he said, once everyone was relaxed and enjoying their tea and delicious dark chocolate chip cookies. He plucked a second treat from the plate and leaned back. "Amaryllis, you finally going to tell me what exactly you're planning on doing with the prototype?"

She jumped as if he'd jabbed her with an electric prod, spilling tea down the front of her pristine white shirt. The liquid saturated the fabric, revealing the edge of the lacy cups underneath. "Dammit, Ivan." She set down her cup and disappeared into the galley, reemerging with a small cloth. "Tea stains, you know, especially on a white shirt." She dabbed at the wet spot. "And, no, I won't tell you."

Somehow, he knew that would be her response. Raising one eyebrow, he said in a fake shocked tone, "But back on Lore's base, in your room, you promised me answers as to what was going on."

She threw down the cloth and flopped back on the sofa with a huff. "I absolutely did not. In fact, I believe what I said was, 'Not here'."

"And I agreed to wait, as long as I got my answers."

"Then you'll also remember that I didn't agree to that."

"It was implied."

"It was not. You merely assumed. And you know what they say when you assume things."

"No, what?" Trick asked, his eyes bright as he watched their interplay of words.

Dagby rolled her eyes and muted the game.

Amaryllis ignored him, slinging her arms over the back of the sofa and propping a booted foot up on the table in front of her. "The answer is no. I will not be sharing my plans with you."

He thought as much. "That's fine. I think I'm smart enough to have put it together myself."

A smirk curled her lips, her dark gold eyes sparking with fire. "Do you now? Well, by all means, go ahead and bless us with your knowledge." She waved a lazy hand at him, the queen giving him permission to speak in her presence.

He popped the rest of the cookie in his mouth, taking a beat to enjoy the bitterness of the chocolate and how it complemented the sweetness of the soft cookie. If Von weren't a part of the *Dog's Day* crew, he might be tempted to poach him for the *Dragon*. Then he washed it down with his strong tea, all the while completely aware of Amaryllis's growing annoyance. Finally, he set his mug on the table at his elbow and dusted the cookie crumbs from his fingers.

"Anytime, Cherry," Amaryllis said, impatience shading her voice.

"Heh. Cherry," Trick said. "Good one."

"Lore wants the prototype, so you were sent to that auction on Vanid Island to retrieve it." He still didn't know why Lore wanted the thing, but given time, he'd figure it out. "Things went wrong."

"You can say that again," Dagby muttered to Von, who gave a grunt of acknowledgement.

"Because it went so wrong, Lore is pissed. If it had just been me getting shot or the mess you escaped behind as you left the island, she would have been mad, but it probably would have resulted in no more than a stern lecture, maybe a slap on the wrist. However, you didn't deliver the prototype." He watched Amaryllis's face tighten and knew he was on the right track. Surprising how well he could read her and her microexpressions.

The room was silent except for the steady hum of the ship. The entire crew watched him with gleaming eyes.

"Because you didn't deliver the prototype, Lore gave the job to someone else."

A muscle jumped in Amaryllis's jaw.

"But you're not the type to leave things undone so you've decided that, after you fulfill Lore's instructions to drop me off at the closest space station, you're going to track down the prototype and steal it before this other crew does." He laced his hands behind his head and grinned at her irritated expression. "How am I doing so far?" He knew he was right. He just wanted her to acknowledge it and then fill in the details.

She looked at her crew. Dagby blew out a breath and gave a slow nod. The men followed suit. With a sigh heavy enough to drown in, Amaryllis said, "Correct."

He wanted to pump his fist in the air in triumph, but he settled for a single nod. He gave her a few beats to continue, to fill in the blanks. Of course, she didn't. "And?" he prodded.

"And what? You're still getting dropped at Gastez. We're going to get the prototype." She crossed her arms over her chest, grimacing as the wet fabric pressed against her skin. "That's the end of it."

"So, you know where the prototype is, then?"

Blowing out a hard breath, she said, "Ship transporting it landed at Cora Station. I'm only telling you that because I'm positive your people already know. Between Dagby and Trick, we'll track it down."

Dagby shook her head, but stopped herself when Amaryllis glared at her.

Trick, however, didn't get the memo to keep his trap shut. "It's been nearly two weeks, Cap. Trail's cold." He shrugged. "It's possible I can pick it up, but only if I get really lucky."

Amaryllis elbowed him. He gave her a wounded look, sliding farther away from her on the couch.

"So you don't know where it is, then." Ivan grinned at her. *Ha. Gotcha.*

"What of it? We'll figure it out." She flicked a handful of braids over her shoulder.

He leaned forward, resting his elbows on his knees. "You might not know where it is, but I do."

She leaned forward, mirroring him. "And what do you want for this information? We can pay."

"I don't need your credits." His grin grew. He was feeling very pleased with himself at the moment, really enjoying poking at her.

"Fine," she said, throwing her hands up in the air. "You go right ahead and dangle that information out there. So you know where it is. So what? We'll figure it out."

He glanced at her crew. Dagby studied the bottom of her mug of tea. Trick shrugged and scratched his chest. Von pretended to watch the muted game. Meanwhile, Amaryllis looked like she was about to tear his head from his neck so she could look inside it for the information she so desperately wanted.

"I don't think you will," he said, giving them all a bright smile. "But don't you worry. I'm happy to tell you where the prototype is."

"Really?" Dagby asked.

Even Amaryllis's dark expression lightened, though it was shaded with doubt and confusion.

"Really," he said with a nod. "I'll tell you."

"Here comes the 'but'," Amaryllis said.

Trick snickered.

"Child," Dagby said, rolling her eyes.

Ivan held up a finger. "But I'm coming with you to retrieve that prototype." He owed it to Bea and Quin to finish the job they started on Badin. Besides, he couldn't let the drive wind up in Lore's hands, no matter the condition. They had no idea why she wanted it. To his knowledge, The Cabal wasn't into engines or ship building. There was something else at play here. Something that made his instincts tingle and his head hurt.

"Absolutely not," Amaryllis said, leaping to her feet and glaring down at him, her hands planted on her hips.

He shrugged. "Fine. Good luck to you, then." He turned to watch the silent rugby game as her crew tromped into the small galley to discuss his proposal.

It took longer than he expected for them to return with their answer.

The Space Dusters had just scored another goal when they returned. Amaryllis stood in front of him, her crew arrayed behind her.

"So? What's the verdict?" he asked. He was enjoying all this far too much, so he took care not to let it show on his face. Amaryllis's paybacks were not something to take lightly.

"We begrudgingly accept your terms." She ground out each word as if they were pulled from the dark depths of her soul.

He smacked his hands on his thighs and got to his feet. "Excellent. Guess you'd better change course to Cora Station, then."

"Fuck," she said. And with that, Amaryllis strode out the door, her crew following behind.

13

AMARYLLIS

Two standard days later and *Dog's Day* was in the queue to dock at Cora Station. Though they couldn't really afford it, she'd burned a jump to get to their destination faster. She justified her decision by telling herself that Christophe and Deno had a head start on them, and they couldn't afford to waste the three additional days it would have taken them to get there without it.

While that was true, she'd actually burned that jump because she was irritated with Ivan and his manipulations and she wanted him off her ship. Not just irritated, but also reactive and snappish with everyone around her. She didn't want to be trapped in this small space with him any longer than absolutely necessary, or she might be tempted to eject him from the airlock. Or worse, fuck him again.

He must have felt the cut of her anger, too, because he stuck to his cabin or the common area in the mess. He didn't come up on the command deck or seek her out, interacting with her only at their daily crew meal.

Even then, he didn't really speak to her. Sure, he told stories and talked rugby stats and player rosters with the others, but she hadn't had a direct conversation with him since he blackmailed them into taking him with them. That irritated her even more because she couldn't work out her frustrations with a loud, old-fashioned argument. Usually, Ivan gave as good as he got, but his refusal to engage with her this time left her feeling antsy and out of sorts. She was all bottled up and, if he wasn't careful, she'd explode all over him and not in a good way.

Grumbling to herself, she stalked into the galley, intent on tracking down something salty and crunchy to bite down on while they waited for the holders of the red tape of Cora Station to detangle it enough to assign them a berth. Not looking where she was going, she ran straight into a warm, immovable object.

"Ivan," she growled, glaring up at the man standing in her way.

"Rilly," he said, with a tip of his chin.

"Move," she said, pushing ineffectually at his chest, noticing how his pectorals flexed beneath her hands. He smelled good, too, the clean sharpness of the soap the guys had given him blending with his natural scent. Her body heated.

"Now, now, Rilly. That's not a polite way to speak to your guest. Didn't Lore teach you any manners?" He was watching her with that annoying half-smile of his.

She clenched her fists, wanting to smack that look off his face. "My parents taught me manners. Lore taught me to survive, even when going up against big, vexing buttheads." She pushed against him again.

"Oh, so now I'm a butthead? Why? Because I messed with your little plans to get rid of me and impress Lore? I hate to tell you, but they wouldn't work, anyway. You have no idea how to find what you're looking for. Or is it something else?" He leaned closer, his warm lips brushing against the shell of her ear. "Is it because when you're in your bunk at night, you're imagining my fingers on your clit and my tongue in your mouth?"

She squeezed her thighs together as a bolt of lust pulsed through her body. Damn him. She tossed her head. "I've had better," she said. She hadn't. And, yes, she thought of him at night. It was part of why she was so frustrated. But he didn't need to know that.

Her breath caught as he slipped a hand around her nape, drawing her closer to him. She let him back her up against the wall, his big body caging hers. The door to the mess slid shut with a gentle shush. She fumbled for the wall panel to lock it and disable the cameras. Locked in a room with Ivan. Oh, she must be a fool. Why was she doing this again?

"Tell me you don't want this, Rilly, and I'll stop." He nipped at her earlobe, sending sparks up her spine.

But she did want it. She wasn't about to tell him to stop. She grabbed the bottom of his beard and pulled his mouth to hers.

His hand tightened on the back of her neck, his strong fingers exerting gentle pressure as he held her in place, his thighs pressing against hers. His tongue delved into her mouth, heat sliding along her tongue. He tasted like the black cherries from dessert, sharp and sweet.

She tugged his shirt from his waistband, running her hand up his back, appreciating the way his muscles flexed beneath her touch. Her hands paused in their exploration to trace the edge of the exit scar left from Andrea's blaster. A little lower and he wouldn't be here, irritating the shit out of her or running his tongue over every inch of her exposed skin.

Shifting his body, he slid his legs between hers until she was on the tips of her toes, straddling his hips, the fabric of her pants rubbing against her clit, creating a delicious friction. "What do you want?" he asked, his voice rough with need.

"More," she whispered, heat pooling in her belly. Her entire body flamed as he kissed his way down the column of her neck, pausing at the dip in her clavicle to nip at her sensitive skin.

He grabbed the front of her white shirt and ripped it open, buttons clattering to the floor around them. With a flick of his fingers, he popped open her lacy bra. Cupping her breasts in his hands, he took one in his mouth, his tongue curling around her nipple as he sucked on it before moving on to the other to give it the same treatment.

She couldn't stop the moan that came from deep inside her as his teeth grazed over the taut peak of her breast. Digging her nails into his upper back, she gasped out, "I need you in me. Now."

There was something to be said about a fast fuck and, after the last couple of days' buildup of tension, she needed it. She needed him. No one else would do.

He undid her pants and shoved them down her thighs. She kicked a leg free. Her fingers flew, unsnapping his trousers and pulling out his cock, already hard and ready for her. She stroked along the thick shaft and grazed her nails over the soft skin of his balls.

His body clenched beneath her touch. "Fuck, Rilly," he groaned.

"That's it exactly," she said. "Fuck Rilly. Do it now."

"Bossy princess," he said, banding his arms under her ass and lifting her, trapping her between his broad chest and the wall. He lined his cock up with her pussy and stroked a finger over her bottom lip. "Hold on."

She wrapped her legs around his waist, shuddering with pleasure as he slid into her, seating himself. His hot, thick length stretched her inner muscles as he pumped hard into her, giving her exactly what she asked for. She dropped her head to his shoulder and sank her teeth into the tendon there, drawing another deep groan from him.

His hands clenched on her thighs as he worked his cock over her most sensitive inner spots, his pelvis pounding out a rhythm against her clit. She wrapped her arms around his shoulders and dug her fingers into his hair, pulling him closer as he drove them to the edge.

He toppled first with a shout, his hips pumping hard. She was so close. She'd kill him with her bare hands if he stopped. He didn't. In an impressive feat of strength and balance, he slid one hand between them so he could stroke her clit as he kept up the pace. With the pressure of his thumb, he coaxed her to join him, groaning as she came, her inner muscles clenching around his cock.

For several brief seconds, they stood there panting, breath mingling, their foreheads pressed together as the last sparks of their desire faded.

After another beat, she unwrapped her legs from his waist. He held her up between his body and the wall for a moment more then let her slide down him to stand on her own two feet before taking a step back.

As they set their clothes to rights, she said, "This never happened."

He nodded. "Absolutely not."

"I hate you, and you're a nightmare to be around," she said.

"Right back atcha," he said, reaching out to tug her shirt into place, fastening the two remaining buttons.

She reached up and ran her hands through his hair, fixing the mess she'd made of it, the red strands silky beneath her fingertips. "And my crew definitely cannot know about this," she added. She cringed, imagining which of the three hells they'd give her if they found out. When they found out. She hadn't told them last time, but somehow gave enough away that Dagby guessed. With a sigh, she began mentally preparing herself for the inevitable.

"This goes without saying, but nor can mine." But his tone held the same sense of inevitability, as if he knew he wouldn't be able to keep it under wraps for long.

Still, they had to try. They looked at one another, exchanged sharp nods, and went their separate ways — him back to his quarters and her in search of something sweet.

AMARYLLIS WAS JUST BUTTONING up a fresh white shirt — one with all its buttons intact — when Dagby hailed her.

"Got ourselves a berth, Cap," she said.

"Finally." Amaryllis slid on her boots. "Gather everyone up. We'll meet by the cargo bay doors as soon as we're secured. We need to get our tickets for the elevator down, and goddess knows how long that whole process is these days."

Cora Station was one of seven major stations that orbited the planet of Melorn. Because of its location and the express elevator that tethered it to the capital city of Waroc, also the busiest. It functioned as the primary hub for the sprawling city-state and docking for visitors and dignitaries alike.

Currently made up of fifty-two layers, Cora looked like a stack of round credits. Each layer's layout was the same, excluding the middle stack, which housed security and crew quarters, and the bottom stack, which contained the express elevator. The outer ring of each layer held docks and long-term ship berths. The second ring was for transportation around the layer. The third ring was filled with merchants. Every layer had its own flavor of food stalls, restaurants, bars, and stores selling basic necessities, medicines, and the like. Depending on which layer you were on, the merchant ring offered everything from high-end mercantile stores and top-notch restaurants to brothels and dive bars. Lifts to take visitors from one layer to the other ringed the fourth layer while the center column of the station was its guts, inaccessible to all but crew.

Cora Station was always packed to the gills with individuals coming and going.

"Um, I think I need to stay on the *Dog*, if that's okay," Dagby said in a shaky voice. They stood at the open hatch watching the crowds eddy around the docks. A dull roar of voices, clanking machinery, and beeping carts filled the air. "I forgot how crowded and busy it is here. Too many people." Her voice grew thin and reedy, and she took a stumbling step back inside to lean against the wide frame of the hatch. "Nope. Can't do it. I'm sorry."

It had been a long while since they'd visited anywhere nearly as busy as Cora Station, and she'd forgotten about Dagby's trouble with crowds of this size. *Ugh, I'm a terrible friend*, she thought. "Sorry, Dagby. I forgot how jam-packed this place is." Waroc wouldn't be any less crowded. She shooed her away from the hatch and further inside. "No worries. Stay here. Honestly, we'll be better served by you staying on board with all your equipment, anyway. Monitor chatter, keep an eye on us, and all that, just like a regular planetside job. We'll handle the ground stuff."

"Dammit," Dagby said, biting her lip. "I was looking forward to getting off the ship for a while. I mean, I love the old girl, but a change of scenery is nice every once in a while." She patted the ship fondly.

"How 'bout after all this, we head to Badin, rent us one of those beachside shacks where we can lie in the sun like lizards, drink far too many slushie drinks, and stuff ourselves on seafood?" Amaryllis said, bumping Dagby with her shoulder.

"That sounds amazing." Dagby bumped her back, giving her a shy smile. "Thanks, Amaryllis."

"Hey. This is what family does; we take care of each other." She shot a glance at Ivan, who was already off the ship and standing next to Von and Trick. She blew out a sigh. "Since you're abandoning me and leaving me alone to deal that annoying man, I guess you'd better add him to our team comm. I don't want to have to loop him in every time you share info with us."

Ivan laughed at something Trick said and swept out an arm, gesturing at the huge cruise liner docked next to them. Trick grinned, slapping him on the back.

"But don't add him to our private chat," she said in a low voice. "Just in case."

"You got it, Cap." Dagby paused, eyeing Amaryllis. "You seem awfully relaxed. Did you two..."

"No!" The word burst out of her before she could stop it. Shit.

Dagby raised an eyebrow, folding her arms over her chest. "Really."

Of course, she didn't believe her. Amaryllis wouldn't have believed her either. But she doubled down. "Really. Come on,

Dagby. When would I even have done that?" Fireworks in less than ten minutes. Of course it was doable.

"Okay." She grinned at her. She didn't believe her. "If you say so."

"I do."

"Fine."

"Fine." Amaryllis tossed up her hands. "I'm leaving. Make yourself useful and see if you can't find out where Christophe and Deno are. I don't want to risk running into them and word getting back to Lore."

"Done" Dagby's grin grew. "Have fun with your little boy toy, Captain."

Amaryllis gave her the middle finger. "Fuck off, Dagby."

Dagby's giggles followed her as she walked down the gangway to join the rest of her team.

Her wrist tingled with an incoming text. She double-tapped to open it.

Liar, Dagby had sent. *I know what you did. The beard burn on your chest is a pretty big clue.*

Shit. Forgot about that. She huffed out a laugh, making a fist to close the comm. Damnable woman knew her too well. She would have figured it out with or without the rasp marks left by Ivan's beard.

Leaving Dagby and *Dog's Day* behind, they wove their way through knots of individuals, skirting around a group of lower mountain trolls in the middle of an argument, their voices clashing together like rockslides, and past a tidy line of river folk, their reed-thin, green-toned bodies swaying as if blowing in an invisible breeze. By the time they finally found the ticket station, Amaryllis was wishing she'd stayed back on the ship with Dagby. Or that she'd been able to pull some strings to get them on a VIP shuttle so they didn't have to deal with the crowds or waste time waiting in queues. Luckily, the line for tickets went quickly. In no time, they had their passes for the elevator down to the planet's surface in hand.

Of course, it wasn't as easy as getting a ticket and then immediately getting on the elevator. With so many people moving through the station, the actual wait time for the elevator was long, which meant they were stuck here while they waited for their scheduled time.

Ivan double-tapped his wrist and pulled up a holo clock. "Looks like we've got about three hours to kill before our time slots. What do you all want to do?"

Amaryllis looked longingly back towards her ship. "We could always go back to the *Dog*. I've got some maintenance checks I need to run."

"Boring," Trick said, drawing out the word. "We're on Cora. When was the last time we were on Cora Station? Like four years ago? You can't go running back to the ship when we've got time in a place like this. I hear they installed a holo board on Level 23, and that one of the programs makes you feel like you're surfing the giant swells of the Fintroth Sea. Ooh, or we could try our luck at the slots on Level 45, maybe hit it big." He grinned and rubbed his hands together.

"I could use a drink," Von said, stroking the spot on his thigh where his holster usually rested. But firearms weren't allowed on Cora or in the city-state of Waroc, so Von couldn't bring his favorite weapons.

Of course, that didn't mean they were completely unarmed. That would be foolish. Besides, despite the illegality of it, there were plenty of places on the surface to purchase what they needed.

Caving to the peer pressure, Amaryllis said, "Fine. But I don't want to waste my time in some virtual reality arcade or gambling. Those places are expensive. Can you imagine how much something like that would cost here?" She shuddered. Because it had a captive audience of people waiting — for their turn on the elevator, for their ship to get fixed, for cargo to be loaded, or whatever — prices at many of the places on Cora Station were eye-wateringly outrageous, more so than most other stations even.

But the guys were right. They came here so rarely. They

should at least find some place not on the ship. Somewhere she could indulge in people-watching. "A drink and some food sounds good," she finally conceded.

"I know a great spot on Level 3," Ivan said. "A little pub Quin and I discovered last time we were here. Tasty fried things. Strong drinks. Not super-expensive. Close to Level 1 and the elevator."

"Sounds good to me. But first, I have to go get parts to fix that glitch," Trick said, consulting his comm. "There's a shop a level up from here that says they have what we need." He raised an eyebrow at Amaryllis. "Meet you there. Okay?"

She nodded. "Von, go with him." Trick protested, but she cut him off. "We're on a job; we stay partnered up. No arguments." Besides, Trick had a bad habit of losing track of time, especially when there were fun, shiny things to distract him. He'd wind up lost in a virtual reality, and they'd never find him. Von would keep him focused and on schedule.

"Fine." Trick sighed. "Send us details of where you are. We'll meet you there."

"Captain," Von said with a nod, nudging Trick forward. The crowd briefly parted, then swallowed them up.

She looked over at Ivan. If she didn't know better, she'd say her crew planned this. But they wouldn't do that to her. Would they? Blowing out a hard breath, she said, "I need a drink."

14

IVAN

"So, Ivan. Serious question. Why are we mortal enemies?"

The bane of his existence sat across from him in the hole-in-the-wall he'd brought them to, twirling her empty pint glass, the moisture on its base leaving rings on the table. She relaxed in her seat, her long legs propped up on an extra chair. The soft lighting accented her high cheekbones and the lightning strike of verdigris along her temple. She'd wrapped her hair in a haphazard bun on top of her head, which emphasized the elegant curve of her neck.

Holding up her glass for the bartender, she signaled for two more. "I mean, I know I claim you as my mortal enemy partly because it amuses me and partly because ever since the first time we met, what four years ago? You've gone out of your way to mess with me and my jobs. So why do you hate me?"

He wasn't prepared for such a dangerous question to be lobbed at him in the middle of a crowded pub. He blew out a breath. "Hate is a pretty strong word," he hedged. He didn't hate her. He might have once, when hate for all things Cabal-related still drove him. In fact, he wasn't exactly sure how he felt about her these days, but it wasn't hate. Not anymore.

"Okay, fine. Dislike, feel distaste for, loathe, revile, abhor, disapprove of... any of those striking a chord?" She rolled the sleeves of her crisp, white shirt up to her elbows and rested her forearm on the edge of the table, waiting for his answer.

"I am not a fan of The Cabal, is all," he said, taking their fresh pints from the bullet-shaped bot who brought them to their table with a bright, electric smile. As Amaryllis placed the empties on its tray, the bot extended an arm and wiped down the table before zipping back into its slot in the bar, ready for its next delivery.

It was more than that, of course. The Cabal itself wasn't the worst organization in the galaxy when it came down to it. Certainly, there were some seriously shitty people and factions who claimed membership. But as a whole, it functioned similarly to guilds, providing a refuge and gathering place for like-minded individuals.

But the person who ran it, who used the guild and its more vulnerable members for her own games and machinations, she was the one he hated. And, for all intents and purposes, Amaryllis was Lore's daughter. Due to that connection and the fact that Lore rarely left the protection of her base ship, it was Amaryllis who received the focus of his ire. Was it fair that he'd taken his anger out on her rather than saving it for the person who truly deserved it? No. Had that stopped him? Also no.

She cocked her head. "And I don't like your goody-goody Shields." She paused, tapping a finger on the table. "Or those overzealous space cops, the Starguard, for that matter. What of it?"

"I'm not part of either of those groups."

"Pfft." She waved her hand, scattering his words to the wind. "At the very least, you're closely connected to the Shields. You use their base as yours, for fuck's sake. And you used to be a member of the Starguard, no matter how you left them, so it counts. I mean, that's how you're judging me, right? Close enough to count?"

He couldn't argue with any of that. While she didn't know that Quin and Rhain were related, she was intelligent enough to recognize that the *Laughing Dragon* crew was tangentially connected to the Knight and his Shields and, yes, used Rhain's space station as their home base.

As for the Starguard, well, after they convicted him and his crewmates of a crime they didn't commit, dishonorably discharged them, and let the captain who'd screwed them over off with no more than a slap on his wrist, they could go fuck themselves. If it hadn't been for Rhain interceding on their behalf, Ivan would be breaking rocks on a prison moon somewhere along with the rest of his crew. So he definitely didn't claim any part of them anymore.

"But that doesn't explain why you don't like me personally." A muscle in her jaw jumped as she studied him. "Your reactions when our paths cross, especially when we first met, they were personal, not merely rivalry between mercenary groups. Why? Do I rub you the wrong way? Do you hate female pirates? Did I do something to you that I'm unaware of? I've done nothing to you specifically that I can recall, so explain it to me."

"Why are we having this conversation now?" He had a strong suspicion why, even as he asked the question. He'd admit it; he was stalling.

Chatting about his feelings and their sources was not something he enjoyed doing. He was more of a "get it done and move on" kind of guy, rarely dwelling in the past. Except when it came to those he loved. Hurt someone he cared about and he would go out of his way to fuck the wrongdoer all the way up.

Her mouth flattened, and she gave him a dark look. "Really? Like you don't know. Even though we said they wouldn't, things have changed between us, Ivan. I think I've earned the right to know."

Godsdammit. She was right. Things had changed. And now that she had him cornered, she wasn't going to let this go, even though this was a conversation he'd rather not have in a public place.

"You're right," he said. "You do deserve to know."

She rolled her eyes. "That's what I've been saying. Now, tell me."

He wrapped a hand around his glass, the condensation wetting his palm. "It's because of Navi." She blinked, opening her mouth to respond, but he didn't stop. If he stopped now, he wouldn't get it out, and she needed to know. He found he didn't like that she thought he still hated her. He needed to clear the air. "It's what your precious Cabal and that Atrax spider of a woman who sits at the center of her web in that ridiculous battlecruiser of hers did to my brother. His involvement in your Cabal and with Lore nearly destroyed him and, because of that, yes, I considered you my mortal enemy."

The ease at which the past tense just slipped out shouldn't have surprised him. No longer did he consider her an enemy. A pain in the ass, sure. But an enemy? Not so much anymore. Lore was still on his shit list, though, whereas Amaryllis had evolved into merely his nemesis and tormentor.

"Because of Navi?" she asked, her eyes wide. "What happened?"

He shot her a look. "Like you don't know."

"Ivan," she said, reaching out and putting a hand on his wrist. "I promise you, I don't. Yes, I knew your brother and his friend, but only a little. My crew and his, we had drinks at the bar when we happened to be on base at the same time. They were fun and made everyone laugh. That was it."

He pulled away, lifting his glass to his mouth and drinking deep, ignoring the wounded look on her face as her hand fell back to the table. With careful movements, he placed the half-empty pint down and leaned back, crossing his arms over his chest. "Don't lie to me, Rilly. Lore's grooming you to take over The Cabal. Surely you know what goes on with all those trapped within her web."

She barked out a sharp laugh. "As if. Lore doesn't even trust me to run my own jobs without adding her own minions to my team. If anything, my crew and I, we're just food for the spider.

Do you really think she's ever going to voluntarily give up control of The Cabal?" She sat up and leaned forward, her arms folded in front of her on the table. "Lore alluded to something when she met with you. What was she talking about? Tell me what happened. Please."

The tone of her voice caught him off guard. She didn't seem to be playing him or stringing him along. Her questions seemed to be truly genuine. Could she be telling the truth? Did she really not know?

He shifted in his chair. "Look, you need to ask Navi if you want all the details." Some parts of the story, they weren't his to tell. But he wanted — no, needed — her to understand why he'd reacted the way he had with her. He felt a pang of guilt about the way he'd just assumed the worst, especially if she truly had no idea what Lore had done.

She nodded. "I can do that."

He scrubbed a hand through his hair. "Growing up, Navi was a wild spirit, running headfirst towards anything that promised him an adrenaline rush. He and his best friend, Pete, were terrible influences on one another, always goading each other to take outrageous risks and go on ridiculous adventures. Somehow, they got it in their heads to join The Cabal."

"What? Why?"

He gave a heavy sigh. "I don't know. They heard somewhere that the life of a space pirate was filled with excitement and challenge and decided that's what they needed to do with their lives. Probably pictured themselves as dashing swashbucklers, swooping in to steal the treasure before heading to Badin to spend it all on wine and women or some such nonsense. Knowing Navi, he thought it would be a daring and exciting life that involved minimal violence and risk but all the adrenaline and reward."

"Idiots," Amaryllis said with a shake of her head. "Sorry, but that's not how it works."

"I know that. Around the time he got this wild hair, I was with Starguard and too far away to knock some sense into his head." It was right around that time Ivan and his crew were dealing with the repercussions from the illegal actions of one Patrick Sevilen, his team's captain in Starguard. He'd been unable to do anything to help his little brother in the moment. Yet another reason to reject all ties with the so-called guardians of space. Hard to support a group that allowed someone like Sevilen to flourish and people like Quin and the rest of the team to take the fall for their former captain's crimes. But that was in the past.

Ivan took a sip of his beer. "Navi, he's never been what we might call a planner. He's always leapt headfirst into anything that took his fancy, usually without repercussions." He said it lightly, as if it hadn't annoyed the shit out of him growing up. Navi had always been the Golden Boy, where nothing could touch him and everything went his way. And if something did go wrong, well, his big brother was there to mop up the mess.

"Until The Cabal." Amaryllis's voice was low, filled with dark, hard-earned knowledge.

He hummed in agreement. "It actually might not have been as terrible if Lore hadn't gotten her hooks into him. She brought him under her wing, claiming she saw something special in him, that she could train him to be the best pirate in the shipping lanes."

"Ah," Amaryllis said. "She's a master at finding those who would 'benefit' most from her attentions." She put air quotes around the word benefit. Lore's attention was not beneficial to those who attracted it.

"She's a master manipulator, for certain. I might even be a little impressed with her skills if she hadn't hurt people I care about." He swallowed down the last of his drink, staring blankly towards an incoming group of travelers whose boisterous excitement at heading planetside raised the noise level in the bar. Folding his arms on the table, he leaned in so they could hear one another over the racket the rowdy group was making.

She moved forward so their forearms were almost touching. "Let me guess. She talked Navi and Pete into taking bigger and more dangerous risks on jobs they were no way prepared for." She tsked. "I knew they were doing stupid shit. Even tried to convince them to slow down, but obviously, they listened to Lore instead."

"I don't think she had to do that much talking." She probably just had to dare them. Navi never could resist a challenge, not even when warned of the risks.

"I know Pete was killed on a job."

His heart clenched. Pete had been a good kid. "He was. A job they never should have been doing in the first place."

"I'm sorry. I liked him."

This time when she put her hand on his wrist, he didn't pull away. He looked down at her long fingers, nails tipped with sparkly purple polished and filed to a stiletto point. Dangerous comfort. That's what she offered and, dammit, he'd take it.

"Lore tried to stick him with the cost of the ship and the money lost when the job went sideways, did you know that?"

Her fingers flexed on his skin. "I did not. But I'm not surprised. She did the same thing to me and my crew. We still owe her. How did you manage to pry him loose from her clutches?"

The sympathy and understanding in her voice struck a chord, shaking loose the wrath and outrage he'd been holding on behalf of his brother for far too long. In its place, a tiny thread of shining copper wove its way around his heart.

"The Knight," he said. Rhain's title garnered another involuntary twitch from Amaryllis. "He struck some kind of deal on Navi's behalf."

"So now you owe him a favor." Everyone knew that, despite the virtues usually associated with his title, the Knight never did anything for free. Every supplicant had to pay in the form of unnamed favors to be collected when the time was right. And gods help those who refused when it was time to pay up.

Ivan shook his head. "Not me. Navi owes him the favor." He hadn't been thrilled that Rhain refused to let Ivan shoulder the burden, but at the same time, he knew Navi needed to take responsibility for his own actions and the cost of them.

"Ah," Amaryllis said again, with a nod of her head. "So. Circling back to my original question: why do you hate me?"

He blew out a sigh. "I don't hate you, Rilly. I've come to realize I may have felt some misplaced anger and taken it out on you once or twice."

"You think?" She lifted an eyebrow.

"Come on now, Rilly," he protested.

"You're not going to apologize for that?"

"When you gave as good as you got and then some? Certainly not. Pretty sure you got in your licks and then more than made up for my lapse in judgment." He covered her hand with his, giving it a squeeze. "But maybe we could call a truce?"

She leaned closer, her eyes sparkling. "Hells no. It gives me far too much pleasure to watch you squirm while I torment you."

He was hoping she'd say that. He shifted so their lips were a hairsbreadth from touching. "Game. Fucking. On." He paused, looking deep into her eyes and added, "Princess."

15

AMARYLLIS

"**O**h, ho ho. What do we have here?"

Amaryllis tore her gaze away from Ivan's to see Christophe and Deno standing next to their table, cocky grins on their faces. She groaned internally, her hand tightening on Ivan's arm. These two chuckleheads were the last people she wanted to see, especially right now. She'd finally gotten Ivan to open up, to tell her why they'd become mortal enemies — a title she completely understood now even though she hadn't actually earned it; poor Navi — and these two had to show up and ruin the moment.

Well, she wouldn't let them. Ignoring their hovering, she leaned forward and kissed Ivan. His eyes widened as her lips met his, but he enthusiastically followed her lead, opening his mouth, his tongue meeting hers in a passionate kiss.

One of the interlopers cleared his throat. "Amaryllis," Christophe said, the irritation clear in his voice.

The grins had disappeared. *Oh, noes. Are they upset that I'm ignoring them?* Amaryllis thought, fighting to hold back a laugh even as Ivan't tongue stroked hers, making her toes curl in her boots.

Ivan's eyes sparked with humor, too. He knew exactly what she was doing, and it seemed he approved wholeheartedly.

She gave him one more gentle kiss before settling back into her chair and picking up the fresh pint of dark beer the bot delivered at some point during their discussion. Making eye contact with Christophe, she took a long, slow sip of her drink.

Neither Christophe nor Deno were particularly tall men. Of course, everyone seemed short compared to Ivan. But she'd put them at maybe 5'10" at most, with athletic builds. Christophe had blond hair that constantly flopped into his face, brown eyes, and lightly tanned skin. As usual, he wore a shirt with a loud print, this one with bright orange and pink birds of unknown origin, and artistically ripped pants that probably cost a fortune. Deno had light brown hair clipped tight to his head, pale white skin, and wore a tailored suit of unrelieved black, not a speck of color to be found. Both of them were smug assholes who firmly believed Amaryllis had been handed everything because of Lore's nepotism and therefore, wasn't a true member of The Cabal because she hadn't earned it. Well, fuck them. She'd earned the hells out of it.

"What are you doing here, Amaryllis?" Deno asked, raising his voice above the noise of the crowd.

"What?" She dramatically widened her eyes.

"Yeah, Lore gave this job to us," Christophe added, trying to get in a dig.

"I had no idea you were coming to Waroc, and I couldn't give two shits about your job. Take it. You're going to fuck it up anyway."

"Like you did?" Deno asked.

She shrugged. "It happens when you're stuck with subpar team members." She gave Ivan a soft smile. "Ivan is taking me to dinner and a show in Waroc," she said, as he lifted her hand to his lips. She looked up at the pair. "What, you planning to run and tattle to Lore that I'm out on a date?"

"No. And we don't tattle," Christophe huffed.

Ivan looked him up and down, distaste curling his lip. "Who are these people, darling?" he asked, playing his part to perfection.

"Ivan, this is Christophe and Deno. They run a third-string Cabal crew." Amaryllis tipped her head towards the pair. "Cock-wombles, this is Ivan."

Red crept up Christophe's neck as he sucked in a breath. "What did you just call us?"

"You heard me. Now, go away." She made a shooing motion. "Can't you see Ivan and I are busy?"

Deno slid a hand into the interior of his suit.

"Tisk-tisk, Deno." Amaryllis waggled a finger at him. "You know weapons aren't allowed on Cora. If you're heading planet-side, you'll have to go through a screening first. If you get busted while on a job for Lore, well, you'd best count your days. I'm sure you heard what happened to Andrea."

He halted his movement, glaring down at her. "We're taking a shuttle."

Amaryllis's hand clenched on her glass. Lore must have pulled some very big strings to get them on a shuttle. Only high-up government officials and gold-star VIPs could use a shuttle. She reached up and squeezed her earring, turning on the team comm.

"A shuttle." She kept her tone casual, though she was seething inside. "Fancy. Who'd you bribe for that, Deno?"

Christophe puffed out his chest. "You're not the only one with connections, you know. We've got people."

"Do you now?"

"Checking all shuttles now, Cap," Dagby said, her voice soft in Amaryllis's ear. "Looks like they're headed down on the shuttle registered to a group called The Obdurate Collective. Huh. No idea who or what that is, but seems they're important enough to rate as VIP. I'll look into it."

Did that connection somehow play into Lore's determination to get her hands on the prototype? She felt a surge of frustration. There was so much she didn't know. Was it important to know? It felt like it, but at the same time, it might be better to focus on getting their hands on Bea's propulsion system before Christophe and Deno could. Leave the machinations to people better suited to play the game.

"Sucks for you that you're stuck taking the elevator down." Christophe sniffed and looked down his nose at them, only able to do so because he was standing.

"With the rest of the rabble," Deno added, his hand resting near his inner pocket as if he was just waiting for them to make a move. "Where you belong."

Amaryllis rolled her eyes.

"Such dicks," Dagby said in her ear. "Let me see if I can do something about that ride they're so proud of."

Amaryllis turned her head to the side to hide her words. "Yes, delay them, please."

"Better still if you can find a way to force these assholes to take the elevator." Ivan held his glass in front of his mouth and gave her a wink when he caught her smiling at him. "Von, Trick, any way you can stick a tracker on one of them? Would be good if we could keep an eye on these two and where they're going."

"You read my mind," Trick said. "Delay them a few more minutes until we get there, would you?"

During their side conversation, Christophe had continued with his shit talking, getting more and more frustrated that he wasn't getting a rise out of either of them.

"You kiss your mother with that mouth?" Ivan asked him.

Ivan's unexpected contribution to the conversation flummoxed Christophe. "I...what?"

"I asked, 'Do you kiss your mother with that mouth?'. Only requires a yes or a no." He looked at Amaryllis. "It's a straightforward question, right?"

Biting the inside of her cheek to keep from laughing, she nodded. "Simple. But then, Christophe struggles to understand even the most basic of concepts."

"Very sad," Ivan said. "Working with simpletons is such a challenge."

"You're telling me." She stretched her legs out, folding one ankle over the other. "This one time, Lore made the mistake of sending Christophe out on a solo job." She cocked her head. "I believe he was supposed to sabotage a Starguard fuel depot on the outskirts of, oh, I forget what town. Some tiny speck of civilization on Cinzia. Doesn't matter because that town no longer exists."

"Oh, no," Ivan said, resting his chin in a palm, his eyes wide as she told her tale. "What happened?"

She watched Christophe through her eyelashes. His face was bright red, his fists clenched at his side. "This one," she jerked her head towards him, "decided that the explosives Lore supplied him with weren't enough; he needed more."

"More?"

She loved that Ivan fell into the rhythm so effortlessly. "More. Ignoramus wound up blowing the depot sky high and setting the surrounding woods on fire with a rain of flaming debris."

"So what happened to the town?"

With a shake of her head, she said, "Small town. Only existed because of the depot, so they all left. It's a ghost town now." She grinned up at Christophe. "Brought the attention of the Starguard, the locals, and everything. Starguard opened an inquiry. Remember that, Christophe? Lore was so pissed."

"What an absolutely spectacular failure, Christophe," Ivan said, clapping for him. "I mean, we all have stories of jobs gone wrong, but wiping out an entire town? That's pretty impressive."

Christophe made a move like he was going to jump them right there in the middle of the bar. Deno put an arm across his chest and shook his head. "Not here. Don't let her goad you into a fight," he said, shooting her a dark look. "I don't know why you're here, but don't get in our way."

"Yeah!" Christophe pointed at them as Deno dragged him away. "Don't get in our way or I will end you!"

Not watching where they were going, Deno ran into Von's broad chest, Christophe piling up behind him and stumbling.

Trick grabbed Christophe's arm, steadying him. "You good, man?"

He ripped away from Trick's grip. "Get away from me."

Holding up his hands, Trick took a step back. "Just trying to be helpful. You don't have to be such a dick about it."

They watched Deno push his way through the crowd, Christophe trailing in his wake.

"Got him," Trick said with a broad smile.

"Excellent," Dagby said. Amaryllis pictured her rubbing her hands together like a villain.

"You ready?" Von asked. "It's time."

"Going down," Trick sang as he trotted along in front of them.

Amaryllis barely noticed, focused instead of the heat of Ivan's hand where it rested on the small of her back.

———

THERE WASN'T another city like Waroc in the entire galaxy. The planet of Melorn had four major continents along with a variety of smaller, scattered groupings of islands, mostly in the southern hemisphere. Waroc, the capital city and glittering jewel of the Melorn empire, engulfed the entire northwestern continent, from sea to sparkling sea.

When she was a teen, Amaryllis used to enjoy coming here with Lore. Back then, it felt like the air was thick with excitement, determination, and the promise of glorious adventure. If Amaryllis behaved herself while Lore conducted business, she'd be rewarded with a gelato — a scoop of double-double chocolate and a scoop of coconut-mango. Many times, it didn't end with her belly full of a delicious treat. Amaryllis couldn't always resist the siren's call for exploration. Bored, she'd wander off and find herself some trouble to get into. Those trips ended with her grounded for at least a month. Sometimes more, depending on how much trouble she found, how irritated Lore was with her, and how Lore's business meeting went.

These days, Waroc no longer held such promise. Amaryllis wrinkled her nose at the cacophony of smells — too-strong perfumes, random bodily fluids, and fetid cheese for some reason — filling the passageway from the elevator to the underground transport hub. If they'd been lucky enough to snag a seat on a shuttle, they would have been delivered to a bright, airy landing pad and greeted with a cool drink from a hovering bot.

Alas, she wasn't one of the fancy people. Just one of the rabble, according to Deno. But fuck that guy. There was nothing wrong with being a member of the rank and file. In fact, she wouldn't have it any other way. Ninety-nine point nine percent of the elite were vicious, backstabbing individuals who obtained their money and power through unethical means and, once they had that status, would do anything to keep it. No way did Amaryllis want to have anything to do with that mess. She had more than enough to handle without money and power to junk it up more.

On the trip down, while the others were watching the city grow closer through the elevator's wrap-around windows, Ivan had been busily typing on his comm. Though she was curious, she hadn't asked what he was doing. Unless it directly affected her or her crew, it was none of her business or so she told herself. At this point, she had to have enough trust in him to tell her if that was the case.

The Waroc Underground Transit System, better known as the Wuts and not just because it was confusing as all the hells combined, had sixty transit lines that circled a primary station on three levels and allowed travelers to get anywhere in the city they needed to go. Thirty minutes or less from coast to coast. Better than most pizza delivery places. As long as everything was in perfect working order, that was. And that was a rarity.

Then there was the challenge of figuring out where to begin. The cylindrical bots roaming the area weren't always the most helpful. The main station, nicknamed the Wuts Nut because of its shape — though locals just called it the Nut — was a warren of corridors, stairs, and lifts, each color-coded to lead individuals to the correct line. Sounded straightforward, but in truth, it was a pain in the ass to navigate.

They paused in front of a massive information board in the middle of the Nut.

"We need a safe place to crash and put our stuff." Amaryllis scanned the board and downloaded the Wuts guide. She'd delete it as soon as they were back on Cora Station. Who needed an app that you used only a few days every four years?

"And we need to avoid anywhere we might run into people we know," Von added.

"True," Amaryllis said. It would be a good idea to avoid any other Cabal members, in case someone got it in their head to report back to Lore. There was already the chance that Christophe and Deno would tell her but, after Amaryllis's goading, she didn't think so. If they did, she'd deal with it.

Ivan looked up from his comm and grinned. "I have the perfect place."

16

IVAN

P unching in the code Quin gave him, Ivan unlocked the door to an innocuous building sandwiched between two enormous storage facilities in Waroc's Warehouse District.

Built on the edge of the Denatil Sea, the district contained the Denatil Seaport, which hosted shipping facilities for a variety of corporate entities and served as one of Melorn's main water-based ports. Besides the seaport, the district also had a variety of open air wholesale markets, subsidized housing for those who worked at the port, and even some bars and restaurants. Mainly though, the area contained warehouses stacked to the rafters with imports and exports.

"First time I've ever been to this part of town," Trick said, scanning the area devoid of sentient beings beyond the four of them. "Not sure I like it. It's a little creepy."

Ivan completely understood. He could take city life in small doses but give him the calm expanse of space with his crewmates any day. The area where they were staying was far from the mixed-use buildings, just silent warehouses.

"Baby," Von said.

"Am not." Trick glowered at Von. "Come on, you have to

admit, all these huge buildings and no people. Just a bunch of bots moving big shipping containers and crates of stuff around… it's got creepy written all over it."

Night had fallen by the time they made it to where they were staying. The daytime workers had long since cleared out. Like most ports, Denatil never closed. At night, when most of the sentient workers finished their shifts and went home, that's when a veritable army of bots stepped in.

"Whose place is this, anyway?" Von asked, dropping the bags he was carrying near the door.

"Quin found it for us," Ivan said with a shrug, tossing his bag next to Von's. "Said the owner was invested in us retrieving the prototype."

The loft's owner was Bea's sister, Dai Farsirus. And, yes, she was very invested in getting Bea's propulsion system back into her sister's hands. In her message, which Quin had shared with Ivan, she'd specifically said not to tell anyone whose it was. Ivan didn't know what that was all about, but he had no problem adhering to that request.

"Very enigmatic," Amaryllis said, inspecting the space. "But, hey, we'll take free digs from a mysterious benefactor any day. Pretty sure we won't have to worry about running into anyone we know around here, and we have easy access to everything we need. Win-win."

It certainly wasn't the most impressive place he'd ever stayed, but it satisfied their requirements: clean and safe. He was practically positive Dai had used it as a bolt-hole during her time with The Unit, the Melorian government's clandestine branch.

He didn't know much about Dai Farsirus other than she was one of their top agents. When they first got the rescue job for Bea Farsirus, Cormac had done some digging on her. As her sister, Dai had turned up in his search, though pretty much everything was redacted. He did learn that she partnered up quite often with Safina Es-Aiit, who he'd had the fortune — misfortune? With someone nicknamed The Viper, things could go either way, depending on which side she was on — of meeting not too long ago. Both Dai and Safina were retired from service now, but they'd lost none of their deadly competence. He had absolutely no desire to go up against either of them.

The warehouse space was set up like a loft apartment, with no walls, everything in one open main room. It smelled a bit musty, the air stale, a layer of dust covering the surfaces. A couple of old, tattered couches in a faded orange flower print faced a bare yellowing plasticine wall that looked like it might have held a panel of screens at one point. Just some holes and screws remained. The opposite wall was also empty, a few scraps of torn paper hanging on for dear life. Pushed up against it was a battered wooden table, four chairs tucked under it.

A kitchenette with nothing more than a mini chiller and a hot plate lined part of the back wall. Three doors filling the rest of the space. The first door next to the chiller was a nearly bare pantry containing a bag of rice, the bottom corner of which had been nibbled open, and a battered box of cornflakes that was no doubt as stale as they came. There was also a large case with a red cross on it. Medical supplies. Always good to have on hand, though considering the layer of dust, he didn't know how useful it would be. He'd have to look through it, see what was still good, and then replace the rest as a small token of their appreciation for the loft's owner.

Behind the second door was a narrow closet with bedding and a folded pile of random clothing. Stacked on the floor were four narrow cases, muddy green in color. He recognized those from his long-past training years in Starguard: pack-and-fold cots. Not at all comfortable, but at least no one would have to sleep on the floor.

The third door led to a bathroom, complete with a requisite toilet, sink, and shower. Amaryllis, who'd been looking over his shoulder as he opened doors, gave a little squee and elbowed him aside so she could turn the shower on. There was a rattle and a couple of spits of water before the flow evened out.

She let the water run over her hand with a happy sigh. "I call first shower," she said, pushing Ivan out of the room.

"Hey, no fair!" Trick said.

"You snooze, you lose," Von replied. He cleaned off the long rectangular table and claimed part of it. Sliding into a chair, he set about turning the seemingly random pieces of crap he'd sneaked through security into weapons.

Trick set up a perimeter that would alert them to unexpected visitors. He claimed it also formed a sort of bubble around them, preventing passing drones or nosy individuals from realizing anyone was inside.

Once his security measures were in place, Trick rigged up a holo display to project on the empty wall in front of the couches and filled in the whiteboard with the information they had. There were a ton of blanks, though. Ivan hadn't shared what he knew with them yet. He planned to rectify that as soon as everyone had settled in.

Ivan pulled the cots out of the closet and set them up near the couches. He grabbed the bedding, setting a pillow and a blanket on each cot before joining Von at the table to help him.

They all moved with a quiet efficiency as they went about turning the near-empty space into their temporary headquarters. It was almost peaceful, the sound of water from the shower sluicing over tile and the clicks of metal snapping together relaxing the tension in Ivan's shoulders.

"So," Von said, snapping the barrel of a blaster into place, "What are your intentions with Amaryllis?"

His muscles tightened back up. Ivan set down the stunner he'd been assembling and looked at Von. "I don't see how that's any of your business. Amaryllis is a grown woman."

Trick abandoned his project and came over to the table, flipping a chair around and straddling it. "See, that's where you're wrong. Amaryllis is our captain, yeah, but she's more than that. She's the heart of our family, the big sister who brought us all together and made us strong. She's smart, she's capable, and she's vicious when cornered, but she's got a squishy heart below that tough surface, especially where you're concerned."

A squishy heart? Ivan's eyebrows winged up into his hairline. That certainly didn't sound like the Amaryllis who'd tormented and annoyed the shit out of him for all the years he'd known her. But now he'd spent time with her one-on-one. He saw the way she treated her crew, the tight bond between them, and how well they worked together. He'd even gotten a taste of her complicated relationship with Lore. Put all that together and he could now see the resilient core of the woman he'd once considered cold-hearted. But squishy? That was pushing it.

"As her family, we look out for her," Von said, sliding the last piece of the blaster he'd been assembling into place and cocking it. "We don't want to see her get hurt, especially if you're just toying with her so you can get your hands on the prototype."

"Yeah. You're like star-crossed lovers or some shit," Trick said. "Opposite factions — our Cabal and your Shields." He frowned. "I mean, I guess star-crossed is the wrong term because any hope of an actual relationship between you to might not be completely doomed, but..." He trailed off, having talked himself in a corner.

After dry firing his blaster, Von took up the thread. "But it might work if you're willing to make sacrifices for each other, to put in the time and effort."

Trick nodded. "Yeah. What he said. So. Are you? Willing to put in the work, I mean? Because if not, I think it would be best if you fucked off right now."

Ivan cocked his head, studying the men at the table with him. "Look, I recognize and admire your concern for Amaryllis. It's important to look out for your family. But as I said, she's a grown adult who makes her own choices and who's responsible for her own actions."

He wasn't about to go into detail about how he was conflicted about what he felt for her or how he might be falling for her despite himself. He was barely willing to acknowledge that to himself, much less people not Amaryllis, her family or no.

Von watched him closely as he rubbed a cloth over his weapon.

Trick opened his mouth to respond, but Ivan continued. "I can promise you that I don't plan to hurt her. Anything beyond that is absolutely none of your business."

The bathroom door opened, releasing a billowing cloud of steam. Amaryllis stepped out, her copper skin glowing. She had on a pair of loose black pants and a t-shirt that read "Done With Today" in sparkly gold lettering. She'd wrapped her hair in a pink silk headscarf. "Trick, Von, while I appreciate you trying to protect me and my heart, I'm going to need you to retreat. This is between Ivan and me. The only thing you need to know is that I trust him." She eyed Ivan. "At least for now."

The pair grumbled, shooting dark looks at him, as if he were responsible for her telling them to back off.

She padded over to the table, the waft of sweet peach drifting over as she approached. She kissed them both on the forehead before giving their cheeks hard pats. "Love you both dearly, but stay the fuck out of my love life. Okay?" She gave them a stern look until they finally nodded their assent. "Good. Now, who's next for the shower? The water pressure is amazing."

AMARYLLIS

They were debating whether to break out the MREs, send someone out, or just go to bed when there was a knock on the door. Exchanging glances, each of them picked up a weapon.

"Trick?" Amaryllis asked in a hushed voice.

"Tall. Probably male. Broad shoulders." He tapped at his wrist comm and threw a vid up on the blank wall.

Whoever was visiting them unexpectedly in the middle of the night had the hood up on his jacket, obscuring his face.

"Doesn't appear armed, but he's angled in such a way that I can't really tell," Ivan said. "Got something in his hands. Bags, it looks like. Can't tell what's in them."

"Trick, no scanner?" Von asked. With a scanner, they'd have information like species and what weapons an unwelcome visitor might be carrying.

"Basic perimeter only," Trick said.

"Which didn't work."

"We're out here in the middle of bot-run warehouses. No one knows we're here," Trick snapped. "Why the fuck would I go to all the trouble of installing a scanner when we won't be here for long? Besides, Ivan said it would be safe."

Ivan rolled his eyes at Trick's attempt to defer the blame.

The person outside knocked again and lifted two large bags. He tilted his face up to the camera and grinned.

He'd recognize that mischievous grin anywhere. "Navi." Ivan put away his weapon and opened the door despite Von and Trick's united protest. He reached out and hauled his brother inside, slamming and locking the door behind them.

Greeted with blasters pointed at his head, Navi raised his hands along with the bags. "Woah, man. I come in peace." He lightly shook the bags. "You all hungry? Thought you might need some sustenance."

Ivan waved them back. "It's just my brother, and I'd appreciate it if you didn't accidentally shoot him in the face. His looks are his only redeeming feature."

"That's hurtful, Ivan," Navi said, a wounded look on his face. "Especially considering your only redeeming feature is that you're the size of a damn mountain."

"Ooh, solid comeback. You think of that all by yourself?" Ivan handed the bags off to Von, who was closest, and pulled his brother in for a hug, smacking him on the back. "Good to see you, little brother. What are you doing here?"

Navi wrapped his arms around Ivan and did his best to crush the air out of his lungs before letting go and giving him a full up-and-down look. "Just needed to see for myself that you were alive and well. Heard that evil harpy of a woman, Amaryllis, got her hands on you, and I feared you wouldn't survive."

"I am right here, jackass," Amaryllis said, moving closer.

Navi released Ivan and grabbed Amaryllis, twirling her around in his arms before giving her a squeeze and releasing her. "Good to see you again, harpy. Wasn't sure you remembered me."

"How could I forget you?"

"Well, you only had eyes for Ivan whenever our crews crossed paths. I didn't even get a hello."

"Sorry." She shrugged. "I can't be expected to remember everyone I drink with."

He faked like she'd shot him in the heart, stumbling back and clutching his chest. "Ow. I'm hurt."

She looked over at Ivan. "Has he always been this much of a jackass?" she asked, a smile curling along the edge of her lips.

Though Navi was the same height as Ivan, he wasn't nearly as broad or built. When they were growing up, Navi had been all arms and legs, coltish and uncoordinated. He'd finally filled out, packing on lean muscle to become a formidable man.

Ivan crossed his arms, watching her interact with his brother. "Pretty much since the day he was born."

"Eh," Navi said with a wave of his hand, "I come by my title honestly. And so do you, Amaryllis." He turned to Ivan. "Do you know that this woman did her damnedest to get me to leave The Cabal? Every time we were on base together, we'd meet up for drinks and every time, she'd make some suggestion about me finding a less dangerous line of work, like joining Starguard." He turned up his nose. "Pfft. Starguard. Sticks up every one of their asses."

So Amaryllis really had tried to help his brother. He'd believed her when she told him that, but it was good to hear Navi reiterate it. The crack in the wall around his heart widened, allowing a little more of her copper light to brighten the darkness.

"Sadly, you were too much of a reckless, adrenaline-seeking idiot to listen to me," Amaryllis said. "But I'm glad to see you got out. You look good."

"Good enough to finally let me take you on that date?" He waggled his eyebrows at her.

With a laugh, she smacked at his shoulder. "Absolutely never gonna happen, not even in your wildest dreams. You are far too much of a dickhead for me."

"Really? Too much dick?" A wicked grin spread across his face. "Why, Amaryllis, you're too kind."

She glowered at him as two flags of color brightened her cheeks. "Too much of an idiot then."

He cocked his head. "But aren't you the one who's gotten

herself tangled up with my brother? He's definitely a bigger idiot than me."

Ivan grunted out a protest.

Amaryllis laughed. "Can't argue that."

Trick watched them banter, a confused expression on his face. "Wait. Did you know your name is Ivan spelled backwards? Why would your parents do that to you?"

Ivan looked at Navi. "Want to field this one?"

With a shrug, Navi said, "Ivan's the oldest in our family, and I'm the youngest. Our mother thought it was both amusing and poetic." He shook his head. "She has a strange sense of humor."

"Which you inherited from her," Ivan said.

Trick mulled this over. "Wait. How many siblings to you have? Do they all have weird names like you?"

"Nope. Just me." Navi grinned. "I think she was tired by the time I came around."

"With four sisters between us, there's no doubt." Ivan snickered. "Little did that poor woman know you'd be the worst of the lot."

"Hey, now! My mama loves me."

"Sure she does, squirt."

Von rooted through the bags of food Navi had brought them, pulling out everything and setting it on the table. "Welp," he said, plucking a bottle from an ezee-freeze carton and popping open a beer. "Man brought us fried chicken and beer. Hard to dislike someone who does that."

"Right?" Navi plopped down on the couch and stretched an arm across the back. "Figured I couldn't go wrong with some of the best fried chicken this side of the galaxy."

"Mama Tanya's?" Ivan asked, his mouth watering. He knew that smell was familiar.

"Of course." Navi accepted the beer Von handed him with a nod. "Nothing but the best for my big bro and some former drinking buddies."

While everyone dove into Navi's offerings, Ivan asked again, "What are you doing here, Navi?"

Navi took a swig from his bottle, dangling it between two fingers. "I wasn't kidding when I said I was here to make sure you were alive and well. No offense, Amaryllis."

She shrugged, tearing off a bite of chicken from her drumstick.

"When Quin came back from the mission all beat to the first hells and you'd disappeared, I was worried. Quin said Amaryllis's team jumped him."

"It was those chuckleheads, Skip and Kenny," Von muttered darkly.

"Yeah, we don't claim them," Trick said.

Navi raised an eyebrow. "Your comms and tracker were down. We had no idea where you were or what happened to you. We were in the middle of organizing a rescue party when Amaryllis contacted Quin and told him what happened." He took a deep breath, his face going serious, anger sparking in his green eyes. "You can't do that to me, Ivan."

"Sorry, Navi." He patted his brother's head. "Won't let it happen again." Ivan plonked down on the couch next to him and rested a box of chicken on his thigh.

"Yeah, neither will I. So I'm here to make sure it doesn't." Navi swigged his drink like he hadn't just inserted himself into their job.

"What?" The question burst out of him.

If Navi thought he was going to join them on this job, he had another think coming. Ivan could take care of himself. He'd been doing it longer than Navi'd been alive. He glared at his brother who was happily swigging his beer. They needed to have a serious conversation before he sent Navi back to the *Laughing Dragon* because there was no way Navi needed to be involved in anything that came remotely close to Lore's sphere of influence. And you couldn't get much closer than Amaryllis, unless it was with Lore herself.

"Um, friends?"

The sudden appearance Dagby's voice in Ivan's head after she'd been quiet for so long made him jump. He caught his chicken box before it slid off his leg and onto the floor.

"Why is there a strange man buzzing the *Dog* and asking to be let in?" Dagby asked. "He says he knows what's going on and that he's here to help. Should I shoot him? Call station security? What?"

Amaryllis paused, drumstick in hand, and raised an eyebrow at Navi. "Who's attempting to get into my ship, Navi?"

"Why do you think I have anything to do with it? Maybe you forgot to pay your docking fee." He snickered at her glare and waved away her concerns. "Kidding. That's Cormac. You know him. Genius with tech. Completely harmless."

Cormac would just love to hear Navi's opinion of him. He already had a complex about staying behind on the ship because he was more useful up there with all his toys and tech close at hand.

Ivan elbowed Navi, rolling his eyes at him. "You're safe with Cormac, Dagby. If you don't want to let him in, you don't have to, but he's one of my crewmates and a pretty smart guy. Could be useful to us."

He still didn't want Navi on this job, but despite being his baby brother and having made some incredibly poor choices in the past, the man was a grown-ass adult who could make his own decisions. He could tell Amaryllis to send both Navi and Cormac away, but then they'd find another way to "keep Ivan safe" which could very well fuck up the entire job. In the end, it would be better to have them close by, where he could keep an eye on them. But it wasn't his decision to make.

He shrugged, looking at Amaryllis. "You're running this job. Up to you if you want to add two more players to the team. One of them is a complete chucklehead, but Cormac could be useful." He grunted when Navi punched him in the arm.

She looked at Trick and Von. "What do you guys think?"

"Couldn't hurt to have two more experienced assets with us," Von said. "As long as we can trust them not to go running to the Knight with any inside information they might come across."

"And what's Lore going to say when she finds out?" Trick asked. "Because you know she'll find out. Do we worry about that?"

"That's a bridge we'll cross when we get to it." She scrubbed a hand over her eyes. "And I trust Ivan. As long as he vouches for his brother and Cormac, I don't see any reason not to keep them around."

She trusted him. His heart warmed.

"Amaryllis? What should I do?" Dagby asked.

"Up to you," she said. "If you don't want him with you on the *Dog*, send him down to us. We could always use a tech geek on the ground as support for you."

Dagby paused. "I guess I'll let him in. But I'm keeping a blaster on him at all times."

"Oh, he's going to love that," Navi said with a cackle.

18

AMARYLLIS

The next morning, they split up. Von and Navi went shopping for supplies. As adept as Von was at smuggling various illegal items through checkpoints and security stations, there were still some things he needed, and Navi had some useful connections in the dark corners of the city.

Trick stayed at the loft to coordinate all their intel on his holo board. True to his word, this morning, Ivan shared the location of the tracker Bea Farsirus had placed on her prototype while it was still up for auction. Navi and Cormac chimed in where they could to answer any other questions. What started as a mostly blank board was filling in quite nicely.

He also shared the other things Bea had done to render it useless to anyone hoping to duplicate it. At the auction, when everyone else was otherwise occupied, she'd managed to upload malware, corrupting both the data and any foreign system that came in contact with it. In a case of what Amaryllis considered intelligent but also tactical overkill, Bea had also stuck a vial of nanites in the tail of the propulsion system's cone. When the vial broke, those hungry little nanites should have scattered and corroded all the metal inside it, turning the prototype into a very expensive hunk of corrupted metal.

Amaryllis wasn't sure how this would affect her plan to use the prototype as leverage. It certainly lowered its value. The question was, did it lower it so much as to render it useless to Lore? If so, they were fucked before they even started. Nonetheless, the crew voted to continue as planned. They still wanted to get it before the other team and still believed it had enough value to Lore to be worth the risk to retrieve it. Amaryllis hoped that whoever purchased it would have some information or something else valuable enough to assuage Lore's anger. She didn't have high hopes.

After some debate, Dagby decided to let Cormac aboard the *Dog's Day* with her. Now that Ivan had given up the location of the prototype, Cormac was tracking down the layout and security measures of the building currently housing the propulsion system while Dagby worked on uncovering who was behind the purchase.

Ivan and Amaryllis were on recon.

The building itself was located in the Creekside Park area, an up-and-coming district composed of mixed-use properties, shared workspaces, and converted warehouses. Like a growing percentage of the mega-city, vehicles were not allowed, only foot traffic, bicycles, and accessibility transports like low-power scooters. This change, which was just being instituted the last time Amaryllis visited Waroc, was part of an initiative to improve the health and well-being of all the residents.

Amaryllis liked it better this way. Without the constant rumble and mechanical hum of a bunch of vehicles, the city felt more peaceful, especially with the greenscaping of trees and flowers replacing the wide roads. She didn't, however, appreciate all the people. This was the problem with metropolitan areas. Too many people.

She growled at a twenty-something who bumped into her, who squeaked and scurried away with her gaggle of friends in tow.

"Stop scaring the locals," Ivan said as they made their way down the crowded street.

"I wouldn't have to scare them if they learned how to share the sidewalk. Did their people not teach them basic manners? You don't walk five across, then expect the people coming towards you to move over. Entitled brats," she grumbled.

"Well, I'm sure you taught them a lesson."

She doubted it. In fact, they were probably trashing her on whatever social network was popular at the moment, not that she cared or even looked at those things. Still irritated, she shoulder-checked a pasty-faced man in a blue suit who refused to get out of her path. He bounced off her with a shocked expression on his face.

Tough shit, man. Learn to share the street, she thought, giving him a sharp-toothed smile that sent him on his way.

Ivan wrapped an arm around her shoulder and steered her towards a shop with a blue sign that proclaimed its name to be "Magic Beans".

"Why are we here?" she asked, looking around. It was a cute little bistro, she had to admit. The exposed brick walls inside hosted a mixture of hanging plants and artwork from local artists. Round tables with comfortable chairs dotted the space. A long, wide counter held glass display cases filled with delicious-looking pastries and other sweeties. The scent of freshly ground beans filled the air. Amaryllis's stomach grumbled.

"I'm hoping that your street-side aggression can be tamed with a good pastry and a caffeinated beverage," Ivan said, looking over the selections behind the glass.

"A little snack and drink doesn't make up for the home training these people are lacking," she said, but pointed at two items and ordered herself a flat white. She wasn't about to turn down a snack, even to prove a point.

"Okay, but your determination to teach them a lesson isn't very discreet. We're here to do some recon, not start a street brawl."

"Fine, fine," she said. "I'll go grab us a table." Since he was the one who claimed she needed a snack, she would let him treat her to it. It was only right.

She found a table outside that gave them a direct line of sight to their target building and settled in. Ivan joined her several minutes later, filling the table with little white plates.

"More like a second breakfast than a snack, there." She reached for her drink.

He shrugged off her grumps. "Hey, I'm a big guy. A single pastry isn't enough. Besides, I couldn't decide. Everything looked good." He took a big bite of a filled donut topped with dark chocolate. A glob of red jam oozed out and plopped on his plate. "Delicious. Want a bite?" He offered her the pastry.

"Not a big fan of jam fillings. I want to try that one." She pointed to a rectangular slice with three layers of different kinds of chocolate.

He waved a hand towards it. "Have whatever you like. I got a selection for us to try."

Her heart gave a little squeeze at the word "us". Were they an "us"? She certainly wouldn't mind if... but no. Despite their ongoing personal conflict, he was a good man, someone very different from herself. Too different, if she had to be honest. He had strong morals and ethics, while hers were a lot more flexible. If her parents hadn't died, if she hadn't been raised by someone with such a loose definition of morality and minimal ethics, then maybe she'd be different enough to fit him better. So her heart needed to just settle down because there was no way he'd ever be hers. They wouldn't ever be an "us", not in the long term anyway.

She shoved aside her deep thoughts, locking them in a corner of her mind out of the light, and took a bite of the chocolate pastry, barely tasting the layers of light chocolate mousse and dense dark chocolate cake. After washing it down with a sip of her flat white, she squeezed her earlobe to activate the team comm. "Dagby, what have you found?"

Ivan finished his jam donut and reached for the chocolate pastry she'd claimed.

She smacked his hand. "What are you doing?"

"Trying yours," he said. He held his hand carefully, like she'd actually wounded him.

"I don't think so, mister."

"But I shared with you. It's only polite for you to do the same."

Over the comm, Dagby snickered. "Amaryllis doesn't share her food. Not with anyone."

Ivan cocked his head. "Really?"

"What's mine is mine." Amaryllis moved her plate farther away from him. The table was small so he could still reach it, but it would leave his arm exposed to retaliation. If he was smart, he wouldn't try again.

"And what's yours is hers, too," Trick chimed in with a laugh.

"Shut it, Trick," Amaryllis growled, irritated at the world. She didn't know why. She'd woken up grumpy with everyone and everything, and those damnable sidewalk hogs hadn't helped her mood. Ivan was right — a snack did usually improve her spirits, but then he had to go and use the "us" word which got her thinking and wishing for things that could never be, and it brought back all the grump. Her friends teasing her didn't help either. "Tell us something useful or stay off the comm. We're here to work."

"Ooh, I don't envy you, Ivan. Amaryllis is in a right foul mood today," Dagby said.

Amaryllis growled again. "Does me being captain have no meaning to you all? I give orders, and you follow them. That's how it's supposed to work." She knew she was being hostile to people who didn't deserve it, but she couldn't seem to stop herself.

"Except that we're equal partners, Amaryllis," Von said, using his patient voice, the one that drove Amaryllis up the wall. "So, no, it doesn't work that way with us."

Ivan gave her a long look. "Dagby, could you mute the team comm? Amaryllis and I need a moment."

"Gotcha," she said.

"What the fuck, Ivan?" Amaryllis glared at him. "You're not the boss of my crew."

"No, I'm not," he said. "But you're picking fights today, and I want to know why. What's going on, Rilly? How can I help?"

She sat back in her chair and crossed her arms, fighting the urge to scream and hit something. Ivan was right there. Her fingers twitched.

But he was also correct. She took a deep breath, forcing the black cloud swirling around her to retreat. She was picking fights when they had more important things to do. What was wrong with her?

"Is it because we decided to let Navi and Cormac stay and help?" he asked.

She shook her head. While she wasn't thrilled at the additions, she knew they'd be helpful in the long run. And she trusted them up to a point, though that might change once they had the prototype in their possession.

She worried Ivan had brought his people here so they could snag the thing out from under her. Was it a valid concern? She hoped not, but she couldn't let go of that niggling little feeling that those guys were being far too generous with their claims that they were only here to check on Ivan and to help. For now, her crew was keeping a close eye on them.

"Is it because you're worried Christophe and Deno will get the prototype first?"

"No." Those two fools couldn't find their own asses with four hands and a giant mirror. It irritated her that they were already planetside and that Lore was helping them more than she'd helped Amaryllis and her crew when they first went after the prototype. But that wasn't the crux of today's crabbiness.

"Then what? It's a beautiful day. We've got a great team working on getting us all the information we need to successfully grab that prototype." He slid another chocolate pastry onto her plate. "You've got a plate full of delicious chocolate pastries in front of you. Why the grumps?"

"It's because you're too godsdamned nice." The statement burst from her, surprising her with its ferocity. "Fuck." She shook her head. She hadn't meant to say that. She wasn't even sure she meant it in the way he would interpret it.

"What?" he said, perplexed. "How am I too nice? If anything, it's the opposite. I basically blackmailed you to come on this job, I fucked up your original heist, I fucked you when you were emotionally vulnerable, and we've been at war since we first met. How can any of that be considered too nice? And what does that have to do with anything that's going on?"

"I don't know, okay?" She threw up her hands. "I just...," she paused, gathering her thoughts. It was so hard to explain when her brain was all swirly, confused about her feelings and completely unfocused. But she needed to figure it out, and he should know the truth of it, whatever "it" was. "Do you know why I'm so dead set on getting my hands on that damned prototype before Christophe and Deno?"

"Because you want to prove to Lore that you can do it." He shrugged. "I understand wanting the approval of parental figures. I dislike Lore, but she's played a large role in your life so, yeah, I get it."

Shaking her head, she said, "It's not that. Well, it's not only that." He wasn't wrong about the need for approval, but that was just a portion of the "it" of it all. "My crew and I, we're at a crossroads. But with this prototype in our hands, we would have options that we never had before."

"What kind of options?" he asked, cocking his head.

She looked at him, sitting there all attentive and truly interested in her motivations and what she had to say. Her heart gave a powerful flutter that rattled her to the core of her soul. A good man. She knew some, had two of them on her crew. They were rare creatures, almost delicate in many ways. She was afraid she'd break him if she played with him too hard. And, despite their differences, she didn't want to do that.

She took a deep breath, trying to loosen the tightness in her chest, then slowly released it. "I don't know if you're aware of how The Cabal works."

He shrugged. "A little. Mostly what Navi told me."

"Okay, you know unless you come in with big money or a big reputation, you're not a full member. The Cabal takes anyone who wants to join, offers them food, a place to live, and the support of a strong group. Gives them a sense of belonging and a purpose. Sounds great, right? We get a lot of runaways, people who've had brushes with the law and Lore welcomes them in with open arms." She sniffed out a laugh. "What she doesn't tell them, though, is that everything costs money. From the moment they step foot on her battleship."

"Basically turning new recruits into indentured servants."

"Pretty much."

"Even you?"

"Even me, though I didn't start owing until I turned twenty, when Lore deemed me useful to The Cabal."

"Very motherly of her." There was sarcasm in that statement, but also a thread of understanding.

"She tries, in her own way." She took a bite of cake covered in chocolate ganache.

Ivan was quiet, letting her talk at her own pace.

"Anyway, we've been saving our money. Our debts are almost paid off and, once they're gone, we can join The Cabal as voting members." She scraped her fork tines over the ganache. "Or, if we happen to have something Lore really wants in our possession, we have bargaining power. We could leave The Cabal entirely." Just saying it out loud eased some of the tension she was feeling. They could leave. She didn't know if the prototype would be a big enough bargaining chip for Lore to let them go, but just the possibility of going their own way lifted her spirits.

"Wow," he said. "No wonder you're grumpy. That's a big deal. A lot of pressure."

Her heart fluttered again. *Fuck.* She huffed out a breath. "Do you have to be so godsdamned understanding?" she asked, with no heat this time. She liked that he understood the scope of the decision that faced her and her crew without having to go into a lot of detail.

He gave her a lopsided smile that made her breath catch. "Can't help it. I've been where you are. When Rhain, er, the Knight helped me and my crew out, he gave us the option of formally joining his Shields or owing him favors. We chose favors because we didn't want to be tied to one large group like that again."

"But you're still tied to them." Rhain? Was that the Knight's real name? Huh. Interesting, but not important. At the moment, anyway. She tucked it away to think about later.

"Those are family ties," he said. "Try as you might, it's nearly impossible to cut all family ties unless you never see them again."

She mulled that over as she ate the rest of the tiered pastry, enjoying the complimentary combination of the white chocolate against the bitter dark. He certainly wasn't wrong about family ties. Unless she decided to move to Caldera on the other side of the galaxy and become a farmer, never venturing into space again, she couldn't ever fully escape Lore and the long shadow of The Cabal.

He didn't interrupt her deep thoughts, allowing her the time to sort her thoughts and work through her grumpy mood with the assistance of a second flat white and a slice of chocolate cheesecake.

He's such an idiot, she thought, watching him scan the area. A gentle breeze blowing on this sunny afternoon barely ruffled those ridiculously red locks he'd coaxed into a high fade. Through her lashes, she surreptitiously admired the flex of his muscles under his tight black t-shirt and the curve of his forearm as he lifted his drink to his mouth. A splash of heat landed in her belly when he licked the foam from his mustache. *No, I'm the idiot.*

Why did her heart beat harder when he did little things like get her another drink without her asking or give her the rest of the pastry he'd bought for himself? Why did she feel like crying when she thought they could never be together, that it would be an impossibility because of how different they were? Why did she have feelings for the big galoot?

But she rarely cried, and she didn't want to have feelings for him. She enjoyed being known as a dangerous woman, someone you did not cross or you'd face her wrath. In fact, she preferred it that way, the strong facade that she'd created to face a cold universe and survive. But her facade was cracking because of him. Ivan, who saw past her mask. She'd shown him the most dangerous parts of herself, and he wasn't phased by them. In fact, he seemed to appreciate them. She didn't know what to do with that. Not yet. But she wasn't letting him go until she figured it out. Fuck him being too good for her. Why would she even think that?

He put the last chocolate treat on her plate as soon it was empty. No comment, no conversation. Just a simple action that showed her he was aware of her even as he surveilled the people entering and leaving their target building.

Yeah, fuck all those negative thoughts and self doubts. She deserved goodness in her life. The man was stuck with her, she decided. Just let him try and get away.

19

IVAN

Ivan watched Amaryllis work her way through everything chocolate on the table, the scowl on her face gradually fading. So, obviously chocolate was one sure-fire way to the woman's heart and a salve to a grumpy Amaryllis. He filed that away for future reference. He'd most definitely need it later.

It annoyed him when she claimed he was too nice. What did that even mean? They'd been at each other's throats since their first encounter. In truth, he'd been an asshole to her for so long because he believed she was aware of and involved in what happened with Navi. Now that he knew better, yeah, maybe he was nicer to her, but too nice? How did anything he'd done add up to him being "too nice"?

He huffed out a frustrated sigh. He decided it was just another way for her to needle him, to try and get under his skin. Well, little did she know she was already under his skin. Like a splinter or the head of a tick that had buried itself deep.

He double tapped his wrist, waking up his comm. "Dagby, you there?"

"Are we all better?"

Amaryllis rolled her eyes, her mouth full of her treats.

"You know, it would go better for everyone if you stopped

poking the bear. I just got her settled down." He winked at her, bracing himself for her reaction.

Amaryllis punched him in the arm. "Sounds like you're about to put me down for a nap."

He waggled his eyebrows. "If I put you to bed, we wouldn't be napping."

"Ugh," Navi groaned. "I don't need to hear my brother's pathetic attempts at flirting. Why did you turn the team comms back on if you were going to subject us to this? What did I do to deserve such torture?"

"Shut up, Navi," Amaryllis said. Her lips curled up into a smile, the first he'd seen from her all day.

"Dagby, Cormac, I do believe we're ready for that report now." Ivan took a chance and stretched an arm over the back of her chair.

She shifted in her seat, gave him a long look, then settled back, her neck warm against his arm. "I second that. What have you found out?"

He tried to listen to what Dagby was saying, but his attention was jagged. Yes, it was important to know that Hegemony Incorporated owned that building and that Dagby and Cormac were still digging to find out what Hegemony was, why they wanted the prototype, as well as the people behind the name. He probably should be glad that they now had their hands on a copy of the building's specs so they could proceed with the job tonight.

But he couldn't stop thinking about Amaryllis peeling back some of her armor and allowing him a glimpse beneath that tough outer shell of hers. Or how every time she breathed, she brushed against his arm. Or how she smelled like crushed ginger and starlight, her bright, sharp scent swirling around him as they sat at their small table with its blue umbrella. He wanted to pull her onto his lap and kiss her senseless, his lips tracing the edge of her lightning strike verdigris marking as it traveled down her neck and disappeared beneath the collar of her shirt.

"...think, Ivan?" Cormac asked.

He blinked at the sound of his name. "What?"

Amaryllis elbowed him in the side. "Are you even listening?"

"Of course I'm listening," he said with a little cough. "I agree with Amaryllis." He wasn't sure what Cormac asked or her response, but it seemed like a safe bet. After all, this was technically her operation and, considering the work he'd done to get her out of her bad mood not ten minutes earlier, he wasn't about to disagree.

She rolled her eyes. "He wasn't listening, but he already agreed, so too bad. No, we're not bringing in anyone else. If you can't uncover the owner of that company, we'll do without. After all, we only really need to get our hands on the prototype. That's what Christophe and Deno are supposed to retrieve. That's what Lore wants. Info on who's behind it would merely be icing on the cake, something we can focus on once we have the prototype and are off this damnable planet."

Okay, so he hadn't agreed to anything too outrageous. That was good. He stroked the nape of Amaryllis's neck, enjoying the feel of her soft skin beneath his fingertips. And she didn't pull away immediately, merely accepted his attentions as she listened to Cormac and Dagby debate the best way to burrow down through the layers of the double-blinds and shell companies that surrounded Hegemony Incorporated.

A steady flow of foot traffic traveled along the tree-lined boulevard between the bistro and the building, people dipping in and out of the crowds as they stopped to window shop or duck into a store. But no one so much as touched the bot-guarded door of the Hegemony Incorporated building the entire time Ivan had been watching.

Until now. Two people exited, pausing between the pair of bots flanking the doorway. A flash of green engulfed them, a visible scan that alerted everyone in the vicinity about the high level of security the building owners instituted on anyone entering or leaving.

Ivan blinked hard, recognizing one of the people. "Safina," he breathed. His body tensed, the tips of his fingers suddenly icy with a fear response as he struggled to maintain his calm outward appearance.

Amaryllis shot him a confused look. "Who?" she asked, her eyes searching for the person he'd spotted. "Are you talking about that old lady with the white hair?"

"Oh, shit," Cormac and Navi said at the same time.

"Wait, what's going on?" Trick asked.

Ivan didn't answer, not daring to breathe her name again. It was as if she was a powerful and deadly mythological creature who would respond to their name spoken aloud with attention you absolutely did not want.

Of course, Safina wasn't a mythological being, but she was extraordinarily deadly in her own right. As strong as he was, with as much training as he had, he wouldn't want to go up against her. Her sweet and soft outward appearance was a deception, a facade hiding a woman who'd spent decades of her life honing her skills. Anyone with a lick of sense knew to get out of her way or face the consequences.

"Safina Es-Aiit. You may know her as The Viper," Navi said. The sound of indrawn breaths and muttered curses filtered over the comm. "She officially retired from Melorn's clandestine branch, better known as The Unit, about five years ago, but that hasn't slowed her down. Oh, no, my friends. As a retiree, this lovely lady still has her fingers in all sorts of pies, though not the kind you'd expect from a woman who looks like your favorite grandmother. Rumor has it that since retirement, she's helped topple corrupt governments and made sticky problems disappear."

"If anything, she's more dangerous now than she was when constrained by the rules of The Unit," Cormac added.

"Truth. I mean, I know I wouldn't want to run into her in a dark alley," Navi said. "So, good luck to you, bro. Stay still and pretend you're not the size of a mountain. Maybe she won't spot you."

"Fuck off, Navi," Ivan said.

"She's coming this way," Amaryllis said from behind her now-empty coffee cup. "What do we do?"

Fighting the urge to grab Amaryllis's hand and walk the opposite direction quickly, he kneaded the tight muscles in her neck, focusing on the feel of her skin and the soft hum she made when he hit a good spot.

From the shaggy haircut to the ill-fitting clothing in a baby shit brown color palette, the man at Safina's side looked like a stereotypical nerd, a prop she was using to get into the building and back out again unaccosted. He gazed down at the petite woman next to him like she hung the moon, a lovesick expression on his face as she nattered on about something or other.

Safina didn't even break stride as she turned her head and winked at Ivan before continuing on down the street.

Fuck.

"OH, yeah, she totally knew you were there," Navi said when they returned to their temporary headquarters in the Warehouse District. He was sitting at the table helping Von assemble mechanical things of some sort, their wires and tools spread across the surface. "You're lucky she doesn't think you're going to interfere with whatever it is she's doing there."

"And how did you come to that conclusion?" It was something Ivan worried about. If Safina was also after the prototype, then they were going to have a problem. Not only could interfering in a Safina job be seriously hazardous to all their health, he didn't want to have to choose between helping Amaryllis and getting out of Safina's way. Was he a chicken? Sure. Go right ahead and call him that. It was a smart move. He had zero desire to stand in the way of either woman.

"Well, you made it back here without your transport

exploding or getting pulled into a dark alley and 'accidentally' bleeding out, didn't you?"

"True," he said, popping the top on the beers they'd brought back with them. He distributed drinks to everyone who wanted one. "But she winked at me. What does that mean?"

"Maybe she likes you." Trick grabbed a chair and straddled it. "Women wink at guys they like, right?"

"Um..." Ivan shot a quick glance at Amaryllis in her spot on the smaller orange sofa. She raised an eyebrow. "I don't think it's that."

"She probably already knows about our job," Cormac said from the holo projected on a wall.

On the opposite wall was Trick's Big Board of Bodacious Banditry. Trick had named it that when they'd left him alone in the loft and refused to let anyone access it unless they called it by its given name. Amaryllis said it was his way of showing his irritation at being left behind.

"Could that wink mean she knows about the operation? Maybe even approves of it?" Dagby asked. She and Cormac had set up camp in the common room aboard *Dog's Day*, both kicked back on the long couch in front of the vid panels, drinks and discarded boxes of random takeaway spread out on every flat surface available.

Ivan was surprised to see they were getting along. Dagby was friendly enough, but Cormac could be prickly at the best of times. Seemed strange, working with the *Dog's Day* crew. The last time this many crew members from both ships were in the same space, they'd gotten into a brawl that left everyone bloody and all the furniture in splinters. That was several years back, though, before Navi joined the crew.

The brawl was Ivan's fault. He couldn't even remember what Amaryllis had said or done to provoke him, but she'd flipped a switch in his brain with it and he'd gone berserk. It rarely happened that he lost control like that, thanks to a stray strand of berserker DNA passed down through generations of Halonens.

He wasn't proud of it, but he couldn't really control it when that veil of red crashed down and set him off. At least he hadn't killed anyone. The bar's furniture took the brunt of the damage. Unsurprisingly, they were banned from ever returning.

He shook his head, glad the dynamics were shifting from "beat the shit out of each other" to "okay, we can work together like mature, rational adults."

They had about six hours to put together a solid, working plan to get into the building, find the prototype, and get back out. Ivan would have liked more time. They needed better recon. They needed eyes inside the building. He really wanted to know why this company bought the propulsion system in the first place. It was bugging him that even working as a team, Cormac and Dagby couldn't find out more information about this Hegemony Incorporated or the people behind it. He didn't know how good Dagby was, but Cormac was one of the best in the galaxy.

They needed more time, but they didn't have it. Despite a delay courtesy of Dagby, Lore's other team was planetside, and they knew Amaryllis was in Waroc. So, if they wanted to get their hands on the prototype before Christophe and Deno, they had to move tonight.

"Don't shoot," a cheerful voice sang out from the wide open front door. "I come bearing food!"

Everyone jumped to their feet and aimed their weapons towards the uninvited visitor.

A bright smile on her face, Safina Es-Aiit calmly stared down the barrels of the five blasters pointed at her. "You know, darlings, if I wanted you dead, you would be," she said, setting her bags on the floor and pulling the door shut behind her. She flipped the lock. "At least you set a perimeter, though I may need to speak with the one who installed it. A child could disable it, for goodness' sake."

Trick spluttered.

"Told you we needed a scanner," Von said in a low voice.

"So, the gang's all here, even your two technical nerds." She waggled her fingers at Cormac and Dagby, who sat so still Ivan thought the feed froze until he saw Cormac swallow. "Ivan, be a sweetie and grab those carry sacks over there. And safely stow that weapon. Someone could get hurt." She blew past him in a cloud that smelled of violet and petrichor, reaching up to pat him on the shoulder. The top of the pensioner's fluffy white head barely came up to his armpit, but he leapt to obey without a second thought.

"Yes, ma'am." He unprimed his blaster and set it back on the low table in front of the couches. What else was there to say? He wouldn't shoot an unarmed woman, no matter what her reputation.

Besides, she was right. If she'd wanted them dead, she obviously knew where they were. She didn't have to come to their doorstep and make her presence known. He picked up the sturdy canvas sacks.

"How did you know where we were?" Amaryllis asked as he brought the bags to the kitchen table, now miraculously cleared of clutter.

Amaryllis brought out a stack of dishes while Trick gathered up enough silverware for everyone. His arms crossed as he hovered beside Amaryllis, Von watched Safina like she was a ticking bomb about to go off.

With a gentle smile, Safina patted Amaryllis's cheek. "You're adorable. Of course I knew you were here. This is my little bolt-hole, after all."

"This is yours?" she asked, whirling to glare at Ivan. "I thought you said the owner was invested in us retrieving the prototype."

Ivan opened his mouth, but Safina answered first. "I am invested in you retrieving the prototype. Bea is my niece, after all. Brilliant girl, though her taste in men is somewhat questionable." She raised an eyebrow in Ivan's direction when he made a sound of protest.

He swallowed down a defensive retort about his friend and

captain. She wasn't completely wrong. He was amazed when he found out their ex-fugitive hadn't moved on to greener pastures and was, in fact, still head-over-heels for Quin, as he was for her. "They are cute together, you have to admit," he said, watching Amaryllis and Navi dole out the food Safina brought them. The spicy scent of stir fry tickled his nose, making his stomach growl.

"Disgustingly so." She nodded. "Even worse than when we were on the boat."

Ivan's first encounter with Safina had been in the hours before they crashed the black market auction. She'd scared the crap out of Quin. It was hilarious to watch his captain tamp down his fear while simultaneously trying to make a good impression and get on her good side. A challenge, especially considering he was banging the woman Safina called her niece.

He handed her a cold beer. "I hear you lent them your murder cabin?"

Navi winced at Ivan's wording and hunched his shoulders, digging into his meal from the relative safety of the farthest couch from Safina. Von took a plate with a chin tip and ate standing with his back against the pantry door, focused on their guest's every move.

Safina giggled, a cheerfully sparkling sound that made the hairs on the back of Ivan's neck stand on end. "Is that what Bea called it? Such a delightful sense of humor. No, no. Merely a little getaway for when I need peace and quiet. They needed a place to work their way through that honeymoon period, so Bea will regain her focus and finish her project."

He wondered what would happen if Bea didn't regain her focus. He didn't think Safina would actually do anything to her, but he'd make Quin aware nonetheless. Better safe and prepared than sorry.

Behind Safina's back, he could see Amaryllis making a hurry up gesture, anxious to find out what she was doing here. He wanted to know, too, but he didn't want to be rude. The last thing they needed was an irritated Safina on their hands. He didn't think she could be assuaged by chocolate alone.

"Thank you for bringing us dinner, Safina." He pulled a chair out for her. "Please, join us."

"So polite," she murmured, taking her seat. "It's almost as if you're afraid of me." She smiled up at him. "Don't worry. I'm not here to ruin your plans. In fact, I'm as invested in removing that prototype from Hegemony Incorporated as you are."

He noticed she didn't tell him not to be afraid.

20

AMARYLLIS

Amaryllis kept a close eye on Safina. For a woman named The Viper, she didn't look like a snake or even all that deadly. Sure, she'd heard rumors about The Viper, whispers in the corridors of Lore's base about a woman so feared and so deadly that just the threat of her presence in the same area gave hardened mercenaries panic attacks. Exaggerations, certainly.

Ivan greeted her politely, treating her like an honored guest, practically bending over backwards to be sweet to the woman. He probably shouldn't have called her beach house a murder cabin, though. Yikes.

Amaryllis ruthlessly repressed the urge to shake Safina and demand to know why she was here and what she was doing earlier, waltzing in and out of the Hegemony building like she owned the place. But that didn't seem like a good idea, considering how careful everyone else was being around Safina.

She looked like a harmless pensioner, though. She wore her Kindly Old Granny disguise with such ease; it didn't present as an act. With her pure white hair styled in a neat bob, her dark brown eyes bright and curious, laugh lines radiating from the corners and wrinkles that could have been erased with a quick visit to a doctor creased her light brown skin. Much smaller than everyone else in the room, she was the exact opposite of intimidating. Even her clothing seemed to be chosen to put people at ease, cloaking her short, sturdy body in soft knits of soothing pastels that were both stylish and comfortable looking.

This was a master at work, Amaryllis decided, chewing thoughtfully on a mouthful of stir fry. And she had good taste in food.

Trick slid into the seat next to Safina and gave her a big smile. "So, what's a beautiful woman like you doing in a place like this?"

Amaryllis sucked in a sharp breath along with a piece of rice. The resulting coughing fit had her eyes watering.

Safina arched an eyebrow at her before turning back to Trick with a sweet smile. "Aren't you just adorable?" she said, reaching forward to brush the hair out of his eyes.

He leaned into her touch, resting an arm on the table. "What are you doing later?" he asked in his bar pick-up voice.

Amaryllis kicked him under the table.

He jumped. "What?" he asked in a wounded tone.

"Leave her alone, Trick," Amaryllis said, pinching the underside of his arm as she said it. "I mean it."

Safina gave a peal of sparkling laughter, waving away Amaryllis's worries. "It's fine. I like his enthusiasm." She traced a finger over the tattoo trailing along Trick's bicep, her sharp eyes noting Amaryllis's own verdigris as well as Von's tattoo peeking out from between the buttons of his shirt. "And I do so appreciate the enthusiasm of younger men, though I believe this one is a little too young for me. Trick, is it?" she asked, cocking her head.

He puffed out his chest. "I'm 29," he said. "And I like older women."

Amaryllis quashed the urge to bang her head on the table. It was a challenge.

"Adorable." A soft smile curled Safina's lips. "But what's the expression? Young, dumb, and full of cum?"

Ivan snorted and ducked his head to focus on the half-full plate in front of him.

"I'm twice your age, darling." She patted Trick's cheek and picked up her beer, tipping the brown glass bottle towards him. "But look me up in a few years when you've gained a little more stamina. I need someone who can keep up with me."

Trick leaned over to Amaryllis and said in a loud whisper, "I think I'm in love."

She smacked him on the back of his head. "Idiot," she said. She was surrounded by idiots.

After dinner, Navi and Von cleaned up while Safina, Ivan, and Amaryllis settled on the couches. Trick stood next to his Big Board of Bodacious Banditry, projected on the wall across from Dagby and Cormac, who'd remained silent since Safina's arrival. For the best. Safina knew of their existence, but there was no need to draw unnecessary attention. Unlike Trick, who continued to play with fire.

"Did you name this yourself, dear?" Safina asked Trick, who nodded and explained how he came up with the ridiculous name. She got him talking, asking a variety of questions, scraping every bit of information they'd gathered without breaking a sweat. Trick preened under her attention.

Amaryllis and Ivan exchanged a glance. While she wasn't opposed to sharing information with the woman, she was both impressed and appalled by how easily she got Trick to give up everything they knew and more. Maybe she should have discreetly ordered Trick to disable the holo and toss a lock on the board. Too late now. She wished that they could have questioned her first, before Trick spilled everything they had in a fruitless effort to impress her. The man was obviously thinking with his little head rather than his big one.

"So. Safina." Ivan's voice crackled. He cleared his throat.

Biting her lip, Amaryllis looked at the ceiling for a moment to compose herself because if she had to watch the slow crawl of red up Ivan's neck as he fought a blush, she was going to break out in nervous laughter. He was so flustered. She desperately wanted to tease him about it. She would have if it were any other person than Safina sitting across from them.

At the same time, she wanted to reassure him that everything was going to be alright. But if she did that in front of Safina and everyone else in the room, that would only embarrass him more. Yes, Safina was supposed to be this scary badass, but she wasn't here to kill them or torture them, so he needed to chill.

She was more concerned about Trick. The man had a bad habit of falling hard for sharp-edged, intelligent women who were quite obviously on a much higher level than him, then moping about it when they invariably kicked his ass out the airlock. Metaphorically speaking, of course. Though with Safina's reputation, she might lean more towards the literal ending of things.

Ivan cleared his throat again. "First, thank you for the food and for letting us use your loft as our temporary headquarters. We really appreciate it."

Safina waved off his thanks. "Being back here, in this place..." She trailed off, gazing around, emotions flitting across her face too quickly for Amaryllis to parse. "Brings back some memories. Good times."

Ivan looked nonplussed but shook it off. "Yes. Well. Um, so we were wondering..."

"You're wondering why I'm here and what I was doing at the Hegemony building earlier today." She crossed her legs and laced her fingers over one knee. "Yes, I saw you over there at Magic Beans," she said with a disappointed click of her tongue. "Ivan, you do realize that not only are you a very large man, but you have both a head of bright ginger hair as well as a matching beard. It's practically impossible to miss you. Why did you choose such a conspicuous spot to do your recon?"

He opened his mouth, then closed it again, looking helplessly at Amaryllis.

"It's because he's a giant knucklehead, ma'am," Navi called over his shoulder. "I swear, the man forgets that he's a colorful walking mountain."

Amaryllis snickered.

"Fuck off, Navi. Do your dishes like a good boy," Ivan barked, his cheeks flaming. He shot her a look of betrayal.

She shrugged. "Sorry. But I agree with your brother."

His entire face crinkled in outrage. "My brother?" he rumbled. "You're taking his side?"

Well, shit. Now I've hurt his feelings. Fucking sensitive-assed men. She reached for his hand, pulling it towards her and lacing her fingers through his. She liked how they fit together, the warmth of his skin seeping into hers. And he didn't pull away. "Don't be upset, Cherry. You can move on cat's feet and fade into a crowd when you want to. It's just that you were more worried about me and my grumpiness than blending in today." She gave his hand a squeeze. "Which I appreciated."

Though his brows remained thunderclouds, he returned the squeeze, his thumb stroking the back of her hand.

Safina watched them with raptor-sharp eyes.

Ivan cleared his throat again. "Safina, we shared our intel. Now, what do you have for us?"

Safina gave another tongue click. "You've already showed your hand. Why should I share with you now? I could walk out that door with everything I learned from you."

"You could try," Von said, his voice hard.

"Oh, Amaryllis, your young men are so delightful. I'm tempted to steal them away for myself," Safina said with a canny grin.

Like she'd ever let that happen. Amaryllis bared her own teeth in a semblance of a grin. "Yes, ma'am, they are. But they wouldn't go quietly. Best you look elsewhere for fresh meat."

She was getting the number of this woman, and she appreciated it. Safina was the type who worked hard, played hard, and respected those who stood up to her. But for those who stood in her way, they would get cut down before they ever realized how much of a danger she was to them. Come to think of it, "Viper" was an appropriate moniker for Safina Es-Aiit. She could learn a lot from a woman like her.

"Pity." Safina dug into her pocket and flicked a thin black card at Trick. "Internal footage of the building, as well as a code that will give you access to most, if not all of the cameras within."

Trick looked from the info card and back to Safina, stars in his eyes. "Thank you," he said, tapping at his wrist, then swiping the card through the interface that appeared above his palm. A checkerboard of still images flashed up on his Big Board. "You are a literal goddess."

Safina tossed her head and laughed. "Yes. I know."

"No access to security, though?" he asked, his brow furrowing as he plowed through the information she'd shared with him.

"For fuck's sake, Trick," Amaryllis said with a groan.

"What? This is amazing, but it would have been nice to be able to access their security from outside, rather than having to chance it once we get in." His head snapped up, his eyes wide as he realized he'd just insulted Safina. "Oh, gods. I'm so sorry. This... this is so awesome. We definitely don't need more... any more. This is perfect." He stumbled over his words, trying to fix the damage.

"No, you're right. It would have been nice to be able to handle security from afar, but that would make the job so much less challenging and where's the fun in that?" she said with a casual shrug, as if the challenge were a drinking contest versus breaking into a protected building.

Frowning, Amaryllis looked at the information Safina shared with them, then back at the woman sitting serenely across from her. It wasn't an equal trade. Her intel from the interior of the building, plus access to the cameras held much greater weight than the schematics and scattered bits of information her team had pulled together. There was something else at play here. "What do you want?" she asked.

Ivan's hand tightened on hers. She glanced over to see a muscle jumping in his jaw. He wasn't trying to tell her to be quiet.

He'd realized the same thing as her. Safina required something more for the wealth of information she'd provided.

Her face lit up as she beamed at them like a proud teacher. "Oh, I was so hoping you'd ask that."

LEAVING her crew to Safina's machinations, Amaryllis stepped outside, needing a breath of fresh air. The air was crisp and held the scent of salt and far-off places carried inland on the cold wind blowing in from off the ocean. She leaned back against the cool metal of their warehouse and looked up at the night sky.

"Anything up there?" Ivan asked, leaning next to her.

She tilted her head to see him, his body outlined in the glow of the building's light. "Too much ambient light to see the stars. There are some clouds rolling in, though."

"That'll provide some good cover for tonight," he said, crossing his arms over his chest.

"Better if it rains."

The low hum of the bots moving around the nearby storage facilities and the calls of nightbirds the only sounds.

"Why are you doing this, Ivan?" Amaryllis asked. "This job, I mean."

He took a deep breath, tipping his head back to watch the clouds. "Much like you, I want to finish a job." He shifted to leaning one shoulder against the wall so he could see her better. "I don't like to leave things undone."

She mirrored his stance, crossing one booted foot over the other. "So what happens when we have the prototype in our possession? What then? Do you plan to try and take it from us so you can give it back to Bea? Or is retrieving it enough to cross this unfinished job of yours off the list?"

A brief frown darted across his forehead. "I hadn't thought that far ahead."

She humphed, not believing that for a moment. "And how are

you going to 'fuck up Amaryllis's little plans'?" she asked, smirking when he drew back. "That's right. I heard you talking to Quin."

"Of course you did." He leaned close and whispered, "I knew you were listening."

"Did you now?" she asked, shifting so their lips were microns apart. "Then you should know I'm on to you. Whatever nefarious plans you have, however you think you're going to fuck up my own plans, I'm ready for you."

Raising an eyebrow, he said, "Are you now." He snaked a hand around the nape of her neck and pulled her to him, covering her mouth with his.

She sank into him, her curves aligning with his, and wrapped her arms around him. Slowly, she teased the shirt from his waistband and dragged her fingers along the v-shaped muscles that crested his hip bones.

He leaned back, eliciting a small whimper of protest from her as he removed his lips from hers. "Nefarious?" he asked.

Sliding her hands down the back of his pants, she grabbed his ass. "It's a good word, nefarious. It means, 'not conforming to a high moral standard'," she said, leaning forward and grabbing his bottom lip between her teeth.

His ass flexed under her touch. He whispered her name as he slid a thick thigh between her legs and wrapped an arm around her waist, pulling her closer as his tongue delved into the depths of her mouth. His fingers circled her nape, his thumb gently stroking her collarbone.

The quiet of the night shrouded them in midnight blue edged in blurred gold. It was as if they were the only two people in the world, wrapped in a cocoon of heat and desire.

She closed her eyes and lost herself to Ivan's touch, the sensation of him enveloping her in his big body, his strong hands holding her tightly to him, his tongue tracing the curve of her jaw, his teeth nipping their way down her neck. She groaned, a soft sound that shimmered in the surrounding night.

His arms tightened around her. "What I wouldn't do for a bed right now. Why are there so many fucking people around?"

She huffed out a laugh. "We'll turn off the feed to the ship. Pretty sure we can take the other three and toss them out on their ears. You want to do it on a cot or the couch?"

Burying his head in the crook of her neck, he shook his head with a laugh. "Probably best to just stay out here and fool around then, don't you think?"

"You're afraid of Safina, aren't you?" she said, stroking her fingers through his silky hair.

"Hells yes, I am. For someone who looks like my Nana Gee, that woman is terrifying." He shuddered, the movement causing his thigh to rub against her core. He peppered her collarbone with gentle kisses.

Sparks lit up her spine, and she dropped her head back. "Chicken," she whispered, humming in pleasure as he pulled her even tighter to him, shifting his thigh again.

He huffed out a laugh as he undid the buttons of her shirt and kissed his way down her chest, his lips hot against her breasts, the slow rasp of his beard tickling her sensitive skin. "See, I'm smart."

"You are?" she asked, wrapping a leg around his waist.

Turning her so her back was pressed up against the cool metal of the warehouse, he grabbed her thigh and ground himself against her clitoris, the fabric barrier between them rubbing over her sensitive nerves. "Absolutely. You have to find out what makes those whip-smart, vicious women happy, you see. Figure out what satisfies them. It's the only way to survive."

She swallowed hard. "Is that so?"

"Incontrovertibly." He gave a little hip-twitch that made her see stars.

"Fuck, Ivan," she said.

"See? Exactly like that." He covered her mouth with his again, his hot tongue searing her senses.

She moaned under his touch and slid her hands under his

shirt, her fingers tracing the curve of his muscles as they carved their way up his back.

So lost in the moment, they didn't hear the warehouse door open until it was too late.

"Are you fucking kidding me right now?" Trick said, his hands planted on his hips as he glared at them. "We're trying to plan a heist and you're out here in the dark, necking like a couple of overly-hormonal teenagers." He threw up his hands in disgust and stormed back into the building.

Ivan and Amaryllis loosened their grip on one another and slid apart. She caught his eye. The corner of his mouth twitched. A snicker escaped from between her lips. He cut off a snort. Try as they might, they couldn't hold back the laughter that overtook them.

"Busted," Amaryllis crowed, leaning against the wall as laughter weakened her knees.

"I haven't been scolded like that since my ma caught me kissing Candy Fitch in the Crone's temple when we were twelve," Ivan said, wiping tears from beneath his eyes.

Navi poked his head around the corner. "By the holy tits of Saint Agnes," he said, rolling his eyes at them. "Get your shit together and get in here."

That, of course, set them off again.

Eventually though, they pulled themselves together. As they followed Navi back inside, Amaryllis realized she never got her answers from Ivan. Sneaky bastard.

21

IVAN

"**I** don't like this," Von said for the seventh time.

And for the seventh time, Amaryllis said, "You don't have to like it. You just have to do it."

Ivan and Navi exchanged a glance. Bickering before a job was something they usually did. Interesting to see it played out in front of them by another team.

"We need more time," he said. "There are too many variables at play here."

"No, I agree, but Dagby said Christophe and Deno are already on the ground. They found that tracker we had on them so we have no idea where they are or close they are to stealing it. They may be on their way here right now. We're out of time. If we delay, there's too great a chance they'll get the prototype before us." She paused and cocked her head. "Unless you no longer care if they get it? We can always cut this party short and head back home."

Von grunted, adjusting the double bandoliers slung across his chest. "Just making sure my protest is on record for when this all goes sideways."

"Stop worrying so much, Von," Navi said. "It's going to be fine."

"Godsdammit, Navi. Not again." Ivan pinched the bridge of his nose.

With the speed of a striking raptor, Amaryllis reached over and smacked him on the back of the head.

Navi rubbed the sore spot, his eyes wide. "What? What'd I do?"

"How many times do we have to tell you to stop saying that?" Ivan shifted the empty padded pack on his back and checked his weapons. Tranqs loaded? Check. Fully charged blaster? Check.

"Tell people to stop worrying?" Navi scooted a few steps away, out of Amaryllis's reach.

"No, you numbskull. That everything's going to be fine. It's a sure-fire way to jinx the mission." Ivan shook his head and adjusted his thigh holsters, making sure they were at a good height for a quick draw. "The last time you said it, Quin got injured, and I got kidnapped by pirates. Now, get a move on." He shooed a protesting Navi across the nearly empty street. The clouds he and Amaryllis had spotted earlier had coalesced, spitting enough of a drizzle to encourage anyone outside to hurry along.

"Hey, now." Amaryllis patted her head, tucking away a stray braid that had escaped from under her black beanie. "We didn't kidnap you. We were making sure you didn't bleed out on the Vanid's stupidly perfect lawn."

"Are you sure it wasn't just an excuse to have me under your control and beholden to you if I wanted to make it off your ship or Lore's alive?"

She smirked. "Added bonus."

"Are we ready to do this? Or do you two need some more time to flirt?" Trick asked, casually leaning out from between two buildings and scanning the street. "Because if you need more time..."

"Shut up, Trick." Amaryllis punched him in the arm.

"Ow. No need for violence. I was only asking."

"I'm here. In position." As their spotter and sniper, Navi was posted up on top of a two-story building catty-corner from the Hegemony offices.

"*Dog's Day* team standing by," Cormac said. There wasn't much Cormac and Dagby could do until the ground team got to security and hooked them into the camera system. For now, they were monitoring chatter and keeping an eye on local law enforcement. They'd already duped and looped footage for the surrounding area, essentially making the ground team invisible to any cameras around the building.

"Unless Von has another complaint to register, we're a go," Amaryllis said.

Von rolled his eyes and gave his bandolier one more tug, smoothing out where it wrinkled his black technical shirt.

"Copy," Navi said. There was a pause. Two quiet pops sounded over the comms. "Clear. Bots on the front door disabled."

"Don't forget to activate your blockers." Ivan double tapped his wrist and flicked on the facial recognition blocker Navi had given them. A present from Bea's sister, he'd said. Hells, anything that helped them stay off the security grid, he'd take it. Facial recognition programs struggled with his beard, but if he had a way to block them completely when involved in illegal activities like breaking and entering and stealing expensive tech, he'd gladly take any help Dai sent their way.

"Let's move." Amaryllis led the team out of the narrow alleyway between Hegemony and its neighbor and up to the front doors.

The two security bots remained dark, taken out with something Von called "splat rounds", his own invention. As he explained it, it was basically an armor-penetrating round that contained nanites programmed to disable any system they penetrated. Small but powerful. Ivan was impressed. He'd have to talk to Von about making some for his own crew.

Three stories high, the building's first floor housed a welcome center with a long desk blocking access to the area beyond, the security office, as well as a cafeteria, break room, and workout facility. The floors above it were offices. Nothing special there that Dagby and Cormac could find.

What was interesting about the building were the two underground floors. It had taken some digging, but Dagby and Cormac eventually found plans for both. Using those specs, along with Safina's images, they had a relatively detailed map that should lead them to where the prototype's tracker indicated. Fingers crossed it was there and not a false trail leading to a trap.

But they first needed to get into the security office. Jacking into the active cameras was a priority. They needed to know in real-time what they were walking into. They were as prepared as possible.

Moving quickly, they entered the building and disabled several patrol bots before reaching the security office. With Ivan and Von on point, weapons out, Amaryllis stepped up and held a semi-opaque white card with gold edges against the locking mechanism. The card's edges glowed, the bright light briefly illuminating the dim hallway. The lock spit a few sparks, then went dark.

She looked at the men and, at her nod, she opened the door. Ivan and Von entered first. Two human guards sprawled in their chairs, chatting and eating sandwiches. They barely had time to swallow their mouthfuls before Ivan and Von shot them with tranqs. The guards slumped over, unconscious.

"We're in," Amaryllis said, shoving a guard out of the way.

Trick stepped up to the bank of surveillance monitors running feeds from all over the building. With a flick of his wrist, he brought up his holo computer.

Ivan wheeled the other guard off to the side, then stood beside the door, his weapon loose at his side. He studied the wall of monitors, showing a rotation of scenes from the floors.

"Multiple teams of guards as well as defensive bots patrolling the floors." Amaryllis pointed to a monitor.

"Minimal civilians. That's good," Ivan said. There were a

couple of people in lab coats wandering around, their faces buried in their devices. As they watched, one paused long enough for the bots to scan them before scurrying off.

"Cameras look like they're covering every inch of the lower level corridors," Von said. "No place to duck out of sight."

"Not one camera showing the interior of the labs." Ivan scratched at his beard. Odd. What was it they were doing in those labs that they didn't want recorded?

"Dagby, get ready." Trick reached into his front vest pocket and pulled out a black card, the one that Safina had given them and slid it into a slot on the security dashboard. It sank into the panel and disappeared. "Anything?"

"Nothing yet," Dagby said. "What's it look like on your end?"

Trick scanned the panel. "No change. Did she give us a faulty key?"

"No way," Cormac said. "She might have a scary reputation, but she's known for being a straight shooter."

"Hey, guys. Did you know the door lock's not work..." a third member of the security team walked into the room and froze as he took in the scene. "...ing?"

Before the guard could reach for his weapon, Ivan wrapped an arm around his neck and squeezed. He bucked and strained against Ivan's hold, his fingers scrabbling against his forearm, trying to dig his nails in but meeting the resistance of a long-sleeved tee. When the man went slack, Ivan let go. He folded to the floor like an empty pair of pants.

Ivan scootched him out of the way with his foot, noting that the man still breathed. Good. He hadn't wanted to kill the guy, just stop him before he sounded the alarm.

Amaryllis and Von stared at Ivan.

"What?" he asked.

"You could've just tranqed him, man," Von said.

Huh. He probably could've done that. Ivan lifted the tranq gun and shot him in the ass. "There. You happy now?"

Von snorted.

"Work, dammit." Trick slammed a fist against the panel.

The lights on the panel flickered.

"There! Yes. Whatever you did, it worked," Cormac said, his voice excited. "We're up."

"Give us a minute," Dagby said. "I want to make sure you have a clear path to the lab housing the prototype."

"Excellent." Amaryllis rubbed her hands together and shot Ivan a grin.

He couldn't help but return the grin. It was infectious. He'd always loved the feel of pure adrenaline that coursed through his veins during a job. With a solid team on your side and a straightforward plan to follow, jobs like this were fun. Even better when things sped along, elements of the plan clicking into place like you'd planned. Yes, you had to anticipate surprises and be ready for when things went very wrong, but skating along the paper thin edge of danger added spice to the game.

That Amaryllis felt the same adrenaline rush... well, what could he say? It was hot. Honestly, if they weren't in the middle of the job with Von and Trick right there and people listening in on comms, he might be tempted to take her right there on the security panel.

But they were in the middle of a job and him thinking about having sex with her, well, that was a serious distraction. He needed to get his head in the game. The big head, not the little one. Distractions like picturing the woman who drove him crazy bent over, panting his name as he made her come, would lead to mistakes. Mistakes could get him and everyone on his team killed.

After, he told himself. Once the job was done, he'd get Amaryllis alone and find out how many times he could make her orgasm in the space of an afternoon. An excellent challenge, if he did say so himself. He gave her a heated look, one that traveled from the top of her beanie-covered head, down over the tight black shirt and pants that hugged her curves, to the thick-soled boots on her feet.

She noticed him checking her out and struck a pose, her hand on her waist. When she licked her lips, he felt his dick get hard.

"By the holy tits of Saint Agnes," Von growled. "You two have got to quit giving each other fuck-me eyes and focus."

Trick glanced back at them and shook his head.

Navi groaned. "For fuck's sake, we're in the middle of a job."

"Shut up, Navi," Ivan said, his eyes still on Amaryllis.

She blew him a kiss before turning back to the monitors.

"Gods, but I'm happy I'm not there to witness all that," Navi said. "I'll take these boring, empty streets any day over that."

"Focus, people," Cormac said. "First floor down is labs. Lowest floor is their testing facility. You're going to want to get to the first floor labs. Tracker says the prototype is in the last room on the left, but you've got some pretty heavy patrols to work through."

Ivan patted the weapons strapped to his thighs. "We've got tranqs and Von's splat bullets. Let's avoid killing anyone unless absolutely necessary. We're not pirates, after all."

Amaryllis raised a hand. "Technically, my crew is."

"Okay, but we don't have to act like bloodthirsty maniacs, do we?" He was trying to clean up his act, after all.

She shrugged. "Some people just need killing."

That sounded eerily like something he'd said before. He narrowed his eyes at her.

She stuck her tongue out, then grabbed a security pass from a guard. "Next up, the elevators. We're going down, boys."

Ivan repressed the urge to make a dirty joke.

Trick and Navi both snickered.

Children.

22

AMARYLLIS

er entire body tingled, and it wasn't just the adrenaline. It was Ivan. The way he looked at her back in the security office, she thought for a second there he was about to kick the guys out and take her up against the wall again. She squeezed her thighs together, remembering.

Fuck. Stop. She needed to get her head in the game. Lusting after her hot mortal enemy was one thing, but actively doing it in the middle of a job when a misstep could get them all captured or killed was a bad idea.

And technically, he wasn't her mortal enemy any longer, but she still have a name for what he was to her. Boyfriend was too tame, especially since they hadn't done anything remotely romantic or couple-y. Arguing, teasing, and fucking were all well and good, but was that enough of a foundation to build a lasting partnership? Was that even what they wanted? Would they even survive a relationship like that, or would they wind up killing one another? Stupid feelings. Stupid relationships. Stupid brain. Why did everything have to be so complicated?

Once they finished this job, she'd get him alone, and they'd hash out the details of whatever this relationship thing was. After a good, sweaty session between the sheets, of course. The man knew how to make her moan in pleasure, and she wasn't about to waste any opportunity to let him prove his talents.

"This guy's no good, either." Von let the security guard slump to the ground outside the elevator.

"Shit." Trick nudged him out of the doorway.

They'd run into a teeny hiccup. The elevator wouldn't travel to the lower levels. Oh sure, they went up well enough, but getting them to head down was a different story. The key card didn't work by itself. The elevator had a biolock, which meant they needed the handprint of someone with the correct clearance before it would go below the ground floor. So far, they'd hauled two of the guards from the security office to the elevator with no luck. The stairs weren't an option — access required not only a keycard and bioprint, but also had a twenty-digit keypad, impossible to crack within their timeframe.

Ivan returned with the last guy. "This one better work or we're fucked," he said, sliding the guy off his shoulder to the floor of the elevator car.

Von shuffled to the side to give him room. "If he doesn't, we'll have to regroup. Maybe lure one of the guards patrolling the lower floors up here."

"We need to hurry this along. It's taking too long." Trick watched them from where he stood outside the elevator between the other two unconscious guards. He shifted his weight from foot to foot.

"We know this, Trick," Ivan said, keeping his voice patient and calm. "Get back to the security office. Get those two out of sight. We don't want to be caught with our pants down."

"Would be nice if someone," Von emphasized 'someone', casting his eyes upwards, "could get this elevator moving for us."

"Sorry, Von," Dagby said. "We're trying. But right now, we only have the cameras. Can't get anywhere else without direct access."

Von grimaced. "I don't like this. Too easy to get trapped if something goes wrong."

"You haven't liked this since we got here," Amaryllis said.

He grunted.

"Trick's in security. Work with him and see if you can't access at least some of the other systems controlling this building." Ivan said.

"On it," Cormac said. "Trick, let us know when you're ready for us."

"Acknowledged."

Ivan grabbed the guy's arm and slapped his hand against the panel.

"If this doesn't work, we could wait until shift change." Amaryllis slid the key card through the reader above it. "But this guy is the one, I can feel it. I mean, look at his little outfit. He's got an extra star on his shoulder and everything."

They held their collective breath.

With a beep, the panel turned green, and the doors slid shut. The elevator car shivered, then descended.

"Thank the goddess." Amaryllis wiped away a bead of sweat from her temple. "Okay, we're on the move. What's waiting for us?"

"Security bot parked itself directly in front of the doors," Cormac said.

"Timing-wise, a pair of guards will round the corner and head your way about when your doors open," Dagby added.

"I'll get the bot." Amaryllis unholstered her blaster and loaded it with a splat bullet. "Von, Ivan, you two get the guards."

The elevator let out a muted chime as it stopped on the first lower level.

She shifted to the right and crouched, gripping her blaster. Taking a deep breath, she slowly released it, focusing on the frame of the elevator door.

There was a pause as the elevator settled, then the doors glided open. As soon as the bot was in her sights, she squeezed the trigger. There was a small pop and a ping as the splat bullet nailed the bot. A second later, its red warning light faded to black.

She slid to the side to let the men flow past her into the corridor. Two more pops and two more security threats were incapacitated.

"Clear." Ivan's low voice in her ear sent a trail of sparks down her spine.

She hauled the bullet-shaped bot over the elevator threshold, using it to prop the door open. There was still security on the other floors. Better to cut off the fastest they could come to the aid of those on this level. Let them take the stairs.

"Looks like there's one more bot and two more security teams on this floor," Cormac said. "Bot's on the opposite hall. Security's checking doors on the same hall."

"One pair stopped to talk to a civilian who just left one of the labs," Trick added.

"We'll take them." Ivan looked at Von who gave him chin tip in the affirmative. "You go get the prototype." He handed her the empty pack he'd been carrying.

"Got it. Last door on the left." She exchanged the blaster for a tranq gun as she set off down the corridor, moving with purpose.

"No alarms. No one has any idea you're there," Dagby said.

"And let's keep it that way," Trick said.

"Movement on the street," Navi said. There was a pause. "False alarm. Carry on. Bunch of drunk university students. Probably kicked out of that bar at the end of the street."

Trusting that Ivan and Von would take care of the remaining security guards and handle any stray civilians they ran into on the floor, Amaryllis picked up her pace.

The door to the lab was sealed, another biometric lock blocking her way. *Shit*, she thought. "Guys, bring that civilian to the lab. We're going to need them to get inside."

"Well, hells," Ivan said. "Just tranqed her."

"Sending Ivan and the civilian your way, Amaryllis," Von said. "I'm going to double-check that these labs are empty. Wouldn't want any surprises."

"Great. Meet us by the elevator. Hopefully, this won't take long."

Ivan rounded the corner, a woman in a white lab coat draped over his broad shoulder.

Amaryllis licked her lips, watching as he stalked towards her, not even breathing hard carrying the weight of another human being. A flashback of him holding her up while he railed her against the wall sent a bolt of heat up her spine. What was it about a strong man that got her going?

No. Bad girl. Focus, she scolded herself. She gave him a serious nod, like she wasn't remembering how he took her in the common room. "Hey," she said. Her voice crackled and she had to clear her throat. "Great. Hopefully, this chick will be the key to this door."

Readjusting the woman, his thick arm wrapped around the scientist's waist, Ivan grabbed her hand and plonked it on the reader. Amaryllis slid the guard's key card along the slot.

The biolock gave an angry beep and turned red.

"Well, shit." Amaryllis looked from the card she held in her hand to the unconscious woman in Ivan's arms. "Wait." She plucked the name badge from the woman's white coat. It was the same size and heft as the guard's key card. "Okay, Yara Be'Llm. Let's try this again."

Sliding Yara's card along the side, she nodded to Ivan, who put her hand back on the panel. This time it turned green, unlocking with a soft click.

"Ha. Thanks, Yara." She pushed the door open and entered the lab.

The lights brightened, illuminating the space, and they were met with a veritable goblin's hoard. Materials of all shapes and sizes were in haphazard but semi-organized piles on the gray tile floor and over every surface. Amaryllis followed a narrow path that led through sheets of metal, boxes of fasteners, heaps of wiring, and stacked metal rods. Someone had spent a long time and a good chunk of credits gathering every material they might possibly need and bringing it to this lab.

The walls were covered in chicken-scratch handwriting, complicated-looking formulas, and bright yellow sticky notes, the white plasticine beneath barely visible.

"Um... how are we supposed to find anything in all this mess?" Ivan bumped into a table, wincing as a stack of washers spilled across the surface with a clatter.

"Better yet, how does anyone get anything done in all this? Or avoid being crushed when they accidentally knock over a stack of metal something-or-others?" Amaryllis shuddered. That would be a terrible way to go. "Are you sure it's in here?"

"According to the tracker Bea placed, yes. This is the last known location of her propulsion system." He looked around. "Highly probable the prototype was disassembled and is now scattered to the four winds." He waved a hand at all the piles. "Or, you know, lost inside this hoard."

"Well, fuck." She poked at another pile, retracting her finger when it wobbled. "I'll do a sweep here, see what I can find. You help Von clear the rest of the labs."

"On it."

"Oh, and take the scientist. We might need her bioscan to open more doors."

23

IVAN

Of course, the damned prototype wasn't where it was supposed to be. Closing the last door of the final lab on the level, he blew out a frustrated sigh. "No joy," he said.

The entire team cursed.

Besides the one goblin-hoard-filled room, the other labs were pristine. Most looked as if they'd never been used. Their biolocks weren't even engaged. Weird. Maybe it was just that Hegemony was a new company with a lot of money to throw around. So why all the security if there was only one functional lab?

He met up with Von in the hall, and they returned to Amaryllis.

"All I found was this," Amaryllis said, holding up a thin piece of metal.

"Tracker?" Ivan asked, easing his way past a box filled with broken plasticine forms.

"Yep. Still doing its thing." She frowned, turning it over in her palm.

"What are you thinking? Trap?" he asked.

"But if it was, why haven't they sprung it yet? There were

guards and security; why weren't they on alert for people like us to come looking for the prototype?" She tossed the tracker back where she found it.

"What if whoever found the tracker didn't care?" Dagby asked.

Amaryllis cocked her head, a small eleven appearing between her brows as she considered the question. "How do you mean?"

"Those piles of junk in there, the scribbling on the walls, it's reading eccentric genius to me," she said. "If that's the case, then the engineer, scientist, whoever disassembled Bea's prototype and tossed the tracker aside because it wasn't part of the system and they didn't have use for it. They didn't care what it was; it wasn't what they needed."

They mulled it over. *Smart*, Ivan thought.

Von's lips tightened. "Whatever the reason, makes me itch."

Ivan grunted in agreement.

"Same, but we need that prototype, if it still exists," Amaryllis said with a shake of her head. "If not that, then something we can bring to Lore or we can kiss our future plans goodbye."

"So, what now?" Von asked as they returned to the elevators.

"I say we check that bottom level," Ivan said, rubbing a hand over the back of his neck. "Might be a good idea to have Trick and Von sweep those offices on the upper floors, just in case." He couched his idea as suggestions, not wanting to step on Amaryllis's toes. She was the one running the job, after all. He didn't expound on what they'd do if they didn't find the prototype at all. Everyone knew they'd be back to square one.

"I'm not leaving you two," Von growled.

"Hey, I can handle a solo sweep," Trick said. "I've been watching and there's no one on the aboveground floors, only a couple of bots."

Amaryllis chewed her bottom lip then said, "Okay. Trick, you say you can handle the sweep, so do it but be careful. Dagby, you're on interior cameras. Cormac, exterior. Let us know if there's anything. Navi, be ready to assist Trick. Von, Ivan, and I will check the last floor and then we're out. Everyone got it?"

Everyone did.

They had about thirty minutes before the tranquilizers wore off, enough time for them to do what they needed to do and get away clean. Of course, that depended on what they found on the lowest level.

"Dagby, what are we walking into?"

"A pair of armed guards stationed to the right as well as a security bot."

Cormac chimed in. "Most recent schematics on file indicate two observation booths facing into two long structures. Testing tunnels. Another lab to the left of them. Walls of that floor are three times thicker than the floor above. Soundproofing, for sure. I mean, there'd have to be, so no one above ground would hear whatever they're doing down here."

"Some seriously shady shit to do in the middle of a crowded area," Navi said.

Von moved the bot door stopper into the hall, and they all piled into the elevator.

When the doors slid open at on the bottom floor, the team exited and split, Ivan and Amaryllis to the right and Von the left. They moved quickly, disabling the security team and bot.

"Doors have biolocks," Amaryllis said.

Von sighed. "I'll get Yara."

Weapon out, Ivan quickly cleared the first observation room and tunnel. There were a few empty coffee cups and a tablet sitting on a table, but no prototype. He picked up the tablet and gave it a swipe. The screen remained black. He stuck it in his pack. There was a risk of it having a tracker or malware, but Cormac could disable it.

He didn't have much hope for its usefulness, though. It sat discarded next to an old coffee cup. Someone who worked in a high security facility would know better than to leave something with classified information on it just lying about. While information would be nice, it wasn't what he was after, anyway.

"Got something!" Amaryllis called.

He spared a glance for the lab beyond the two testing areas, waving at Von to keep searching. "You found it?" he asked, joining her in front of the glass that separated the observation room from the tunnel.

Amaryllis gave him a bright smile and pointed. "Looks like."

Through the glass of the observation booth, he saw a familiar looking cone-shaped object that tapered to a wide tube, flat circular panels ringing its surface. It was smaller than he remembered, small enough they could easily transport out in the backpack he brought.

It still amazed him that something this size would one day power ships that could travel across the entire galaxy and possibly beyond. Granted, this was only a prototype. Even the smallest functioning propulsion system was several times bigger than this, and closer to the size of the labs for the massive long-haulers who required multiple jumps to get from one end of the galaxy to the other. Although, maybe Bea's system was different. What did he know.

He narrowed his eyes at the prototype. Bea said she'd rendered it nonfunctional, infecting it with malware and injecting the internal workings with nanites. So how was it that her prototype sat in the testing tunnel of a secret facility? A testing tunnel would indicate that it was working, unless they'd put it there for safekeeping. Seemed counterproductive though.

With Amaryllis at his heels, he opened the door to the tunnel and approached the small system.

"I thought you said Bea damaged it?" she asked, cocking her head as she tapped a fingernail against one of the circular panels.

"She did." Ivan crossed his arms over his chest and frowned down at it.

"So, why is it in a testing tunnel?"

"My question exactly." He shook his head. "I don't think this is Bea's. The outer body of hers was all one material." He pointed at a bright stripe swirling around the cone. "This one looks like it's got an alloy fused to it as well." They'd have to test it to be sure.

"Shit," he said softly. If someone had found a way to replicate Bea's original work despite her sabotage, she needed to know about it. Within the United Body of Planets' legal system, it was necessary she be the first to claim ownership of the design. If she lost control of that, it could be disastrous. Ivan was by no means well-versed in the legalities of it all, but he did know that first rights were the ones that counted the most, giving the claimant the most control and power over their design, product, whatever it was.

But again, none of that was his focus here tonight. His job was to retrieve the prototype and destroy or collect any physical records he happened to come across. There was already a plan in motion to handle everything else.

"Whether it's the original or something new, we're definitely taking it." She tugged at one of his pack's straps. He took the bag off and handed it to her. She opened the pack and looked from Ivan to the empty bag. "Well, go ahead. Stick it in."

He coughed, feeling the creep of heat up his neck.

Rolling her eyes, she said, "Just do it. I know you want to. You're practically foaming at the mouth."

"That's what she said." He snickered. He tried to hold it in, but he couldn't help it. She set him up perfectly.

"You're an idiot," she said, flapping the pack at him. "Well?"

"Yeah." He picked up the prototype and maneuvered it into the pack with a grunt. "This thing is a lot heavier than it looks."

"Aw, too heavy? Poor Cherry. You need me to carry it for you?" she asked, batting her eyes at him as she held up the straps for him.

"No," he growled, shoving his arms through the holes and getting it settled on his back. "I was just saying."

"Well, you do know it's made of metal and whatnot. Bound

to be heavy, even though it's small." She patted him on the shoulder. "Let's go see what Von found in the lab, then get the hells out of here. I don't love being trapped underground any longer than I have to be."

Von was standing beside a long table, his hands on his hips. "Take a look at this," he said.

This lab was the exact opposite of the first they'd encountered. Everything was put away in flush-mounted cabinets that were neatly labeled. The entire room's white surfaces sparkled under the bright lights it was so clean. The only visible item was disassembled and under a sealed clear plasticine hood, its parts organized from smallest to largest, each piece neatly labeled.

"Pressure control assembly, interface ring, propellant tank, pyro valve, thermal control...," Amaryllis read off the labels as she moved down the table. "These are all parts of a propulsion system," she said. "Bea's work?"

"Pretty banged up," Von pointed out the corrosion, entire chunks eaten away.

So Bea's nanites had worked after all. Just not well enough to render it as completely useless as she'd hoped.

"Couple of servers tucked away in those cabinets, too," Von said, nodding towards the cabinets on the wall behind Amaryllis.

"What are we doing with it?" Trick asked. "Not leaving it there like that, I presume."

"If the nanites are still active, they could continue to eat away at the metals," Cormac said.

Amaryllis pressed her nose up against the clear covering. "Well, it's under a sealed hood and doesn't look like anything's moving or changing. I'm thinking the nanites are either destroyed or disabled."

"Pretty big chance to take, though," Ivan said.

Bea didn't actually need to have her prototype back in her hands; she just didn't want it to stay in someone else's. She had all her notes and everything and, according to Quin's latest update, was already hard at work on a newer version of the thing.

"So what's the plan, then?" Trick asked.

"Grab it," Amaryllis said.

"Destroy it," Ivan said simultaneously.

They eyed at each other.

"You don't need it, Amaryllis," Ivan said. "If you destroy it, you still thwart Christophe and Deno because they won't be able to complete Lore's job."

She huffed. "But if we grab it, I'll have more leverage to pry ourselves free of The Cabal."

"You can't just hand this over to Lore, especially since you don't know what she wants it for. Something like this in the hands of someone like her..."

"Like her? Don't you mean like me? You've got the other prototype in your bag, and you don't want me to have this one. Okay," she said, drawing her blaster and smashing the butt of it against the protective hood. A small crack spider-webbed over the surface. "I see your game. Thought you'd weasel your way into my job by holding that location over my head."

"Game? Hold on now," Ivan asked, taking a step back and holding up his hands. He didn't know where she'd gotten that idea, but she had it all wrong. He wasn't playing games. In fact, he thought he'd been pretty honest with her. Maybe not right at the beginning, but certainly later.

However, Amaryllis was in no mood to take questions. She slammed the weapon down again. "And then when we find what you were looking for, you try and take it for yourself." Smash. "Mother." Smash. "Fucking." Smash, smash. "Son of a biscuit-eating bulldog!" The plasticine gave way, and she tore into it, ripping out the shattered material and throwing it onto the floor. "Von, bag," she barked.

He whipped an expandable bag from a zippered pocket on his pants and handed it to her.

The lighting changed from soft white to a dull red as an alarm sounded.

"Lockdown initiated. Please proceed to your assigned locations." A soothing male voice repeated his instructions. "Lockdown initiated."

"Uh, team?" Trick said. "Which one of you set off the alarm?"

AMARYLLIS

"Perfect," she growled, turning around to glare at Ivan.

"Hey, this was not my fault." He cast a glance over the smashed hood now decorating the shiny white flooring.

She growled again, clenching her fists.

"I'm on my way to you." Trick raised his voice to be heard over the sound of the alarm.

"Don't come down here," Amaryllis barked.

"Uh, people?" Navi said. "The building is locking down."

"Yes, we know that, Navi," Ivan said, his voice shaded with impatience.

"No, what I mean is the building is literally locking down — there are metal panels dropping over all the windows and doors. Place will be completely sealed in maybe a minute."

Well, fuck, Amaryllis thought, stuffing pieces of the dismantled prototype into her bag as quickly as she could. Why were there so many damn parts to this thing? She had no idea what was important. It would be just her luck if, after all this, she left behind something small but crucial.

"Heavily armed security teams arriving on the scene. A lot of them," Dagby said.

"Shit. Where in the three hells did they come from?" Amaryllis shoved something labeled 'interface ring' into the bag. She'd let her temper get the better of her and now they would have to fight their way out.

"Trick, you need to get out of there now," Dagby said. "ETA three minutes."

Trick protested, but Amaryllis cut him off. "Agreed. Trick, get out of the building before you're trapped."

"Not the front door. They're coming in," Navi said.

"Copy. Heading up to the roof now," he said.

"Once you're there, jump to the building with the red roof. There's a fire escape on the far side," Navi said. "I'll cover you."

"Amaryllis, stop shoving stuff in that damn bag. We don't have time for this. Drop a charge and let's go." Ivan put a hand on her wrist. "We need to get off this floor while we still have access to the elevator."

She growled at him and snatched her hand away. "Back the fuck off, Ivan. If you're not going to help here, go secure the hall or something. Just get the hells away from me."

Ivan gave her a long look, then stalked out of the room. The door slammed shut behind him, followed by several loud bangs.

Dickhead. She ground her teeth as the lockdown instructions continued to repeat. She needed to pull herself together and think because right now, they were trapped two stories underground in what was essentially a bunker built by a paranoid engineer. Even if they held off security right now, they wouldn't be able to do it forever. By now, local law enforcement might even be on its way. At some point, her team would run out of blaster charges and ammunition, and Hegemony security would bust in and drag them out kicking and screaming if they didn't shoot them on sight. They needed an exit strategy and fast.

Von checked his weapons, reloading his tranq gun and slapping a fresh charge into his blaster.

Blowing out a sharp breath, she set the half-filled pack on the table and looked at Von. "We're so fucked," she said.

"Yep."

"I overreacted, didn't I?" Her hand clenched on the pack's straps. She forced it to loosen.

"Yep."

She eyed the now-closed door Ivan had stalked through. "I'm going to have to apologize, aren't I?"

"Yep."

"You're so helpful."

He grinned at her. "Always."

"Asshole," she said.

"Yep," he said with a wink.

"Ivan," she said. "Please come back into the lab."

No response.

"Come on, Cherry. I apologize for yelling at you, okay? I don't really think you're going to steal the prototype out from under us."

The comm crackled but there was still no response.

Amaryllis growled, smacking a fresh charge into her weapon. "Okay, now you're just being childish. Get your ass back in here. That's an order."

"Um, Cap? Looks like you didn't completely knock out those guards the first time 'round. One of them zapped Ivan with a taser," Dagby said.

"Well, shit," she said. Must be why he didn't answer her.

"Armed response will be on your floor in less than a minute," Cormac said.

She chewed the inside of her cheek, thinking fast as she finished packing up all the pieces on the table and zipped the bag. "I mean, there's got to be another way out of here, right? Certainly someone wouldn't build a place like this with only one way in or out, especially when working with things that have the tendency to blow up. That would make it a death trap if everything was on fire and they had to wait for the damned elevator."

"Whatever you're thinking, make it quick," Dagby said, anxiety raising her pitch an octave.

"We're missing the something that will help get us out of here in one piece and preferably not aboard a ship bound for a prison moon." An idea glimmered in the corner of her brain. Something she'd seen or read… "Cormac, when you pulled the schematics for the building, you pulled all of them, right?"

"Yep, grabbed 'em all," he said. There was a clap, like he'd smacked his hand on something. "Ooh, I like where your brain is headed, and I'm on that train with you. Give me a second."

"Fast as you can." She tapped a fingernail against the table. "Von, you got something that will take care of this?" she asked, gesturing at the lab as a whole.

He raised an eyebrow.

"What was I thinking? Of course you do." She paused, then said, "Would be even better if you had something that will wipe those servers, too, in case the underground blast leaves something recoverable behind." She'd taken care of Safina's favor in the lab, but she didn't think Safina's team knew about everything that was down here.

He nodded, pulling items from his pockets and getting to work.

She moved towards the lab door, intent on physically dragging Ivan into the lab with them. She shouldn't have sent him away. They were better together. When security reached their floor, they'd hold them off as long as they could from within the lab. "Cormac, anything?"

"Yes!"

She winced as he shouted in her ear.

"Dude, too loud," Navi complained.

"Sorry. But I do believe we have an out. Sending you something now."

Her comm beeped. She paused to double tap her wrist, swiping up to 3D it. Cormac sent the new schematic with an older one layered over it. "Where am I looking?"

"At the back of the lab, the bottom cabinets against that back wall. See that?"

Amaryllis squinted, then pinched open her fingers to enlarge it. "What is that? A tunnel or ventilation shaft?" Her heart sped up. She knew she'd seen something when they were making their plans and tucked it away in the back of her brain for just such an occasion. A tunnel meant they could get out of here. She grabbed the handle to the lab door, but it didn't open.

"Part of a very old sewer system, actually. Don't get your hopes up yet. Might be they filled it in at some point between the old plans and the new. But, if we're lucky, might be your way out of there. I know I'd keep an egress handy, in case things went bad with one of my experiments."

"Welp, fingers crossed, then." She hated depending on luck. You never knew when it would turn on you. She pulled at the lab door again, jiggling the handle, but it wouldn't move. Pounding on it, she called, "Ivan. Door's stuck on our side. Open it and get your stupid ass back in here. Cormac may have found a way out."

"Amaryllis," Dagby said. "Elevator just opened on your level. Six guards, heavily armed, and three security bots. More on the stairwell and seconds away."

And Ivan was out there. Alone. Because she'd lost her temper and sent him away.

"Ivan." She tugged at the door. Jammed. She pounded on it again. "Open the damned door. We can secure it from this side, hold them off until we get our exit."

Muffled shouts penetrated the door. She took a step back when something heavy landed against it, stumbling as her heel caught. She looked down to see Ivan's pack, the one with the new propulsion system, propped up against the inside door frame.

"I've got this, Rilly," Ivan said in her ear. "Take the prototypes and get out of here. I'll hold them off until you and Von are safely away." He let out a pained grunt.

"No, Ivan," Amaryllis said. "We don't leave our people behind. Open the damn door and get your stupid ass in here. There aren't that many of them. We can take them together." She looked back to see Von tearing the doors off the back cabinets and setting another charge.

"Listen to her, Ivan," Navi said. "You might be as big as a mountain troll and as tough as one, but even you can't hold your own against an armed force like that. At least with all three of you, you stand a fighting chance."

"What your brother said." Amaryllis kicked the door with her heavy boots. Why wouldn't the stupid thing budge? What had he done to it? Did he plan this? She growled. She was going to kill him for putting himself in harm's way like this.

"Time to take cover." Von flipped over an empty table and pulled her away from the door, dragging her down beside him. "In three, two, one..."

She covered her ears against the percussive reverb of the blast, then peeked over the edge of the table. At the other end, the once-pristine wall had melted away from Von's shaped charge, cinderblock, and rubble spread over the floor in a half-circle.

"Did it work?" Dagby asked.

Von left the protection of the table, fanning away the settling dust. "Worked! Let's go."

She shook her head. "Not without Ivan."

"Go, Rilly," Ivan said, his voice heavy with exertion. "Von, if you found what you were looking for, get her the hells out of here. And take my pack with you." His comm fuzzed with static before going silent.

"No!" She fought off Von's attempt to steer her toward their exit. "You don't leave your team behind. Ivan, what the fuck? Just open the damn door." She kicked at it. "Ivan!"

"Amaryllis," Dagby said in a gentle voice. "Ivan is down. They tased him, shocked him until he lost consciousness. Zapped his comm, too." She blew out a breath. "Man broke the biolock to the lab so they won't get that door open without a torch or some explosives."

"He bought us time, Amaryllis. Time we need to get away."

Von picked up Ivan's pack and slung it over his shoulders with a grunt. "We can't waste it."

"Don't you worry too much about Ivan. He's a strong motherfucker," Navi said. "They didn't shoot him outright. He's still alive."

"Besides, I tagged him with like three different kinds of trackers," Cormac said, his voice oddly chipper. "No way will they be able to find and disable all of them. Not like last time." He paused, then added, "Amaryllis, that was you last time, by the way. Don't think I've forgotten about that."

She sniffed out a short laugh. "Yeah, EMPs will do that to you."

"Oh, is that what it was? Huh. Well, I've accounted for those this time around."

"Reinforcements coming in hot," Navi said. "Looks like a full squad of them, all decked out in fancy armor with lots of weapons. Whoever Hegemony is, they haven't gone for cheap on the rapid response team, that's for sure. I'm going to head out before they sweep the surrounding buildings."

"Go. Where's Trick? You two need to get back to the loft," Von said. "We'll meet you there."

"He's here."

"Yeah, I'm here. And we'll get Ivan back, Amaryllis," Trick said. He sounded out of breath. "But it'll be extremely difficult to mount a proper rescue operation if two more of our people get snatched along with Ivan so, please, get the fuck out of there now."

She put a hand on the door and closed her eyes, as if she could touch Ivan one more time. "Dammit," she breathed.

"Come on, Amaryllis." Von gave her arm a squeeze, tugging her away from the door. Away from Ivan. "Let's go."

She gave the door one more solid kick before heading into the narrow escape tunnel, the explosions Von'd set to destroy the lab and the information it held lighting the way.

25

IVAN

Ivan came to with a splitting headache and the taste of blood in his mouth. He rolled to his side with a groan, working to gather enough liquid to spit out the metallic taste.

Pushing himself up to a sitting position, he took in his surroundings. Boring white box of a room with no handle or lock on his side? Check. Complete lack of creature comforts? Check. Eerie sounds coming from outside the room? Check.

Great. So he was in a prison or a holding area of some sort. At least no one was screaming. Maybe he slept through the torture portion of the day. Or was it night? Didn't really matter.

Actually, this room looked a lot like the "Me Time" room on board the *Laughing Dragon*. Was he on a ship? The gravity felt the same as if he were planetside, so if he was, they weren't running on low grav, like many ships did to conserve power. The air was a little stale, but that could be a crappy circulation system that needed maintenance. Whoever had him disabled his comms so he couldn't contact his people or scan the area for more information. He could still be on Melorn, on board a ship, or somewhere else entirely. He had no way of knowing while he was stuck in this room.

So, his first priority was to see what he was working with.

After scrubbing his hands through his hair and down his face, he got to his feet and did some stretches to assess the damage to his body. Not too bad, considering. He made sucking owie sounds as he prodded the dark purple and deep red injuries peppering his body, checking for anything significant. Some serious bruising. The multiple prong burns from where they'd tased the shit out of him earned a wince or two. A sharp, shooting twang in his side when he tried to take a deep breath suggested a cracked at least one rib. Not surprising.

Those guards had been none too pleased when they realized he'd destroyed the biolock and fucked up the door in such a way that they couldn't get inside without some serious explosive efforts. They'd been even less happy when he knocked out almost half of them before they finally took him down.

He stumbled over to the corner to piss in the drain, sighing with relief. He slapped a waist-high panel to activate a wall spout, leaning over to scoop some of the cold water pouring from it into his mouth, rinsing away the remains of the metallic flavor and quenching his thirst. His headache eased as well, though there was nothing he could do about the myriad of aches and pains he'd accumulated.

It was worth it though, if Amaryllis and Von made good their escape. He'd heard Amaryllis pounding on the door, ordering him to open it so they could fend off Hegemony security as a team. But there was no way he'd let them get their hands on her, not if he could help it. Her safety and security came first for him. And her getting away with the new propulsion system they'd found in that testing tunnel was icing on the cake.

He dropped back down onto the sleeping slab, pondering his line of thinking. He should be mad, right? After all, she'd yelled at him and kicked him out of the lab when he suggested they destroy Bea's prototype.

But he wasn't. That was just Amaryllis letting off some steam before she cooled down long enough to ponder the wisdom of his words and realize that he wasn't trying to screw her over or play games like she'd accused him of doing in the heat of the moment.

Okay, so expecting her to think he was right was probably a step too far. But he hoped that she now realized he wasn't trying to sabotage her efforts to work her way free of The Cabal. In fact, he wholeheartedly supported her efforts. Even if she wanted to stay with The Cabal, to buy a full membership, he'd support her. He wouldn't like it, but he could work his way around to understanding her reasoning, if that's what she wanted.

Because he wanted her to be happy. She was a complicated, headstrong, hotheaded woman who made his blood boil and who frustrated the hells out of him, and he wanted her to live her best life in whatever way she chose. He just hoped he'd be in the picture somehow.

Antsy with both his line of thinking and the need to figure a way out of his predicament, he pushed to his feet again and paced the small space. Five strides in one direction, pivot, five strides in the other. It did nothing to calm the noise in his brain, though it loosened up the muscles that had stiffened when he'd been knocked out. He shook out his arms, pumping his fists down. The stabbing pain in his side reminded him that, when the time came, he'd need to fight smarter, not harder, if he didn't want to get taken out because a broken rib pierced his lungs.

Amaryllis. He imagined the fury on her face when she realized he'd locked her in that lab so she'd have a chance to escape. Shaking his head, he said, "I'm such an idiot." An idiot for having feelings for a firebrand like Amaryllis, who was either going to leave him here to rot or kill him the next time she saw him. Even when he disliked her because of what he thought she'd done and who she represented, he'd still had feelings for her. Pretty straightforward, woman-he'd-like-to-fuck feelings coupled with anger and irritation, but yeah, feelings. These days however, it was so much more complicated.

He'd been quite deeply in love before. That connection between him and the woman who would have been his wife if not for Starguard had been a steady, warming glow rather than a raging wildfire. Neela had made him feel safe and loved, right up to the point where she decided she couldn't handle the loneliness of being a Starguard spouse and quietly slipped into the arms of another while he was on the other side of the galaxy.

Amaryllis, on the other hand, frustrated him, inflamed him, tormented him, and challenged him. Every step of the way forward in their long relationship felt like a battle, with both of them fighting the steady pull between them. But was it love? *It could be*, he decided. Would the relationship last? Including the years they'd been mortal enemies, this counted as the longest relationship he'd had, outside of his crew and family.

Maybe they needed time to work each other out of their systems before going their separate ways. They'd never had a chance to truly spend quality time together. They'd had a few sips at the font of truth and openness, and dammit if he didn't like her even better for it. But not enough. He craved more.

If for no other reason, he needed to get his ass out of this room and away from wherever he was being held so he could get back to Amaryllis. They deserved to figure out what exactly they had together and meant to one another. There were, of course, other reasons to escape, but Amaryllis topped the list.

Loud footsteps and voices outside had him squaring his shoulders and planting his feet. He cracked his neck, mentally preparing himself for whatever they threw his way. He was ready.

The door slid open with a whoosh, and a band of dark blue flashed over the open doorway. They'd set a wall. If he tried to run through it, he'd bounce off with a nasty shock. Walls could be overloaded, though. If he absolutely needed to, he probably could withstand the jolt long enough to burn it out. A shitty escape plan. He wasn't at full strength at the moment, and he'd most likely be flat on his ass afterward.

On the plus side, it meant they weren't coming in. So, no torture. He sketched a rune of luck, sending thanks along with it. Torture was not on his to-do list. He'd experienced it before and would happily never participate in it again, thankyou-verymuch.

A man with pale white skin and slicked-back brown hair stood in the hall, flanked by two heavily armed bodyguards. Both guards had their "I'm a badass" faces on. Ivan swept a look over them, pegging them as low tier mercs. There was absolutely no need for that much hardware unless the body you were guarding required it of you, usually for show or because it made them feel safer. A good bodyguard carried enough weaponry to handle business, but not enough to slow them down when things went bad and they needed to move.

Ivan studied the pale man. Dressed in a tailored dark blue suit, a sky blue cravat wrapped and double-knotted around his neck in the current style, the man had no outstanding features, nothing to distinguish him from any other brown-haired white man out there in the galaxy. Flat brown eyes, average-sized nose, round face, average height. The clothing stood out more than the man himself. He looked familiar and simultaneously utterly forgettable.

"Ivan Halonen. Member of the *Laughing Dragon* crew. Former member of Starguard, dishonorably discharged after being convicted of sales and distribution of illegal narcotics," the man said in a bored tone, as if reading from a file.

Ivan crossed his arms. "We were set up, but otherwise yeah, that's me. And you are?"

The man cocked his head. "You don't know who you stole from?"

"You mean retrieved stolen property from?" Ivan said, conveniently leaving out that they had, in fact, stolen that other prototype.

"I do not." The man tugged at his suit jacket lapels. A gold signet ring flashed on his left hand. "You may call me Mr. Martin. I represent the Obdurate Collective."

Obdurate Collective. Ivan stored away that bit of information. Seemed like he'd heard that name recently but how were they related to Hegemony then? Their parent company maybe? The group who ran it? Something to add to the file of information they were slowly collecting to pass along to the Knight and his Shields. Let Rhain handle it in whatever way he saw fit. Dealing with the powers behind this collective or the ramification of another player entering the ongoing race to control space travel was above his pay grade.

Ivan was guessing, but he didn't get the impression that Martin was the big boss. It was possible he was somewhere up the food chain, if that fancy suit was any indication. No matter who he was or where he was in the Obdurate Collective hierarchical structure, Martin's name and any tidbit of information he let slip could be important.

"That building's owned by Hegemony, Martin," Ivan said. "Not Obdurate."

Martin's lips flattened when Ivan purposefully left off the 'mister' but didn't take the bait. "It is my job to do whatever is necessary to retrieve our property. At present, you are my collateral for getting it back."

"Collateral?" Ivan cocked his head. Did they think to exchange him for the prototype?

The man gave him a patronizing smile. "A pawn in the game, if you will."

"Game?" Ivan asked. He sounded like a fool, repeating the man's words back to him. Getting information out of people in this manner was not his forte. He was better with weapons than words, and his hands itched to wrap around Martin's throat so he could squeeze the intel out of him.

Martin adjusted his cravat, his finger brushing over a sapphire clasp. "Only the most important game of our lifetimes. Whomever controls the space lanes, wins."

His bodyguards looked bored.

"So, you believe that this propulsion system will give your group the advantage in this game?" A wash of anger swept over him. It wasn't a game. They were playing with people's livelihoods and, in many cases, with their lives. But to these big conglomerates, it was all about power and money, rather than what was best for their fellow sentient being and the galaxy as a whole.

Martin huffed. "Obviously, whoever hired you to steal it from us believes the same."

He was mistaken about Ivan's reasons for stealing it. Ivan didn't bother to correct him. "And you think you can use me to get it back?"

"Exactly."

Ivan rocked back on his heels. "Okay, I get it. You think that the people I broke into your secret building with are really going to trade what they took in exchange for me. Ha." He shook his head. "You do realize that they're a bunch of pirates and pirates, well, they don't do ransom or exchanges. Your property and the people who took it are long gone."

Martin's patronizing smile never wavered. "From what I understand, the female in that group was rather put out when we took you down. My people reported she yelled at you that they didn't leave people behind, or some such sappy nonsense. So, pirates or not, I believe they will choose to cooperate."

Strange that Martin didn't call Amaryllis by her name. Unless he didn't know who she was, and this first meeting was to gather information. He was attempting blackmail without having all the pieces. Ivan had time to turn the tables.

He shrugged, playing it off like he didn't care what Amaryllis said. "Yeah, that woman, she's got a temper, for sure. But, once she cools down, she'll forget about me and go about her business." His heart squeezed when he said that. Hells, he hoped it wasn't true. That would really suck. "You won't get any type of cooperation from her."

A small frown flickered across Martin's face. Ivan allowed himself a moment of triumph. The moment didn't last.

"You'd best hope she cooperates," the man said. "Or we will

have to do things the hard way, and I don't think you want us to take that route."

He flicked his fingers at the guard to his left. The door to Ivan's prison slid shut, sealing him inside.

"Yep," Ivan said, lacing his hands behind his head and rocking back on his heels. "That went well."

26

AMARYLLIS

"Well, that was a disaster," Amaryllis said, flopping onto the couch and covering her eyes with her forearm.

"Not a complete disaster," Trick said. "We got what we went in there for."

"And lost Ivan in the process." Navi distributed bottles of beer to everyone present.

"We'll get him back from those fuckers. That, I guarantee. Even if we have to take down everyone in that building to do it." Amaryllis lifted the cold drink to her mouth and downed half the bottle. Her anger burned right through any effects of the alcohol.

From the safety of the *Dog's Day*, Cormac cleared his throat. "It appears Ivan is no longer in the Hegemony building. In fact, he's no longer on the planet."

Her hands tightened on the bottle as a drop of condensation landed on her chest. "Where is he then?" It had only been a few hours since they made their escape, leaving the lab smoldering behind them. How in the three hells had they gotten Ivan off the planet so quickly?

"Not sure." Cormac tugged at his earlobe. "We lost his signal several times along the way."

"Cormac, the fuck, man. What about those three trackers you were so proud of, huh?" Navi practically quivered, his muscles were so tense. He looked like he wanted to punch something. Hard.

Amaryllis completely understood.

Dagby looked up from her holoscreen. "We figure they transported him from the lab to a dock in something that blocked our trackers' signals." She glanced at Cormac, who looked grim. "They then loaded him onto a shuttle that took him directly to a ship."

Amaryllis sprang to her feet. "And so? Where is he? We need to get after that ship, board it. With extreme prejudice." She itched to get moving. The longer Ivan was in their hands, the larger the chance they'd hurt him or kill him, if they hadn't already. She needed him alive.

Dagby licked her lips and glanced at Cormac again. "Well, that's the thing. We don't know where the ship went after it left its orbit around Melorn."

"All our trackers died bare minutes after the shuttle docked on that ship," Cormac said.

Her heart in her throat, she swallowed hard. "Tell me you were able to tag that ship or at least get an identifier off it so we can find it?"

Cormac shook his head. Dagby said, "If it had been docked on Cora with us, maybe. But it was in orbit over the western edge of the city, too far from our location."

"Shit!" She threw her bottle at the plasticine wall, splattering beer and foam across the white surface. The bottle clinked to the floor. Made of a plasticine composite, the bottle didn't even give her the satisfaction of shattering like one made of real glass would. "Godsdammit all," she said, slumping.

Navi slipped an arm over her shoulder. "Ivan's a tough bastard, and he knows we'll come for him. It just might take us a little longer than we'd hoped."

She felt his tension, like heat rising from his body, and

wrapped an arm around his waist. Together, they took a moment to breathe. "Ivan's going to be fine," she whispered. "We'll find him."

"We'll find him and, if they've hurt him at all, we'll make them pay," he whispered back, planting a kiss on the top of her head.

"Sorry, everyone," Cormac said, looking shamefaced and upset. "I really thought at least one of those trackers would survive."

Dagby patted his arm.

Still leaning against Navi, Amaryllis stared down at her hand, wet with condensation from the bottle. She couldn't believe that he'd sacrificed himself so she could get away. On top of that, he'd left the other prototype with her. She'd been so wrong when she told him he was playing games, that he wanted to keep the system for his own purposes. Her yelling at him was the last thing he was going to remember of her.

Von drained his beer and tossed the bottle in the recycler. "We need to get off this planet."

"Strip it down and pack it up," Trick said, grabbing his duffle bag. He picked up one of the half-finished explosives Von had been putting together. "Guess we have to leave this stuff behind."

Cormac brightened, waggling a finger at him. "You're not the only one who wants that prototype back, which means the faster we can get you off the planet, the better," he said. "There's a shuttle waiting for you at the dock."

"Who?" Von asked.

"Sweet." Trick gave a fist pump. "VIP service. Now, we won't have to leave anything behind. Thanks, man."

Von adjusted his pack, checking the weight. "Good thing, too, because there was no way security would let us on board the big elevator with everything we took from Hegemony."

"We definitely do not want people asking us those types of questions," Dagby said.

"You can thank Bea's sister and the Knight for that," Cormac said, a smirk curling his lip.

"Some day," Amaryllis said, "you're going to have to tell us how you know the Knight so well."

"Ask Ivan," Navi said.

Von opened his mouth then closed it and shook his head. "You know what? I don't even want to know. As long as we have a ride, I'm good."

Letting the chatter wash over her, Amaryllis gave Navi one more squeeze before she picked up her bag and began packing. Her mind focused on Ivan and how they were going to find him, much less rescue him. They could trace the origin of the ships that docked at Cora Station those in orbit over Waroc in the last twenty-four hours. They could dig deeper into Hegemony, try and connect that company to the shuttles. They could break back into Hegemony and download all their data on the off chance there was a piece of information that would lead them to where they were holding Ivan.

But all that would take too much time. Time Ivan didn't have. She had no idea why they were holding him prisoner. It would have been easier to turn him over to the Melornian authorities for the myriad of crimes they'd committed in that building. There had to be a reason they took him when the easiest solution was to remove him from the equation completely.

Her heart clenched. No good would come of her thinking that. Ivan would be fine; she'd just have to do something horrible to get him back, the last thing she wanted to do. She was going to have to ask Lore for help.

Back on the *Dog's Day*, Amaryllis locked their prizes away in the armory for safekeeping. She might need one or both to do what needed to be done.

As soon as they arrived on board, she'd sent out her messages, putting into motion what her crew claimed was a ridiculous plan.

"Are you sure about this, Amaryllis?" Dagby studied her friend's face with a worried expression. "What if, I don't know, Lore's feeling uncooperative and, instead of being helpful, makes what we have to do even more challenging?"

"She's always feeling uncooperative, Dagby. That's her standard M.O. You know this." Amaryllis stood in the common room. They'd cleaned up the mess Cormac and Dagby had made during their time docked at Cora Station, the room put back to rights. "It'll be fine. Don't worry." But the muscles in her shoulders were so tight, she felt like they were up around her ears.

"If you're sure." Dagby gave her a long look. She must have believed what she saw there because she sighed and said, "Fine. We trust you to do what's best for the crew. Don't burn any bridges." She dragged her friend forward and wrapped her in a hug.

Amaryllis sank into the affection, needing the comfort Dagby provided more than she realized. The tension didn't completely leave her, but at least she felt like she could take a deep breath again. "I'll do my best."

"I'm serious," Dagby leaned back so she could look Amaryllis in the eyes. "You'd better count to ten, put away any explosives, and back away. Don't let Lore goad you into losing that infamous temper of yours."

"I don't have a temper."

"Haha. Very funny." Dagby tightened her arms around Amaryllis's middle, squeezing her tightly.

She tapped her friend on the back. "Struggling to breathe here."

"Sorry." Dagby released Amaryllis from her clutches. "I'm worried about you. Ivan is the first person besides us that you've let get close to you since I've known you, and now he's in danger. You have every reason to not be thinking clearly."

Amaryllis leaned a hip on the arm of the sofa. "I'm fine, Dags.

Recent events have crystalized some things in my brain. I have a plan, a good plan..."

"A ridiculously wild plan that has maybe a one percent chance of succeeding," Dagby muttered, narrowing her eyes.

She ignored her. "A good plan," she reiterated, "that, yes, might come with some risks, but the rewards will set us up for an even better future than we dreamed." At least, that was the idea. Dagby was being pessimistic with her one percent chance of success. It was more like an eighteen percent chance. Maybe twenty-two percent.

"Fine. Fine!" Dagby threw up her arms and turned to leave, but not before pointing a stiff finger at her. "Just be careful. Think before you open that big mouth of yours."

"I don't have a big mouth," she shouted after Dagby, the common room door swishing closed behind her.

With a groan, she flopped back onto the sofa and stared blankly at the ceiling. What if she was wrong about all this? What if they killed Ivan before she could put her plan into action? What if he was already dead? What if Lore never responded? What if she didn't take what Amaryllis was offering in exchange for her help? What if Lore didn't know what was going on and couldn't give any help, no matter what Amaryllis promised her? What if Ivan wasn't on that ship still, and everything she was doing was for nothing? Too many questions. Zero answers.

She dug the heels of her palms into her eyes, rubbing them until she saw sparks on the back of her eyelids. "What am I doing? Why am I doing all this?" She had the two prototypes. If she let Ivan rot, she could hand the original albeit junked one over to Lore and sell the other, probably make a very tidy profit that would set her and her crew up for a good long time.

But she couldn't make herself do it. Maybe, if she were actually the cold-hearted pirate Lore wanted her to be, had tried to teach her to be, she could leave Ivan to his fate without a qualm or a pinch of conscience. Maybe, if she didn't love that big idiot, she could leave it up to his own crew to rescue him.

She sat up, her eyes wide. She loved him? *Fuck*, she thought. She did. She loved him. From the top of his ginger head to those giant clodhoppers he called feet, she loved every ridiculous part of him.

And it scared her to her very toes. Loving someone meant baring your soul to them, sharing the darkest bits of yourself with another individual. It meant trusting that person implicitly, knowing that person looked out for you and had your best interests at heart and vice versa.

And she trusted Ivan. He put his life on the line to protect her. He gave her the new prototype with no strings attached, jammed that lab door behind him knowing that she might grab it and walk away without a backward glance. Such a fucking idiot.

A gentle chime sounded, pulling her from her thoughts. She got to her feet. It was time.

"Lore's on the line," Von said over the ship's comm system. "Do what you have to do. We're with you, no matter the outcome. And watch your temper."

Why did everyone keep saying that to her? She patted her head, checking her hair, and ran a finger under her eyes, clearing away any dampness that remained. Tugging at the hem of her shirt, she took a deep breath and said, "Put her through."

A three-dimensional image of Lore blinked into the space in front of her. She looked much like she always did, dressed in a tailored pantsuit that nipped in at the waist and fell in a straight line to the floor, her blonde hair twisted into a chignon at the base of her neck. Amaryllis pictured her standing in her cold office, the wall of weapons arrayed behind her. She wondered if there was anyone else present, but there was no way to know for certain. Lore had shared only her own holo and nothing else for this call.

"Amaryllis," Lore said, sweeping her eyes over her adoptive daughter. "I heard about your little adventure."

Deep breaths. She's trying to get you off kilter from the get-go. Don't lose your temper, she reminded herself. *You have a plan.*

Follow it. "Lore. Thank you for meeting with me. And yes, we had an adventure. A successful one, in fact."

Lore raised one perfectly plucked eyebrow. "Explain to me how losing one of your team members could be considered a success."

How in the three hells did she already know that Ivan had been captured? She knew for dead certain that no one on her team or Ivan's had said anything. She'd have to sweep the ship for bugs again, even though Von already did that the moment they left the *Ephemeris*. "Losing a team member is not ideal, no. However, we did manage to get our hands on the prototype."

"Wonderful. Bring it to me." Lore reached forward, as if to disconnect from the call.

"Not so fast, Lore. There are a few things to settle before I even considering turning the item over to you."

She straightened, folding her arms over her chest. "Is that so?"

"It is." Amaryllis swallowed hard, trying to dislodge the lump in her throat. She'd never been great at standing up to Lore, especially not face-to-face. All her rebellions had been sneaky ones, less under Lore's nose and more behind her back. She generally avoided head-on confrontations with her. But she'd do what had to be done for the sake of Ivan and for the sake of her crew. Her family.

"Well?" Lore asked, cracking out the word like the snap of a whip.

She squared her shoulders. "First, I want to know where Ivan is."

"And why do you believe I have this information?" Lore studied her nails, pretending to be bored by the whole conversation.

But Amaryllis knew better. This was how Lore tested her, acting as if she didn't care what Amaryllis did, how she got her intel, or solved the puzzles set before her. Fine. She'd play Lore's game, for Ivan's sake. "He was taken from a Hegemony building. On Cora Station, you arranged for Christophe and Deno to use a shuttle owned by a group called The Obdurate Collective. Hegemony is one of their subsidiaries."

Cormac and Dagby had been busy. There was definite high-fiving when they found that intriguing connection.

"Maybe I just bought them a place on that shuttle."

"Possible but not probable. You don't spend money unless absolutely necessary and, because you're working with the people running this company, you merely used your connections."

"If what you say is correct and I'm working with these people, then why would I want to steal the prototype from them? It would make more sense if I let them have it," Lore said.

"Not if they were shutting you out." Amaryllis knew she was on the right track when Lore's eyes narrowed ever so slightly. "You invested time and money in this company. Probably resources, too. I figure it all started when you somehow learned of this new propulsion system and its potential — you've got connections everywhere, after all — and decided that it would be a smart move to make sure The Cabal wouldn't be left behind when the new tech wave came."

"How?" Lore asked.

"I have some very smart people on my team," Amaryllis said with a casual shrug. Much of it was guesswork, but, based on Lore's reaction, they'd gotten it right. "Honestly, it's not such a surprise that a rogue company working with stolen technology would try to weasel out of its promises to its investors. Unfortunately for them, they didn't realize The Cabal doesn't take betrayal lightly."

Lore tipped her head. "Very good, Amaryllis. I'm impressed."

No matter her age, no matter how much she tried to distance herself from Lore, those words never failed to make her stand taller. She and her people had impressed Lore. But that didn't change the situation they were currently in. "And now that I've satisfied your curiosity, where is Ivan?"

Lore shrugged. "I don't have that information and even if I did, I wouldn't give it to you."

27

AMARYLLIS

Amaryllis's heart sank. "What?"

Lore laced her fingers together behind her back. "I know you heard me, Amaryllis. Now, understand this: you cannot go after that man. I forbid it."

Her brain stuttered. Surely, she'd misheard. "What?" Amaryllis asked again, though she didn't expect the answer to change.

"That man is far too closely linked to the Shields," Lore said. "We may have a cease fire with them, but that is barely worth the ink it took to scratch it out on the back of a napkin."

"But..."

Before she could get more than a word out, Lore cut her off. "I allowed you time to scratch the itch, to work him out of your system. I even allowed you to use his talents to steal back my prototype. But him getting caught is not our problem. Let the Knight deal with that. You, I want back here at base along with my item."

"No." Just saying the word made Amaryllis feel like she'd grabbed a live wire, giving her the jolt of her life.

For a scant second, Lore looked just as shocked as Amaryllis felt. "What did you say to me?" Her voice was low and deadly.

Amaryllis squared her shoulders, planted her feet, and looked Lore in her holographic eye. "I said, 'No'."

Lore rocked back on her heels. "No, what?"

"No." Amaryllis swallowed hard. *Be direct*, she reminded herself, *and most of all, keep your temper in check*. There was nothing to be gained from losing her temper and yelling. It would make her look like a child having a tantrum, not the strong, capable woman she was. A loss of temper had its time and its place, and this was not it.

With every muscle in her body clenched tight, her spine stiff with resolve, she said, "No, we're not going to leave Ivan to rot. No, we're not going to bring you the prototype. No, we're not going to follow your orders any longer." Lifting her chin, she took a deep breath. It was now or never. "As of today, my crew and I are no longer part of The Cabal. We are cutting ties and going solo."

The barest hint of a smile crossed Lore's face, so fast Amaryllis would have missed it, had she not been watching her every facial twitch. "Is that so." The tone was so low and deadly, she wondered if she'd imagined the smile.

Amaryllis gave a slow nod. "It is."

"We'll see about that." And with that ominous statement, Lore ended the call.

Her legs suddenly jelly, Amaryllis sank to the couch and put her head between her knees trying to remember how to breathe properly. What the fuck had she done? Would they even survive a day on their own? What if Lore loosed the full force of The Cabal on them and made their lives more difficult and dangerous than the lowest of the three hells? *Oh, gods.* Had she condemned them all?

The common room door swished open, and Dagby wrapped her in her arms. "You did so good. I'm so proud of you."

Another set of arms joined Dagby's as Trick sank down on her other side, enveloping her in physical support and comfort.

Amaryllis snorted out a thick giggle.

"Amaryllis?" Dagby said. "You okay?"

She giggled again, slapping her hand over her mouth as it turned into a snort.

Trick coughed out a laugh and then it was all over. All three of them were laughing hysterically, holding onto one another for dear life.

"Oh, gods. I've as good as signed out death warrants," Amaryllis said between cackles.

"At least we'll be free." Dagby giggled, her head pressed against Amaryllis's arm.

"And we'll go out in a blaze of glory," Trick added, giving the pair a squeeze.

Finally, the mad laughter died down, and they all took a deep, cleansing breath. The arms loosened enough to let her sit up. Though Dagby and Trick remained pressed up against her, a show of moral support.

Navi crouched in front of her, his hands on her knees. "It had to be done. This is a good thing."

"Is it?" She put her hands over her face. "I don't know. What if this backfires spectacularly? No one up and quits The Cabal. They won't let us. You heard her." She pitched her voice lower and in her best Lore impression said, "We'll see about that."

Navi shook his head. "It will be okay."

"Just because you got out, and you're still alive and kicking doesn't mean the same thing's will happen for us. Everyone thinks that Lore's been grooming me to take over The Cabal. She won't let me go. She'll lose face, and we all know how she feels about that."

Dagby and Trick exchanged looks.

"Yeah, see." Amaryllis pointed at them. "You know what I'm talking about. The woman does not like to lose her toys. Ask Navi."

Navi patted her knee and got to his feet. "It'll be alright," he repeated. "I have the feeling this is the path that you were meant to take."

"What if I've doomed us all? Have you ever head of anyone

excluding Navi who left The Cabal? No? That's because they're all dead. Either Lore went after them or someone else in The Cabal did. We do have enemies, you know."

"You might, but not me." Dagby sniffed. "Everyone likes me."

Amaryllis scrubbed her hands over her eyes. "Doesn't matter. You're a deserter now. We're fair game."

Dagby rolled her eyes. "Deserter? What is this, Starguard?"

"Hey, don't pre-worry about stuff that might not happen," Trick said.

"Exactly. And if it does, well, we'll handle it like we always do. Better than average, even." Dagby gave her another squeeze before letting her go.

Von burst into the room in a very unVon-like fashion. He pulled up his comm and flung something at the room's panels. "This just came in, routed through a bunch of back channels. It's Lore's signature."

"Are those coordinates?" Dagby tilted her head as she squinted at the image.

Von nodded. "Think so. And it says Amaryllis should check her messages."

With a frown, Amaryllis double tapped her wrist, waking her comm. There was a message from Lore. She closed her eyes for a second to steel herself for what was inside before accessing the message.

Amaryllis,

From the moment we found you on that ghost ship, a survivor despite the odds, you had my heart. I know I don't show it to you, that I make you work for every morsel of approval and affection. That is for your own safety. If they have any idea of how much I care for you, you would become a bigger target than you already are.

If you truly want to part ways with The Cabal, I won't stop you. In fact, I encourage you to follow your own path. You never were bloodthirsty or cold enough to thrive in this environment, and that softness will get you killed someday if you stay. You are smart to have surrounded yourself with strong, dependable people who believe in you and support you.

However, I cannot let you go without some form of trade or payment to satisfy not only the board but the other members. They must believe I squeezed you and made it painful before I kicked you to the curb. You said you have the prototype. That will satisfy them. Credits would, too. You know the cost to buy in; it's double to cash out. Your choice. But make it quickly, before The Cabal decides for you.

I will be keeping my eye on you. Don't think you've gotten out of our little talks just because you are no longer under my thumb.

-Lore

P.S. I sent you a small going away gift. Fetch Ivan. His connections may very well keep you alive long enough for you to give me grandchildren.

"Um, Amaryllis? That is the palest I've ever seen you," Dagby twisted in her seat so she could get a better look. "What is it?"

She opened her mouth to answer and closed it again. How could she possibly distill what Lore said down to answer that question when she wasn't even sure how to parse it herself? With a shake of her head, she threw it up on the screen for all to read. No point in hiding anything from her crew now. Better that they know what they were truly in for by staying on this ship and continuing down the new path they were blazing.

The room was silent while everyone read Lore's message.

"Here, you look like you need this," Navi said quietly, handing Amaryllis a glass with three fingers of whiskey.

She took a big slug, the drink burning a path down her esophagus.

"Oh... shit," Von breathed. "That's intense."

"Grandchildren? She wants you to give her grandchildren?" Dagby asked, grabbing the glass from Amaryllis and knocking the rest of it back. "Holy cats."

"Right?" Amaryllis accepted a fresh glass from Navi with a nod. She took another mouthful, appreciating the burn as it morphed into a warm glow that eased her tension. She sank deeper into the soft couch cushions, staring at Lore's words on the big screen.

That message rocked her entire worldview. Cold, scary, perfectionist Lore truly cared for her. Not that Amaryllis thought Lore hated her, but Lore had never been one to show emotion, much less affection. She had a bare inkling of Lore's feelings, formed over time as she got better at reading her microexpressions and responses. But, since Lore never fully dropped her mask, not even for Amaryllis, she hadn't been positive. This message, though. Wow.

"Well, that's certainly something. And here I thought Lore was just icy as the second hell. Incredibly effective as the leader of a bunch of pirates, pretty shit as a parent," Trick said.

Navi refilled Dagby's glass before setting the half-full bottle of whiskey on the coffee table. "I would never have even suspected that Lore was interested in grandchildren. Especially from Ivan." Navi shuddered. "Of course, there's no accounting for taste."

Dagby reached over and punched him in the arm.

"Thank you," Amaryllis said.

"Of course. That's what friends are for." She shrugged. "So, are we going to talk about this?" She gestured at Lore's message.

"No." Amaryllis drained her glass and pulled the message off the big screen. "In fact, the contents of this message are never to be discussed outside this room. Is that understood? That includes you two." She pointed at Navi and Cormac.

Cormac nodded.

"No idea what message you're talking about," Navi said. "Let's get my brother home safe and sound, okay?"

She paused, making sure she had confirmation from everyone else in the room. They sat in silence for a moment, absorbing the massive shift-change that had just happened.

"Now, we have some time to decide how we're going to handle her requirement for cutting ties. We'll decide what's best for us as a crew. It'll be okay," she said, reassuring her crew as much as for herself. Right now, she needed to believe that everything was going to work out, or she'd wind up in a ball on the floor.

"It will be." Dagby reached over and squeezed her hand.

"Like I've said, we're with you. One hundred percent," Von said.

"And I have some thoughts about those requirements of hers," Dagby said, then waved them off when she saw the look on Amaryllis's face. "But they can wait."

"They'll have to because right now, Ivan needs us." Taking a deep breath, Amaryllis tucked her thoughts and emotions about Lore into a corner to deal with later. Ivan's predicament took precedence over her mommy issues. There would be time to process after he was safely back with her. "Cormac, little help?"

He jumped up, rubbing his hands together. "Right. The coordinates." Cormac drew a red box around them and moving them to the top right corner while Dagby got to work, tracing their trajectory.

"We can't rush in there, wherever there is. We need a plan," Von said.

"Coordinates are for a quadrant of space not far from Badin." Cormac narrowed in on a sector of the star map.

Dagby's fingers flew over the holo keyboard floating in front of her. "No stations or structures there. None registered, anyway."

"A ship?" Von asked, watching the screen as their tech duo zoomed in on the area.

"Most likely." Cormac said. "We're not close enough for a scan, but those coordinates are a ways off the main space lane between Badin and Cinzia, but close enough that they could make it planetside in a few hours. If I had to guess, I'd say our Ivan-nappers are parked over here, either waiting for instructions or meeting up with someone."

Her brain still not running at full speed after Lore's bombshell of a message, Amaryllis nodded, letting the team pull on the threads and see where they led.

Navi jumped to his feet and started pacing. "We need to bust in there and get him. What are we waiting for?"

"Well, for one, they'll probably toss him out the airlock and jump away if we did that." Cormac shook his head. "No, we need to be smart about this. Take it slowly."

"Why not do what's worked for us in the past?" Trick asked. "We jump in somewhere nearby, disable their drive, sucker onto the side of their ship, and take it before they realize we're there."

"No way." Navi slashed his hand through the air. "That pirate shit is dangerous. By cutting the hull, we run the risk of depressurizing the entire ship. Add in the fact that we don't know exactly where they're holding Ivan and..."

Tuning out what was devolving into a mercenaries versus pirates argument, Amaryllis tugged at her bottom lip, her eyes distant as she ran scenarios in her mind. Navi was right. They couldn't go in there, guns blazing. That would be the fastest way to get Ivan killed. No, they needed to get onto that ship with stealth. But Trick also had a point. They needed to move quickly before the other ship had a chance to react.

When they finally settled down, Amaryllis said, "I have an idea."

28

IVAN

His arms folded behind his head, Ivan lay on the hard sleeping slab and stared at the flat white plasticine ceiling as he considered his options. One, he could stay here and let them try and make a trade with Amaryllis. Even if she agreed to the exchange, he didn't trust these guys to keep their word. Something told him that they were more the "crush any opposition beneath their boot heels" kind of people rather than the type to stick to their agreements.

Two, the next time they opened his door, he could rush them. However, if they got the wall in place before he crossed the threshold, he ran the risk of taking enough of a jolt that it would knock him out or kill him. He was pretty sure he'd survive, but gods, that did not sound like much fun.

What did sound like fun was option three. As he choked down the rock-hard protein bar someone shoved through the food slot at the bottom of his door earlier, he remembered something. When they'd first brought Bea on board the *Laughing Dragon* after her rescue, Quin had the bright idea of locking her in the "Me Time" room for a cool-down period. Because his captain had well and truly fucked up that job, Bea was pissed, fighting Quin every step of the way, culminating in a devastating knee shot by her to his twig and berries. Even more unfortunately for Quin, Bea was much smarter than him, freeing herself from the holding cell by carving into the plasticine to access the locking mechanism and disabling it. She then sabotaged their engines and absconded in one of their escape pods. Seriously, Quin was so far out of his league with Bea. He'd better treat her like a veritable goddess or he'd risk losing her.

Ivan decided to take a page from her book.

As soon as another protein bar slid through the food slot, Ivan was on his feet, pressing his ear to the door. The sound of boots paused in front of one more door, then carried on down the corridor. When they dumped him in here, they'd take his boots, his belt, and all his weapons, leaving him with just his shirt and his pants. No doubt they thought they'd stripped him of everything useful, but they didn't have access to someone like Safina.

During their preparations to crash the black market auction, she'd outfitted Quin, Bea, and Ivan with all kinds of fun little items that looked innocuous but actually served other purposes. Like the dragon tattoo running up the outside of his left calf. While he was a big fan of dragons — his clan had a red fire-breathing dragon as part of their crest — this particular dragon tattoo wasn't real but it hid a very useful secret.

Pulling up his left pant leg, he peeled back the top of the drag-on's head, wincing as the tattoo's adhesive pulled away from his leg hairs to reveal a slim piece of metal underneath.

But it didn't neatly slide out when he pulled on it. He frowned, giving it a tug. The skin on his leg stretched, but the metal remained firmly stuck between the fake tattoo and the skin beneath. He cursed. The tattoo was supposed to act like a sheath, one that fooled scanners into thinking it was real skin. He'd used something like it before and it'd come off with a gentle tug at the leg hairs. But this time, it was well and truly adhered, the metal he needed inaccessible. If he were on his ship, he'd hit up the medi-bay and get a solvent to unstick it. Alas. And he needed that damn metal shim or he'd have to go with one of the other much shittier options if to get out of here.

He tried to slowly peel it back a bit more, hoping that by revealing more of the metal, he could work it free. But that slow peel only resulted in tingling bursts of pain as his leg hairs plucked out one by one. The metal wasn't budging.

Fuck. He didn't have time for this. Someone patrolled through the area on a regular rotation, and there was no telling when that weasely little man, Martin, would visit again. He needed to get on with his escape project before that happened.

He'd have to rip the fake tattoo off all in one go.

Sucking in several short, sharp breaths to prepare himself, he gripped the top of the dragon tattoo's head, holding his skin taut with his other hand, and gave an experimental tug. The bolt of pain had him cursing Safina for giving him this torture device. She probably did it on purpose, knowing it would basically wax his leg when he went to remove it. Sadistic woman.

Giving himself the worst pep talk ever, he chanted under his breath, "Fuck. Just do it. Just pull. Pull hard and fast. Get it over with. You have to do it. Fuck."

He sucked in a couple more sharp breaths. Then, holding the last breath, he gave a mighty yank, ripping the adhesive free from his calf along with all the hairs beneath it. Tears sprang to his eyes, and he had to rest his head on his knee for a minute before the pain faded to manageable levels. Holy shit, he never wanted to do that again.

But the dragon tattoo was off, the thin strip of metal accessible. He had a smooth strip of skin on his calf, his reminder to never trust Safina's smile when she handed him a present, especially one that attached to his body.

He tugged the metal free of the adhesive and began the slow process of chipping away at the plasticine to access the door lock.

IT TOOK one more pass of a guard down the corridor before Ivan had his access point. He dug into the locking mechanism, manipulating the wires so a jolt of electricity zapped the lock. The door popped open an inch. Tucking both the tattoo and the metal shim into a pocket, he pried the door open the rest of the way. After a quick check, he stepped out into the empty corridor and slid the door back into place.

He didn't have a lot of time before the guard came back through on patrol. With the door back in place, there was a good chance no one would notice he was gone until they tried to open it. But the way his luck had been running, he didn't want to test it. Better to move forward with his plans before the whole ship was alerted to his escape and looking for him.

It sucked to work with so little intel. He had no idea how many crew members were on board. If absolutely necessary, two people could fly the *Dragon*, as long as everything was functional, and they employed the autopilot. But it could hold a full crew of twenty. He thought this ship was a similar type as his, though he'd only seen the holding cells, so he couldn't be sure. At the bare minimum, there might be six other people on board — Martin, his two bodyguards, the person patrolling the corridors, and two people flying the ship. At most, twenty. And he wouldn't be taking them all on at once. He could work with that.

Pausing in front of the cell next to his, he put his ear against the door. He was practically positive there was someone in there. The patrol had stopped there like they'd done by his, and it sounded like there was someone moving around in there. Should he take the chance and open it? His escape plan would go much smoother with a second pair of hands to help make it happen. On the flip side, it could be disastrous if he released the individual in this cell and it was, say, one of the crew tossed in there to sleep off a bender.

Ivan managed to bite back a yelp when a hand shot out through the food slot in the bottom of the door and grabbed his bare ankle.

"Get me out of here," a voice said in a harsh whisper.

"Let go of me," Ivan said, keeping his voice quiet as he yanked his ankle out of their grip. That voice sounded familiar. Where had he heard it before?

"You gonna let me out of here?"

"Maybe," Ivan said. "Who are you?"

"Christophe. If you let me out, I'll put in a good word for you with The Cabal," he said. "I know people. I've got connections to people at the top."

Ah. That's why he knew the voice. The shitty dresser from that bar on Cora, the obnoxious one in the pair Lore had sent to retrieve the prototype. How in the three hells had he wound up here? He frowned, his brain processing the implications of Christophe's presence. Better to leave him or risk freeing him?

Christophe hadn't left Ivan with a positive first impression and Amaryllis hated the guy, but leaving him here would only give these Obdurate people another pawn to play with or, when Lore refused to play, another body to dispose of. *Fuck.* He should have kept moving, ignored the fact that there was another human being in Martin's hands. He had to spring him and bring him along.

He pressed a hand to the biolock. It beeped angrily and turned red. Of course it did. Couldn't be one of those locks that merely needed a sentient being on the proper side of the door to open, could it? It would be really nice if luck swung his way for once instead of him having to brute force his way through things. He pulled out his trusty piece of metal, jammed it into the base of the lock, and gave it a sharp twist, shorting it out. The door popped open an inch.

Christophe wrapped his fingers around the edge and gave it a hard tug, peeking through the opening. His eyes widened when he saw Ivan on the other side. "You," he said, stuttering to a halt.

"Hey." Ivan gave him a chin tip. "No time to get into it all. Guard will be back around soon, and we need to be gone from here," he said, forcing the door open the rest of the way. This wasn't a good idea, but he didn't want to leave someone locked in a cell and at the mercy of these guys, even if that someone was Christophe.

Christophe slipped through, and together they slid the door back into place. "What's the plan?" he asked. "Escape pods?"

"Not yet. First, we need to disable the engines so they can't come after us," Ivan said, noting that Christophe looked a little worse for wear. They'd stripped him of everything but his ratty flower print shirt and ripped pants. Cuts and bruises covered nearly every inch of visible skin.

"Right. No point in taking a pod if they can just scoop us right back up." Christophe paused, then added, "Or shoot us out of the sky. Ship has a weapon system, too."

"Well, shit." He should have expected that. The *Dragon* had one as well, though it was pretty basic. Quin was always complaining about not having enough funds to upgrade it. "You saw it?"

He nodded. "You didn't?"

"I was out when they brought me on board. Woke up in that white room, no idea where I was."

Christophe rubbed a hand over the back of his neck, wincing when he touched the large bruise blossoming there. "They worked me over pretty good, then threw me on a shuttle. Saw a handful of weapon ports as we approached. One shot from those, and any escape pod would be reduced to scrap."

"Okay." Ivan took a deep breath as he saw his simple, straightforward plan disappear in a puff of smoke. Typical for plans like that — they started out on track but swiftly went off the rails — but frustrating, nonetheless. He'd have to plan on the fly. At least he had plenty of practice at it. "First, let's hit engineering, slow them down. We'll figure the rest out from there."

"Right behind you."

They moved down the corridor, their bare feet sliding silently over the cool flooring.

"You know where you're going?" Christophe whispered.

"Like the back of my hand," he said, taking a right turn and heading down a ladder to the bottom level. He knew well enough where he was going. Like he thought, this ship was a Vanid design like the *Laughing Dragon*, which meant the layout was similar. And thank the goddess because it made what he needed to do a whole lot simpler with a ship type and systems he was familiar with. It was bigger, though, and newer. Maybe one of the updated E-classes. Maybe his luck was improving. He sketched out a rune to give it a boost.

He took a quick peek around the corner into engineering, then held up two fingers for his fellow prisoner. He indicated he'd take the one on the right, then signaled for Christophe to take the one on the left.

Christophe nodded, his body tensed for action.

Silently, Ivan counted down. At the signal, the two of them sprang forward, taking the engineers by surprise.

"That was easier than I thought," Christophe said, his hands on his hips as he looked at the men unconscious on the floor.

"Get them out of sight. Storage lockers." Ivan pointed to the other end of the room. "You do that while I disable the system."

Ignoring Christophe's complaints about having to do the grunt work, Ivan got to work on the drive. Since it was a Vanid and they all tended to be the same no matter the size or what ship they were in, he had little difficulty messing things up enough to take the propulsion system offline while allowing the important bits like life support to keep functioning.

"You done yet?" Christophe asked, coming up behind Ivan to stare over his shoulder.

Ivan caught a glimpse of something in Christophe's hand. Seemed the man had found a weapon. Ivan chided himself. Stupid to have let Christophe have access to the space and the crew members without checking for weapons first. Amaryllis would call him an idiot if she found out.

Still focused on the guts of the ship, he narrowed his eyes. Unarmed, he didn't trust the man. Armed, he trusted him even less. Son of a... He should have asked more questions before letting Christophe out of the cell, like why he was in there in the first place and where his partner was. Hindsight and all that. For his own safety and so he didn't have to conk Christophe on the head, he needed to disarm the man immediately.

"Almost done." Ivan flicked a switch to disable the emergency lighting before slicing through one more component with his handy dandy metal shim. Then he shifted his weight, bracing himself as the ship shuddered to a halt.

Caught off balance, Christophe stumbled backwards into a workbench, his arms flailing.

Ivan spun on the balls of his feet and lashed out, kicking the weapon out of Christophe's hand. He grabbed him by the neck and hauled him up to his face, the man straining to find his balance on the tips of his toes. "And what were you planning to do with that weapon?" he asked, his voice low and deadly.

Christophe made a croaking noise, his fingers scrabbling against Ivan's iron grip around his neck.

"What?" He tilted his head. "I can't quite hear you." He loosened his fingers slightly, allowing Christophe to drag in some air. "That's a lovely shade of red you're turning, by the way."

"Wasn't going to do anything with it," he gasped, his hands wrapped around Ivan's arm in a sad attempt to pry Ivan off of him. "I swear."

"Why didn't you let me know you found a blaster, then?"

Christophe kicked at the bigger man, his bare feet doing nothing but irritating Ivan. "Was gonna."

"You know, Amaryllis told me that you and your partner were not to be trusted. She said you two were always looking for the easy job with easy money and, if that score happened to come from legit source or at the detriment of a fellow Cabal member, well, you didn't care much either way." He gave Christophe a shake. "What was going through that empty head of yours when you came up behind me with a weapon in your hand, huh?"

"Wasn't..." Christophe choked out.

But Ivan was done. He shook Christophe one more time, then let him go, shoving him back against the workbench. "You. Don't move." He bent down and picked up the small blaster Christophe had found. "You've got one more chance to tell the truth before I knock you out and shove you in the storage lockers with the others. What were you planning on doing?"

Christophe gulped. "It was only to make sure that you would take me with you when you left, I swear."

"And what made you think I'd leave you behind or that I'd need a blaster in my back to make it happen?" Ivan shook his head. What kind of life was it when you couldn't trust the one person who was helping you in your time of need? He felt a little sorry for the guy. Not sorry enough to apologize for half-strangling him. But a teeny trickle of sympathy.

He blew out a tired breath. He wanted to get out of here and back to Amaryllis. Back to his life. He didn't want to have to deal with this man or Martin or any of it. What he wouldn't give for a little shack in the middle of nowhere with Amaryllis where they could fish, drink some beer, and make love as often and as loudly as they wanted to without anyone pointing a blaster at them or annoying them. "I got you out of that cell, didn't I?"

Christophe nodded, staring at the ground in front of him. "I just... needed to be sure." His shoulders slumped, lank blond hair sliding over his face.

Ivan frowned down at the defeated-looking man. It wasn't the best idea, keeping Christophe with him, but after that display of pathetic wretchedness, he couldn't just abandon him. "Okay. Don't do it again, right?"

He nodded.

"Look, we can't stay here. No doubt someone's already on their way down here to figure out what happened to their system and get everything back online and moving. I've got a place we can hole up for a bit, figure out our next steps." He needed to get his hands on a tablet or a communication access point so he could contact Amaryllis and their team. Hells, he'd be happy to talk to

Navi at this point in the adventure. "Agree to come quietly, to follow my directions, to answer some of my nagging questions about why you're on this ship in the first place, and I'll let you tag along."

"And get off this ship?" Christophe asked, his voice hopeful.

Ivan nodded. "And get off this damned ship."

"Agreed."

"No more going for weapons? No more trying to shoot me in the back or betray me or whatever it was you thought you were doing?"

He shook his head so hard, Ivan worried what little brains he had would come flying out his ear holes.

"Fine." It would have to do. He'd have to trust that Christophe meant what he said. He took two steps forward, then whirled around and stuck a finger in Christophe's face. "Do not fuck me over."

Christophe held up his hands in surrender. "Won't. Promise."

"This is an exceedingly bad idea," he grumbled to himself as he slid along the quiet corridor towards his destination. If this fool killed him because he was too trusting, he'd never hear the end of it.

29

AMARYLLIS

"Ship's called the *Stoneheart*. Looks like an E-class, a Vanid build. One of their newer models," Cormac said, consulting his comm. He stood on the command deck in front of the wide wall of screens, his keyboard hovering at waist-height as he worked with Dagby to pull together as much information as possible. "They're not moving."

Once Dagby had pinpointed the coordinates Lore sent them, they'd moved from the common room to the deck. The plan they compromised on — a more refined, less blow-'em-all-up version of the original plan — required a mix of stealth and boldness plus a healthy dash of luck. Amaryllis didn't like depending on luck at all, but sketched out a rune for it just in case. Better to be safe than risk the wrath of whatever forces existed in the universe that enjoyed thwarting even the best laid plans. She preferred not to be a cosmic joke when at all possible.

"Scan says life support and other systems are still functioning, but their engine is currently disabled," Dagby said, spinning in her chair to look at Amaryllis. "What do you think happened?"

Amaryllis leaned on the armrest of her captain's chair, her nail tapping against its edge. "I'm hoping Ivan is what happened, that he's found a way to muck things up for them."

"That sounds more like a you thing," Trick said, flashing her a grin before turning back to his station.

"She must be rubbing off on him," Cormac said.

"She's certainly been rubbing something on him." Navi ducked, though not fast enough to avoid a smack on the back of the head from Cormac.

"No. Bad Navi," he said.

Amaryllis rolled her eyes. "Children, if we could get back to it? Trick, you got a flight path for us? The secret squirrel stealth us, I mean?"

The plan was that she and Navi would pilot a tiny ship, essentially a retrofitted escape pod, over to the *Stoneheart*. Her crew had used the tiny ship, which they'd named Lil Bit, several times, twice as a lure to other ships who thought it actually was an escape pod and once as a stealthy way to gain access to a larger ship. It was so small, most scanners dismissed it as space junk unless the homing beacon was activated.

"Yep. Sent it to your comm. It's pretty straightforward, aided by the fact that the *Stoneheart* is currently drifting in space. We don't have to worry about chasing after them or slowing them down," he said. "You will need to keep an eye on their weapons, though." He pointed to the ports lining the sides of the ship. "One shot from those, and you're space dust."

"That's what you and the *Dog* are for," Amaryllis said, standing up to pace. She needed to burn off some of her nervous energy. Though they'd run jobs similar to this multiple times before, this one felt different. It was different. It wasn't just them boarding a ship to steal cargo or capture a fugitive or whatever. Ivan was on that ship. It was his life that was on the line.

She clenched and unclenched her fists, trying to find some semblance of calm. Usually before a job, she had a little nervous energy, but then it morphed into adrenaline, and they were off. This time, the anxiety kept building and building. Without a good outlet, her brain churned through all the ways this could go wrong and all the ways Ivan's life would be at risk.

He's a big boy, she told herself. *He can take care of himself.*

But she needed to know that everything was in place. "Let's go over it one more time." She could feel their internal groans, but her crew were professionals, so they'd save the bitching until she was out of the room.

"The *Dog's Day* is going in weapons hot," Dagby said. "The *Stoneheart*'s engines are already offline, so we'll focus on distraction and drawing fire until you're on board that ship."

"Once that happens, we'll zip in, set the clamps, and sucker on before cutting through their port side to gain entry," Trick said. "That's the opposite side of where the holding cells are. Though, if Ivan's not in them anymore..."

"Okay, I'm still not happy about cutting into the hull. If we can find another opening, let's do it," Navi interjected, before picking up the thread. "Let's assume Ivan escaped the cells and is the one who disabled the *Stoneheart*'s engines. His next moves depend on how many people are on board, how much hardware they're packing, and if they know he's loose. Personally, I'd find a place to hole up, somewhere defensible, figure out what I'm up against. With my comm out of commission, I'd see if I can't get my hands on a tablet so I can make contact with my people." He leaned over to Trick. "That's us, if you weren't sure."

Trick rolled his eyes.

Cormac said, "They may not realize he's out and tearing shit up, but when they do, they'll come for him."

Amaryllis listened to them run through the plan, nodding along at the appropriate spots. She held up a finger. "Not to throw a wrench in the works, but it'd be nice if we could avoid damaging that ship any more than necessary."

"Captain?" Trick said, cocking his head.

Dagby gave her a hard look. "Not really the best time to be changing up the plan, Cap."

"Just putting it out there," Amaryllis said, waving a dismissive hand in the air. "Ivan comes first, of course. He's our primary focus. But a mostly undamaged ship like the *Stoneheart*? Well, it would be a nice score for a newly emancipated crew with minimal funding at their fingertips."

Dagby and Trick nodded, following her line of thinking.

But both Cormac and Navi turned to her with frowns on their faces. "But Ivan," Navi began.

"I know, Navi," she said, catching his eye and holding it. "Ivan is the entire reason we're here. If the *Stoneheart* gets damaged or winds up blown into a zillion pieces so we can safely extricate him, so be it. I'm just saying. That ship would be a nice little bonus for us from this whole mess."

And it would be. A nice score like that would keep them running for a good while and wouldn't leave them scrambling for jobs at the start of their new freelance careers. If they couldn't sell it as a whole ship, they could always salvage it and sell it off piecemeal, keeping the rest as scrap for future repairs to the *Dog*. But if she had to choose between Ivan and a salvaged ship, she'd choose Ivan every time.

Navi narrowed his eyes at her. "Just know that if anything happens to my brother because you're more interested in preserving the integrity of a stupid fucking ship than saving his ass, you and I are going to have a serious problem."

"Agreed. Good thing you're coming with me on this rescue mission of ours. You ready?"

He gave her one more long, hard look before rising to his feet.

The deck door shushed open. She turned back to her crew, giving them a bright smile. "Oh, and people? Please try to keep *Dog's Day* all in one piece. We just got her running the way we like."

"Safe home, team," Trick said. The others echoed his words.

They walked out the door and headed down to the shuttle bay where Von was prepping their little pod.

"Took you long enough," Von grumbled. Dressed from head to toe in black tactical gear, he looked ready to take on a veritable army. "Get into your suits while I run a final check. Don't forget to activate team comms before you suit up."

Though *Lil Bit* was engineered to firmly attach to the side of a ship and equalize the pressure and atmosphere so as not to kill its passengers when they opened the hatch, only a fool completely trusted technology. Too many things they couldn't control. So, though they were binding and Amaryllis hated wearing a helmet, especially since most of them didn't fit over her hair comfortably, spacesuits were a must. She just knew that the one time she decided to go without would be the one time a seal failed and that would be the end of her.

Von stepped out of the tiny ship and gave her a nod. "Ship's ready to roll." He twirled his finger. "Turn around so I can check your suit."

She spun, holding her arms out so he could inspect the seams and seals. No point in wearing a suit with a leak.

He did the same for Navi, then jerked his thumb towards *Lil Bit*. "Load up," he said. "I'll see you safely off, then head up to command. Fly well, Captain. We'll see you on the other side."

"Fly well, Von," she said, giving him a cheeky salute and a grin before climbing into the ship after Navi and sealing the hatch.

As they got strapped in, Von secured the inner cargo bay doors. "*Lil Bit* is ready to fly on your word, Dagby," he said over team comms.

"Send 'em out," Dagby said.

There was a loud clang as the outer bay opened. Amaryllis took control of the joystick and they blasted out into the stars, the bay sliding shut behind them.

30

IVAN

Ivan hunkered down in the ship's citadel and wished for the nine hundredth time he'd left Christophe in that cell. Not that the man was doing anything wrong at the moment, but holy fuck, he was annoying. If he wasn't complaining about the small space they were currently holed up in, he was whining about the temperature of the room or the boots he'd scavenged from one of the engineers pinching his toes. At least he had boots. Ivan's feet were too big to fit in any of the available footwear, so he was still bare-footing it.

Doing his best to tune the annoying gnat out, Ivan pulled the tablet from a charger and tried once again to get it to turn on. He'd scrounged the tablet from amongst a pile of broken electronics in one of the storage lockers. It was a little worse for wear and had no power when he found it, but as it was Ivan's only option, he'd tucked it into his pocket before they headed to the citadel.

This particular ship still used it like the panic room it was originally designed to be, a safe place for the crew to withdraw and hide during a pirate attack. It was stocked with enough MREs and water for ten people to survive a week.

The citadel's walls were an amalgamation of plasticine and

metal, built to withstand heavy weapons fire. If the entire ship was destroyed, it would provide those inside with at least an hour's worth of air, depending on how many were within. Time to possibly survive if there was a ship close enough and brave enough to take on whomever attacked the ship in the first place. Also, enough time to watch everyone around you die horrible deaths as you asphyxiated. That part was not ideal.

There was also an emergency beacon that, when activated, would alert the nearest Starguard outpost or carrier — neither Ivan nor Christophe would be using that. Bringing Starguard into the situation wouldn't do either any good.

The *Dragon* crew had repurposed its citadel to store munitions, spare fuel, and other things that could possibly blow up the ship. Quin figured that, if it got to the point that they needed to hide and call for help, pretty much everyone was dead anyway, so why would they need a panic room? He might change his mind now that Bea, the love of his life, was on the scene but, at the time, it made sense.

The tablet gave a garbled squeak as it did its best to warm up. Cracks spider-webbed their way across its surface, the text barely legible under the breakage. Ivan tapped on the surface with a frown. No holo. No video. But it looked like it he might be able to send out a message via text, so at least there was that.

He typed out a quick message to the *Dog's Day*, telling them he was alive and sharing his location according to the tablet's data, which he really hoped was correct and hadn't reverted to factory settings. The thing was on its last legs, so it was in the realm of possibility. *Fingers crossed*, he thought, clicking send. He stared at the tiny notification triangle flipping from green to red and back to green as it did its best to pass Ivan's message along.

"Is it working?" Christophe asked, grabbing for the tablet.

Ivan palmed his forehead and pushed him back onto his side of the small room. "Fuck off, man. This is not for you."

He huffed, crossing his arms over his chest. "I figured I'd have better luck contacting my people than you. The Cabal is everywhere, after all."

Ivan rolled his eyes. "They might be everywhere, but they're also a bunch of pirates who wouldn't lift a finger to help you and would sell their own grandmothers if it meant credits in their accounts. You planning on paying them to come save you from this situation?"

Christophe's face turned red. "If you think that, then you must realize Amaryllis and the *Dog's Day* crew are pirates, too. Some of the worst The Cabal has to offer, in fact."

Somehow, he doubted the man's veracity. The worst of The Cabal? From what he'd seen, Amaryllis and her crew were pretty shitty pirates with little of the true bloodthirstiness required to be truly awful. But he wasn't going to argue with Christophe about it. Let the man have his opinion. Ivan knew Amaryllis's heart.

"And?" Ivan asked, raising an eyebrow.

"And that's who you're trying to contact, right? I saw how you looked at each other at that bar on Cora."

"And?" Ivan asked again. His love life wasn't up for discussion, especially with a shitheel like Christophe. And he certainly wasn't going to give him the satisfaction of responding to his inane probing and attempts at wrangling a reaction.

"She's a pirate, you imbecile. Like you said, she won't raise a finger to help you. Unless of course, you pay her buckets of credits." Christophe tapped a finger on his arm, his irritation apparent. "Or maybe you have something she wants. Those are the only reasons she'd even bother to try and find you."

"Okay," Ivan said.

The man huffed again.

The tablet's triangle finally stopped flipping, landing on the green side. Message sent. Now, he just had to wait for a response.

Shifting on the uncomfortable slab seating, Ivan leaned his head back against the smooth wall and settled in to wait. Now that they were inside, no one else could get into the citadel unless he let them in. No weapons' fire could penetrate the walls. If he wanted, he could hole up here until Amaryllis or someone on the *Dog* responded to his message and came to rescue him.

Rescue him. He snorted out a quiet laugh at the thought. Like he was some helpless being who couldn't do some very serious damage to the individuals on this ship if he wanted to. Thing was, he didn't really want to hurt people most of the time. He had the potential for violence, had used that potential to its full effect when required by his commanders in the Starguard. Used it as part of his job on the *Laughing Dragon* crew, when it was called for. He was good at it, too. But he didn't particularly like it.

Besides, he didn't have any real beef with the crew of this ship. They were just following orders. Granted, he didn't approve of their life choices, working for a group like Hegemony — or was it Obbligatos or Obstreperous or Obliviously or whatever stupid name they'd called themselves, he couldn't remember it at the moment for the life of him — that conducted business in a shady manner, but hey, gotta make a living. So, he'd hurt them if necessary, but preferred to avoid it unless they got in his way.

Amaryllis would get a kick out of riding to his rescue. Hells, most likely the woman would lord it over him for the rest of their days. His lips curled up into a grin at the thought. The rest of their days. This thing between him and her, he no longer believed it was short term. He didn't want to let her go. Ever. And he needed to tell her as soon as he saw her face. He hoped she felt the same.

The tablet shimmied in his hand, squeaking out a weak buzzing notification that someone had answered him. Coaxing the machine awake, he pulled up the short message:

Glad you're alive. We're here & coming to get you. Hang on.

Short, sweet, and to the point. Whoever wrote the reply didn't call him names so not Amaryllis. In the grand scheme of things, it didn't matter who aboard the *Dog's Day* answered him. He'd take it. Without meaning to, he flexed his hand, and the screen cracked the rest of the way, the tablet crumbling to pieces with one final, sad croak.

"Well, shit," he said, opening his hand and letting the pieces fall to the floor.

Christophe jumped to his feet. "Fucking meathead. You just busted our only means of communication." He glanced at the emergency beacon, as if actually considering employing it.

"I wouldn't if I were you." Ivan'd knock the fool out before letting him call the Starguard for help. "Sit your ass down and relax."

"Relax? Relax?" Christophe's voice rose to such a high register that it hurt Ivan's ears. "The fuck I will. You pulled me out of one prison only to stick me in another. Well, I won't have it. Do you hear me, meathead? I. Won't. Have. It."

The ship rocked as something hit it.

"What was that?" Christophe screeched, tugging at his hair.

Ivan smiled at him, all teeth and attitude. "That's my honey. Come to rescue me."

Christophe let out an incredulous laugh. "Amaryllis? You think that's Amaryllis? She does know that you're on board, doesn't she? Is that why she's shooting at us? She want you dead? What did you do?"

He shrugged. "No, she doesn't want me dead." He hoped. "Part of her plan, no doubt. My woman does enjoy a good explosion."

Most likely, the attack on this ship by the *Dog* was a distraction, diverting the command deck crew from noticing whatever else was going on. That's how he'd do it anyway. He trusted that Amaryllis and the rest of the crew had employed such tactics before.

"Well, I'm not sticking around to find out." Christophe turned and twisted the handwheel on the citadel's only door, spinning it towards the open position. "I'm getting out of here."

Ivan rose to his feet and put a hand on the man's shoulder,

tugging him away from the door. "And going where?" he asked. "This is the safest place on the ship."

"Let me go." Christophe elbowed Ivan, breaking his nose with an audible crunch then spun and kicked him in the solar plexus.

Caught off guard by the sudden violence, Ivan stumbled back into the wall, cracking his head against the hardened plasticine, jarring his broken nose, and sending a jolt of pain through his entire face. "Fuck," Ivan growled, tipping his head back to stop the bleeding. Bracing himself against the pain, he placed a thumb on either side of his nose and, with a sharp jerk, snapped it back into place.

By the time he'd recovered his breath and his vision cleared, Christophe was gone, the citadel's door wide open. "Jackass. No wonder Amaryllis doesn't like him," Ivan muttered, bracing himself as the ship rocked against another barrage. "Good riddance." He wasn't going to track him down. Christophe was a grown man. He could look after himself and if he couldn't, well, he should have listened to Ivan. Can't fix asinine.

He stepped out into the corridor, not surprised to see the bodyguards hustling Mr. Fancy Suit Martin towards the citadel. They must have headed in this direction as soon as *Dog's Day* appeared on their sensors. After all, it was the safest place for him.

Ivan waggled his fingers at Martin as he neared. "You weren't planning on hiding in here, were you?"

Mr. Martin's eyes widened, and he skidded to a halt so quickly, the guard behind him crashed into him. Slapping away the guard's hands, he wheeled around and ran in the opposite direction.

"Your body is getting away from you," Ivan said to the bodyguard, who was still headed in his direction with a grim look on his face.

As a bodyguard, there was only so much you could do when the body you were guarding refused to cooperate, especially if they were also the one paying for your services. One of the myriad of reasons he truly disliked the job of bodyguard.

The guard's eyes widened, and he looked back. Cursing, he turned and ran after Mr. Martin and the other bodyguard.

The outer walls of the ship hummed. *Godsdammit*, Ivan thought. He knew that hum well. It was the sound of large weapons being primed. Christophe mentioned this ship had weaponry, enough to repel other ships and keep them from boarding.

He had to believe the *Dog's Day* knew about those weapons and was prepared for them, but Ivan wasn't about to sit in safety while his people were facing that level of danger. Sure, it would have been amusing to see Amaryllis's face when she rescued him and found him in the citadel, but he couldn't risk the possibility of any of their people getting hurt because he was playing around.

He needed to get to the command deck and shut this shit down before someone he cared about got injured or worse.

31

AMARYLLIS

"Word from Ivan," Dagby said. "He's alive and currently hunkered down in the ship's citadel."

"Like, locked in a citadel and awaiting rescue like one of those old fashioned fairy princesses?" Navi asked with a snort. He double-checked that the seal between *Lil Bit* and *Stoneheart* was airtight. "Two minutes until the pressure equalizes."

Amaryllis snickered, imagining Ivan holed up in a safe room, waiting for them to save him. "I don't think it was fairy princesses that needed rescuing. Just regular human princesses who were supposedly too helpless to do it themselves." Amaryllis triple-checked the seal behind Navi. Not that she didn't trust him, but it would really suck if, when they opened the hatch, they blew off the side of the *Stoneheart* and tumbled directly into the path of its weapons. And, yes, it was a fear, but also something she'd heard of happening. An old Melorian myth maybe, but she didn't want to chance it.

"Yeah, it's always the humans that were the dumb, helpless ones in those books." He tapped a finger against a sensor. "One minute."

They braced themselves as a nearby blast rocked their little ship. Both of them rechecked the seal. "Still good," she said. "And if we find that man hiding in a panic room, I'm never going to let him live it down." She shook her head. "Ivan. In a panic room. Got to be a joke."

"Right?" Navi said. "I mean, I kind of expected him to have already taken the ship and be kicked back in the captain's chair, waiting so he can tease us for being worried." He poked a couple of buttons. "Pressure equalized. Popping the hatch."

Amaryllis drew her blaster, checked the charge, and held it against her thigh as Navi opened their hatch. She bounced on her toes as he reached forward and got to work unlocking *Stoneheart*'s hatch. As much as she wanted to tell him to hurry, a process like this couldn't be rushed.

There were several ways to open the hatch of a ship. The first and easiest way to be invited. If only. The second was to use one of the skeleton keys that tricked the computer into thinking you'd been invited and, thus, happily open. The third was to brute force your way aboard with the use of a torch and sometimes explosives. While explosives might open the *Stoneheart*'s hatch, the blast would also blow *Lil Bit* off the other ship and straight-up kill them.

So today they were opting for number two, using a skeleton key. They had several to try, courtesy of the combined efforts of Cormac and Dagby. If none of them worked, they'd have to reassess their choice of entry.

"Got it." Navi popped larger ship's hatch open. He pushed it forward, the hinges pulling it inward and locking in place. "Second key worked."

Amaryllis slid past him to assess the situation. The escape hatch opened into a hidden compartment within the cargo hold. Holstering her weapon, she pulled herself through the round opening and crawled into the closet-sized space. Thank the goddess it was empty, and they didn't have to deal with trying to shift things around to make room.

As Navi joined her and got to work on closing up both *Lil Bit* and the escape hatch, Amaryllis found the edge of the paneling and carefully pushed it forward. As soon as she could, she wrapped her fingers around the edge to keep it from falling outward. It was heavier than she expected.

"Navi, help me with this," she said.

Together, they quietly removed the panel and propped it up against the inner wall. They pulled out their weapons, holding them at the ready. "Stun only," she reminded him.

He gave a sharp nod, following her lead as they slipped along the wall of the cavernous and very empty cargo hold. Odd that there was absolutely nothing in the space, not even a stray crate of supplies. For the majority of beings, space travel was too expensive not to make use of every spare nook and cranny during a trip. Whether coming or going from a place, a smart captain made sure to pack their hold with materials or products or they wouldn't be able to recoup the cost of fuel, much less make a living.

But not this one. Someone must have paid the *Stoneheart*'s captain a great deal of credits to venture out here without cargo of any kind. Hells, there wasn't even an emergency shuttle. It was weird.

"There's something really unsettling about that empty cargo hold," Dagby said. They'd opted for both audio and visual for this job. Navi knew his way around the ship but the crew decided that, since only two could travel in *Lil Bit*, it would make sense to have the rest of the experts traveling with them via first person cams.

Amaryllis was holding her judgment on the decision. She loved her people and respected their expertise in their areas, but having all of them both seeing and hearing everything she did and then commenting on it when she was trying to focus could be a serious pain in the ass. They tended to forget that one person — Amaryllis, in this case — was running the job, that it wasn't a group effort. If it got too bad, she'd have to cut them off and deal with their bitching when she got back to the *Dog*.

She braced herself against the wall as the blowback from another explosion rocked the ship. "Come on, people," she growled. "Time to pull back a little on the playing with the big guns."

"Yeah, last one was a little close for comfort," Navi said from behind her. "Unless you're actually trying to take us out and then I'd have to say that maybe Von needs to get his vision checked because he missed."

"Haha," Von said, his gravely voice low in her ear. "My vision is fine. But the *Stoneheart* has finally remembered they have their own weapons and that they can use them on the pirate ship harrying them."

"Took them long enough," Trick said.

"Hey, chill on the swoops and swirls, man," Dagby complained. "You're making my stomach icky."

"Would you rather be blown into a zillion little pieces because I held back on the evasive maneuvers?" Trick asked. "Maybe just take a pill and get over it."

Amaryllis traded a glance with Navi. "Is your crew as bad as mine when it comes to bickering?"

"He's the one's who usually the main bickering culprit," Cormac said.

Navi gasped, pressing a hand over his heart. "You dare cast blame on me? Pretty sure you're right in there with me."

Regretting the impulsive choice to ask the question in the first place, Amaryllis let out a loud sigh. "If we could all just focus here. Everyone does remember that Navi and I are on board a foreign, hostile ship with gods only knows how many opponents between us and Ivan, right?"

Low mutters sounded over the team comms.

"Great. Then let's concentrate on the job at hand and save the bickering for when everyone is safe and sound and not in danger of getting blown up or shot, okay?"

Silence.

"I would like everyone to verbally acknowledge that they are focused on our current job," she said, feeling very much like a primary school teacher.

Various versions of "Yes, Captain" echoed through the comm link.

"Excellent." She pulled out her second blaster. "Trick, can you get the *Dog* close enough to sucker on like we'd planned?"

"Not with the barrage we're currently facing," he said. "We're in evasion mode at the moment. It would be easier if we were actually trying to hit the ship, but since we're not, we don't have any way to stop them."

"Understood." *Shit*. She frowned, thinking through the possibilities. "Keep it up. We'll work on it from this end."

"Acknowledged," he said. "Dagby, I hope you have a barf bag close by because I've got to do some more fancy flying here." He paused. "Sorry, Cap. Habit."

She rolled her eyes but didn't comment. He'd managed to restrain himself for two whole minutes. A record in Trick's world. She turned her attention to the man at her side. "Navi."

He jumped at the sound of his name, his eyes wide. "Captain," he said, straightening as he snapped out the start of a salute before he caught himself and lowered his arm.

She swallowed a grin at his response. "Lead the way to the *Stoneheart*'s command deck."

"The deck?" He swallowed hard. "But Ivan...?"

"I know." She did. She was itching to find Ivan and make sure he was safe and unharmed. "But we need to shut down those weapons before they destroy my ship." She paused and put a hand on his arm. "Last we heard, Ivan is safe and sound in the citadel. If for some reason he left it, then we have no idea where he is on board and no way to get in contact with him. If we take the command deck, we'll be able to access their systems. *Dog's Day* will be out of danger from those weapons, and they can help us secure the rest of the ship." She took a deep breath. She was working to convince herself as much as Navi that this was the best choice they had at the moment.

He considered her words, then gave her a nod. "Agreed. I'll lead the way." He raised an eyebrow at her double-fisting blasters. "You still thinking stun versus something more permanent?"

She nodded. "I'd prefer not to kill or maim anyone, if at all possible. Except maybe those jackasses who took Ivan in the first place." A surge of anger swept through her body, priming her for action. If anyone had hurt Ivan, they would pay dearly for it.

32

IVAN

"Why are there so damn many people on this damned ship?" Ivan growled to himself, stunning yet another crew member. The man slumped to the floor, and Ivan quickly disarmed him, disabling his blaster and dropping it down a trash chute in the wall rather than stuffing it in his waistband with the other one.

Seriously. Though this ship was larger than the *Dragon*, Ivan had hoped for fewer individuals on board. So far, he'd disabled eight, not including the engineers who were probably awake by now and trying to find their way out of the storage lockers. He hadn't even made it to the command deck yet.

No matter the size, it didn't take a full crew to operate a cruiser and generally, when you're transporting someone you basically kidnapped — two someones, if you counted Christophe — you did that on the down low, with minimal crew members. Not a bunch of untrained, unprepared individuals who barely knew which end of a blaster was which.

This whole operation felt off, like whoever was running it was flying by the seat of their pants and just reacting to whatever situation came their way. Mr. Martin had been pretty cocky when there was a force-field between him and Ivan, but it was entirely possible that he was winging it. After all, ransoming someone to a bunch of pirates? What kind of sense did that make? None, that's what.

Ivan dragged the downed crew member into a room where he'd already stowed two others. Both of those people were awake, hands and feet wrapped in the same duct tape that covered their mouths. The women's eyes widened at the sight of their limp crewmate. One of them, a pale girl with pointed ears, squeaked and huddled behind the other, who squared her shoulders and tossed the black hair from her face as she glared at him.

Ivan pulled the duct tape from his pocket and using his teeth, tore off two strips and set about binding the unconscious man. When he was done, he crouched down in front of the pair of women. They shied away from him.

"I've already told you I'm not going to hurt you," he said, carefully pulling the tape from the black-haired woman's cheek.

Once free, she licked her dry lips. "What about Gary?"

"Who?"

Nodding at the guy, she said, "Gary."

He spared a glance at the downed man. "He'll be fine; he's just unconscious. Shot me, so I had to stun him."

Gary's shot barely grazed the outside of Ivan's thigh. Irritating after the day he'd already had. Maybe he should have waited it out in the citadel. Having Amaryllis tease him forever might have been less annoying than trying to make his way past these untrained but enthusiastically bloodthirsty crew members. It was taking forever to disable and disarm them, then tuck them away somewhere safe so they'd be out of the way and not keep trying to kill him.

"Who are you?" the woman asked. "Are you a pirate? Are you going to kill us?"

"I was your prisoner," he said, sinking into a low squat, his forearms resting on his knees.

She shook her head. "We're a science vessel. We don't have any prisoners."

"You had two," he said. "Me and another guy." A science vessel. Sort of explained why there were more people than he expected. Definitely explained why they were such shitty shots. But it raised a whole lot of other questions.

She frowned and shook her head again. "I don't believe you."

"Okay. You don't have to believe me, but it's true." He shrugged. Whatever. He didn't have the time or energy to try and convince her. But he did want more information, if for no other reason than to add it to the knowledge they'd gathered so far. "Who are you and what is it you're science-ing out here in the black of space?"

"Science Officer Lani Tran'al." She tipped her head at the woman using her as a shield. "That's Junior Science Officer Chanan Washa. And the man you tied up is Gary Rimas, one of our medics." She clenched her jaw for a moment, then said, "I can't tell you what we're studying out here. You don't have the clearance."

Ivan choked. "Clearance?" What the fuck did that even mean, clearance? Of course, yes, he knew what it meant in the definition sense, but what kind of experiments or studies were they doing out here that required clearance? And why didn't the ship's officers know about their prisoners? A ship full of secrets, that what this was. Annoying. "Okay, so let me ask you this: how are you connected to the Obdurate Collective?" He'd remembered the actual name. Amazing.

She shrugged. "Never heard of it."

"What about Hegemony?"

But she was clueless about that, too. Ivan felt his frustration growing. Far too many tangles, threads, and knots for him. He liked things straightforward, not all mish-mashed together and puzzle-y. He took a deep breath and let it out slowly. No point in getting mad at the science officer. It wasn't her fault he was here or that her bosses didn't tell her anything useful. He tried again. "Who signs your paycheck? Is that classified, too?"

"I don't think so..." She paused, considering. "We're working on a three-standard-year grant from the Melorn government. So I guess technically, the Melorn government signs my paycheck."

Well, that was something at least. A grant from the Melorn government could be traced. This situation was aggravating and made his brain hurt. "Do you know Mr. Martin? The short guy with the two hulking bodyguards? Kind of impossible to miss on a ship this size."

If she said she didn't know who he was, he was going to let out a wild barbaric yawp loud enough to bring anyone else not currently unconscious or tied up to this very room. And he didn't particularly care. His building irritability needed an outlet. Punching some annoyingly clueless scientists in the nose would do the trick. Not Lani but, you know, someone.

She nodded. "Sure, I know Mr. Martin. He's on our board of directors. Rumor has it we're dropping him off on Cinzia, though why anyone would want to go there is beyond me. Sand and trolls and heat are not my cup of tea." She gave a delicate shudder, her glossy black hair glimmering in the dim light.

A nearby explosion rocked the ship, eliciting a surprised yelp from Lani. Chanan let out a low moan, burying her head in Lani's back.

"Is it pirates? Please tell me it's not pirates," Lani said. "Why would they attack us? We don't have anything they want."

"Who knows why pirates do anything," Ivan said, reaching forward to restick the duct tape over Lani's mouth. Though he would have preferred to take a moment to address her concerns, that explosion meant he'd spent too long here and needed to get moving.

Making little mewling noises of protest, she tried to shift her mouth away and avoid the tape.

"Sorry, Lani. Can't have you calling for help yet. Your crew doesn't know where I am at the moment ,and if I lose that element of surprise, someone — someone not me — might wind up dead and we don't want that," he said, patting the tape into place and getting to his feet. "But don't worry. It will all be over soon. Then you can go back to whatever super-secret experiments you're conducting."

Lani yelled at him from behind her duct tape, calling him all kinds of horrible names, he imagined. At least her anger had snuffed out her worry about the pirates.

Scooping up Lani's unbroken tablet and tucking it in a pocket, he exited the room, blasters at the ready, and made his way towards the command deck.

33

AMARYLLIS

"Are we shooting at the escape pods leaving the *Stoneheart*?" Cormac asked. "Or letting them go?"

"What escape pods?" Amaryllis loosened her grip on her weapons and cracked her stiff neck. Too much tension had her muscles locking up, which would do her no good if she had to more quickly. "Who's escaping?"

"Unknown. One left a few minutes ago and, uh, there go two more. None of them are responding to our hails. Currently on a trajectory to Cinzia, if no one intercepts them."

"Let them go. Ivan would respond to you if he were on one of them. But track them, please. If the people responsible for taking Ivan are on board, I want to know exactly where they landed so I can find them and kick their asses."

"Acknowledged," Cormac said. He sounded relieved she hadn't ordered their destruction.

"Uh, another ship just joined the party," Dagby said. "No overtly aggressive moves, no use of weapons as of yet."

Shit. Not turning from her position guarding the short corridor leading to the command deck, Amaryllis nudged Navi with a hip to get his attention.

Crouched in front of the biolock mechanism, he was so

focused on getting the locked door open, he'd tuned everything else out. He dropped a small pick tool and cursed. "What?"

"How much longer?" she asked.

"As long as it takes?" He flung out a hand, gesturing wildly. "It's not like there's a buttload of people for you to hold off or anything. Relax."

"We've got another ship on the scene, and they might not be as gentle with us as *Dog's Day*."

The ship rocked again. "You call this being gentle?" he groused. "They do remember who's on board here, right?"

"We can hear you, you know," Trick said.

"They do." She nudged him again. "Hurry up."

"Hey, I'm doing the best I can. It's not easy when your own people are shooting at you. Someone has completely gummed up the works of this stupid lock." He muttered expletives at it under his breath.

"Dagby, any ID on the other ship? What are they doing?"

"At the moment, they're just sitting there, watching. They're far enough away I can't get a solid scan," she said. "Cormac says not to worry, that it's the *Laughing Dragon*. He's hailing them as we speak."

"Unless they make some aggressive moves against either ship, let them enjoy the show for now," Amaryllis said. But if it was actually the *Dragon*, and they weren't doing anything to help, she was going to be highly irritated with Quin. Did they come here to lend a hand? Were they on a clean-up mission from the Knight? What? "And let me know when they answer our hails."

Out of the corner of her eye, she caught a shadow of movement. She crept forward to where the short corridor dead-ended into a t-junction, her blaster at the ready. Scooting to the edge, she took a deep breath and snuck a quick peek. Her forehead cracked against a hard chin and she danced back with a curse.

When she saw who it was, the pain evaporated like it was never there. "Ivan!" She shoved her blasters into her holster and jumped at him, wrapping herself around him like a spider monkey.

"Rilly," he said in a deep rumble, sliding his arms under her ass and burying his face in the crook of her neck. He took in a long, slow breath. "You're here. You came for me."

She ran her fingers through his soft locks and peppered his face with kisses. "Of course I'm here, you idiot. I told you I would find you and here you are."

He released his grip on her backside, letting her slide down his body. Framing her face with his big hands, he gave her a soft smile and kissed her lips. "Here I am."

"Really enjoying this up-close view at Ivan's chest, Amaryllis. I totally get what you see in the man," Dagby said.

Amaryllis rolled her eyes, repressing the urge to mute the team channel, at least for a little while.

The stomping of boots echoed down the corridor behind him.

"Seems you're not alone." She took a regretful half step back from him and pulled her weapons.

"Nope. Unfortunately." He bent back to take a quick glance around the corner. "I swear, these people are multiplying," he growled.

"You sound tired. You look like shit." She stroked a gentle hand over his cheek. He flinched when her finger hovered too close to his nose, which looked like it was recently broken and reset. "Don't you worry, Cherry. I'll take care of it."

"Of course you will, princess." He planted a kiss on her forehead. "Stun only, please. They're just a bunch of annoying scientists and, as much as I'd like to punch at least one of them in the nose, it's easier to knock them out until we decide what to do with them."

"Wait." Her brows drew together. "Scientists?" How was this a science vessel, and how did they not know this? Why in the three hells would scientists want with Ivan?

"Scientists?" Several of the crew echoed via team comms.

He shook his head, scrubbing a rough hand through his hair. "Long story. Confusing one, better solved by smarter and less exhausted brains than mine," he said, giving her hand a squeeze.

She squeezed back, reluctant to stop touching him. But there was a job that needed doing, and, as much as she wanted to, she couldn't drag him into a closet and have her way with him just yet. *Soon*, she promised herself. "Go say hi to your brother and see if you can't help him get that command deck door open. Those people need to stop shooting at my ship before they do real damage to it or the crew."

"Why the hells did you bring Navi with you? Man is hopeless with tech."

"I heard that," Navi said, not turning his attention from his work on the lock. "Though you're not entirely wrong. But I wouldn't let Amaryllis go without me. You are, after all, my only brother. An annoying one, but I'd miss you if you were gone."

"This whole reunion thing is so very touching," Trick said. "But can we wrap it up? Like, aren't there dangerous scientists headed your way that you need to stun into submission?"

Dagby chimed in. "And I would really appreciate it if we could stop loop-de-looping around to avoid the *Stoneheart*'s weapons fire. Getting them to stop all that so Trick stops flying like a squirrel high on Pink Moon would be great."

"At least they're poor shots. Can't aim worth shit, even with the help of a computer," Cormac said.

Amaryllis poked her head around the corner to see two determined-looking individuals headed in her direction. Both were armed. She double-checked that she had enough charge and that her weapons were still set on stun. Good to go. Planting her feet and steadying her arm, she took aim and fired off two shots, stunning both of them before they could even lift their weapons in her direction.

She shook her head at the ease with which she'd taken them down. They really couldn't handle their blasters. Someone really needed to send these scientists through a weapons training program, if for no other reason than to keep them from accidentally shooting one another. The next set of pirates to board them would not be using stun or merely shooting near their ship to distract and draw fire.

She scanned the area for anyone else. "Clear," she said. "Cormac, what's the word?"

"Confirmed. It's the *Dragon*." There was a pause, then he said, "Quin's here and ready to lend a hand. Oh, and he's pretty pissed that you let Ivan get captured on your watch."

34

IVAN

"Put down the tools and step away from the door, oh useless brother of mine," Ivan said, laying a heavy hand on Navi's shoulder. "I think you've done enough damage here for one day."

Navi jumped to his feet and pulled Ivan into a bear hug, pounding his back with an open hand. "Big brother! You're alive. Boy, am I glad to see you." He pulled back and gave Ivan a once-over. "Why aren't you wearing shoes? And what happened to your face?"

He tried to answer, but Navi just kept running his mouth. He smiled at his brother.

"What?" Navi asked then shook his head. "Doesn't matter. Get in here and get this door open for us, would you? They're pounding the hells out of the *Dog* and unless we actually want that ship to become space dust soon, we need to stop whoever is operating that weapons system."

"Luckily, they really suck at aiming and don't seem to trust the computer enough to let it do the work for them," Amaryllis said, coming up behind Ivan and stroking a hand down his back. "You'd think that scientists would have a little more faith in technology."

He desperately wanted to pull Amaryllis into his arms and kiss the hells out of her. Poor timing. But he took the opportunity to check her out. Even in an evac suit, the woman was stunning. She'd unzipped the top half of the suit, letting it dangle behind her, the sleeves knotted around her waist. Underneath, she wore a white tank top, the curves and plains of her muscled arms glistening in the harsh overhead lighting. She'd pulled her hair back into a tight braid, her edges laid flat. The severe hairstyle only emphasized her high cheekbones, those wide golden eyes, and her full lips while doing nothing to convince him he shouldn't leave Navi to his poor attempts at lockpicking so he could greet Amaryllis properly and fully.

Navi snapped his fingers in front of his face, bringing him back from his dreams of peace, quiet, and a naked Amaryllis.

"Brother, you'd better get that sappy look off your face and focus," Navi said, returning his attention to the mess he'd made of the biolock.

Amaryllis gave Ivan a disappointed look, her bottom lip popping out a fraction before she raised an eyebrow and gave him a rueful grin. "I hate to say that Navi's right, but, yeah, he's right. It's even more crucial now because your captain's here."

"Quin?" Ivan said, surprised.

"The *Dragon*?" Navi asked, looking up at them with wide eyes.

"Yes to both." Amaryllis leaned against the wall, turning her head to watch the corridor behind them, her weapons cradled in her hands. "Cormac says Quin said he's here to help. At the moment, he's not doing much of anything besides lurking out of range of the *Stoneheart*'s guns."

Ivan grunted. "Most likely there to protect our flank from anyone who might pop in and try to cause trouble." Quin must have seen the *Dog* harrying the *Stoneheart* but not actually landing any shots and decided he'd be most helpful on protection detail. "Let him know if you want him to jump in or do something else."

"Probably the best place for him at the moment."

"Who even knows we're here?" Navi asked. The man was concentrating so hard on that mechanism, his tongue peeked out of the corner of his mouth.

With a loud sigh, Ivan kneed him lightly in the side, knocking him off balance and out of the way. "You're making a mess of things. Move it."

Navi's eyebrows drew together as he glared at his brother from his position on the floor. "You could've just asked."

"Would you have moved?" Ivan bent to look at the mangled biolock.

"I almost had it."

"So no." He poked at the mechanism's exposed innards and held out his hand. "Gimmie."

Navi smacked his roll of tools into Ivan's hand harder than necessary. "Doubt you can do any better. These scientists of yours, they must have done something to it. Otherwise, I would have had it figured out ages ago."

Ivan grunted as he stripped the casing off several wires, twisting a few together and reseating a couple others in the housing. He jiggled a data chip, twisting off a bead of solder before popping the panel back on. Digging out an ident card he'd snagged on his way here, he swiped it over the lock.

It beeped red.

"Ha," Navi said. "And here you thought you'd make a few tweaks, and it would work for you. Guess you're no better at lock picking than me."

Amaryllis smacked him on the back of his head. "Dude. We need to get in there, remember? Don't be a dick."

Ivan ignored his brother and hammered a sharp blow to the center of the panel. Then he scanned the card again.

This time it beeped a happy chime and turned green. The door slid open.

He barely had enough time to move his bulk into the corner, push Navi out of the doorframe and throw an arm across Amaryllis's chest to protect her before someone inside shot at them.

The blast winged the door, melting the plasticine into slag.

"Hey, no heavy ammo, you dipshit," he yelled at whomever was shooting at them from the deck. He popped his head around the edge of the door, taking a quick look before tucking back out of the line of fire. "Did no one teach you the rules? You'll melt holes in this ship, we'll lose atmospheric pressure and oxygen, the walls will collapse and we'll get sucked into the black of space." More dramatic that what would actually happen but as long as it got them to stop using weapons on that setting, whatever. "I thought you were scientists, for fuck's sake. You should know this."

Shaking his head at their obtuseness, he signaled to his small team that there were ten people inside, spread throughout the space. Only four were armed at present, the others seated at various stations around the deck. He hoped that, if they could take out those who were armed, the rest might surrender. He fully expected those hopes to be dashed, however.

He pulled out both of his blasters, checking their charge. Amaryllis adjusted her grip on hers. Ivan pointed at Navi and made a stay and play sniper motion. The man was the best distance shot out of all of them. He'd cover Ivan and Amaryllis.

Pulling a gun with a long, narrow barrel from his holster, Navi flattened himself against the edge of the doorframe. He then pointed at himself, signaling he'd take out the armed targets on the right.

Ivan gave him a thumbs up, then checked with Amaryllis, signaling that he'd take the one farthest from the door on the left.

She gave him a broad smile and a sharp nod, practically dancing with anticipation.

Holding up three fingers, he counted down. Go time.

35

AMARYLLIS

Ivan took point, crouching low and scooting around the door into the room, Amaryllis on his heels. The command deck was much larger than *Dog's Day*'s but it had a similar layout: three stations with swivel chairs on either side, the pilot's station directly in front of the massive wall monitor and the captain's chair slightly elevated behind it. The space was comfortable enough for eight people. A little squished with the additions.

The wall monitor's display was currently in split screen mode. Half displayed *Dog's Day* darting around, bright shots blazing from their weapons ports. The other half showed the *Laughing Dragon*, still disengaged and watching from a distance. Amaryllis noted her *Dog* looked worse for wear. These jackasses had hurt her baby. A bolt of anger shot through her, adding to the adrenaline already coursing through her veins.

The armed crew members fired off several shots as soon as Ivan and Amaryllis crossed the threshold. Most missed their mark, but one hit, striking Amaryllis. She gasped at a blaze of pain that seared her forearm.

Ivan's head whipped around, his eyes widening at the sight of blood trickling from her wound. Before she could assure him she was fine and to get his big ass out of her way so she could take her shot, he'd backed her out of the space to safety, his arm around her waist, a hand cradling her face. "You're hurt?"

She glanced at her arm. The shot hit her left arm, digging a deep furrow along her bicep. While it hurt and it looked bad, what with the blood and crispy skin along the edges of the wound, but she'd survive. "I'm fine, Ivan. They barely got me. An easy fix."

But Ivan's face turned a furious red. "Which one did it? Who hurt you?" He turned back towards the deck and roared, "Who shot her?"

Everyone on deck froze for a hot second before some fool shot off another round.

With a bellow of anger, he dropped his blasters and crashed into the closest armed man. He smashed his fist into his face before tossing him to the side and moving onto the next. Growling, he grabbed another armed crew member, a woman nearly as tall as Ivan, and headbutt her as she tried to shoot him point-blank. Her weapon slipped from her limp fingers as she slumped to the ground.

Frozen with her mouth stuck open, Amaryllis watched in awe as Ivan bare-knuckled his way through anyone who wasn't already laying on the floor with their hands up in surrender. Navi tugged her over to him to check her wound.

"What is that?" she asked, pushing against his grip. She wanted to make sure Ivan wasn't hurt while he was going through whatever it was he was going through.

"Berserker rage. Your injury sparked it. He would have settled since you were still standing and talking to him, but then someone went and shot at you again. That spark turned into a full-blown conflagration." Navi pulled a quick-fix patch from his pocket and placed it over the wound, holding it in place for a few seconds so it would adhere properly.

"I thought berserkers were a myth, a lack of impulse control on the part of the individual." She watched Ivan tear things up. She noticed he only went after those who were armed or attacking him. Anyone unconscious or with their empty hands visible he ignored. "Hurry up, Navi." She shot the armed woman hiding behind a chair who'd been aiming for Ivan's head.

Pulling a cloth from his pocket, Navi wiped off the rest of the blood and wrapped up her arm. "Okay. Good to go. Show him you're completely functional so he won't kill everyone in that room because someone had the audacity to shoot you."

She stared at Navi. "Really?"

He pulled a face. "He's only fallen into a berserker rage four times that I know of — twice when he was a kid, once when his team was betrayed and ambushed, and today. It would destroy him if he went too far before he's stopped. We can shoot him on stun him, but that most likely won't work because his adrenaline is so high. You're our best bet at snapping him out of it before he damages anyone beyond repair."

She moved back into the room, stunning the man who'd leapt on Ivan's back and was actively trying to strangle him. "Ivan," she said, her voice sharp. "Stop. Look at me. I'm fine."

He paused as if he'd heard her, then leapt over the captain's chair and smacked a blaster out of a crew member's hands. It shattered into pieces where it struck the wall. The shooter was a good foot shorter than Ivan and out of shape, but he put up his fists ready to fight. Ivan grabbed him under his arms and shook him, growling in the man's face. The man's light brown skin paled to a brownish-green shade, and he fainted, going limp in Ivan's grip.

"Ivan." She raised her voice, his name echoing across the deck. "Stop it. It's over."

"Rilly?" He spun to look at her, breathing hard, his face red from a combination of rage and exertion. He dropped the man in his grasp, letting him fall into a crumpled heap at his feet.

Ignoring the people splayed out on the floor, either injured, unconscious, or cowering, she moved over to him and put a hand on his arm. "I'm fine, Ivan. It's over. I'm pretty sure they're done." She raised her voice again, addressing the room. She didn't take her eyes off Ivan. "Right? You surrender, and we don't need Ivan to ask you again, correct?"

"Yes, we surrender," the intelligent ones said in chorus.

"Good." She patted Ivan's arm. "See, honey? You single-handedly crushed their spirits with your bare fists and rage. Excellent work."

The tension drained out of Ivan. His shoulders slumped, and he took a deep, shaky breath, looking at the destruction he'd wrought. "Oh, gods. I didn't kill anyone, did I?" he asked, wrapping an arm around Amaryllis and pulling her to him. He gently touched the edge of her bandage. "You're hurt." His arm tightened.

Stroking a calming hand over his back, she shook her head. "It's nothing. Barely even a scratch. Navi slapped on a quick-fix patch and wrapped it up. Probably won't even need a trip to the medi-bay."

"Oh, you're going to the medi-bay," he said, frowning down at her.

"Only if you join me," she said. She reached up and gently pressed at his bruised knuckles. He flinched away, then sighed and let her check out his injuries. "Pretty sure you're more banged up than I am."

"It's not a competition, people," Navi said from where he was slapping a quick-fix patch on one of the crew members. "And, no, you didn't kill anyone, though you did manage to break a lot of noses in a very short period of time."

Amaryllis squeezed Ivan's waist. "Impressive. I mean, you mentioned you wanted to break a few scientists' noses and, look, you got your wish."

"Haha." He pressed a kiss to her forehead. He kept hold of her hand as he bent to check on a man leaning against one of the stations. "That was a lovely little scenario I was imagining, not something I thought I'd actually be doing."

The man recoiled, hunching into himself.

"Sorry," Ivan said to him, his cheeks flaming. He gestured for

Navi to come over with his supply of quick-fix patches. "Don't worry. You've surrendered. I'm not going to hurt you anymore."

"Unless you were the fool who thought turning the blaster all the way up and firing it while aboard a ship in the black of space was a good idea." Navi crouched next to the man. "If so, we're going to have some words about proper weapons' usage on board."

"The whole batch of them could use training." Ivan got to his feet and wrapped an arm around Amaryllis again. He seemed reluctant to be away from her for long. "All these scientists and not one of them properly trained. How does that even happen?"

"Hey, Cap. Hate to interrupt," Dagby said, "But the *Dog* took some fire…"

"Anyone hurt? Is my ship okay?" She glared at the woman who'd moved to sit at the weapons station. Whether she was the original operator or just looking for a comfortable place to sit, Amaryllis had no idea and didn't particularly care. In her mind, they were all responsible. "Do I need to kick someone's ass because they hurt my ship? I'm pretty sure I can follow Ivan's example and go all berserker on them."

The woman shrank in her seat, preemptively raising her hands again.

Rolling her eyes, Amaryllis cut a hand through the air and turned away. It was no fun when they cowered like that.

"No injuries over here, but we've sprung a leak on the second level, and the engine's making some rather interesting noises," Dagby said. "Everything's currently working, but we're going to need more than Von's patch job if we're traveling any kind of distance."

Sounded expensive, but still repairable. Shit. "Okay. We're close to Cinzia. Lay in a course that'll take us to the nearest port." Cinzia was mostly sand, rocks, and criminals, but there were a couple of decent, semi-trustworthy places where they could put in for repairs.

"Got it," Dagby said.

"Cormac, what about Quin? What's his plan?"

"Let me ask."

She shook her head. "No, scratch that. We're not doing this third party conversation thing. Just let him know I'm contacting him."

"Good idea." Ivan moved over to a station. "Contact that ship," he said, pointing to the *Dragon*.

"Yessir." The officer had short, spikey blue hair, pointed ears wrapped in polished metal rings, and light pastel purple-toned skin, indicative of the peoples native to the southern continent of Dathria. Interesting, considering Dathria was a closed planet, one that no one was allowed to visit without explicit invitation. Very few of the inhabitants ever left and even fewer chose to live off-planet.

Interesting, but not at all pertinent to the issue at hand. Amaryllis moved to the middle of the deck, skirting around two unconscious people and one man still cowering under his chair. She turned her attention to the man on the screen in front of her. "Quin." She gave him a nod of greeting.

He returned the nod. "Amaryllis. I see you found Ivan. Oh, and Navi, too. Good. I was a little concerned that you'd run off with him and the rest of my crew forever."

She gave him a half-smile and a shrug. "What can I say? You have good taste. Navi and Cormac, you can have back. Ivan, though." She cast a glance in his direction. "I think I'm keeping him."

Quin laughed. "Are you now? And what does Ivan think about that?"

Ivan met Amaryllis's look and gave her a slow smile. "I think I'm keeping her, too."

Bea popped on screen, clapping her hands and bouncing on the balls of her feet. "Oh, goodie! That's exactly what I was hoping would happen. Quin, weren't you saying they should get together?"

Quin pulled her to his side and planted a kiss on her lips. "No,

Daisy. I said they should get together and bang it out, not that Amaryllis steal my Number One out from under me."

"Well, too bad. He's mine now." Amaryllis folded her arms over her chest, setting her jaw. She'd fight him, if necessary. She wanted — no, deserved — the same happiness she saw in the looks Bea and Quin traded, in the small intimate exchanges between them. She and Ivan deserved their own version that.

"Ooh, she looks so scary when she does that." A smile lit Bea's face. "Hey, think you could teach me how to do it? I need to know how to better intimidate people, especially these annoying men around here." She poked Quin in the side.

Amaryllis laughed, unable to hold on to her aggressive pose in the face of Bea's enthusiasm. "Maybe. But only if Quin will come to some sort of arrangement." She had thoughts about what that arrangement might entail, too. It could be so valuable if it all worked out.

Quin snorted. "With pirates?"

Unless Quin was going to be an ass about it.

Ivan moved up beside Amaryllis, sliding a hand up her back and giving her nape a gentle squeeze. "I'm sure we can work something out. Right, Quin?"

Though she wanted nothing more than to sink against him, she stiffened her spine. While Bea might be eager to see them together, Amaryllis had the feeling that Quin would use any iota of weakness or intimacy against her when she proposed her idea to him.

Quin blew out a breath. "I suppose we'll have to, won't we?"

36

IVAN

Ivan flinched as Amaryllis ran a diagnostic wand over his face.

"Don't be such a baby," she said, gripping his chin. "You got to make sure my arm wasn't about to fall off from that one little shot. Now, it's my turn. Just sit there and let me fix you up."

He took the opportunity to run his hands up the backs of her thighs. They were such a tempting target, what with her standing this close to him.

"Stop it, you big idiot," she said, batting his hands away. "You didn't set your nose properly, and it's going to heal crooked." She looked him in the eye. "Unless you want to have a big ole bump on the bridge of your nose and struggle to breathe properly because you've jacked up your air passages? Up to you."

He grumbled, shifting on the hard chair she'd shoved him into.

"That's what I thought. Now stay still." Not waiting for him to say he was ready, she reset his nose with a quick jerk. There was an audible click as the bones popped back into place.

He let out a pained grunt, his eyes watering, but he didn't wrench free of her less-than-gentle grip and run away like he wanted to. He sat still, making only minor sounds of protest as she slapped a plaster over his nose to help speed up the healing. The woman was not the most gentle of doctors.

She rewarded his bravery with a soft kiss on the tip of his injured nose. "Good boy," she whispered, nipping his bottom lip.

They were back on board *Dog's Day*, limping towards Cinzia for repairs, with the *Laughing Dragon* as their escort. Amaryllis had a bit of a shit fit when she saw the damage done to her ship, and it had taken the entire crew to talk her down from wanting to shoot the *Stoneheart* to "even things out".

Still dead in the water so to speak, the *Stoneheart* did not earn any new holes thanks to Amaryllis and her temper, but it did gain Rhain and some of his Shields as its temporary security. Bea's sister Dai was there with Rhain, which told Ivan that the science vessel and whatever they were doing must be part of the grander scheme Rhain and Dai were involved in.

He was curious, but not enough to interfere. Definitely not curious enough to forego dragging Amaryllis back to her ship so he could assess her injuries. She was his priority, not some galaxy-shaking game the big dogs were playing.

Quin had waved away Amaryllis's demands for an explanation, telling her that they were all better off letting Rhain and Dai do their thing and to not worry about it. Ivan knew then that Quin wasn't any more informed about Rhain's plans than the rest of them. Rhain liked to keep his cards close to his chest and, considering Dai had been a member of Melorn's clandestine branch for years before retiring, Ivan guessed she wasn't one to share information with just anyone, either.

"You know, your bedside manner could use some work," he said, wincing as she pressed along his ribs.

"You know, you could have died," she said, slapping a healing plaster on his torso with more force than necessary. Since he refused to spend any more time in a medi-bed, the plaster was the next best thing. It would stabilize his ribs and help speed healing.

"But I didn't die." He stroked the curve of her hips. "I'm here.

I'm fine. You're the one who was shot." His fingers tightened on her waist. "You're the one who could have died."

"Neither of us did. We're both here, in this room." She put her hands on his shoulders, her fingers tightening. "I'm still mad at you for what you did at the lab. Don't think that your brush with death is going to let you off the hook so easily. Payback is a bitch."

"So, no thanks for saving you and Von and helping you get away with the prototype, then?" He meant it in a teasing manner, but as soon as he said it, he knew it was something that needed to be addressed or they wouldn't be able to move forward.

Her nails dug into his skin. "I don't need saving. I can do it myself."

And there it was. "I know you can, Amaryllis. You're one of the most annoyingly capable, determined women I know. But you don't have to do everything yourself. You don't have to prove anything to me or to anyone else, for that matter."

The green flecks in her eyes churned, a swirl of emerald in a golden pool. She swallowed hard, absorbing his words. "And you're one of the most frustrating, steadfast, honorable men I know. You don't have to take on the whole galaxy, to shoulder all the risk to prove yourself, especially not to me."

Tugging her closer, he wrapped his arms around her waist, resting his head against her breasts, and inhaled deeply, breathing in the spicy-sweet scent of her. She stroked her fingers through his hair. A sense of peace flowed over him and the final band of copper slid into place, encasing his heart in its fire.

He looked up at her. "I love you, Amaryllis."

Her hands stilled, her eyes widening.

"My mortal enemy, my nemesis," he said, taking another deep breath, filling his lungs with her scent. "You hold my heart in your hands. It's yours. You have the power to utterly annihilate me if you so choose."

A smile kicked up the corner of her mouth. "Damn, Cherry, you can be beautifully poetic when you want."

Then she went quiet. He rested his forehead on her chest and listened to her steady heart beat. If this was it, if this was the end of them before they ever really had a chance to get started... No, he didn't want to think that way. She'd come for him when he was on that ship. She'd risked her life and that of her crew, risked her own ship to find him. That had to mean something. She was a part of him now, wrapped around his very soul. If she wanted him to leave, he would, but she couldn't stop him from loving her or looking out for her. He'd do that until the end of time.

"Ivan," she said, her voice soft.

He steeled himself. Whatever it was, he could take it. He tipped back his head to look at her. "Amaryllis," he said, breathing out her name like it was a benediction.

"You're such an idiot," she said, framing his face with her hands, her thumbs tracing the edge of his lips. "Of course I love you, too. How could I not? My mortal enemy, now my lover. It's as poetic and ridiculous as you are." She bent and pressed her lips to his, tender and soft. And then she bit him. "But if you ever put yourself at risk like that again, try and shove me behind you so you can take the hits rather than accepting that I will always fight beside you, I will cut out your heart and eat it in front of you."

The enormity of their declarations filled the room, a future rife with possibilities splaying out before them.

He nipped her finger. "I'll bring the hot sauce."

"Good. I like it spicy," she said, her eyes lighting up.

Everything except the glorious woman in his arms faded away. Whatever was going on with the *Stoneheart*, Obdurate, Bea's prototype, and everything else, Ivan didn't care. At the moment, he was with Amaryllis, and she loved him. She loved him.

He stood, backing her up a few steps. "Don't tease me, Rilly," he growled, grabbing the back of her neck and pulling her lips to his. "I'm injured."

"Too injured to show me the appreciation I earned rescuing you from those evil scientists?" she asked, pressing the length of her body against his.

His cock twitched. "Well, we don't know for certain that they're evil," he said, sliding his hands down her back to cup her ass. He continued to walk her backwards until she was pressed up against the wall. "But you definitely need some appreciation. I can give you that. I can give you all the appreciation you want."

"Most excellent. I deserve it. I worked hard for it." She wrapped her legs around his waist, confident in the knowledge that he would support her weight and not let her fall. "But not against the wall again. I want your full and total appreciation back in my quarters, in my bed." She nipped his earlobe. "With clean sheets," she whispered. "And soundproof walls."

Needing no further convincing, he wrapped his arms under her backside and walked them out the medi-bay doors.

"Godsdammit, you two had better be going somewhere private," Trick said. He got out of the way to let them pass. "My sensitive ears can't take any more of your lovey-dovey crap."

"Get some earplugs, Trick," Amaryllis said, locking her ankles around Ivan's back and wrapping her arms around his shoulders. "Because there's about to be lovey-dovey crap all over this ship."

Their laughter drowned out Trick's cry of dismay as they turned the corner toward her cabin.

37

AMARYLLIS

They undressed like their clothes were on fire.

Amaryllis kicked off her panties and stood naked in front of Ivan. Her nemesis. Her love. What seemed an antithesis was, in fact, a counterpart. Her heart floated out of her chest and into her throat, her entire body prickling under his gaze.

She swallowed hard and took a deep breath, her heart settling back into place, though it still beat too hard, too fast. And all because of the man who stood in front of her, as naked as she was.

Battle scars criss-crossed their way around his big body, a map of what he'd endured and a testament to his survival skills. From the finger-tousled ginger hair on top of his head, his broad shoulders and wide chest, to the ripple of ab muscles and erect cock at the juncture of his thick thighs, Ivan made her mouth water. And if the heated look he was giving her was any indication, he felt the same about her.

He was hers, and she was his.

Without words, they moved at the same time, coming together in a clash, their lips reuniting in a blaze of passion. She ripped the comforter off before they fell onto the bed in a tangle of limbs.

"Ivan," she said, running her hands along the rippling muscles of his back.

"Amaryllis," he growled, sliding a big thigh between her legs, the rasp of his leg hairs against her sensitive clit sending sparks up her spine.

He rolled her onto her back, taking infinite care to caress every inch of her body, as if he were tracing a tactile map, the dips and mounds of her skin landmarks he needed to memorize. The weight of his thigh against the core of her, the length of his hard cock sliding over her hip as he moved, the touch of his hands against her breasts made her feel desired, cherished.

When his lips met hers, she welcomed him, her tongue meeting his, wet heat sending sparks down every nerve in her body. She ran a hand up the back of his head, the velvety feel of his short hair giving way to the softer silk of the longer locks on the top of his head.

Ivan wrapped his arms around her and pulled her closer, the weight of his body pressing her into the mattress. "Rilly," he whispered, placing gentle kisses along her jawline and down her neck, his beard rasping over her sensitive skin.

Her fingers tightened in his hair at the sound of her name on his lips. She was already slick, her body in flames at the very idea that this man loved her, that he gave her his heart openly and fully. How was it that some words could have the same effect as talented fingers and tongues? Whatever. She didn't really care because Ivan had kissed his way down her body and was sucking on her clit, pulling it into his mouth and teasing it with his tongue. By the holy tits of Saint Agnes, she could come on this alone. Her entire body bowed up, her hands gripping the sheets as the sparks along her spine exploded into a myriad of colors behind her eyes.

From between her legs, he gave her a lazy smile, proud of what he'd done.

She licked her lips, trying to remember how to speak. "Good thing you're so talented with your mouth or..."

He squeezed her ass, making her squeak. "Or what, princess?"

She growled. "Or I might have to kick your ass for calling me princess again."

"You're on." With a snicker, he added, "Princess."

She waited until he was kissing her stomach before she wrapped her legs around his torso and rolled him onto his back. With a grin of triumph, she immobilized him, her knees pinning his upper arms, her hands pressing his wrists to the mattress. "I win."

His eyes lighting with delight, he returned her grin. "Are you so sure about that? Because, from where you're sitting, I'm pretty sure I win." He tilted his head forward, his tongue darting out to taste her clit.

Fuck. That tongue. She attempted to growl at him, but it came out sounding more like a rough moan. Giving up what she now realized was not the immobilizing position she originally planned unless she wanted him to dine on her again — not that she was opposed to it, but she wanted more than just his tongue in her at the moment — she planted her hands on his chest and slowly slid down his body.

"Where are you going, Amaryllis?" he asked, using a now-free hand to wrap her braids around his fist, though not enough to restrict her movements. "Come back here and let me taste you again."

"I have other plans," she said, shifting to rub her clit along the hard shaft of his cock.

He groaned. "Please tell me those plans involve more than just teasing me and giving me blue balls."

She leaned down and nipped his ear. "That's not a thing, you know."

The corner of his mouth kicked up. "Feels like it, though. My cock aches for you, Rilly."

The way he whispered her name made her shiver with desire. Reaching between their bodies, she encircled his cock with her fingers, running her hand along its thick length. "Sounds painful," she said, giving it another stroke and pulling a deep growl from Ivan.

Sitting up, she positioned herself above him, guiding the tip of his cock to her entrance. "Maybe I can do something about it." She sank down an inch before rising again. She smirked. "Maybe not."

He grabbed her, his fingers kneading her ass. "Why are you always so mean, Rilly?" He let out a low groan as she hovered above him, just the tip of of his cock in her heat. He twitched his hips in encouragement.

A slow smile made its way across her face as she lowered herself leisurely down his shaft, enjoying the tight stretch of her body as he filled her all the way up. "You like me that way," she said, her voice low and rough with desire. And she began to ride him, tossing back her head at the delicious glide of his cock within her.

"Goddess help me, but I do." He pressed a thumb against her clit, a firm pressure and stroke that matched her rhythm. "I like it even better when you come around me, though."

"Oh, gods." She sped up, rocking her hips, the feel of him in her, the stroke of his fingers upon her skin, dancing over her clit. The pressure between her legs built, pushing her higher than she'd ever been until she peaked with his name on her lips, shattering against him as he tumbled after her.

She collapsed on top of him, her head on his chest.

His fingers traced along the dip of her spine as he stroked her back. "Still mad at me about the lab?" he asked.

Luckily for him, she was too sated and boneless to move. "Absolutely. Especially since I did all the work."

He grunted. "Did you now."

"It was hard work, too."

"Damn right it was hard," he said, wrapping an arm around her waist and rolling them over so she was beneath him once again. "Give it a few minutes, and it'll be hard again. Until then, I guess I'd better get to work."

"I do so enjoy the fruits of your labor," she said with a laugh before giving herself over to his delicious ministrations.

38

AMARYLLIS & IVAN

A knock on the door and a mellow voice that said, "Room service" was the only thing that got Ivan up off the giant bed where he'd been laying in a boneless heap with Amaryllis. He cinched the belt of the deliciously soft complementary robe around his waist and opened the door of their hotel room to find a cylindrical bot loaded down with covered dishes.

"May I come in?" it asked, blinking up at him with bright electric eyes.

Ivan stepped to the side to let the bot roll past him.

"Where would you like this?" the bot asked.

He had the server bot set the dishes on the dining table and shooed it out of the suite, declining any more of the services it offered.

"Bring me my steak, Cherry," Amaryllis bellowed from the other room. She was hungry, but had no desire to move from the comfort of the bed. They were in a hotel room, one paid for by Quin, so why couldn't she be decadent and eat in bed?

Ivan raised an eyebrow at Amaryllis, burrowed in her nest in the suite's bedroom. "It's not sanitary to eat in bed." He dropped a sealed envelope next to her. "Bot delivered this for you. Why don't you read it while I set out dinner in the other room?"

She picked up the envelope, turning it over in her hands. It looked a little battered, its edges bent and discolored, but the seal wasn't broken. There was nothing written on the outside to tell her who sent it. No one outside of her immediate circle even knew she was here. Unless you counted Safina, who'd been on Cinzia when they were stuck there waiting for repairs to the *Dog*, and she highly doubted Safina was spreading her location around.

Sliding a finger under the flap, she broke the seal and pulled out a handwritten letter. She couldn't remember the last time she'd received a handwritten anything, not when it was so much easier and convenient to comm whoever you were trying to contact. Her breath caught when she read the signature at the bottom. Lore. Of course Lore knew where she was.

Right after she'd been rescued by Lore, she used to find handwritten notes on her pillow. Sometimes it was a line of poetry or a quote. Sometimes it came attached to a small piece of candy. Nothing special, just random notes. Lore's way of making sure Amaryllis knew she was there for her, that Amaryllis was safe now. She covered her mouth, tears prickling her eyes. She'd forgotten all about that until now.

Taking a deep breath, she read Lore's note.

Amaryllis,

With the delivery of my prize, the Dog's Day crew is officially separated from The Cabal. You played an excellent game, one worthy of a master.

A smile crept across Amaryllis's face. They were free and clear of The Cabal. Amaryllis had Bea to thank for manufacturing a dupe of her prototype, one that she felt comfortable handing over to Lore, one that wouldn't function no matter who tried to reverse engineer it. It seemed Lore understood what Amaryllis had done and not only accepted it but complimented her on the sneakiness of it. Wow.

While you may no longer be a member of The Cabal, you will always be my daughter. I expect regular communications from you as well as you and your partner's presence on high holidays. This is non-negotiable. Should you not acquit yourself as expected, I will be forced to either seek you out or have you delivered to me.

Congratulations on your new company. It is good you have people watching your six.

-Lore

"Get out of bed, lazybones, and come eat," Ivan called. "I'm not serving you dinner in there."

She grumbled and threw aside the covers, pulling on a robe that matched Ivan's. "So mean to force me out of bed. That thing is so damned comfortable." Her stomach growled. She padded across the thick pile of the carpet and pulled the two beers from the chiller, setting one in front of his place at the table. She put Lore's note next to it.

"Hey, you're no good to me if you're weak from hunger." He placed a full plate in front of her and kissed the top of her head. "Now, eat up because I need dessert."

A flag of rose gold bloomed on her cheeks. "You're insatiable."

"Only for you, princess."

She threw a roll at him, whapping him in the shoulder. "Hey, I am a queen, dammit. You would do well to remember that, lest I not allow you to visit my palace anymore."

He snickered. "I do love your palace." He handed her back her roll and sat at the table next to her. "What's this?" he asked, picking up the note.

"Just read it."

She started in on her steak, watching him read through her eyelashes.

When he was done, he blinked at her.

"Well?" she said.

"It's a very Lore note. Giving you praise while also threatening us."

"It is." She shrugged. "And you're stuck with her now, too."

He blanched. "Is it too late to reconsider this whole 'I love you' thing?"

"No. You'll have to make your peace with her."

"I still don't like her or the way she does things."

"You don't have to. But you do have to be polite to her. She is your mother-in-law now." Technically, they weren't legally bound, but she did so enjoy watching all the blood drain from his face when she informed him of that.

"Bite your tongue, woman." He sketched a rune of protection.

With a roll of her eyes, she said, "Idiot."

"Your idiot." He lifted her hand and grazed his lips over her knuckles. "You're stuck with me, even if you do come with some serious baggage."

She shivered at the contact. "Hey, I can still throw you out the airlock anytime I like. My crew wouldn't say a word."

He tsked. "They might not, but what would your other business partners say? Or did you forget about them already?"

Waggling the mouth of the bottle at him, she said, "I knew I'd regret teaming up with your crew."

While the *Dog's Day* was in port getting the repairs it desperately needed, its crew and that of the *Laughing Dragon* had met in Toro at a little dive bar named Tits Out. There, they banged out a partnership, two freelance mercenary crews banding together to form a company they named "Rogue Justice".

Ivan was thrilled. Not only was it a smart move for both of their small crews, but he had the feeling they could do some real good out there in the galaxy. Oddly, the company name had come about because of Safina, who had helped facilitate the merger. They'd been talking about their last jobs, the ones with Bea and her prototype, and how much they'd liked setting things right. Returning a stolen item to its rightful owner, bringing a wrongdoer to justice, clearing someone's name. It felt good.

Safina, who was doing something similar in her retired life, got a glint in her eyes as they spoke. "You know," she said, "I could use the services of a company that doesn't mind working outside the boundaries of the law at times, one that provides the kind of rogue justice our galaxy needs but is sorely lacking."

And just like that, their company was born.

"This is the start of an amazing partnership," Ivan said.

"The company or us?" she asked, popping a crispy seasoned potato into her mouth.

"Both," he said.

She swallowed and lifted her bottle of beer. "To new partnerships borne of strife and forged in fire."

His eyebrow rose. "Now who's the poet?" He picked up his bottle and clinked it against hers. "To love, success, and righting wrongs."

She beamed at him. "Cheers to that."

SOME TIME LATER, the pair of them lay sprawled on the bed, naked and panting, satiated to the point of barely being able to move.

"So," Ivan said, idly running his fingers over her shoulder. "Remember that crown thing you wanted to steal from the auction?"

She rolled to her side and flung a leg over his thighs, rubbing her foot against his leg. "Crown thing...," she muttered. "Do you mean the Ibiana Diadem?"

"The one with flame stones and black opals," he said. "That's how Dagby described it anyway."

"Yeah, that's the Ibiana Diadem." She propped her chin up on his chest. "What of it?" She was still mad Andrea interfered in her theft it that night. Poor Andrea. "How do you know about it?"

He shrugged. "I guess that, while they were holed up on the *Dog*, Dagby and Cormac were talking about the auction. Somehow, the diadem came up, about how it was stolen from your people and how you wanted it back." And, of course, Cormac told him all about it. Said Ivan should retrieve it for Amaryllis, that would be a symbol of his love for her. He hadn't realized until that moment what a romantic Cormac was. But he had a better idea, one he knew she'd appreciate more than him just handing it to her.

"Okay..." She drew out the word until it was a question.

"Well," he said, "what would you say if I told you I had a line on it?"

She gasped. "Really? I'd say tell me more and tell me now."

"So demanding." He laughed as she smacked his chest. "There's not much more to tell. Except I have a very good idea of who bought it and where it is now." He grinned at her, loving how the thought of righteous thievery made her glow with excitement.

She pushed up to her elbow, looking down at him. "You'd better not be joking with me." Did this man really track down some jewels because he knew she wanted them? Her heart swelled until it felt like it was about to burst in her chest.

"Wanna go on an adventure with me, my queen?" he asked, waggling his eyebrows.

She tweaked his nipple, eliciting a squeak out of the big man. It always made her giggle when he made noises like that. "I'll adventure with you anytime, Cherry."

Join Amaryllis and Ivan on their heist
to retrieve the Ibiana Diadem!
Get your free book, CROWNED, at:
https://dl.bookfunnel.com/kr58oqyayr

Or sign up for my newsletter and get CROWNED as well as other free stories, giveaways & release news at
www.maryashe.com

AUTHOR NOTE

First off, thank you so much for reading my space pirates and their adventures. I'm having so much fun writing them.

You may have heard this before but, while writing can be an isolating, solitary job, the act of creating a book isn't. So thank you to everyone who read my first book and especially thank you to those who left a review or told me they enjoyed it. Your kind words gave me the boost I needed to power through the 90+k words in this story (not including the 30k or so that ended up on the proverbial cutting room floor).

I can only hope Ivan and Amaryllis's story entertained and I do have plans for more Rogue Justice, including shenanigans with Safina and her Old Lady Danger Squad (OLDS for short and, yes, I amused myself with that moniker) and a bunch of spicy novellas.

What also helped was that I found a community to write with every day. So, to the women of The Office, thank you for your support, your help (ugh, those darned blurbs, I tell you!), and your presence on the Zoom calls. Hanging out with a bunch of hard-working writers, seeing those squares of people doing what they do best, is so inspirational. It gets me in writing mode every morning and helped me finish this second book.

And thank you to Becca Syme and her entire Write Better-Faster team for providing us the space to connect, for encouraging writers to find what works for us, and to always question the premise. You've helped me more than you'll ever know.

For those curious as to what my top five Clifton Strengths are,

I'm Input, Intellection, Futuristic, Learner & Discipline (yeah, I go hard on the thinking strengths and if you know me, you're not at all shocked by this lol).

With so much going on in the world, it's a necessity to have a place to escape to and to dream. Books have always been that place for me. So, brew yourself a cup of tea, snuggle into that warm blanket in your favorite chair, and get lost in a good book. Happy reading, friends!

DID YOU ENJOY VOLATILE CONJUNCTION?

Please consider leaving a quick review on Amazon or the site where you purchased the book. Reviews help other readers like you find new books and authors to scratch that reading itch (you know the one).

Thank you for reading!

Be the first to hear about new releases, exclusive giveaways, and to get access to bonus content

Sign up for my newsletter at
www.maryashe.com

ABOUT THE AUTHOR

Mary Ashe is the author of science fiction and fantasy romances packed with humor and adventure and featuring protective, growly heroes and the smart, capable heroines who bring them to their knees.

When not lost in fantastical worlds of her own creation, Mary can be found attempting to grow a veggie garden, starting new craft projects and discarding them just as quickly, or snuggling up with her geriatric diva dog and a good book, a cup of tea close at hand.

To learn more about Mary or her books, visit her at www.maryashe.com